A
Lion
is in
the
Streets

The slothful man saith, there is a lion in the way; a lion is in the streets. As the door turneth upon his hinges, so doth the slothful upon his bed.

Proverbs 26, 13-14

A
Novel
by
ADRIA
LOCKE
LANGLEY

A Lion is in the Streets

THE BLAKISTON
COMPANY

Philadelphia

PUBLISHED BY WHITTLESEY HOUSE
A division of the McGraw-Hill Book Company, Inc.

Printed in the United States of America

THIS BOOK IS FOR MY MOTHER,
HENRIETTA LOCKE,
AND FOR MY DAUGHTER,
FAITH LOCKE LANGLEY.

1

FOR TWO DAYS, ever since Hank's death, she had been in a daze of numbness, held in a strange waiting on some inner knowledge. Now she stood at her bedroom window in the executive mansion of the Magnolia State staring across the tops of palms, live oaks and magnolias, at the high tower of the magnificent Capitol which Hank had caused to be built. The tower stood bright and gleaming, its windows and marble reflecting the very sheen of midday, and the tall pole with its flag at mourning mast let the sun run down its polished roundness with bright little tongues of flame.

And then, Hank came alive to her as she heard again the words with which he first admired the tower from this very window:

"Lookit there, Sweetface—lookit there—ain't that purely a thing a' beauty, though! There it is, Sweetface, the pinnacle I been a-climbin' to, all marble 'n shinin'!" After a moment of silent admiration, he added, "But now I look on it, I see it ain't big enough nor high enough for t' satisfy Hank Martin." He beat his chest with his fist, grinned broadly; then sobering, he dropped his voice to the tone of intimate confidence. "No, sir, Verity, I see now I gotta climb to that round glitterin' dome in Washington. I purely have."

But now Hank Martin, the Big Lion, lay in state at the foot of that pinnacle in the magnificent rotunda of the Capitol, in a silver casket guaranteed to protect him from the worms and maggots of the earth. Over the casket lay a blanket of orchids which had been bought by the pennies and nickels and quarters of calicoed women and barefoot men, the hillbillies and the swamplanders. As in life, so now in death, Hank's richest gifts came from the poorest people.

As she pondered on the qualities that made up his greatness, such desolation poured in on her that she fell on her knees. Selah opened the door quietly, locking it against the horde of great and near-great who filled the house. She stood looking on Verity with love showing in every line of her broad black face. Then coming to her mistress she knelt on the floor, took Verity in her strong arms, cuddled her to her big soft bosom and swayed rockaby fashion.

"Y'all jes' plain got ter let yo'se'f go, Miz Verity," she counseled urgently, softly. "Y'all got ter cry. Many's de time I'se seed you cry. Folk been a-hollerin' at you fo' ter git some iron in yo' guts till now it plumb seem lak dat iron gwine choke de life outen you, honey." She smoothed Verity's thick blond hair. "Law, honey, Mistuh Hank, he got ter go some time, an' he got ter git hisse'f kilt, too, seem lak. Shu' 'nuff. An' iffen Mistuh Hank can see all dis yere hullabaloo"—she nodded at the newspapers strewn over the big gracious room—"all dem papuhs, an' all dem movin'-pitcher fellers a-grindin' at evabody, an' all dem million uv folkses a-mo'nin' fo' him, an' heah all dem fellers on de radio—lawdy, honey, it'd shu'- pleasure him somepin' special." Selah managed a little chuckle. "Yas-m, I bets iffen Mistuh Hank's spirit lookin' on all dis—um-umph! dat man plumb cakewalkin' up dem golden stairs! Um-umph! You reckon dey gwine ketch de feller whut shot him?"

A great wrenching shudder tore Verity. "Oh—oh—" she moaned, "I get to thinking—and I can't bear it! I asked God to kill him! Ten years ago—"

But Selah covered Verity Martin's mouth with a big, gentle hand.

"You didn't! No sich a thing!" she declared firmly. "I 'members plain eva word you say. You says, cryin', 'Gawd, I'd ruther see him kilt than see him killin','—dat's whut you say." Selah nodded wisely. "So dat's whut keep you lak a walkin' ghost since Mistuh Hank kilt! Dat's whut keep you fum seein' yo' own baby, an' dat's why yo' very own baby, she got ter take all her comfort fum Mistuh Jules—Lawd bless dat man. Mistuh Jules, he say tell y'all dat Mistuh Saber gwine start tellin' de whole United States 'bout Mistuh Hank any minute now! Law, I near 'bout fo'git!"

Selah rose and taking Verity's hands helped her to her feet.

"Mistuh Saber, he start talkin' in—" she studied the face of the small boudoir clock and, making out the time, she announced with pride, "in 'zactly fo' minutes. Yas'm, zactly fo' minutes he startin'." And she left as quietly as she had come.

Tears began to fall from Verity's cheeks. Selah had punctured the ice wall around her heart. Wise, all-knowing Selah. Verity knelt beside her bed. "God," she prayed, "God, forgive me. I said I'd rather see Hank killed than killing and I meant it, God. I meant it! I meant it! But now —oh, God—maybe I'm the guilty one—not that man!"

She beat the ivory bedspread with her clenched fists. She had to find that man before the police did. She had to know who it was—it would surely lead to the records—the records—the records. . . . She felt the numbing terror of the past two days creeping in on her again. Then she heard Hank's own words plainly counseling her: "Breathe deep, Sweetface. Ain't nothin' so curin' as pulled-in guts a-shovin' up on a chest full a' air. Sends somethin' t' the brain that's right confidence-givin'. Ain't you never watched animals when they're a-feared? Animals know lotsa things."

She rose, breathed deep, thinned her abdomen in conscious imitation of Hank, then went to the pile of newspapers. Their great scareheads screamed blackly, HANK MARTIN DEAD! BIG LION SHOT! GOVERNOR ASSASSINATED. But she did not see the printed words. To Verity they all read, HANK MARTIN, NICTITATER, DEAD.

She wiped the tears away and picked up the latest extra. There were hundreds of pictures: Hank, looking vital even in death; the crowd on the Capitol grounds; the line of mourners, which filled the streets for blocks and blocks.

The people had started coming in the night, and now the line had crept forward for five long hours to get a last look at the man who had first made national headlines when he shouted, "I'm the Big Lion! 'Cause the lion's king a' beasts, 'n I'm king a' this here jungle!"

But the Big Lion had been bagged by a sure bullet fired by the hand of an unknown big-game hunter, described throughout the land as a blond, black-coated, dark-bespectacled man. Just as Hank stepped from his car, the unknown man fired and then disappeared into the Capitol before the very eyes of the four men who were Hank's bodyguard. Before the very eyes of hundreds, for the great rotunda was filled in a twinkling. People poured from their offices, from the art gallery and the assembly chambers. Swith had got through the crowd and fired at the assassin, but the excited crowd had jammed against the huge bronze doors and one had almost swung to, catching Swith's bullets.

There was a picture of the bronze door with the bullet marks among the magnolias which were so handsomely done in bas-relief. There was a picture of the bodyguard. All four of them, Swith and Flower, Jep and Vince. There was a picture of Lieutenant Governor Kirkendall who must now take over the reins of the Magnolia State. There were pictures of Guy Polli and of Robert Castleberry and of Marcus Davol.

There was a picture of the little share-crop house where she and Hank had lived for years; and many pictures of her, Verity, his wife, and of his child. There was a fine picture of Jules Bolduc, old friend of the family; a stunning likeness of Sylvia Hylen under which was the caption, "She headed the women's organization against him." There was a picture of Jenny, captioned, "Swamp woman who has been with Hank since his beginnings." But in not one single paper had there been a picture of the Little Flamingo. How had the papers missed the Flamingo?

The papers had everything, it seemed, except some hint which would help her to find that unknown black-coated, dark-bespectacled man.

She felt she should be able to pick out from her memories the one person who would be bitter enough or desperate enough to do this thing. Was it revenge? Or desperate need for Hank's secret records? She must listen to Saber. She twirled the dial of her radio and from it came a male voice, smooth and rich in its emotional quality, but with a brilliant conciseness which was different from all other voices.

Yes, it was "Saber" Milady talking. He was speaking into a microphone that was set up not more than fifty feet from the dead body of Hank Martin. The only newsman whom Hank had ever really liked and the only newsman whom Hank had really feared. The man whom Hank had named for a shining sword was giving the world a word picture of the Big Lion's life and death.

Verity sank into a chair and listened tensely. Saber Milady had a genius for knowing the secrets of the great. She could not afford to miss one sentence. Now his remarkable voice came in with:

> *It has always seemed to me that Hank Martin's career began in earnest with marriage to Verity Wade, young Yankee school-teacher. When they met she was nineteen and Hank was pushing twenty-four. That was back in 1922. . . .*

1922! Why, in the instant of Saber's speaking her mind had encompassed years! His oration carried her back to almost-forgotten scenes. She relived many emotions, many events, with every sentence he uttered. Saber knew so much—so much that was off the record, and yet, in the total he knew so little; and the life he pictured for the world was incomplete and far different from the one relived by Verity, Hank's wife. She listened eagerly:

> *Yes, it is hard to believe, as we see the body of Hank Martin lying in state in this magnificent capitol with thousands paying homage to his memory, that he started as a peddler with a pack on his back. . . .*

A pack on his back! Big and handsome and vital, Hank stooped slightly to enter the schoolhouse door. She noticed, as always, that the door was actually high enough for him, but he seemed to feel himself too big for small places. He shifted his pack, and its bulging sides told her he was off again with a new load. Off to the back country and the swamplands, trudging miles upon miles to farmhouse and swamp hut, bringing laughter and news along with bright gewgaws, calicoes, and Sizzle, his special cooking fat.

He paused in the doorway. She had a feeling, akin to the excitement she felt at the theater, that the star of the show was making a carefully planned entrance. Silhouetted against the setting sun, she saw him not as a dark bulky man in cheap ill-fitting clothes, but as a magnet with a warm radiance. His thick, dark, wavy hair glistened in the strong light, giving him a copper-and-purple crown. His ruddy outdoor face glowed with vigor and eagerness, and his beaming eyes spanned the distance between them, embracing her.

After the long look he strode toward her, slipped the pack from his shoulders to a chair.

He straightened, looked with tolerant disdain about the small school-house; and suddenly the place was horribly drab. Until she met Hank, she had loved the squat little building, painted with the enduring barn red, with its rows of cheap scarred desks. The cheesecloth curtains which she had made with precision were rags not fit for this glowing god to see. She touched her hair, pulled at her prim little collar, longed to be clothed in something lovely, something with a graceful fullness instead of the plain skimpy dress.

He seemed to sense her wish.

"Someday, Sweetface, you'll have silks 'n satins 'n velvets. Things fitten for a lady like you." He strode back and forth before her desk. "I'm gonna have me a horse 'n wagon next trip, Verity. I'll cover more ground that-a-way. I'm gonna have me some catalogues made withen pictures a' things I can be a-gettin' cheap, 'n take orders for stuff I can't be a-haulin' alla the time. I'm a-tellin' you, Verity, it's gonna mean everythin' t' me, this here peddlin'. I know near 'bout every damn swamp angel in this here state. 'N someday," he paused before her and shook a finger at her, "now remember this, Sweetface—I'll run this state! 'N d'you know why? 'Cause I'll know what folks think. I'll know what they feel. I'll know what they want. 'N what's more, I'll be a-knowin' just how much they gotta have give to 'em afore they'll be a-givin' their vote t' me."

He flung his arms heavenward and boomed, " 'N every vote means power, Sweetface, power—power!"

The crescendo of his words made her head ring. She was hypnotized with his nearness. Every nerve in her answered his call of desire, and his eyes glowing into hers showed, suddenly, an awareness of her yearning. He came slowly, intently, toward her, savoring the nearing minute. His two big hands cupped her white face. He swayed her head gently beneath his—a connoisseur luxuriating in the bouquet.

"I like y', Sweetface," he whispered huskily. "I'm a-honin' for y'. Purely a-honin'. Hell, I wanted y' first time ever I seed y'."

"Saw, Hank," she corrected him in a weak murmur and thought how silly to correct his English instead of his conception of her.

Looking steadily into his eyes she saw his face coming slowly nearer and nearer. He brought her to her feet, pressed her tightly against his body, and suddenly she could wait for that minute no longer. She put her hands on his cheeks, brought his lips to her own, and let herself melt against him curve for curve. Then, as suddenly, she pushed him from her.

"Lord save us!" breathed Hank in awe. "Lord save us!" He backed away and eyed her with a new wonder. "I was a-wantin' to marry y' first time ever I seed y', 'cause you was a lady. But you're even better'n that, Sweetface. I want a lady alongside me when I'm a-runnin' this state." He lifted her hand, ran his lips shiveringly up her arm, and grinned at the sight of her wide, frightened eyes. "But like allus, I get better'n I ask for—I'll show the world a lady on parade and take home a passionflower."

He dropped her hand abruptly, pushed up a creaking window, beat his chest with his fists.

Verity, clinging to the desk for support, tried to find in herself the Verity Wade she knew.

"Hank, Hank," she rasped desperately, "I'm not like that. Not really. Honest, I'm not. It's you—you make me feel terrible things, Hank."

"Wonderful things," he boomed at her. "Wonderful things. 'N the best is still a-comin'."

He came slowly toward her, cupped her face once more and swayed it beneath his own, savored deeply of her, and said, "I ain't a-goin' t' kiss you agin, Sweetface, 'cause iffen I know Hank Martin, was I t' do it, I'd not be a-gettin' off on this here journey."

He shouldered his pack and started for the door. There he hesitated, turned.

"Farewell, my lady," he said with native courtliness, "I gotta get a-goin'. You got a date six, mebbe eight weeks from now, to go a-marryin' in a new wagon 'n behind a new horse."

For a long moment his eyes devoured her. Verity felt he was memorizing her likeness to carry with him and that he cherished this picture of her, bewildered by love. Nervously she smoothed her hair, pulled at her waist and cuffs. Hank laughed at her efforts to become the schoolma'am again, lifted a hand in salute.

"Lord save us!" he whispered, and lunged through the doorway.

It seemed impossible that this pulsing excitement could be contained within her, Verity Wade, until two months ago of Meyersburg, Pennsylvania, where the Pocono Mountains were probably still capped in white. But here she was in the lush South in a village called New Cross, where nothing was new, where the people resented a Yankee teacher, and where, she had found after getting the place, the school was open only three or four months each year. She lived in a little room in back of the schoolroom and cooked her scant meals on the school stove.

Often, as she fixed her sweet potatoes or beans, she thought of her mother, her wonderful mother, dead now almost a year. How she would love to hear what her mother would say about Hank. She felt she would love his sense of self-sureness, his feel for people, his intense desire to lift himself up to a high place where he could benefit others. She had enjoyed talking to Hank about her mother and the big brick orphanage, the Sheltering Arm, where her mother had been cook and general assistant.

Sometimes her little room in the back of the schoolhouse felt much like the big room off the kitchen in the Sheltering Arm, and sometimes, as the few children who could afford to buy school books took their places at their desks, she repeated her mother's words to them. "You don't have to feel alone because you have no father or mother," Mrs. Wade had told many a lonely child not her own, while Verity sat by feeling proud and generous for sharing her mother with so many. "No, indeed, not while we all have an Uncle Sam." Oh, yes, her mother would see how wonderful Hank was.

She ran now to the doorway of the school to watch Hank. There he was, the man who, in three short weeks, had become the very sun of her world, swaggering gallantly even though slightly stooped under the weight of his pack.

How startled she had been the first time she saw him. She had answered a most demanding knock, and there was Hank, big and beaming, a can of Sizzle in one hand, his great pack upon his back. Slowly the beaming look turned into unbelieving, almost reverent amazement, making her aware of herself in a way she had never before known.

"Yes?" she had said in a sort of breathless query.

"God'lmighty!" he had said prayerfully. "Lord God Almighty allus gives me His best." Then bringing himself out of this mood, he asked, "You ain't actual the new Yankee schoolma'am?"

She knew then that this meeting had the mark of destiny in it. "Why, yes, yes, I am," she managed to say. "Can I do something for you?"

A teasing twinkle, which made him at once like a very young boy and a most assured young man, lighted his eyes. "Yes, ma'am," he laughed, "I got a feelin' you can do more'n anybody else in the world. I purely have. How come you t' these here parts anyways?"

She was confused and deliciously self-conscious. "I—well, the teaching requirements aren't so high here. You see, I had only one year of college."

"College!" he exclaimed. "College!" He looked at her with awe.

It always made her laugh when she remembered that look and the look of exultant gratitude which followed it as he said, "Hank Martin allus gets better'n he asks for. It's just like's if the Lord says t' me, 'Hank, m'boy, yore eye just can't envision the treasures I have laid up for thee.' Yeah, it purely is."

Dour old Preacher Polder who railed about hell and eternal damnation each Sunday back home would have condemned this peddler to the burning fires forever and ever.

Her heart went out to him as he trudged with his load. Oh, she would miss him! From the first she had accepted him in her heart as her own, almost as quickly as he had recognized her as the answer to the prayers of youth and hope. The sun was lowering behind the cypress trees, the first insects of evening began their buzzing. Hurry back! hurry back! her heart called after him. And as though hearing her, Hank turned before taking the bend in the road. He waved delightedly, his arm swinging in a wide arc, an upside-down pendulum ticking, "Six weeks, mebbe eight—six weeks, mebbe eight—"

2

Hank Martin took his bride to a sharecropper's farm, for which he paid rent in the coin of the realm, because Hank would not sharecrop for anyone. One of the best stories about Hank Martin concerns his first day in his new home.

Hank Martin always wanted the best. In a single day—the day after his marriage—he transformed his house.

It was the usual tenant place on the lovely old plantation, Cypress Bend, owned by Jules Bolduc. . . .

SHE WAS Mrs. Hank Martin jogging home behind a big black gelding in a shining new wagon. Jogging home! To a home she had not yet seen, in a place called Cypress Bend.

It was a perfect wedding day. White clouds danced over the sky's bluest dress, casting varicolored shadows on a lush world. Verity snuggled closer to Hank. Leaning down he looked up under her big hat.

"Sweetface," he murmured.

Clasping her knee with a strong brown hand he snuggled her leg against his own and held it there possessively and with promise. She felt a running fire through the small of her back. It leaped around the walls of her stomach, danced along the nerves of her legs, to die down as it reached her feet where they rested on the little iron footrail in front of the dashboard.

She moved, leaned forward, in an attempt to regain her poise. Her bride's bouquet of three huge magnolia blossoms, still clutched in one hand, sent up waves of perfume which the wide brim of her white straw hat seemed to pocket and hold in her face. She felt a great need for fresh Pocono Mountain air, the clean smell of pine. She was half hypnotized by a strange expectancy, smothered in perfume. She pushed her hat back and pulled air into her lungs. It was no use. The perfume was thicker than the air.

The narrow red road twisted between the mournful cypress, glistening holly, and flowering catalpas.

Ahead she saw a clearing. They climbed to slightly higher ground. She was glad to leave the heavy timber. The fields of cotton and cane spread before her. The bare earth between the rows made her feel somewhat better. They spoke of hard work, and the perfume was not so potent. She breathed a little freer. This was more nearly a world she understood.

Cypress Bend, she saw, had once been a fine plantation. There was the great old manor house, its once-gleaming white sides now gray and scaling, two of its shutters hanging at absurd angles. It stood in the midst of magnolias and moss-hung live oaks, its pillars facing the unseen bayou. It had an immense dignity in spite of its slightly uncared-for look, serene with its heritage of splendid traditions.

A man not quite thirty lounged on the gallery steps. His white suit was immaculate, his black hair lay in smooth measured waves, his athletic leanness somewhat belying his attitude of dreaming indolence. He was simply enjoying the weather.

"Lookit him!" exclaimed Hank scornfully, "a feller as smart as him just a-lazin' 'round 'n it a-not sundown yet."

"Who is he, darling?" She experimented with the word "darling" and Hank responded with the intimate pressure of his leg against hers.

"Jules Bolduc, last of a great family," Hank sneered. "But the feller's smart—smart in books 'n such. But it won't never do him no good 'cause he's too dog-lazy to follow up withen action. Says he's one a' life's spectators, not one a' its actors. Ain't that a hell of a thing for a smart man to say?"

"Oh, you know him then?" She was surprised that Hank should know so elegant a person. Somehow she'd always thought of Hank simply as knocking on the doors of the poor.

"Yeah, I know him." He hesitated and then added, "In fact, Verity, he's purely the reason we're gonna live in Cypress Bend."

This caught her attention fully.

"But why?"

"Well, fact is, I'm a-hopin' he'll lemme use his lawbooks someday and sorta guide me in my studyin'. I already asked him 'n he said he'd be glad to. Looked down his nose at me whilst he said it. But what the hell do I care 'bout that s' long as he does it!"

He waved at the approaching man.

"Howdy, Jules," he called.

Verity saw the man's head go back in a slight start and she knew Hank had never called him Jules before.

"Good evening, Hank." His cultured voice held only a hint of the South. "You chose the year's finest day for your wedding."

"Lord God Almighty's allus good to me. Allus gives me His best."

Jules Bolduc's eyes were on Verity. She was conscious that she looked very well. She knew her big hat pushed back made a startling halo for her face and hair, and though she had wished for a beautiful gown of satin she knew the sheer dotted swiss was most becoming. She had made it carefully in a rather tailored fashion with a little long-sleeved jacket. She saw that Jules Bolduc also approved.

"He does indeed give you His best," Bolduc said fervently. He bowed gallantly to Verity. "Jules Bolduc, at your service, madam."

Stepping over to the cart, he held out his hand to Verity. She put her hand in his and he lifted it to his lips. She was nervous and overwrought and Bolduc's little mustache prickled her fingers. She wanted to giggle. She half turned her head toward Hank to give him a wink of amusement, but Hank was looking at Jules Bolduc's bowed head with pride. Suddenly she was annoyed with both men. Hank for his pride, and Mr. Bolduc for his obvious surprise that Hank Martin, peddler, should have such a wife.

"My husband tells me you will let him use your lawbooks," she said, trying to hide her annoyance.

"Law, Mrs. Martin, requires a great deal of studying before the law itself can be read with understanding." He gave her a quizzical one-sided grin. His dancing black eyes almost jeered as they swept over Hank and the peddler's cart. Verity was, for the first time, acutely aware that Hank's shoes were a bright yellow, that his ill-fitting suit boasted a gaudy purple stripe, that his tie was a dazzling purple. None of these grotesqueries hid Hank's strength and purpose from her, but she knew that to men like Jules Bolduc smooth surfaces counted. She was hurt and resentful.

She lifted her head proudly.

"Either you overestimate the law, Mr. Bolduc, or you underestimate my husband." Bolduc's face sobered. She saw that he regretted his thrust but she was not mollified. "We will go now. Good evening." Her tone was final and one of complete dismissal.

Hank slapped Beauty's rump with the reins. "Giddap," he clucked to the horse as he turned and waved to Jules. "So long, Jules, I'll be a-seein' y'."

Hank was laughing. "That was sure pretty, Sweetface. Mrs. Hank Martin a-goin' highfalutin' on the last Bolduc. But, Sweetface, you got a heap t' learn by the time we get int' politics. You gotta learn never to let nobody catch you takin' a insult. Laugh it off. Allus remember you can kiss their ass today 'cause you're a-plannin' to kick it tomorrow."

She was shocked. But she would not take time to argue about niceties. Bigger things were bothering her.

"And you have something to learn before you go into politics. How much actual schooling have you had, Hank?"

"Went through the fifth grade. Hadda quit then. Worked like to a nigger on the farm. Couldn't 'a gone nohow. No money for schools. The goddam governor cut down expenses and us hill folks found there wasn't money for schools in our districts. Christ! What a way to cut down expenses!" He snorted with indignation. "I'm a-tellin' you, when I'm governor I'll . . ."

"I begin to see there is a long way to go before you can think of being governor, Hank."

Hank seemed to shrink just a little. But he saw the problem and was willing to conquer it.

"If you're a-thinkin' 'bout what Bolduc said—why, he's right. Hell, I picked up one a' his lawbooks 'n I couldn't hardly read it."

Verity patted his knee in a consoling, motherly way.

"Don't you care, darling," she said softly. "Don't you care. You have brains and push and you can do it. We'll map out your education just as soon as we can get the books sent out here."

"You mean you'll help me, Sweetface?"

"Of course." She was happy. Here was something she could do for Hank.

"Mrs. Hank Martin, you're wonderful. I thought mebbe you'd help your old man that-a-way."

So, he'd thought of all that before. Funny Hank! Planning on their wedding day for his ambitions. She had not been mistaken in him. He could do fine big things someday.

"We're home, Sweetface. Whoa, Beauty, whoa!" He pulled on the reins, wound them around the whip, and jumped to the ground, ran around the cart and held out his arms to her.

She stood up in the cart and looked at her home. There it stood, an unpainted shack of a house. One of the tenant sharecropper houses on the Bolduc place, ugly and dilapidated. It had one beauty—a great live oak strung with Spanish moss graced the yard, giving deep and restful shade.

And suddenly the tree took on a special meaning for Verity. She looked again at the run-down shack. It sat on the western edge of the tract of land that went with it—a sharecropper's farm. To live here would automatically mark her as "white trash."

She turned and looked wonderingly down at Hank. His uplifted arms invited her to be carried into that house—into the emotional turmoil of marriage. And what would she find there—torment or fulfillment?

She felt that perhaps the huge live oak offered her surcease from either. If torment, she would come to that tree and find peace. If fulfillment, she would lie beneath it with her face in the thick, sweet grass and take counsel from the earth.

Her steady look, her immobility, made Hank impatient. He did not understand her hesitation.

As she looked back into his urgent eyes, she felt that her appearance was a disguise. Fresh and untouched she looked as she stood in the full glow of the low red sun, and the fever which suddenly burned in her middle, shooting a paralyzing weakness down her legs and a delirium of desire up to her brain, should not be in a body which was clothed in chaste white. Only a half of her mind was still cool and she wondered if she dared surrender it, too. She wondered if all brides knew their robes to be a courteous lie. She hoped so, for that would make her experience less strange, less terrifying.

For a little second she thought of picking up the reins and driving away. But as she continued to look into Hank's urgent eyes, she felt complete surrender. He leaned over the wheel of the cart, arms still outstretched. Her knees sagged and with a sweet intoxication she went into his arms, her white skirt dragging over the cart wheels, leaving a smear of dust. She thought that was better, more honest, somehow.

Hank let his lips glide lightly across her forehead, temple, and cheek, then buried his face in the curve of her neck. Her nerves rippled a thrilling message. Hank tightened his hold as he strode across the small yard.

"Sweetface," he murmured against her ear, "we begin livin' now. Livin', Sweetface."

He kicked the sagging door wide and carried his bride over the threshold.

A cool missing of Hank's body caused Verity's hands to feel of her wrinkled, sweat-damp petticoat and push it down to her knees, to pull her open corset cover over her breasts. Somewhere an imp giggled with a gleeful sinfulness, "I knew it would be messy," and tried to prod her into words and laughter. But her body felt rich and grateful and clung to this sweet, new sense of being both rebuilt and spent. The moss-filled mattress crackled as she turned slightly and the little imp laughed, remembering the many small cracklings of a while ago, cracklings that had grown rhythmical as if they were tapping a million drums—little, secret, earthy drums.

Her wedding dress lay over a roughhewn cypress stool where Hank had put it after pulling it over her head, and her big white hat lay upturned on the floor, the bowl of its crown filled with the drooping, brown-turning magnolias. From the top edge of an open door hung a pair of bright green galluses, from which Hank's trousers dangled. The gaudy purple stripe stood out plainly, for the moon came through uncurtained windows and spread the rough floor with sheer white, and the reddish tar-paper walls hid their afternoon blotches.

With whitewash and paint and percale from Hank's cart, I can make our room quite nice, she thought. Our room—our room.

The light, sure tread of Hank's unbooted feet brought her eyes to the doorway. Fascinated astonishment at his nakedness, and a placid sense of the rightness of seeing him so, filled her. His palely gleaming skin, emphasized by the dark, hour-glass design of hair from shoulders to groin, chased the rich lassitude from her. He lifted her in his arms in one quick, fierce movement.

"I got a supper cookin' fitten for a queen. Corn pone a-bakin', 'n pot-licker a-stewin'. How many bridegrooms cooks his bride her first married meal, d' y' reckon?"

She rubbed her nose on his whiskery cheek.

"Hank, you're joking. You can't cook!"

"I can't cook! Lookit, I been a-sellin' Sizzle—it's made a' cotton seed. You think I could sell it t' folks that's oozed sowbelly for five generations without I could go t' their stoves 'n show 'em?" He laughed and danced a few steps. "Yes, sir, Sweetface, I get fed 'n sell 'em somethin' too. Not for years has Hank Martin's food 'n bed cost him a picayune. I'm their friend. Hell, I'm a event in their lives."

He sat her on a big pine table beside the coal-oil lamp. Its chimney was spotless, the table top had a scraped cleanness, the open cupboards displayed a few dishes, and on a worktable back of the little wood stove was a pecan pie.

"That pie—now you didn't make that! And who cleaned this place?"

"Well, now, I'd like t' be a-tellin' y' I done it. But the fact is I says to Tim Peck—he's the smith here—I says, 'Tim, y' damned old iron pounder, congrat'late me. I'm 'bout t' be the bridegroom a' the most beautiful lady in the Magnolia State. A lady, mind. 'N beautiful,' I says. 'Her cheeks,' I says, 'is just the color a' the pink underdown a' the flamingo. Not red like the top feathers, Tim,' I says, 'but just pinkish like to the underdown. 'N her lips is a brighter pink liken fresh boiled shrimp, an' her eyes is flashin' blue-gray—like to the river way out where it's almost ocean 'n got storm riffles in it!' " He ran his hands through her hanging, waist-length hair. " 'N that ain't all I says, Sweetface. I says, ' 'N, Tim, her hair's as yeller as a jasmine bell, 'n she walks high-steppin' 'n proud, like to a thoroughbred trotter that's got spirit but wears harness good.' Yes, sir, b' God, that's the way you are. Only there's somethin' else 'bout you I can't say exactly. Reckon that's why I call you Sweetface."

Flipping up her ruffled petticoat he kissed her knee, then ran to the stove, lifted the potlid, and stirred vigorously, grinning at her. The glow of the fire through the cracks between lids and open draft played over his nakedness.

She jumped from the table and went to her luggage.

"For mercy sakes, Hank," she said, "put some clothes on!"

He threw back his head and roared. Slowly she tied the sash of a straight little kimono of cashmere dotted with small pink flowers.

"Y' like me naked 'n y' know you do," Hank declared.

"Well, certainly not in the kitchen!"

Hank laughed and shook the long wooden spoon at her.

"Now ain't that just what I said—y' wear harness, but you wear it pretty. Throw me m' pants. They're jus' behind y' on the bedroom door."

She lifted his trousers from the top of the door, found his pink shirt on the doorknob under his coat, and brought them to him. As she held them out to him he took her in his arms and clasped her tight against his body.

"Lord save us," he whispered passionately, "Lord save us."

"Hank, Hank—is it right to love so much? To feel like this?"

"A-course it is, Sweetface, a-course it is. Lord God'lmighty made us this-a-way." He tipped her face up to his. "Ain't it wonderful? Tell the truth now."

She tried to turn her head away. She felt shy and frightened. Not of Hank, but of the glad, primitive urge which throbbed in her.

"Ain't it," he insisted, "ain't it wonderful?"

"Yes," she whispered, "yes, too wonderful."

She pulled away from him. He laughed and let her go. She went to the cupboard and tried to study its contents while Hank put on his clothes. Why was she scared? What did she mean by too wonderful? She wished she could think of something to talk about. Something commonplace, something known.

"You—you never did tell me who cleaned the place, or where the pie came from."

Hank walked over to her, buttoning the fly of his pants.

"Well, it's like I was a-sayin'. I says to Tim Peck—the smith—'You find me a healthy nigger wench 'n send her down t' my place 'n have it shined up for my wife.' 'N Tim says, 'Hank, y' well know niggers don't like to work in them tenant houses. They're most all field niggers hereabouts.' 'N I says, 'Tim, I'm askin' y'. You git that there place all proper clean 'r I'll brand y' withen one a' yore own damned horseshoes,' I says. So Tim he grins 'n says, 'I'll be a-sendin' m' old woman down 'n let her do her neighborly duty.' 'N sure 'nuff it looks like she done it."

"Why don't the Negroes like to work in the tenant houses, Hank?"

"Aw, niggers has a stuck-uppityness a' their own. They 'druther work in the fields for most nothin' a-tall than work for the white trash. But we're different. There ain't nobody gonna think Hank Martin's white trash. Not nobody. I'm gonna go up. We're here for a reason, Sweetface, for a reason!"

She knew he would go up. He had what her mother would have called "the get-up-and-get." Hank would go up. But it would take some doing. She thought of Jules Bolduc's dancing, jeering eyes, and walked to the window to look toward the manor house. The live-oak tree in her yard stood like a great armored friend, its dark leaves shimmering silver like a coat of mail. It had a noble height and width and its supporting roots would have to spread deep and wide in the earth—the strange earth which thrived so queerly. She suddenly saw her mother, herself, and the other orphanage children carrying buckets of manure, which had been carefully saved to spread over the garden and around the fruit trees, could hear her mother patiently explaining each fall and spring that every living thing grew better for having fertilizer. Why, maybe that was the purpose of sex in human life. Maybe it was an enriching fertilizer—maybe it served some deep design other than children, other than pleasure—some deep design of growth. Maybe it stoutened the top growth of spirit and mind. Yes, maybe, oh, maybe it did.

A sense of alive, strength-giving heat from the calves of her legs up her back to her shoulders made Verity realize in a soft awakening from the deepest sleep she had ever known that she was lying with Hank's body curled around her, line for line. He gives off heat like the sun, she thought, and curved her back outward, burrowing a little deeper into the cradle of his stomach and thighs. She felt his stomach ripple with a laugh-pushing breath before she heard his chuckle.

"I been a-layin' here harmless as a milk adder just a-makin' bets with myself that the first move you made'd be t' try to get closer." He slipped his tongue along the curve of her ear.

She felt again that odd fear. She was not afraid of Hank. What was it then? The sun glared in where last night had been the moon, and the blotches on the tar-paper walls were a clear and readable story of poverty —or were they the story of folk who sank into miasmas of sensation?

She struggled, but he held her tight.

"Hank, for heaven's sake, it's broad daylight."

"It shore is. Broad daylight on our first married mornin'. Lay still and get the feel a' it, 'cause, Sweetface, you ain't never goin' to have another first married mornin'." His face became serious though his eyes still danced. "No, sir, you ain't never goin' to have another, 'cause this here marriage is one that's took, Sweetface. This ain't no lark we're off on. We're good 'n married for the whole world t' see."

He lay back and stretched, pushed his arms from under the cotton blankets above his head. He sniffed, raised his head from the pillow to put his nose nearer his underarm. Looking at Verity, he grinned widely, took hold of the edge of the blanket and fanned it up and down. His nostrils pulled downward and flared, making white indentations as he drew through them, long and slow.

"Like all animals we got our own scent come ruttin'. Excitin' smell, ain't it?"

Almost terrified, she jumped from the crackling mattress, grabbed her kimono, and ran from the room. He went after her instantly, the tails of his knee-length nightshirt flapping comically with his long strides. He jack-knifed, grabbed the back tail of his gown and pulled it up between his legs diaper fashion.

"Helluva lookin' sight," he muttered.

With the other hand he grabbed Verity's hair.

"Whoa, there, whoa!—" he pulled her to him. "Don't you never run away from me, Sweetface," he said softly. He patted her head with firm long strokes, like a master gentling a scared filly. "What's a-itchin' you that y' run that-a-way?"

She kept her eyes low, watching her hands slowly fashioning a bow from her sash streamers.

"You—you make me ashamed, Hank."

"Ashamed! Why, hell, Verity, don't never be 'shamed a' yore nature. That's purely silly. Damnedest waste there is. Makes fools a' folks." He whirled her about, but she kept her head lowered. "Might's well smother yoreself 'cause it ain't proper nice to be a-breathin' in good air 'n breathe out poison. Yes, sir, that's what a doc tolt me we're a-doin' alla the time." He tipped her chin up and held it high between pinching thumb and fingers.

"Be glad—be proud, b' God—that y' got a body that's a-livin' every second 'n that ain't a-lettin' you miss airy a tingle."

She felt better, but she must also make her point clear.

"Yes, but—look at this place! Just look at it! Maybe the people who've lived here before just—just—well, tingled." Her face flushed but she went on. "Grew slovenly. Thought that was all that mattered. And just look at this place!"

He looked around and laughed.

"Don't bother me none. None whatsomever. I aim t' live in a palace some day. All marble 'n shinin'. 'N it just don't matter none what I gotta take a-gettin' there. We ain't white trash, no matter what."

"Well, if we're not white trash we better prove it. I want some decency between now and that palace."

"Prove it, huh? Right now, you mean? Well, we ain't white trash." His tone was stubborn and bewildered. "But this here's a share-crop house 'n how you goin' to make it different? What you a-wantin'?"

"I want this place painted or whitewashed inside and out, the doors hung straight, and curtains at the windows."

"Well, b'God'lmighty you get it all come nightfall. That'd make this place right smart different, it would. You're a-askin' the right man, Sweetface." He chuckled. "I'm a-beginnin' t' catch on to you. You wasn't shamed a-tall. You was just plumb scared lovin' was all you was gonna get in this marriage. Lemme tell you Hank Martin can work more hours 'n love more hours than any god-damned day can cram into itself." He shook a finger in her half-smiling face. "On yore first married day, Miz Martin, you're a-goin' t' get a sample a' what it's gonna mean t' keep up with yore man. Now where the hell's m' pants so I c'n get a-goin'? You get busy 'n fry us some grits whilst I'm gone for that whitewash 'n paint."

"Silly," she chided, "you can't get paint. It's Sunday."

"What's that gotta do with it? I'm just a-goin' up to old Squeeze-nickel Noady's house—he runs the store for that lazin' Jules Bolduc. Cheatin' right 'n left, too. 'N I betcha, Verity, them long, skinny, shitepoke legs a' hisn'll run him all the way from his house t' the store for a chancet t' steal another dime. Nope, ain't goin' t' be no trouble gettin' paint. Then I'll make him come down 'n help with the paintin'. Sermons don't do that thievin' Squeeze-nickel no good, nohow."

He pulled on his trousers.

"But we're a-goin' t' Sunday meetin' ourselves hereafter. Ain't fitten not t' be 'mongst them as harks t' the words of the Lord. Ain't y' allus a-readin' 'bout the President 'n governors bein' churchy folks come 'lection time?" He stood still, studying the room a minute. "Don't seem t' me this here floor's no better'n the walls. Don't y' think the floors should oughta get painted too?"

"Oh, Hank, it would be nice."

"Shore. What color y' a-wantin'? Red 'r yeller? Or purple, mebbe?"

"Mercy no! Brown."

"Aw, brown's what things turn when they're a-dyin'. What's the matter with green? Yes, sir, that's it, green. God's got green on His floor. Now why ain't green all right?"

"Green—dark, dark green might be fine. And, Hank, while you're at the store buy some food, dear. We brought so little with us."

"Shore." He pulled his coat over the glowing pink shirt. "That there wood stove makes this place hotter'n hell. Reckon I'll hafta get one a' them coal-oil jiggers I seen in Loder City. It's got big tin chimneys 'n wicks like to a lamp. 'N a woman c'n cook withouten the sweat a-runnin' down her legs come summer."

He strode to the door. Verity ran after him.

"Aren't you going to kiss me, Hank?" She lifted her face.

"Now lissen here, Sweetface," he said, half scolding, "you ain't never gonna get no habit pecks from me. Them habit pecks ain't got no flavor. Me, I like my kissin' with laughin' after lovin', 'r I like it with teasin' afore lovin', 'r I like it in earnest with lovin'. Now we ain't got time. I done promised a painted house come nightfall."

He grinned down at her a moment, then jumped over the steps to the ground.

She leaned against the doorjamb, feeling annoyed and a little foolish. "No habit pecks, indeed," she said aloud. And then, "Now, we ain't got time. *Now,* we ain't got time." Then suddenly she laughed. Wasn't that just what she wanted? The little weight of fear was dissolving. She would never have to worry about Hank's sinking into those miasmas. She must be dressed and clean and pretty when he returned. She took a big galvanized pail and went down the rickety back steps and out to the pump. The iron handle shuddered with the effort she put it to and the rusty plunger squealed against the cylinder sides. Her body bent and straightened, bent and straightened, pushing down and pulling up on the big old handle. Her hair fell forward over her shoulders and the warm morning sun plotted with the pump to make her feel sticky. "Everything is a sweating job. Cooking is—just as Hank said. And pumping, and—" The little imp giggled. She straightened, laughing, and looked out at the fields. There lay the acres that went with this house. Did Hank intend to till them? she wondered. Right here would make a fine green garden patch. One of the things that had astounded her in the South was the fact that the poor so rarely had table gardens. Many of the sharecroppers tilled the soil for market produce only and bought their food dried and canned in the company stores at prices which kept them forever tied to the company for debt. She would have a fine garden, a garden as fine as her mother's. She began pumping again.

She bent and straightened, bent and straightened, listening for the gurgle which would announce the coming water, wondering if it would need priming; and all the while way back in her mind thoughts tried to take form, to come to life for her future use. Finally the water gushed out and over the bucket sides, dampening the splintery platform. The freshening feel of it on her bare feet made her realize anew that only a bath could make her feel remotely like Verity Wade, spinster. She tipped some of the water from the bucket, getting it down to a level which would not slop out on her new kimono, as she carried it up the wobbly steps.

Inside, she took the water to the bedroom, draped the thin cotton blanket over the window, dipped water from pail to basin, and stripped. As she lathered herself with a cake of perfumed soap and enjoyed the sectional freshness of first neck and arms, then legs, then midriff, her mind still worried with the unformed thoughts.

She reviewed their morning conversation word by word. She knew that Hank's every word, every look, every touch could be relived in her memory in fifty—a hundred years. "Now, we ain't got time." She stopped in the act of fastening the stiff front stay hooks of her corset and laughed. Hank was unquestionably going to be a great man. Why, she could feel his greatness now in a way. Jules Bolduc and people like him could laugh at Hank, but they were wrong. They had no vision. A seed must contain all the elements of the thing it will grow to be. Within the seed lies that which determines the bloom. How else could the oak and the cypress grow side by side, the gum and the hickory, the ash and the elm? They had the same earth and air and rain. But with humans there were those great unknowns, the will and the mind. What of them? Had Hank already swayed her will, colored her mind somewhat? She examined that thought and rejected it. No, they had come together a mating pair, man and woman, and who could say that in the mating each did not simply make it possible for the other to live fully?

With a determined effort she pulled her mind away from such muddling thoughts. Now, we ain't got time! She put on a starched blue dress with puffed sleeves and a prim white collar, fluffed her hair about her ears, and coiled it in a big loose knot low on her neck.

She carried her bath water to the kitchen door and threw it out, scoured out the basin, and put it back of the stove. She poked more wood into the stove, stirred the grits, and measured out the chicory and water for the brew which passed for coffee. Carefully she repacked her clothes so they would not get spattered with whitewash, rolled the moss mattress, and covered it with the blanket. The slightly sagging ropes woven from frame to frame surprised her. It had seemed such a good bed.

She saw nothing more to do until Hank came, and so went out into the knee-high grass and weeds to the oak tree. Its moss draperies hung still and solemn, seeming to know it was Sunday morn. Happiness and a love for this tree welled in Verity, and she rubbed a leaf on a low-hanging branch between her fingers like a shopper testing silk, pleased with its tough, leathery resistance.

From down the road came men's voices singing, wagon wheels squeaking on their axles, hoofs plunking with the slow stolidity of plow animals, and over all she could distinguish Hank's voice, jubilant and loud.

> "Work, for the night's a-comin',
> Work through the sunny noon;
> Fill brightes' hours with labor,
> Rest comes sure 'n soon."

Hank stood, his back to the seat, facing the men in the wagon bed who were standing or sitting on the edge of the sides, waving his arms like a band leader. Everyone swayed with the music, and their scythes and hoes caught the sun's gleam darkly on their earth-blackened blades.

"Come on there, Squeeze-nickel, 'n you too, Picayune Potter. Lemme hear y'. Beller out good 'n strong like a bull a-rarin' t' go. Ain't more'n a hundred paces afore we get t' the work a' the Lord. Come on, now, beller out!"

> "Work, for the night's a-comin',
> Under the sunset skies;
> While their bright tints a-glowin'
> Work, for daylight flies."

She wondered where the men were going. Hank was certainly giving them quite a sendoff.

The driver pulled on the reins and stood up. His huge torso, too long and too broad for his legs, made a mammoth frog of the man as he leaped to the ground. All the other men climbed down from the wagon bed.

"There it is, just a-hungerin' for paint. Slap 'er on thick, boys. 'N remember, the bargain is come nightfall. I wonder oughten that t' go for the barn, too?"

A little man not five feet high, with a round face and a round belly, scratched his slick bald head and drawled jovially, "Now look-a-here, Hank, ain't none a' us hearn you say nothin' 'bout the barn ner the privy yonder. Ain't airy one willin' t' paint yore barn 'n privy." His laugh wheezed and whistled.

"That's right, Hank."

"No barn 'n privy."

"Well, shore not—no privy."

Hank threw back his head and laughed, gave the little fat man a wallop on the back.

"So you think you're too good for t' paint a privy, do y'? Lemme tell you, Picayune Potter, you're a-goin' t' paint that privy personal. You men done gone 'n forced me t' make a decision in favor a' paintin' the barn 'n privy. 'N, Picayune, mebbe y' better plane down the seat smooth 'n splinter-free, cause iffen I was t' hurt m' treasured parts I'll set you in the middle a' the biggest dung pile in Delamore Parish." The men roared. "Now ain't that a threat t' scare you t' death, Picayune?"

"Hit shore is." Picayune laughed. "You shore air a holy terror, Hank," and his stretched shirt and pants showed every wobble of his laughter-shaken body.

Anger flared in Verity, almost choking her. The men turned to take supplies from the wagon and she ran to the house, around to the other side and in through the back door.

Hank came through the front door from the yard.

"Well, Sweetface, yore house is shore a-goin' t' be painted come night-fall. I got it all fixed. I got friends organized to get a-goin'. They'll be a-comin' in to make their kowtow to you 'n t' say howdy. Ain't that fine?"

"I can't see them." Her white face set and her eyes filled with tears.

"What's the matter? What's been a-happenin' whilst I been gone?"

"It's happened when you returned! How can I meet your friends when they talk about—about—" She waved her hands helplessly.

Hank laughed. "You mean you heared the jestin' 'bout the privy? How come you heared that? I don't hear them men a-talkin' now."

He stood in listening attitude, looking at her questioningly.

"I was out by the big oak."

"God'lmighty, Verity, you ain't a-tellin' me you're a-holdin' talk agin men that's aimed for private conversation? Them men's plumb full a' respect. 'N it's plumb persnickety to feel that-a-way 'bout a privy. God'lmighty! Brother Moulton's a-bringin' his entire flock here today.

We're a-havin' the services—holdin' 'em right out there in our own yard soon's Brother Dady scythes it down."

"You mean the entire congregation of a church is coming here?" Her amazement rang out and bounced back in a small echo.

Hank nodded vigorously.

"That's right, Sweetface. The whole congregation's a-comin' 'n is a-goin' t' work."

She leaned against the pine cupboard and stared at him.

"But why—why?"

Enjoying her bewilderment, he chuckled, "Well, it's this-a-way. I don't never talk through m' hat. And so I get a-figurin' on my way to Squeezenickel's. An' I says t' myself, 'Hank, y' damn fool, you're fast, 'n y' ain't one for takin' time out to be allus a-restin', but even if y' can do it yoreself, ain't this the perfect time for t' be makin' yoreself felt in this neighborhood? Ain't it now?' I asks myself. 'N then I answers myself 'n says, 'Course the best way t' do anything is t' make other folks wanta do it!' 'N that seems like as if 'twas the right answer 'n then I remind myself it's Sunday 'n I gotta make these here folks see they're a-helpin' the Lord iffen they was to work for me. 'N right there, Verity, I think 'bout the last time I was here 'n about the womenfolks a' the church a-bakin' and a-cookin' an' a-peddlin' their stuff to get a strip a' carpet for the aisle. 'N right then I remember the Catholic priest in Loder City 'n the red carpet he's took outta his rich church 'n I know I can mebbe get it for nothin' or sure not much—'n there's my answer! I hustle 'n catch Brother Moulton 'n tell him how his flock can earn that there carpet 'n enough mebbe for his own parlor. 'N there y'are, Sweetface. Everythin' y' wanted is gonna be done come nightfall. 'N more. We got ourselves good church standin' just throwed into the bargain."

She could not answer for a second. He beamed down on her, waiting for her to grasp the full meaning of all he had done.

"Oh, a sort of picnic!" she said slowly.

"Shore, a picnic," Hank exclaimed. "Y' don't think Hank Martin'd expect folks to work happy 'thouten no food in their bellies? I fixed it all up with Brother Moulton to be a-sendin' back the folks that don't live too far off for to fetch their own Sunday dinner 'n tolt him I'd be a-gettin' some vittles. 'N then I tells Squeeze-nickel, an' Tim Peck, 'n Picayune Potter to have their women load on some big syrup pots 'n bring some chickens or some hawg meat, 'n come ahead. We're a-goin' to have ourselves a great gatherin' first day we're in Cypress Bend!"

Verity looked around the bare, ugly rooms in a sort of panic.

"But I—I—have nothing to do with. How can I cook and serve—" Her voice faded out.

Hank laughed.

"Sweetface, y' ain't got a livin' thing to do. Not a livin' thing. 'Cept tell

21

all the womenfolks what's to be done, withen the curtains 'n things you said you was wantin'. M' cart's in the barn. We'll go look at the yardage bolts so's you can get yore choosin' done. Got a right pretty bolt a' stuff withen a red stripe down it 'n a green vine a-climbin' up it. Rest a' it's white. Prettier'n a pelican it is. But afore we see the stuff I'll beller to the boys."

He stepped to the door and howled, "Hey there, fellers, come on in! The missus is plumb anxious t' be a-knowin' y' all." Turning to her, he dropped his voice to a low whisper. "Lookit them a-hustlin' here all in a herd. Ain't airy a one got the gumption of nutted cockerel, but in herds they fancy theirselves t' be gamecocks. It's funny," he mused thoughtfully. "Y' know it—but I see plain ain't a one a' 'em worth a dang. Not a dang. But in herds they got a use to a man like me. I been a-thinkin' on it for years. 'S funny, ain't a one worth a dang, still 'n all, I'm right partial to the dumb sonsabitches. B'God, sometimes I think I'm full 'n runnin' over withen love for 'em."

He took Verity's hand.

"Come on, Sweetface. Better mebbe you should come outside like as if you was anxious t' meet 'em. Actual, I mean."

She wanted to cry out in protest that she was truly anxious to meet people friendly enough to help a neighbor, childish enough to call it working for the Lord. They must be a lenient and lovable people. She thought of Preacher Polder's dour face, his fist shakings, and the threats in which he clothed religion. Painting for red carpets was much to be preferred. She rebuked herself for a prude, censured herself for lack of understanding that she had judged these men by words not meant for her ears. Her fingers tightened about Hank's hard, warm hand. She was Mrs. Hank Martin. These men coming toward her were her first guests. The weeds bent under their oncoming feet, leaving a triple pathway to the barn, and their silence told her they were taking her measure, using as yardstick their love for Hank—Hank who was like these men and yet so different. Pride in Hank, pride in being his wife, combined with that new and glorious physical joy, made her feel weightless. She was happy, so happy that she was light and floaty.

She went down the steps toward the men. Picayune's bright blue eyes twinkled out from little wells of fat and suddenly the imp in Verity laughed and laughed—"plane it smooth 'n splinter-free," it laughed.

"Sweetface, this here fat runt's Picayune Potter; 'n this long-legged shitepoke's Squeeze-nickel Noady. 'N this is Brother Dal Dady, deacon a' the church. Reckon I ain't knowin' him well enough t' be a-callin' him names yet, 'n wouldn't likely call a deacon names on Sunday nohow, specially seein' as how he's here on church duty kinda like. 'N the feller behind them peaked whiskers that's been scissored up so fancy says his name is Orn-rye Mee-no, account he's a French hang-over, but once't y' see his name spelled out y' know he's plain Henry Minot, same's his face is ugly more'n likely back a' them whiskers. Yes, sir, Orn-rye Mee-no is a man as is given to dudin'."

She shook hands with them, murmuring each name, wanting them to feel her welcome, wanting them to feel Hank had made no mistake.

"'N this giant's Tim Peck, Sweetface; Tim Peck, a extra special friend a' mine."

The calluses of Tim Peck's hand pressed into her palm. Like squeezing a horned toad, she thought, but she liked him immensely. The naturalness of earth was in the man. His eyes and hair and skin were the cinnamony brownness of fine and flexible leather. He said nothing, just let his eyes look into hers long and steadily.

"I want to thank you and Mrs. Peck for your kindness to Hank and me," said Verity. "For the pie and everything."

His great froglike body relaxed as she spoke, and his cinnamon eyes half hid as his heavy cheeks pushed up in a smile.

"Hank tolt me poetical how you was beautiful, 'n his description was well-nigh perfect, I 'spect, him bein' the most describin' talker in the state most likely. But it don't seem's though even Hank could tell it all. Hank's purely lucky."

His sincerity was simple and profound. She knew he loved Hank like a son, believed in him as she did.

"I am the lucky one," she said. "Hank's going to be a great man someday."

"Goin' t' be!" Hank exclaimed in protest. "Goin' to be! Roarin' thunderbolts! I'm a-doin' all right right now!"

"You're a-declarin' the truth, boy." Tim's voice was most reverent.

"That I am," Hank declared. "But you snails in human form had better get a-movin', bearin' in mind the bargain is come nightfall. Tim, God bless yore iron-poundin' right arm, get busy 'n take them doors down and fix them hinges. Picayune, get that there paint mixed. No, reckon we'll whitewash the innards a' that house first, so's the ladies can have a fitten place for t' set and sew curtains. Get mixin' that stuff now 'n take five, six in with you 'n slap it on quick 'n neat. Go easy on them brushes, too, account Squeeze-nickel only rented 'em to me for 'bout the same money as the sale price. But he 'spects to sell 'em for new 'n we wouldn't want him to feel bitter 'bout a good Sunday's work."

Their laughs rolled up from their bellies as they went off toward the wagon, slapping Squeeze-nickel's thin, narrow back.

Hank turned to the other men.

"Brother Dady, iffen you'll be so kind as to scythe down the weeds in this here yard so's we can have a fitten place for picnickin' 'n preachin', I'll be mighty grateful. 'N, Henry, you get them tools a' yoren and start fixin' the steps front 'n back so's they won't teeter even under Tim Peck.

Then fix the windows good afore we get to the outside paintin'. You boys with them spades get a-diggin' out back by the pump 'n make the hollers for the fires, 'n get things set 'n ready withen the poles for to steady the syrup kettles, so's the womenfolks can stew up chicken 'n hawg enough for t' feed all Delamore Parish. Now get a-goin' whilst I take my wife down t' the barn where m' cart is, to do her choosin' for the stuff the womenfolks is to sew on."

The men seemed to understand the instructions perfectly. Hank put a hand under Verity's arm and guided her to the barn.

He opened the door and they stepped inside. Turning to her, he ran his fingers lightly from her chin up her jawbone and twiddled the lobe of her ear, gazing down at her earnestly.

"Y' got the kindlin' power in y', Sweetface. All different kinds a' kindlin' power. Them men felt it, Tim specially. Y' kindled 'em plumb full a' respect 'n good manners." His eyes went half closed and his head came a fraction nearer and moved ever so slightly, a small smile lifted to meet the whitening line from his nostrils. "In me, a' course, you kindle everythin' I got. Smell that blend a' horse 'n hay. There ain't no sweeter place to lay for lovin' than in a haymow," he whispered.

His head came nearer and nearer with a slow, slight sideways movement as if he were nuzzling her neck. His body tensed, his finger moved faster, faster, back and forth in a small flipping motion on her ear lobe. Her heart beat faster, her throat tightened. The dim half-light of the barn seemed wavering with its thickness of pungent smells, wavering faster and faster, keeping time with Hank. A part of her longed to fall against him with boneless and giving laxity, a part of her stiffened in outrage. Suddenly outrage froze into anger, her hand darted out and landed a sharp slap on his cheek.

"Now we ain't got time," she said acidly.

His eyes lost their languor and came sharply into focus, his finger ceased its odd caressing. He stood with a breathless stillness for a second, studying her white anger; then throwing his head up and back he roared with laughter.

"I allus rejoiced that you was one woman couldn't be raped. 'N like allus Hank Martin was righter'n right. You're one woman as can't be raped afore nor after marriage."

He picked her up and cakewalked over the straw-strewn floor to the cart standing tarpaulin-covered in the farther stall, put her on her feet and stood back admiring her.

"Sweetface," he said softly, "ain't nothin' I like better'n t' bite unexpected into pepper. You're plumb a-flavorin' my life with sugar 'n spice 'n everything nice. But you gotta be rememberin'," his eyes twinkled, "that even in them jingles for babies they start off explainin' how boys is made a' tails."

He turned to the cart and jerked the tarpaulin off.

" 'N when girls as is made a' sugar 'n spice 'n boys as is made a' tails get together for t' do a little earnest mixin' a' their charms, they want curtains t' hide behind whilst they're a-cuttin' their didoes."

He leaned down and looked up into her face with the beguiling, teasing smile of a naughty young child.

"So in view of them didoes we're aimin' t' cut, oughten y' t' be a-doin' yore choosin'?"

He lifted the lid of a rough pine box and pulled out six bolts of material, deftly flipped bolt after bolt, flaunting with pride purple, pink, and yellow fields of flowers; orange, magenta, and blue checkerboards.

"But this'n I was a-tellin' you 'bout is mebbe more to yore likin'. That vine is like to the swamp somewhat, 'n that red stripe's citified as a barber pole. It'll gay yore house up right smart."

It was really very pretty. It had a clarity of color, a sort of unmixed purity which appealed to her. But the remnants of anger were in her. She clutched a wagon wheel, hunting for composure, knowing she must find it if she was to get through the day—a day filled with strange neighbors, and a stranger husband, able to combine passion and sermons, picnic and curtains, and the painting of house, barn, and privy, all in the name of red carpets for the Lord.

Hank sobered, seeming to feel her perplexity.

"Breathe deep, Sweetface," he advised. "You upset right easy. You gotta get over that. Don't never let nothin' upset you. Ain't you never watched the animals when they're a-feared? They stop 'n breathe their-selves deep 'n full."

He lifted his head and breathed deep, pounded his chest, pulled himself up to his tallest. His chest pushed out, his lower torso thinned and stretched.

"Ain't nothin' so curin' as pulled-in guts a-shovin' up on a chest full a' air. Sends somethin' t' the brain that's right confidence-givin'. Try it, Sweetface. Animals know lotsa things. Like this."

She watched again—the expanding chest, the thinning abdomen. He lifted his head and sent up a joyous howl to echo in the rafters. He stopped, stood very still, his lithe, stretched body reminding Verity of something—but what?

"Lissen—they're a-comin'. Hear them wagons down the road? The whole damn herd a' them's a-comin'. Let's get outta here 'n greet 'em proper. This is a-goin' t' be a day t' remember. Yes, sir, by God'lmighty, a day t' remember!"

He grabbed the bolt in one hand, Verity's arm in the other. She shaded her eyes from the dazzling sunlight.

Five wagons rattled and shuddered over the washboard road. The first one held only two huge black syrup kettles. The others were jammed with men, women, and children, many of them holding squawking, terrified chickens.

"Roarin' thunderbolts," cried Hank, "looks like a funeral procession. Them big black kettles in the front!" He laughed. "First time ever I seen coffins empty 'n the victims a-follerin' it live 'n squealin'. Them chickens'll be plumb glad t' have it over."

A big fat woman in red-and-white calico shifted her hold on her rooster's feet to a firm hold on his head and leaned over the wagon side.

"My rooster'll be the first 'un ready fer the pot!" she screamed. Her huge strong arm whirled round and round. The brilliant red rooster whirled round and round, his neck stretching, turning, wringing smaller and smaller. His body parted from his head and fell flopping its last agony, the bloody shreds of neck sopping up the dust.

Thrusting the curtain material into Verity's arms Hank ran to rescue the red body from two lean dogs who had suddenly abandoned their peaceful following of the wagons.

She held tightly to the bolt. There was no doubt but that her house would be painted come nightfall. Clearly she sensed that the slow, quiet bringing about of a beauty would never be her privilege. This is my life, my own choosing. There was humor in it at least. She sent a smile to her lips. Yes, sir, a day to remember!

3

Probably many a great idea was born in that little newly white house, for Hank has said he even then wondered and dreamed and thought on the amazing and catching ideas we now know as Divide the Earth's Riches.

He tells us that, like most of his ideas, they came to him from the word of God—"The earth is the Lord's and the fullness thereof. . . ."

LITTLE sounds of stove lids and oven door, of potlids and muffled scrapings of a stirring spoon prodded persistently at her luscious sleepiness. Each little impingement of sound struck on her consciousness and sent sparks of awareness through her brain. Through half-closed lids she peeped at the early morning. Like glowing new silver it shone on the world meeting the up-steaming ground mist just above her window's level. Like the beginning of time, she thought, and all framed by stripes of barber-pole red and the green swamp vine. The drapes were nice, but they sagged. That would all be corrected when she got some rods. She looked at the opposite wall. Three stains still sketched themselves grayly through the fresh whiteness. They annoyed and mocked her. The sun was not yet up and still they showed. She had to be rid of those stains if she whitewashed that wall every day of her life.

It was silly to be superstitious about a stain. She had to forget it. She raised herself on her elbow and looked out the window. The mist lay over the earth like a shallow sea, the trees seemed rootless and unreal. She wished she could sail that sea and imagined her body from thighs to toes as the prow of a ship, knifing through the mist at gale speed, causing no displacement spray ahead of her and leaving no riffle of wake behind. She could feel herself rushing through the waterless foam creating such a wind in the stillness that her hair waved out like a masthead flag. She wished she could make it a reality, but the reality came from sounds beyond the closed door. Hank was singing. It was a strange tune and she listened to catch the words:

> "Oh, there's pork on the table 'n grits in the pan,
> An' the pone's oozin' grease through the crust.
> My gal's cookin' is fitten for a king,
> An' I'm fixin' for to eat it till I bust."

He sang it with a drum rhythm, lightly, yet heavily accented on the third beat. She surveyed the green floor and smiled. She liked its green cleanness and there, clear but faint, were the prints of Hank's heel and toe marks from bed to door.

She didn't want to make another set of marks, so she scooted to the foot of the bed where Hank had climbed over her and carefully set her right heel in Hank's right-foot imprint. She lifted her gown and stretched her stride to match his. At the door she looked back. She had only succeeded in messing up his unmarked instep spots. The chipped black china doorknob turned quietly. Still in his nightshirt, Hank squatted before the oven. He had the front tail of his nightshirt pulled high from his body, using it to pad his hand against the heat of the iron handle; the back fell straight and free from his waist. His brown buttocks and thighs glistened with sweat. Clothes to Hank were not made for the sake of modesty. He wears them as a horse wears a silvered bridle on parade. Verity giggled inwardly. She wondered if she would ever get used to him. She swung the door wide.

"Hank, Hank," she laughed, "you haven't any more modesty than a horse!"

"Nary a bit more'n one a' them waltzin' circus horses," he laughed.

He rose to his feet, held his nightshirt high in hands that pawed awkwardly in the air; then went into a stiff-kneed dance, crossing his feet back and forth as he sang:

> "Oh, my gal's table's got a checkered cloth
> An' her stove is greased free of rust;
> Yes, my gal's cookin' is fitten for a king,
> An' I'm fixin' for to eat it till I bust."

At the close of the verse he stopped, feet crossed, and with hands still pawing the air he bowed his back and neck stiffly and whinnied plaintively.

A feel, as of an enlarging of her capacities for gaiety and loving, spread through her. She felt like a queen—oh, a very young queen, a playful and pampered queen. Hank had that quality. Why, yesterday every woman who sewed and scrubbed and cooked took on color when Hank approached. And it was she whom he loved! Lucky—lucky—her arms raised themselves and, feeling like beauty and rhythm, she whirled. From the deep wells of her being bubbles rose and foamed out on the air as laughter.

The green floor of this room was dry. Not the least sticky as was the bedroom floor. Her laugh grew deeper, fuller, as she remembered the reason. The bedroom floor had not been painted until they were ready for bed. Hank, with his nightshirt safety-pinned around his loins, had painted the floor, beginning at the living-room door and crawling back and back until they were imprisoned in bed by the wet green paint. This floor was clean and dry against her feet and she danced round the room admiring it.

"Oh, I like my walls and my lovely drapes and my green, green floors!" she repeated over and over happily.

Hank gave his voice the undulating wavers of a neigh and chanted:

> " 'N I like that filly with th' yaller mane
> Her 'n me could prance down any lane,
> If I can't ketch her I'll be dyin' of pain,
> Oh, I like that filly with the yaller mane."

She ran to him and paddled him almost sharply. "Is that one of those funny folk songs? Or did you make that up?"

"I made it up. Like that." He snapped his fingers. "I like words. Allus did. Someday I'm gonna learn every word there is." He pulled her to him. "Now I got me a horse 'n cart I c'n be a-settin' up there with one a' them dict'naries a-learnin' words by heart. Or mebbe a-learnin' them school books we're a-gettin' me."

The intent of approach crept into his eyes.

"Lord save us," he murmured softly. He sniffled, looked toward the stove. "My pone's a-burnin'!" He howled.

The little stove was red-hot. Smoke crept out through the oven cracks and a grease smoke puffed from the skillet. Verity rose and minced elegantly to the table.

"I can see I'm going to be a lady of leisure. My house is painted, my meals are cooked for me. You're spoiling me, Hank."

"Wisht you didn't never have to do nothin' 'cept think of me." He lifted the blackened pone from the pan and held it for her to see. "Reckon we'll have to whittle it some. It purely hurts to see food a-wastin'. Been hungry lotsa times. Lotsa people half-hungry all their lives, I reckon. Take m' maw. She was plumb gaunted. Had that there look on her t' make you remember the bones to a body."

"Your mother," she said wonderingly. She'd never thought of Hank as being a member of a family. Her whole thought had been on Hank himself. He had seemed to stand alone like the live-oak tree, needing no explanation of growth and parenthood.

He put the pone and sowbelly and coffee on the table and sat down.

"I hadda feelin' for Maw. Maw's eyes was big 'n askin'. It was right seldom she seemed to get a answer. When she did, then her eyes was big 'n seein'. A-seein' of things not there."

He held a steaming piece of pone, not noticing its heat.

"Then there was Maw's maw. Grammaw Kelts. She was allus a-settin' by the fireplace 'r the window a-readin' her Bible 'n a-sneezin' on her snuff. Y' know, Verity, when I was a little feller I allus thought of Maw 'n Grammaw as captives. It puzzled me powerful. When Maw was despairin' she'd go to the door 'n look out, 'n right pitiful she'd say, 'How shall we sing the Lord's song in a strange land?' 'N then Grammaw'd say it over faint, like a echo. 'N then she'd come out strong with 'We want t' go back to Zion, Lord.' Why, Verity, when I was scarce past my didy years I use t' wake up 'n sneak outta the house so's I could think on it.

"Sometimes in the fall I'd be out so early the rime was still a-shinin' on the grass. Didn't have no proper clothes so I'd go a-runnin' to get some blood warmth. The little things of the earth all scurried 'n it pleasured me. 'N all the time I was a-thinkin' it was a right nice country 'n why want for a place called Zion? But by the time I was eight 'r nine—God'lmighty! I was a-wantin' a Zion, too."

For Verity it had the proportions of a revelation. A revelation she wanted to understand.

"But being captives—what did they mean?" she urged.

"Oh, it all come of Grammaw's readin' 'n readin' her favorite psalm. 'By the rivers of Babylon, there we sat down, yea, we wept, when we remembered Zion. We hanged our harps upon the willows in the midst thereof. For there they that carried us away captive required of us a song; 'n they that wasted us required of us mirth, saying, Sing us one a' the songs of Zion.' Then comes Maw's question—'How shall we sing the Lord's song in a strange land?' "

His voice had a rich solemnity to match the majestic complaint, giving it the emphasis of quotation; and yet it sounded just like Hank. It seemed to have his rhythm.

"You know the Bible pretty well," she said.

"Hell, I was suckled on it, Sweetface. Thing 'at got my mind set on bein' a talkin' whiz-bang was them camp meetin's. First off, I was set on bein' a preacher. But time I got twelve years on me I knowed I wasn't endurin' enough to stand up there exhortin' for coppers. A man that's purely in a lather from movin' folks to go thou 'n sin no more is worth more'n a picayune."

"What about your father, darling?" she asked.

Contempt curled his lips.

"Paw was a pulin' man," he said simply. "Allus a-cryin' the mouths he hadda feed kep' him pore. Maw done more work in the fields than ever he done. Borned him seven young'uns, too. Just three of us was a-livin'. Y' see, Verity, we was in the pine hill country where the earth ain't a-yieldin' up like here. Still, there's a-plenty to eat iffen y' jus' happen to be the sort as can get it." He stared out the window.

"Twelve years I was when he bound me out to Farmer Plinkham. He wasn't the starvin' kind. God'lmighty! I was out a-workin' afore the stars left the sky, 'n I was still a-workin' come their first glimmer in the night. God'lmighty!"

Twelve years old, just a baby! Tears burned her eyes. And people were sorry for orphanage children! Hank grinned at her.

"Don't be a-lettin' it salten yore eyes, Sweetface. It done a-somethin' for me. A whole year I was with Plinkham a-workin' f' my grits 'n pone 'n for my pallet in a outshed, 'n for a dollar cash a month to be give me the followin' harvest." His voice hardened. "Th' somethin' it done for me was to make me know no matter what I hadda do, I was gonna go up! At camp meetin's I watched the preacher 'n what he done to folks. It was then I knowed I was gonna move folks too—but not preachin' for no picayune!"

Her eyes saltened in spite of her best efforts, pity for a young Hank spread her chest and throat to hurting.

"Damn if the pone ain't stone cold," he growled. "Helluva note. Bridegroom a-cookin' his bride her breakfast 'n a-lettin' it burn whilst they play's one thing but a-lettin' it go grease soggy whilst he drools on what's done 'n over is another."

"I'm glad you did, Hank," she said softly. "Please tell me more about . . ."

"Lissen!" He tilted his chair to look out the window. "There's a starched nigger a-comin'. Looks to be Jules Bolduc's nigger."

Resenting this interruption she rose from the table to don her kimono. She must know more of Hank's childhood. Must know why he had never mentioned it before, why she had never thought of him as one of a brood.

Seeing Hank about to open the door, she exclaimed in an urgent whisper, "Hank, you're in your nightshirt!"

With a great show of quiet and stealth he tiptoed back to her, put his lips against her ear.

"Wouldn't s'prise me none," he whispered, "iffen he's seen a nightshirt afore. Wouldn't s'prise me none iffen I went up in his eyes, seein' I don't sleep in m' underpants."

The well-bred, short little knock sounded on the door again. Grinning back at her, Hank went to the door and flung it wide.

"Mornin'!" he said heartily.

"I'se Moses, suh." The stiffness of his white coat and trousers made little crackles as he bowed. His close-cropped white hair seemed as starched as his suit. He looked past Hank at Verity and bowed again. His fine long black hands with fingers interlaced were held in front of him away from his body, giving the effect of offering something when he bowed.

"Moses, huh?" There was a slight query in Hank's voice.

"Yassuh. Is you Mistuh Hank Martin, suh?"

"That's me."

"Mistuh Jules Bolduc's compliments to you, suh. He wantses to know would you an' Miz Martin honor him by comin' to dinna tonight? Seb'n o'clock?"

"T' dinner?" Plainly Hank could hardly believe his ears.

"Yassuh. Seb'n o'clock." Moses half turned to leave.

"Moses," said Hank as if speaking to an old friend, "I'm plumb fulla puzzlement."

Moses turned. His eyes on Verity were gentle and knowing. He bowed again and his hands seemed to make a physical offering of his courtesy. Then turning to Hank he grinned.

"Mistuh Jules say he liken ter fall off his hawse dis mawnin' wen he see dis painted house." He bowed again. "Seb'n o'clock, Mistuh Hank, suh."

Hank stood quietly watching Moses. The fine long hands swung at his sides now as he strode under the live-oak tree and on over a little rolling swell in the earth toward the manor house.

" 'Mistuh Hank, suh,' " repeated Hank slowly, tasting the words. " 'Mistuh Hank, suh.' Y' know, Verity, I like the sound of that. We're gonna hafta git us a nigger."

Three flies buzzed and circled over the table. Verity shooed at them ineffectually.

"We'll get some screens, first," she said absently.

"That's a right likely notion. Wouldn't 'a dreamed a painted house'd make a impress on Jules Bolduc. His own house needs a paintin' iffen he was to ask me."

He grabbed a dish towel, flipped it at the flies. They escaped to the ceiling. With a corner of the towel in each hand he skipped about waving it vigorously, finally maneuvering the flies out the door.

"Dinner. At Jules Bolduc's!" he gloated. "It makes a real beginnin'. All 'cause a house gits painted." He shook his head. "Don't know oughten I t' swaller that whole 'r not."

"It's just a neighborly gesture," said Verity.

"Neighborly, hell. Tim Peck'n all them others 's been neighbors since they got borned—since their grandpappies got borned—'n they ain't et their dinner there yet. A-course, we're different."

But her mind was not on Jules Bolduc nor his invitation. She was trying to picture Hank as he might have looked at twelve.

"How much money did you have coming to you the following harvest? And what did you do with your money?"

"What'd I do with it! I went into bizness. That's what I done. After Maw sent me away—well, I wasn't gonna do farmin'. Hell, farmin' makes a mule outta a man. Weren't nothin' else I could do 'ceptin' start a little peddlin'. 'N I been a-thrivin' ever since." There was pride in his voice.

"Your mother sent you away? But, Hank—"

"It's this-a-way, Sweetface." He turned from the door and began pacing the floor. "Like I said, Paw was a pulin' man. Come harvest, Paw come, too. T' collect the money I sweated 'n slaved for. Fourteen dollars. Looked t' be a sizable fortune t' me, Verity. I watched him pocket m' money 'n I follered him out t' th' gate.

" 'Gimme m' dollars,' I says. 'N he tells me that all I earn till I'm a man growed b'longs t' him. I screamed 'at it don't neither. But he turns, 'n I watched him a-walkin' the road t' home. I set on the rail fence a-feelin' doomed. Till I was a man growed looked t' be a long stretch, Verity. 'N then a rebellion hottened in me 'n pushed my throat 'n ribs most to bustin'. I run cross country to home. Spite a' it bein' a coolish day the sweat was a-runnin' down m' britches.

"I caught up with Paw just as he got to our woodpile. 'Gimme m' dollars,' I says agin stubborn 'n fixed. 'N he picks up a old ax handle 'n starts t' lay it on me." He whirled to Verity. The fierceness of old hurts flared across his face.

"But the fields gimme strength in them fourteen months 'n I jumped in 'n bust him in the belly 'n the chin. Paw went prone agin the choppin' block 'n laid there. Maw 'n Grammaw Kelts come a-runnin' out. I leant over Paw 'n took m' dollars outen his pocket. 'You're a-takin' yore earn-in's back t' yoreself,' Maw says, just that calm. 'Yore brothers ain't a-comin' till sundown,' she says. Then Maw 'n me lugs Paw in to his bed. Grammaw Kelts looked him over close. 'He's gonna live,' she says like as iffen it's a great pity."

He sat at the table, quiet for a minute, then chuckled.

"I'll never forget Grammaw Kelts then. Account she's got no teeth she gums her words as well's her vittles. 'N d'you know what she says, Verity?"

He pounded the table.

"B'God, I put a store in them words a' hern."

Verity sat spellbound, not daring to risk a question.

"Grammaw Kelts says," he drew his lips inward, his voice quavered in imitation, " 'You're liken to m' maw's paw. Him as had the name a' Breck-inridge. Him as built a town in Virginny. M' maw use'n to be allus a-tellin' of him when I was a tyke. Reckon m' maw was the first a' our tribe t' git took to a strange land.' "

His voice took on its natural fullness again.

"All the time Grammaw's a-talkin', Maw's a-fixin' a poke a' hoecake 'n such, 'n she brought the poke to me 'n she says, 'Son, you're the child of my heart. Them others is purely the childern of m' loins. 'Ceptin' for you I birthed a pulin' litter.' "

Hank shook his head as though trying to come out of some unhappy hypnosis.

"I can see her plain," he went on softly, "like as if she was here a-standin' afore me now in a wore-out black calico liken all the pine-hill women. But that was oncet she stood straight 'n sorta uplifted. That was oncet she got a answer 'n was a-seein' of things not there, 'cause she says, 'I want y' should go away. Fur away. I want y' should fergit us. Stand up, son,' she says, 'you got t' git a-goin'. I'm a-thinkin' I birthed one as c'n mebbe git back t' Zion.' So I got a-goin'." He ended simply.

His hand on the table clenched and opened and clenched.

"Maw was a somebody, spite a' everything. Maw should oughta had somethin'. Leastways a purple dress."

Verity leaned over the table and kissed his warm hand, but his hand, feeling the still warmer tears, lifted her face.

"Lord save us, Sweetface," he admonished softly, "you looky here— don't never salten yore eyes for what's done 'n over. Yore bridegroom likes 'em best with storm riffles."

Shoving the crocks and dishes aside, he leaned far over the table, then belly-bustered slowly across it to her. His lips touched each eyelid gently, then whispered, "D'you know what kind a' kissin' that is?"

She shook her head.

"It's kissin' afore lovin'," he said low and soft.

A nervous uncertainty about going to dinner edged her mind all the while she was dressing. After much hesitation, she had decided her wedding dress was the most appropriate thing she owned. She knew its full skirt and trim little jacket were becoming. But it did not give the confidence she had hoped it would. She had done her hair three times and knew it lay in smooth waves and coils, and yet she half dreaded to meet Jules Bolduc.

Now as she walked with Hank under the live-oak tree she felt lacking in dignity. "Too much love," the imp in her mind warned, "too much, too much." As the thought came to her she touched her cheeks and wondered confusedly whether it had left its mark on her. She was glad to be out of the little house. Hank put his hand on her back between her shoulder blades, and even in the midst of such thoughts, all her being seemed to rush to that one spot to meet his touch.

"Ain't it beautiful!" he exclaimed, drawing a deep breath and swatting a mosquito at the same time. " 'Ceptin' for skeeters 'n moccasins 'n such, God'd live in this here country Hisself 'n call it heaven."

Turning her head she studied him. He didn't look different. Why then should she? He looked just as he had yesterday when he called "Howdy, Jules." The little house had not marked him.

Walking with him made her feel better. They were going someplace together. She was not just a woman to be kept in a house and loved. She was his partner.

From the top of the knoll the manor house glowed with windows of flame reflecting the reds which still warmed the sky. The dark slick leaves of the magnolias in the manor lawn glistened, almost shaming their big white blooms. On the gallery in a green slat chair sat Jules Bolduc, his white suit faintly pink with sky color. He rose and came down the walk to greet them.

"Evenin', Jules," Hank called.

"Good evening, Hank."

He did not call to Verity, but came on down the walk to her, held out his hand to receive hers, then touched it lightly with his lips.

"Thank you for coming, Mrs. Martin."

The nerves in her stomach unlaced themselves and she was comfortable. Somewhere the evening damp was pulling perfume from out the jasmine and spreading it like a tangible thing.

"I don't see the jasmine," she commented.

"There is a hedge out back," Bolduc said. "Sometimes one can smell them a mile away. Rather wonderful, isn't it?"

She laughed. "I never really liked jasmine until tonight."

"I prefer to take that as a personal compliment," said Jules.

"B'God'lmighty, lookit there!" Hank pointed at the house. "Them two dispairful shutters is nailed up straight 'n perk!"

"It is completely due to you, Hank. You stirred me out of a five-year lethargy. When I saw a snug white house where only the day before had been a gray, run-down . . ." He shrugged and smiled. "By the way," he continued, "it is just possible that Mr. and Mrs. Castleberry of Loder City may be here this evening. I had a note this afternoon saying I could expect them tonight or tomorrow."

"Robert J. Castleberry the fourth?" asked Hank with heavy sarcasm.

"Yes. Do you know him?"

"Naw. I been plumb pertected. Up t' now, leastways. I reckon he's a-drivin' through the country now a-lettin' his eye rove over the cotton fields, a-judgin' how much kin he be expectin' at all the gins he owns, come pickin'." Hank's voice was broadly casual. " 'Spect he's a-makin' loans for his bank, too. 'Spect ninety per cent a' the ownin' planters has gotta borry off him to see 'em through to fall."

"Hm-mm." Jules made a noncommittal sound. "You're from the North, aren't you, Mrs. Martin?"

"Yes, Pennsylvania."

"Mrs. Castleberry is also from the North. She was on the New York stage a season or two before she married Robert. She was Mavis Easton. Did you ever happen to see her?"

"No, I was never in New York, Mr. Bolduc. I never went anywhere until I came down here," she said simply.

"I hear tell," said Hank, "that this here Miz Castleberry's right well worth lookin' at. There's folks in Loder City as says he just natcherly hadda add her t' his collection. Didn't make no sense seein' as how he's allus been plumb skittish 'round th' womenfolks."

"Ah, well, I suppose people did a lot of talking." Jules laughed. "I can see what they meant, though. Mr. Castleberry collects rare old jades."

"Old jades!" exclaimed Hank. "Sounds plumb floozy."

They were on the gallery now and Jules opened his wide front door.

The gracious hall welcomed Verity with the dulcet tones and gleamings of old mahogany. The curve of the stair seemed almost a curtsy. Curbing an impulse to return the bow, she stood still, curious and enchanted. Never had she dreamed a big house could feel like this. It was bigger than the orphanage, yet it had no feeling of emptiness, though it housed only one man and his servants.

The huge living-room rug was a thing of many colors, and two splendid candelabra on the marble mantelpiece made a shrine to a dark-eyed, lovely lady who sat pensive, and at peace, in a wide gold frame. Every-thing here had a fine old pride. This place stands for something, she thought, like a big silk flag that's been through battle and comes out waving and a little frayed.

Hank walked through the house quite at ease. He didn't even look out of place here. His purple striped suit, his pink shirt were in themselves a rude insult to the rooms, but Hank was as completely himself here as in his own house, or on his own cart. He had none of the chameleon in him. He was here to impress, not to be impressed.

"Let's go into the library," suggested Jules.

Hank stood in the doorway and glared at the long high walls lined from ceiling to floor with books.

"Christ!" he exploded. He strode across the room to the little mahogany stepladder, looked up at the rail on which its wheels ran. His fist gave it a vicious whack on its siding and the little ladder went skittering the length of the room. Verity's knees felt weak.

"Hank!" she protested. But he didn't hear her.

"Won't you sit down, Mrs. Martin?" Jules Bolduc was undisturbed by Hank's outburst. "There, please, by the window. The flowers will furnish just the right background."

His smile reassured her and she sank into a chair of leather, old and pliable as chamois. Hank strode around the room glaring.

"God'lmighty, what the hell right you got to all these here books whilst kids can't get ary one to git a edgucation. No money in this state for books!" he stormed. "Roarin' thunderbolts! Why the hell didn't they take some a' these!"

"But, Hank—"

Jules interrupted her. "Do you think I haven't the right to these books, Hank?"

"You read all these here books?" Hank demanded.

"Well, no, I haven't."

"It ain't right! God'lmighty, here you're a-settin' hoggin' books y' ain't read 'n thousands a' kids withouten learnin', withouten ary book."

"I see," said Jules, his one-sided smile spreading. "Are you a disciple of Saint-Simon?" He gave the name its French pronunciation.

"San Seemawn," Hank mimicked bitterly. "What's that?"

"Perhaps I should give it the English pronunciation—Saint-Simon!" Jules picked up a book from his desk. "Odd you should have this attitude toward my books, Hank. I was just writing a little satire on that very subject." His lips curled downward. "It has seemed to me that all the so-called poor and downtrodden are bitter and wishful. Short on working and long on wishing. Not wishing to acquire through their own efforts, but wishing to see someone else divide his riches with them." He sighed heavily with mock despair. "I had thought you different, and here you are thinking I should divide my books."

"You thought I was different, 'n I am. I think books is different, 'n they are," Hank declared loudly. "Ain't no man got a right t' be a-hoardin' knowledge jus' 'cause he's got the money to pay fer the paper 'n the leather it's a-hidin' in." He leaned over Jules's desk and jounced up and down on his heels with the air of a preacher in the throes of a conviction. "Not no man! 'N I'm a-tellin' y' when I'm governor a' this here state every young'un in it's a-goin' t' git free books!"

"Governor, Hank?" Jules tilted back in his chair looking into Hank's eyes earnestly. "I would not set my heart on that, Hank."

"Why the hell not?"

"I'm sure you would be as good a governor as most," replied Jules placatingly. "But you could not possibly get elected in this state. The voters here have a passion for paying compliments only to members of the old families when they go to the polls."

"That's purely a habit I'm a-goin' t' break 'em of someday." He laughed. "Hell, Hank Martin don't never talk through his hat. Ain't that right, Sweetface? I'm gonna make lotsa folks voters as ain't never voted afore. Hell, as ain't voted in generations!"

She sat entranced as by a show.

"Ain't that right, Sweetface?" he repeated.

She could not bring herself to answer like an echo to Hank, as if she had been trained to heel; but she smiled in his direction. Jules was studying Hank.

"But," their host pointed out, "we have a literacy and property law in this state, I believe. I have never looked up that law, but I have always understood from those in politics and government that voters must be able to read and write, or they must own property worth at least three hundred dollars."

"Yeah," said Hank. "Allus I'm stuck on that. But," he grew very intense, "I'm gonna change that, too. I purely am. How is pore folks a-goin' to learn iffen the rich as can vote don't never vote money for schools? 'N whilst a book costs 'em two, three whole dollars!" His voice was a moving blend of pleading and outrage. "How the hell are sharecroppers gonna get three hundred dollars' worth a' property!" He shook a finger under Jules's nose. "But I'll be a-findin' a way. You'll be a-seein' someday. I'll be a-findin' a way iffen I gotta test a white man's right to vote in every goddam court in this here whole country—come time I'm a lawyer."

The thought disturbed him and he paced agitatedly up and down the room while Jules watched him with interest and Verity watched him with some apprehension.

"The worst a' the whole thing is a feller has gotta stir folks as ain't mebbe had enough vittles 'n hope for to grow some gumption. Gotta stir 'em into holdin' together for a aim. Yeah, that's mebbe the sticker. Aw, hell!" he exclaimed, frustrated and angry.

Verity leaned forward. "Mr. Bolduc," she needed a change of subject, "the satire you said you were writing—I didn't quite understand."

"Yeah," said Hank, "what was you a-talkin' of anyhow?"

"I can't claim it as original with me." Jules picked up a sheaf of typewritten papers and turned on his desk lamp.

Hank snorted. "Lookit that, Verity. Even his own power plant a-buzzin' somewheres to save Mr. Bolduc's eyes. 'N the rest a' us still a-pourin' coal oil. 'Lectricity's like books. It had oughta be everybody's."

Jules smiled ruefully.

"Dear me, I had hoped you would enjoy yourself tonight."

"I'm a-enjoyin' myself right smart. I'm a-gettin' m' mind made up to lotsa things." He slapped Jules on the shoulder and grinned. "Go ahead, Jules, read them bright thoughts a' yoren. Expand yoreself. I'm a-goin' to be p'lite the rest a' the evenin' iffen it busts me."

"Please do read it, Mr. Bolduc. Don't mind Hank," Verity urged as Hank perched on the arm of her chair.

"Well, it is amusing to realize how many people have been willing to tell the world what is wrong with it. Saint-Simon, for instance. Although he was a French count, he lived for a time in America. At sixteen he came to this country to fight with Washington's army against the mighty Cornwallis." He stopped for a second while his eyes looked bitterly back on a dream. "Yes, it was to Saint-Simon I spoke, not to Lafayette, when our transport nosed into Calais. I lifted my bayoneted gun. 'Saint-Simon, we are here!' " He sighed. "Were you in the World War, Hank?"

"Nope. They didn't draft fellers under twenty-one years tillst 1918. But that there armistice come along the follerin' November 'n they didn't never get t' me." He fell silent a second, seeming to study on the matter. "Didn't never enlist. I've ofttimes wondered iffen 'twas 'cause I hadda do so dang much fightin' just t' keep alive right here."

Jules nodded. "I can understand that. Didn't you say you'd be twenty-four this fall? In some ways you seem much older."

"Why wouldn't I!" Hank jumped up and flailed his arms. "Been a-fightin' m' way through 'gator swamps for to sell a packet a' pins since m' thirteenth year. God'lmighty!" He whirled on Jules. "You tryin' to bust me with being p'lite? God'lmighty, we come to eat 'n y' stuff us with this here Saint-Simon. Is there a point t' this Frenchie, 'r ain't there?"

To Verity's amazement Jules laughed heartily. He rose, and going to Hank he took his hand and clasped it.

Still laughing, he said, "Against my better judgment, I like you, Hank."

" 'N agin mine I'm a-likin' you, too." Hank grinned. "Don't reckon you to be a bit better'n Picayune Potter. Mebbe not so good. Leastways he's helped to clutter the country withen eight young'uns." His hand slapped Jules's shoulder genially. "Dang if it don't beat me how many fools I gotta plumb likin' for."

Jules laughed and Verity told herself she would have to get used to this sort of thing. It was Hank's way. And it seemed to be a good way. Never would she have guessed when Jules stood beside their cart that these two men would like each other.

Her own laughter ran out to join theirs and she settled deeper in her chair telling herself seriously that she would learn to enjoy Hank's ways.

"Evenin', Miz Martin." Moses' rich voice blended in the laughter like a bass-fiddle note. "Evenin', Mistuh Hank, suh. Dinna's served, Mistuh Jules."

"Now, lissen, Moses," said Hank, "you keep that there dinner hot for a spell. I'm gonna swaller Saint-Simon first. Hours on end, seems 's though, I been a-tryin' to make the master a' this here house come t' the point. He's the sidetrackin'est man ever I knowed. What y' got fer dinner, Moses?"

Moses rolled his eyes and made a great mound with his hands. "Ham, Mistuh Hank. Stuff ham. I done make hunderds pockets in dat ham. I done tamp in spice, den mo' spice, an' Annabell keep sayin' ain't 'nuff. Dat ham done swole to twice its size."

"Well!" Hank glowed. "Y' reckon, Jules, I c'n swaller ham 'n Saint-Simon at one 'n the same time?"

"I think you can, Hank. I'd like to have had cocktails or a julep. But these prohibition times limit one. I must have faith in my liquors. Will you take my arm, Mrs. Martin?"

As they reached the hall she hesitated to admire again the lovely stair. "You like my house?" asked Jules.

"Yes. There's something wonderful about it."

"The most wonderful thing about it has been its ladies. Sometime—perhaps—I'll show you the loveliest lady who ever stepped into it."

"Ain't none a' 'em lovelier'n Verity."

"Exactly," replied Jules, smiling down at her.

Hank, following Moses, saw the table first.

"Back t' candlelight. Ain't there no 'lectricity in this room, Jules?"

"I prefer candles," said Jules simply.

Hank pointed. "Lookit them azaleas, Verity. Reckon I'll endure them candles after all, Jules, seeing they're set like to pickets a-fencin' them flowers." He sat in the chair Moses pulled out and watched Jules seat Verity. She thought, He's remembering exactly how Mr. Bolduc's doing this.

"I got a plumb admiration for them there flowers," Hank went on. "Mind me a' good women. Yes, sir, I been a-noticin' as I tromp the woodlands 'at they're a-flourishin' best when somethin' bigger is a-shadin' 'em. Azaleas is particular flowers. Ain't a-wastin' their substance, like some. Ain't a-givin' careless. See all them there things fluffin' liken to lace on a woman's collar?" He chuckled. "Them's really stickers as keeps th' ants 'n such from depravin' her honey. Azaleas ain't a-givin' 'ceptin' to bees 'n butterflies, as do right by her pollen. Some a' them'd be right fitten in yore hair, Verity."

With the eyes of both men upon her, Verity felt pink as the flowers. The little moment of silence seemed puffed with meaning. Deftly Moses placed before Jules a huge silver platter bearing a mountain of something brownly glazed and steaming.

"Iffen that's ham," said Hank wonderingly, "the hawg as growed that there haunch musta been bigger'n a horse."

"Stuff ham," said Moses. "Usn proud uv our stuff ham."

Hank sat pulling deeply of the air.

"It would shore been a pure disaster iffen the Lord'd stopped short a' givin' us a smeller. Reckon after He stirred us outta dust He felt kinda sorry for such a unflavorsome lot 'n throwed in a smeller. Like addin' a sprinkle a' salt."

"The picture you draw of a casually generous Lord!" said Jules between laughs. "Believe me, Hank, I have always been afraid He threw us together just that way."

When Moses put a plate before Hank, he said, "That's purely beautiful. I gotta be gettin' a lesson in the makin' a' stuffed ham." He looked at the forks beside his plate, then grinned impishly. "Eeny, meeny, miney, mo—you're it!" And he grabbed up one with the quick swooping motion of catching a fly. "I'm purely a one-fork man, Jules," he said.

Confusion flushed hotly through Verity, but honesty compelled her to remember that there was no reason why Hank should be expected to know about forks or pretend to know. She didn't know, either. His way might be better than sitting uncertain and watchful.

Hank took a big mouthful of ham and smacked loudly.

"Hum-m-ummm! Stuffin' 'r no stuffin', no common hawg ever growed hisself a ham liken this, don't seem's though. Iffen one did, I'm a-goin' to take t' liftin' my hat to 'em."

"I think you promised us Saint-Simon with the ham, didn't you, Mr. Bolduc?" She felt she must say something, take some part.

"That's right," said Hank. "Iffen you c'n keep yore mind on a Frenchie, go right ahead. With the likes a' this afore me I ain't gotta pay you no mind."

"Saint-Simon believed riches should be better divided through the reorganization of society, taking labor for the basis of the new hierarchy. He declared, 'No man has a right to free himself from the law of labor,'" Jules's one-sided grin turned downward with disdain. "Now in the little satire which I was writing for my own amusement, I point out that Saint-Simon may have known what was wrong with the world, but failed because he did not know what was wrong with people." He paused, almost expectantly.

"And do you know?" asked Verity politely.

"Why, yes, they are all like Hank." Jules's voice was smooth yet brightly baiting. "They want the successful to divide their riches with them."

Slowly Hank lowered a filled fork to his plate. His nostrils widened, whitening with reined-in anger, his lids dropped and lifted jerkily.

"You're unfair, Mr. Bolduc," said Verity stiffly. "Hank thinks knowledge should be free to all. I think so, too."

The tenseness left Hank's face; it became again laughing and genial. Verity felt his eyelids had swept the anger from his eyes only to store it in his brain.

"All I gotta say, is," said Hank jovially, "iffen everybody was like to me, this here world'd be purely Heaven." He held out his plate. "Iffen you're a-wantin' to hit me on the button that-a-way, Jules, you oughta leastways lemme bulge it out withen another hunk a' ham. Make it easier for y' to land one."

As Jules filled the plate he said slowly, "I think I'll take it back, Hank. It is the average person who wants the capable and fortunate to divide with them."

"Still 'n all, the average man, 's you're a-callin' 'em, ain't so bad. The average man's bound to be the pore man 'cause there's so dang many more of 'em. 'N mostly, they ain't worth a dang, mebbe. Not a dang." He leaned toward Jules. "Now it's my turn to see can I land one on yore button, so I'm askin' you straight—would you be worth a dang iffen you wasn't all cushioned with yore grampaw's money?" He paused, enjoying the situation. "Now you answer this honest, Jules. You think it's any more right you should stay rich 'cause yore grampaw was than it is for me t' stay pore cause m' grampaw was?"

"You're going to extremes, Hank," Jules laughed.

"Extremes, hell!" exclaimed Hank.

Moses entered.

"Mistuh an' Miz Castleberry done come, Mistuh Jules."

"Well," said Jules and smiled at Hank. "You must have had me spellbound. I usually hear the knocker. Excuse me a moment, please."

He rose to leave, but then all three of them, seeming to feel a demand for attention, looked toward the doorway. Mrs. Castleberry stood there with both hands extended, waiting for Jules Bolduc to come and take them in his. Behind her was Mr. Castleberry's tall silhouette.

Verity was scarcely aware of him then. The hall light behind the two was brighter than was the candlelight they faced and for a moment Verity couldn't see them plainly. Instead, she felt Mrs. Castleberry's presence. Some quality of her hurt Verity.

"Moses failed to say you had guests." Mavis Castleberry's voice was clear and carefully pitched like a good bell. "I do hope we are not a nuisance barging in this way. But I could not endure to stand on ceremony with you, Jules."

She stood waiting, poised, sure of tribute.

"Foolish indeed, Mavis," said Jules cordially, and taking both her hands in his he drew her into the room.

An awareness of her own beauty held Mrs. Castleberry like a tangible brace. Her gown, an off shade of green, snugged her figure, shadowing and high-lighting delicate curves. A slim white neck lifted her lovely head to a haughty height, so haughty as to give it a slight backward tilt, so that the great dark eyes pulled their lids at quarter drape as they looked down on the world.

As Jules greeted his guests, Verity decided she had never before seen such people. Long thin bones carried Mr. Castleberry with arrogant assurance. His teal-blue tie and kerchief, his tropical worsted of black and gray dressed him as naturally and handsomely as feathers dress a bird. His lower lip protruded in a full wide curve, and in the candlelight it shaded out his flat upper lip and made a beak of his narrow nose. He looked at Hank as he might look at a freak, and such resentment clutched at Verity's throat that she couldn't speak to acknowledge the introductions and was grateful to Hank for his boisterous, "Howdy, Castleberry."

Mr. Castleberry's lip jutted, his eyes, round and green like gooseberries floating in cream, studied Hank.

"And what is your name again, sir?" he asked.

"Hank Martin's the name. 'N don't never forget it." Hank grinned. "Someday mebbe you'll be a-hearin' a' me much as I been a-hearin' a' you. Robert J. Castleberry the fourth," Hank laughed. "What's that 'the fourth' mean, anyhow?"

Mr. Castleberry looked at Jules, but getting no help, he cleared his throat and answered stiffly.

"Er—aa—fourth in my line, Mr. Martin." He emphasized the "mister."

"Only three forebears afore you, huh? That comes to me liken a blow, Castleberry," Hank said mockingly. "Only three forebears! Well, well, 'n here I was a-thinkin' everybody's forebears went a-stringin' right back to Adam. Leastways to Cain 'r Abel."

"Just now," said Jules, coming at last to his friend's aid, "the only important one in the line is Robert the fifth. Isn't that right, Mavis?" He turned to Mrs. Castleberry.

"Of course it is right, Jules. I am worried about him right now. Robert says it is silly to worry about Bobby, that old Rosa wouldn't let anything happen to him. But—" She shrugged and looked about appreciatively. "So wonderful to be here again, Jules."

"You'll have dinner, of course. Moses will fix you up at once."

"Well, the fact is, we have had—"

"We have had a longing for a dinner here." Mrs. Castleberry finished the sentence, committing her husband.

Hank pulled out a chair for her.

"Lemme help y' t' set," he said, and put a fine flourish in his bow.

She looked a little startled, then her clear laugh ran the scale with trills. "The South is wonderful. Simply too wonderful! I am always being surprised."

"I'm allus a-bein' surprised," said Hank, "but I oughta be plumb ust to it."

"Really? Are you a Southerner, Mr. Martin?"

He grinned at her. "I'm a Southerner, awright, awright. Got birthed in the pine hills in the north a' this here state. God'lmighty, I'm a part this state like as iffen I was made a' the pine-hill clay 'n the bottom-lands mud."

"Oo-oo." Her nose wrinkled daintily with distaste. "So nasty-sticky when wet, so wretchedly rough when dry." Her eyes twinkled into her husband's curdled stare.

"Now you're a-speakin' the truth plain 'n fine, Miz Castleberry. We got roads in this here state shouldn't oughta be trod by nothin' but the feet a' mules. You come out here from Loder City in a autymobile?" She half nodded and seemed to fold in the waistline, giving a dramatic suggestion of utter collapse. "Feelin' powerful jounced, ain't y'?"

She laughed.

"Yore husband should oughta be shamed to jounce the insides t' such beautiful outsides as you got."

Mr. Castleberry choked.

"Do you hear that, Robert dear?" Mavis Castleberry teased. "You are entirely right, Mr. Martin. Never have I seen such roads. And did I not say, Robert, that they are more than the human frame should be asked to endure? Positively uncivilized."

Both Mr. Castleberry and Jules started to speak, but Hank gave them no chance. He leaned over the table and looked squarely at Castleberry.

"Why'n't y' tell yore beautiful wife why we ain't got good roads?"

"Why, damit!" exploded Castleberry, "any fool knows it takes money to build roads. The taxes would be exorbitant."

Hank chuckled. "Why, damit," he mimicked softly, "any fool is a-knowin' full well that iffen we had good roads the sharecroppers 'n even the owning planters, liken my good friend Jules here, could haul their crops somewheres 'sides local gins—most a' which is owned by you 'n yore crowd, 'n the rest is owned by the Newtons. Now them Newtons is a passel a' snides." He looked blandly at Mr. Castleberry's purpling face, at Jules's startled stare. Then softly he said, "Nary a bit liken you 'n yore crowd, a' course, Castleberry. Them Newtons' scales weigh powerful light, come cotton-pickin' time."

Mr. Castleberry rose with dignity and finality. Turning to Jules he said, "Really, Jules, you must excuse us. Never did I think the day would come when I would sit at the Bolduc table with a clown."

"Iffen I'm a clown why ain't you a-laughin'?" asked Hank, grinning broadly. "Iffen my words is a-makin' yore gorge raise, iffen they're a-gallin' you, I'll be a-sayin' my so-sorry's t' you in any way you're a-choosin', Castleberry. I never knowed you was friends with them Newtons. Roarin' thunderbolts, I allus thought you 'n them Newtons was agin one 'nother!"

"That's a dreadful thing to say about anyone." Jules's voice was reprimanding. "The Newtons are a fine old family."

"Yeah, it's a right dreadful thing to be a-sayin'," Hank agreed. "But the most dreadful thing 'bout it is the plumb pure truth a' it."

"Hank!" Verity protested. "You're making everyone unhappy. Why talk about those people!"

"God'lmighty, Verity," Hank exclaimed innocently. "You ever knowed me t' wanta make folks unhappy? I was just a-tellin' Castleberry somethin' he should oughta knowed long ago 'bout them thievin' Newtons. Why, Verity, Mr. Castleberry should oughta mebbe own all the gins 'n give the growers a chancet t' git a honest price."

Mr. Castleberry seemed to be swallowing Hank's soothing syrup. His long bones relaxed a little.

"Although the Newtons are competitors of ours, it seems impossible they would cheat in weights. Have you proof of this, sir?"

"No," Hank pursed his lips judicially, " 'ceptin' the fellers say they weigh it on little scales a bag to a time. Lessen their 'rithmetic's off, them Newtons' scales is. A-course it could be their 'rithmetic seein' as how—like

I'm allus a-sayin' t' Jules 'n Verity—the pore ain't gittin' rightful learnin' in this here state."

"Verity?" asked Mrs. Castleberry, trying to turn the conversation. "Such an old-fashioned name."

"Yeah, ain't that a meaningful name, though," said Hank proudly. "Verity's paw come a' Quaker folks, she says, 'n he named her for her grammaw. Cain't make out just what the Quaker religion can be. Seems t' be a-plenty of 'em in Pennsylvania. Seems a little like to the Holy Rollers, 'ceptin' not mebbe so noisy."

Mrs. Castleberry laughed. Obviously she was enjoying Hank Martin.

"Mr. Martin, you are delightful!" A playful note danced through her trained voice. "Quite the best dinner party I have attended in the South, Jules."

Hank beamed, but into Mr. Castleberry's gooseberry eyes came a soured look of utter distaste. He rose, bowed stiffly and ever so slightly to Verity, turned to Jules and said curtly, "You will excuse me? And—ah—is it asking too much of you to put us up?"

"What nonsense, Robert!" exclaimed Jules. "You have been welcome here since you were born."

Mr. Castleberry fixed his commanding eyes on his wife. "Coming, my dear?" But it was not a question. It was a command. Into Mavis Castleberry's eyes came a haunted look and Verity thought, That's why she gives me that hurt feeling. But the haunted look lasted only a second, then was replaced by the imperious, haughty air. She rose, said a gracious good night and swept from the room followed by her husband.

"Excuse me, Mrs. Martin," said Jules, "I will be right back." And he followed.

Verity sat very quiet until she no longer heard their steps on the stair.

"Hank, what on earth is the matter with you?" she asked tensely. "It started out to be such a lovely evening. It would have been all right about the books," she added in justness, "but why did you affront Mr. Castleberry?"

"Affront, huh? That's a right good word, Verity, but too dang tame for what I wanta be a-doin' to the likes a' him!" He chuckled. "D' you see the sonuvabitch a-coddlin' his feelin's? A-makin' hisself believe I was a-talkin' only 'bout the Newtons, a-pridin' hisself 'cause I'm a-kissin' his ass, seems 's though." He strode back and forth kicking out his right foot viciously. "When I get 'round t' kickin' that thin setter a' hisn, it's gonna get such a jolt it'll plumb take off for the moon."

Verity sighed, feeling completely lost. Could she cope with this man, this husband of hers? Could Mr. Castleberry really be dishonest?

"Practicing football?" asked Jules a bit sarcastically from the doorway.

"You c'n call it that." Hank grinned. Then suddenly he laughed heartily and loud.

Jules closed the door.

"Yes sirree, more I think on it, Jules, the more I incline to that there notion a' yoren 'bout dividin' the riches." Half dreamily he added, "Often I catch m'self a-thinkin' the Lord creates the critters a' the earth 'n sky so's him that hath ears to hear 'n eyes t' see can watch 'n learn 'n judge the human critters rightly." His eyes half closed and glinted with fiery points. "Now, this here Castleberry—I shore would like t' make him do some dividin'. First time ever I seed a black skimmer I found myself a-wantin' desperate bad to squeeze him hard so's he'd hafta spew back into the water the little things he'd been a-skimmin' into his gullet." He looked slyly at Jules. "The black skimmer ain't agin swallerin' bigger critters as is a-flounderin' on the surface, either."

Hank stopped and sat watching Jules's studying, remembering eyes. Verity did not understand, but wondered why Hank's words seemed to take on such meaning to Jules. When Jules spoke it was hardly a whisper.

"A black skimmer," he said thoughtfully.

"Yeah." Hank's voice was low. "Now I been a-noticin' how some owners, even big owners, is a-gettin' smaller 'n a-flounderin' more every year. Take last year. This here country was purely blest. Plumb bountiful it was, as it stood in the fields. The cane growed high, 'n a hungry man could keep strength in him just a-gnawin' on a snibben he could snipe with his pocketknife." He put out a hand in a gesture which brought visions of far fields. " 'N the cotton rows stretched white 'n woolly, their bolls fair bustin' with their wideness. The niggers 'n the pore whites chopped the cane, 'n picked the cotton, a-haulin' ahind 'em the many pounds, that, come weighin'-in t' mill 'n gin, wasn't so many pounds after all."

He walked back and forth kicking out his right foot at some imagined object.

"Yeah, Jules," he said slowly, intently, "yeah, you gimme that there paper you was a-writin' on dividin' the riches. It's like to prove the aim as will give folks gumption. I aim t' read it careful. You got a plumb sneerin' way a' lookin' at things as is like to be right revealin', seen backside to. 'N I got a plumb natural hate for a bird as can fly so low as t' keep his bottom beak in water 'n force th' little things down his gullet 'thouten never lessenin' the swiftness a' full flight. Yeah, I got a plumb hate for the way the black skimmer feeds 'n fattens hisself."

4

*Where Hank got his ideas on Divide the Riches probably no
one will ever know. What kind of mind did this amazing man
have that he could stir loyal belief in him with his very first
speech?*

*Yes, Hank's organization began long, long before the world
knew there was such a man in it. He loved to tell how his first
meeting was held, not in a stable exactly, but the next thing to
it, for it was held in a blacksmith shop. And he loved to point
out that he was one prophet who was honored in his own land,
for his first disciples were signed when. . . .*

THE SECOND night Verity lay in their bed alone she recognized Jules's
satire as a signpost in her life. An unreadable signpost just now, because
Hank had not yet decided in which direction he would point the arrow.
She lay there listening to the rain and to Hank's footsteps in the next
room, the squeaking of the old pine floor boards, the muted cadences of
his voice as he read and reread Jules's satire.

He's starting on the first page again, she thought. She knew it so well
she could fill in the phrases she couldn't actually hear.

"The chief difference between the animals of forests and fields and the
human animal is simply this: the animals of forest and field live upon
meat they hunt for themselves, but the human is not content to do this.
The human wants to live on meat which is procured for him by the
labor of others.

"Now, since only the labor of man saves man from nesting in ground
holes and tree hollows; since only the labor of man produces, it is the
ambition of men with ability to make a number of men with less ability
work for their profit. But it must be admitted that this is more admirable,
since it has been proved through the ages that it is more constructive
toward the good of all than is the ambition of the man who is poor in
ability and stamina, and therefore, in worldly goods. For the poor man's
ambition is exactly the same as the rich man's—except that the poor man

secretly realizes he is indeed a poor, inadequate thing. But his ego, wishing to strut, declares all men are born equal—and any fool can see they are not—so what does the poor man do? He covets what the rich man has acquired. He wants to find a way to make the able man divide with him.

"Now every great thinker and philosopher who has delved into the laws that go beyond physical life . . ."

Verity sat up in bed, tense and nervous. Would Hank do it again when he got to the next sentence? She listened.

". . . whether he be Chinese or East Indian or whatever, tells us that covetousness will keep us poor. Our own Christian Lord gave us a commandment, 'Thou shalt not covet thy neighbor's wife nor his ass, nor . . .'" Yes, Hank did it. He kicked the table viciously.

"God'lmighty!" he said fiercely, "the sneerin' sonuvabitch! He should oughta go withouten no vittles for three, four days. God'lmighty!"

She wanted to scream—I can't stand it! I can't stand it! But another part of her brain told her harshly to shut up and demanded: What is it you can't stand? Yes, what is it? She asked herself. She struggled to find the exact balancing spot on her teeter-totter. One minute she was up in the air with love and pride in Hank, and the next she went down with a terrifying jolt from his bitterness, his fierceness, his intensity.

Night before last they had walked silently home from Jules Bolduc's. Hank clutched the satire in one hand swatting a mosquito with it, or hitting out at a lightning bug. Clouds to the west and south were heavy and aching to burst, and the air seemed dull and inert. She wondered if she really smelled the bayou or just imagined she did.

With her first glimpse of their little white house she felt better. She had been so glad to get out of it, and now was so glad to return to it. As Hank lit the coal-oil lamp she felt a real pleasure in the room. Handing Verity the sheaf of papers, Hank said, "Read me this here thing. Don't reckon it says nothin' worth the hearin', though."

"Is there a real bird called the black skimmer?" she asked.

"There shore is, Verity. There shore is. Right purty in his high flying he is, too. More gray than black he is. Reckon as how it's his way a' feedin' made folks think a' him as black." He snorted. "Go on, read me that thing whilst I do a few chores."

She began. In a few sentences she caught the feel of Jules's smooth cynicism. Hank picked up the water bucket and with a motion of his head asked her to follow. Still reading, she went as far as the doorway, stopped where she yet could see by the lamp light, raised her voice to speech-making pitch so that he could hear above the squealing of the pump. As he entered with the full bucket she read: ". . . tells us that covetousness keeps us poor. Our own Christian Lord gave us a commandment, 'Thou shalt not covet thy neighbor's wife nor his ass . . .'"

He dropped the bucket. The water in it rose like a geyser, then plopped out on her fresh green floor.

"God'lmighty! So all a' us pore folks is a-breakin' a commandment 'cause we're a-wantin' a-plenty t' eat! Why, Jesus Christ hisself figgered a belly should oughta be full. Didn't He do a miracle to feed five thousand not countin' the women 'n childern? Didn't He turn water into wine? Didn't God send manna in the wilderness? Didn't God command Moses to be a-leadin' His people promisin' a land a' milk 'n honey?"

So many emotions pounced on her consciousness she could not choose the path her mind should travel. Simultaneously they jumped on her and began their tug of war. One exulted that Hank should champion the unfortunate; one shrank from the savage bitterness in his voice; one longed to rock him gently and give him comfort; one cried the futile wish to be a god for just one omniscient glimpse of truth; and one resented the entire business of marriage and Hank and Jules and essays, with a dull red madness. But through and over these emotions was the calm knowledge that all she could do was the thing necessary at this moment; so she laid the papers on the table back of the stove, took a gray rag from a low nail, and began mopping the floor to keep the new paint from becoming pocked and leprous.

Kneeling there mopping she watched Hank grab up the sheaf and stride to the table. The full light showed her the humiliation, the pain and bewilderment, as well as the fury in his face, and the mother in her softened her, shooing away the madness and shaming her for longing, however fleetingly, to abandon this man. "He needs me," the mother in her said to the rest of her being, "he's so hurt. He never had a chance, poor darling. He needs me." And then she had her omniscient glimpse of truth. Not the kind she had wished for. Not the kind to show the rights of all men. But the kind that comes to a woman. She saw that this man would weave the picture that was to be her life and destiny, and she hoped to God she would have the strength and wisdom to help him with his colors and design.

His voice read on, turning Jules's sharp barbs into blunt cruelties. Jules Bolduc, she felt sure, had no hate for poor people, had not meant to say that they were all covetous. Jules Bólduc, she felt, was sitting—not on the fence—but comfortably, upon a turnstile, laughing slyly at the folk on each side.

Through her thoughts she heard sentences about banks and money systems and rediscounts, and all the meaning it had for her was the knowledge that Hank was mad over what it implied and mad because he couldn't understand the systems at which the words poked fun.

" 'It is the nature of the human animal,' " Hank read haltingly, " 'to try to get to a high place in life, and when a man gets on a pinnacle, or even a little mound, he schemes to make the less fortunate or unsuccessful work to keep him there.' "

Hank stopped and read that sentence over and over before continuing.

" 'Actually, it is simpler and easier to stay on a pinnacle of prominence and power than for the poor man to get just enough to eat; for all the laws have been made by the men on the pinnacles and the mounds.' "

The floor had long since been mopped dry but she still knelt there with the wet gray rag in her hand. After he had reread that sentence the ninth time his eyes lifted from the paper.

"I'm a-goin' t' git on that pinnacle iffen it takes every gut in m' body!" He made the pledge to himself solemnly, tensely.

"Oh, Hank," her voice was only a tired whisper, "Mr. Bolduc meant only to laugh a little at everybody."

He turned toward her blinking like a wakened sleeper.

"Sweetface! What y' a-doin' a-squattin' there like as if you was a Chitmacha squaw?"

"I was mopping the floor," she said, feeling very foolish.

He came to her and helped her up. Her whole tired body seemed to rush appreciatively to greet the touch of his hands, to thank them for their warm pulsing promise of comfort.

"You should oughta be abed, Sweetface."

He lifted her up, carried her into the bedroom, and put her on the bed. He unlocked her clinging arms.

"Now we ain't got time," he said softly. Turning abruptly he left her and closed the door without a backward glance.

Now as she sat in bed waiting for him to read again, and hearing the rain on the roof and walls, she felt an anxious pity for his tiredness. He had not slept these two nights, had eaten only an occasional hoecake or a bit of cold fried salt pork which he picked up automatically from the stacked plates she left temptingly upon the table. She knew a new admiration for him, felt him struggling to produce in himself a new growth.

"God'lmighty!" His voice was different. What did the exclamation mean this time? She jumped from bed, ran to the door, and opened it quietly.

"God'lmighty!" he repeated. Jubilance and light were in his face. "A-course! God'lmighty, ain't I been dumb! Why, that's the greatest campaign stuff ever wrote, I bet!"

She had meant not to intrude herself into his thoughts, but she exclaimed unbelievingly, "Campaign!"

"Yeah, campaign—campaign," he exulted. His red-rimmed eyes danced and his grin looked extra white in the weary, whiskery face. "Verity, them there pages is the key t' m' future! Yes, sir, the key t' m' future! When Jules Bolduc said poor folks'd like to make the rich divide he shore knowed what he was a-talkin' about. He shore did. But it plumb makes the blood to boil t' be a-hearin' it from the likes a' him. Covetous, he says we are. Well, I'm plumb gonna take the covetousness outta wantin' to make the rich divide the riches. I'm plumb gonna make it a political campaign!"

"But you can't campaign for anything! You won't be ready to campaign for years and years. Why, Hank, you need . . ."

"You watch, Sweetface! You watch. Tomorra I start a-campaignin'. I ain't mebbe gonna run for nothin' for years 'n years. No office, I mean. But, by God'lmighty, I start a-campaignin' tomorra."

It had no meaning for her. How could he campaign?

"I'll fix you something hot," she said, crossing to the stove.

"I ain't a-needin' nothin' but a spell a' hibernatin'.'"

Going into the next room he toppled onto the bed without removing his trousers and shirt. Grinning groggily he said, "I ain't got the words for it tonight, but I got the feel for it clear 'n plain. Tomorra I'll have th' words 'n I'll start a-campaignin'. D'you know who's gonna be m' first disciple? Tim Peck. Yes, sir, Tim Peck." His last words slowed down with sleep.

The next day, as they walked toward the village and Tim Peck's blacksmith shop, Hank's lips moved on the words he had to have. The hot sun pulled steam up into the air, big drops of rain the sun had not yet reached wetted their ankles, and water sloshed into their shoes as they crossed the fields.

The world seemed to have enjoyed the beatings of wind and rain. The grass stood up again and plants bore tiny green buds to make up for broken blooms. The softened earth let new sprouts creep out to the sun.

"Tim'll be a-workin' day like this," Hank remarked. "Won't none a' th' men be a-wantin' t' toss horseshoes. Mud'd be knee-deep out back a' th' shop."

How strange it was, she thought, that in any place men could find games to play. But when their women gathered, they sewed or cooked for the church.

As they reached the road they must cross to get to Tim's shop, she stopped. Mules had pulled wagons down this road, and instead of an innocent glazed blackness it had the look of churned and steaming tar.

"Helluva note in this day 'n age. Jus' cause men was a-flyin' like birds in the war don't mean a sight a' us ain't still a-troddin' the earth." He grunted disgustedly and stooping, took off his wet shoes and socks and rolled up his pants legs.

Verity made no move to follow his example. She couldn't imagine herself going into Tim Peck's shop holding her skirts up from muddied legs. Hank grinned and lifting her up in his arms, looked at her wet brown shoes, her wetly clinging brown stockings.

"Can't have mud a-oozin' up them," he laughed. "I purely worship them golden calves. Here—" He handed her his shoes. "Hang onto 'em, now."

She laughed and hoped no one would see them. With one arm around his neck and one hand dangling his wet shoes she felt gay and silly.

Hank walked into the road sinking deep in the mud. Looking at her feet he chuckled and chanted, "How beautiful are thy feet with shoes, O prince's daughter! 'N th' joints a' thy thighs are like jewels. Thy navel is like a round goblet which wants not liquor . . ."

She squirmed, but his arms tightened. "Hank! Hank Martin! What on earth are you saying?"

"I ain't a-sayin'. I'm a-singin'. Song a' Solomon, 's a matter a' fact." He cleared his throat, stopped in the middle of the road and chanted softly, "Thy belly is like a heap a' wheat set about with lilies. Thy two breasts are like young roes that are twins. Thy neck is . . ."

She struck him half earnestly across the shoulders with his shoes. Hank lifted his head to laugh, then called loudly, "Howdy, Tim!"

She turned her head and, seeing Tim Peck and several others in the doorway of the shop, felt a hot red creep over her face.

"You fellers seen m' wife hit me," Hank called out, shaking with laughter. "I want y' all to be a-'memberin' that blow."

"I bet she should oughta hit y' with a crowbar," Picayune Potter wheezed at them shrilly.

Struggling to pull a foot up from the black glue, Hank teased softly, "Allus thought Solomon got his five hundred wives on that there chapter 'n here I ain't able to woo one t' a state a' soft givin'."

"Do shut up, Hank!" She hissed it almost fiercely.

"Why, a feller dassn't stop whilst his love's a-spittin' fire. I'll give it another try," he teased, then chanted softly, "Thy stature is like to a palm tree. I said, I'll go up the palm tree. Come, my love, let's go forth 'n lodge in the villages—" She gave up the struggle. How strange, she thought. We started out so earnestly. She had been upset at the idea of campaign. Surely he wouldn't be capable of saying anything sensible to those men. These were not the words he said he would have clear and plain. Thinking then of the long, tiring, tense time while he studied Jules's sheaf, the thought came to her that she should be grateful that he could concentrate so intensely and come out of it laughing and playing. She patted his shoulder lightly, feeling strangely shy.

"So I'm finely a-gettin' some'eres with you," he laughed, taking the last steps to the green field but continuing to carry her, chanting softer and softer, ". . . 'n at our gates are all manner a' pleasant fruits, new and old, which I have laid up for thee, O my beloved." At the narrow plank walk he put her on her feet.

She stood uncertainly a moment, feeling a wealth of mixed enjoyments —the peculiar sense of life's fullness which Hank's nearness always gave her, pride in the pleasure in men's voices as they greeted him, the inviting smell of fresh green things of the earth blending with the smells of forge and hot irons, of the old wooden building which gave out from its un-painted porousness the odor of horses which had been shod here for almost a century.

"Howdy, Miz Martin," Tim Peck greeted her, and the prickly, callous feel of his hand pleased her as it had before. "You're shore powerful welcome here. Picayune, make yore howdy-do's quick 'n run t' the house 'n tell Maw. Tell her m' fire's hot 'n to bring her mixin's."

"Howdy, Miz Martin," grinned Picayune. "You're a-lookin' right peart."

"Good afternoon, Mr. Potter," Verity said.

"Call him Picayune, Sweetface. These here folks is friends 'n neighbors."

Tim called after Picayune, "Ask Maw where is the young'uns. They should oughta make their kowtows t' Miz Martin."

"Aw, let the young'uns alone, Tim. That is, iffen they're a-playin'. Iffen they're a-workin'," he grinned, "then tell 'em Hank shore wants to be a-seein' 'em. B'lieve in trainin' the young t' think a' me with pleasure, Tim." He winked. "They'll mebbe be a-votin' time I'm a-runnin'."

Everyone laughed.

"The rest a' you fellers has met m' wife, too. But seein' 's how, Sweetface, y' met so many at our paintin' party, reckon it'd plumb strain the brain a' giants t' be a-'memberin' 'em all. So I'll tell you over agin."

Clapping one man after the other on the shoulders he named them.

"This here rosy-cheeked bald-headed good-for-nothin's Harry Disbro. He ain't never done nothin' worth a tinker's damn 'ceptin' t' marry Jenny. You shore 'member Jenny, Sweetface. She come t' our paintin' party in a pink dress. Hair's pret' near the color a' yores. Little bitty thing she is 'n this here lunk 'lowed her to do all the totin' a' them big fat twins."

Harry Disbro glowed with pleasure at Hank's flattering remarks about his wife.

"I do remember your wife, Mr. Disbro." Verity smiled.

"Reckon it won't be no harm t' go fetch her," he said almost shyly. "I'll tote her 'n the twins, too, crost the road."

"That'll plumb put me t' shame," said Hank. "This here little squab with the picked look's Hannibal Swithers Dupree. Call him Swith, for short. Takes the little fellers t' grow them long names. But liken all squabs, Sweetface, he's choice. Yes, sir, Swith, you're a choice a' mine."

She liked Hannibal Swithers Dupree. The sparrow-boned little fellow had big, intelligent eyes.

Picayune came in puffing. "Sophy'll be here soon's she gathers up her mixin's."

" 'N this here four-by-seven's Whale Cruze," Hank went on. "What's yore rightful name, Whale? Don't reckon I ever heard it."

Four-by-seven was almost an accurate description of his dimensions, and the big man roared.

"Iffen y' won't never tell a soul, I'll admit m' maw named me Cuthbert."

Laughter doubled and redoubled in volume. Even Tim, who was doing mysterious things at the forge, stopped his work of fitting a grill-like thing of iron over the fire. Seeing Sophy coming Hank hurried to her and took the huge clothesbasket loaded with bowls and boxes and bags.

"Sophy," he said, almost bowing as he took her burden, "ain't nothin' like you in the whole state. Ain't 'nother woman could think up nothin' half so nice as these here parties in the shop."

"You 'n yore syrup," Sophy chided. But she beamed on him.

Verity held out her hand to Sophy, but Sophy put her arms around her and hugged her tight.

"Sweetface, he calls you, 'n Sweetface y' are." Sophy's voice held the warmth of real affection. "It's right glad we are to be a-seein' of y'."

Nodding her head for emphasis she released Verity and bustled across to the forge, seeming to crackle with energy as her dress crackled with starch. Opening the boxes and bags which Hank had put on a bench, she began pouring and mixing while Tim finished adjusting his handmade top oven and grill.

"We didn't mean to put you to so much bother," said Verity.

"Pshaw, now," said Sophy Peck, "ain't no sich a thing 's bother when it comes t' doin' fer friends." She smiled. "Well, here comes Harry withen Jenny 'n th' twins."

Little Mrs. Disbro, in a dress all wilted and soiled with the abuse it had taken from the twins, came in and drooped onto a bench, sticking her muddy feet and legs out straight.

"Yore old man crawfished, Jenny. Said he'd carry y' crost the road." Hank grinned at her. "I was plumb anxious he shouldn't be a-doin' it, too. Planned you 'n me'd wash our feet in the trough together. Seein' y' wore shoes I plan now to carry m' mud home with me."

Verity sat down beside Jenny and took one of the babies. Sophy poured a creamy corn batter over stewed fruit and stuck the pan in the oven.

"My, my," she said, "this forge saves me a lotta hot hours alone in m' kitchen! It purely gives me pleasure, it does."

"Hang onto yore pleasures, Sophy," advised Hank solemnly, "folks like to us don't get a heap."

"Why, we-all have right good times, Hank," said Sophy.

"Yeah," said Hank, " 'n this is shore one such time. You-all know I ain't one for bellyachin'. Ain't nobody can squeeze out more joy'n I can. Nobody. I'm a singin' fool. But by God'lmighty, that ain't no sign I don' want more'n I got, 'n it ain't no sign I don't want more for any young'uns I might be a-havin' than what m' maw 'n paw was able to give t' me." He paused. "You'd like for yore young'uns to have some learnin', wouldn't y', Sophy? Hell, I 'member when you was a-feelin' so bad cause y' couldn't find the money for all the schoolbooks."

"That's right, Hank," said Tim.

"Just what'd y' mean, Hank," asked Swith, "when y' said you was gonna find a way t' divide the riches a' this earth?"

"Iffen I ever get on the top, iffen I get in a place where I can make laws, I'll be a-makin' some laws that'll change things so's the bankers 'n the money loaners can't be a-keepin' you down year in 'n year out. Why, I betcha iffen the rich a' this here state hadda spew into one pot all the money they got, 'n it was divided even 'mongst everybody, you folks'd get enough t' be a-ownin' yore own land."

"Wouldn't that be a wonderful thing!" exclaimed Sophy. "Wisht I could vote fer y', Hank."

"Why, you can vote, Mrs. Peck," said Verity.

"Pshaw, hear you tellin'!"

"Why, women vote," said Verity with some heat. "My goodness, it almost makes me mad. Why, women voted in Wyoming in 1869. Since almost the Civil War. And women all over America won the right to vote two years ago, in August 1920. Why—" Hank was beaming on her with such elation she was startled.

"Ain't she wonderful!" he boasted. "Ain't she wonderful! I plumb forgot that women was a-votin'. Roarin' thunderbolts, ain't that fine now!"

"Votin' ain't women's business. Polls ain't no place fer womenfolks," said Tim.

"Tim, I'm purely dis'pointed in y'," said Hank. "Lemme tell y' somethin'. I allus figgered Sophy was jus' 's smart 's you. Allus figgered it took just 's much brains for a woman to make th' mite a' money feed you 'n all yore young'uns 's it took for you t' get a-holt a' that mite a' money in the first place." Sophy and Jenny nodded vigorously. "'N then, lookit, take that there oldest boy a' yoren, Tim. Spit 'n image a' his maw. Iffen the women ain't fitten for votin', then all the men 'at looks like their maws should oughta be ruled out, too."

"Poorest argymint ever I heerd y' put up, Hank," grinned Tim. He jerked his head toward Sophy and Jenny, winking heavily. "Blind man kin see y' ain't gonna have no trouble a-fetchin' the womenfolks."

Hannibal Swithers Dupree sat through all this with a dreamy, studying air and after the laughter he said, "It's gonna take years mebbe, you say, Hank. I can see that plain. 'N mebbe you'll be a-gittin' tired a-tryin' 'thouten no hope a' help 'tillst we git a chancet at the polls." He looked at everyone timidly. "When the day comes, mebbe you'll be a-needin' some extry dollars." He squared his shoulders and blazed, "'Twouldn't bother me none t' be a-owin' th' Black Skimmer a dollar more ev'ry year." The steam went out of him again as he added apologetically, "A mite a' hope's plumb worth a dollar a year, it is."

"A mite a' hope's worth a dollar a year," repeated Hank softly, hunting the meaning. "You aimin' t' say you'd put a dollar a year on me, Swith? A actual dollar?"

Stunned by the effect of his words, Swith could only look up at Hank with expecting devotion like some noble dog.

"D'you mean a actual dollar every year?" Hank asked again, softly, urgently. "Speak, man!"

Something about Swith's muteness caught them all in a mesh of stillness, suspended them until sound should come from this human. They stood, like anxious relatives waiting the wail of a new baby. Suddenly Swith gulped air into his lungs.

"I mean it," he cried. "I wanta see them riches divided someday, iffen it ain't 'tillst the day I go t' m' Maker! I'll bank a dollar a year in y', Hank. 'N so'll others. Lotsa others, I betcha!" Blood pinked his thin, sallow flesh and his eyes praised the new world they visioned.

"God'lmighty," said Hank prayerfully, "God'lmighty!"

Hank's friends looked at him with adoration, their voices blended in agreement like a joyously solemn hosanna and over all was Tim's fine bass, "We'll see y' through, boy, iffen th' Lord'll let us." Verity looked at Hank. Through the prayer in his eyes there crept a canny computing, a self-pleased glow. Within Verity something new stirred to life to protest this scene.

"But this is homage," she cried. "This is homage!"

But not loud enough. No one heard her. No one at all.

5

Hank Martin, peddler, was welcome everywhere he went. He always came with glad tidings, always offered a helping hand, always had time to help solve a problem, to listen to troubles.

In this state, where there is much religious intolerance, Hank was loved by Protestants and Catholics alike. Hank Martin is the only man I have ever known who could persuade the bigoted, uneducated hillbilly or swamplander to put a bright and promising child in a convent. A convent offered education and. . . .

USUALLY Hank helped with getting meals, if indeed he didn't do most of it. But tonight was different. The afternoon's triumph was wine to the head. He strutted. He flailed his arms.

" 'N did y' see the way they was a-lookin' when I said. . . ."

She heard again, with embellishments, his afternoon speech, his own description of how Swith looked, and what Sophy said.

"God'lmighty, Sweetface, it was purely wonderful yore 'memberin' 'bout women a-votin'. Where I was a-thinkin' 'bout one vote, dang if y' didn't speak right up 'n start me thinkin' on how I could be a-gettin' me two!" A chuckle grew into a howl of laughter. "Oh, sweet day that's a-comin'!" he cried. "Oh, sweet day that's a-comin'! Iffen ever them uppity swells a' Delamore, 'n Loder City, 'n Sherman, 'n Crescent City— them fine fellers that rides t' the polls in nigger-drove autymobiles—ever sees them sunbonneted women a' the hills 'n swamps a-stompin' in t' mark their ballots! I'm a-tellin' y', Sweetface, strong men'll faint. Yes sirree, they'll be a-faintin' t' the right 'n a-faintin' t' the left!" he howled. "Liken Tim said, polls ain't no place for women. 'N the womenfolks a' them uppity swells ain't a-votin'. Not yet they ain't," he added thoughtfully.

"But women should vote. I'm going to vote in the next election."

"You ain't a-goin' t' do no such a thing!"

"I'd like to know why not."

"Lookit, you ain't a-goin' t' give out no such idea. Y' go t' the polls 'n vote when all the other womenfolks goes t' vote for me!"

She laughed. "All right. I'll wait and cast my first vote for you, darling. But what about the literacy and property law Mr. Bolduc spoke of?"

Leaning across the table he ran his finger down her arm.

"I'll do something 'bout that—somehow," he said caressingly. "Yeah, I'll find a way."

He lifted another great forkful to his mouth. "God Almighty allus gives me His best."

He was eating prodigiously and she was concerned.

"Darling, don't eat so much. After three days of scarcely eating at all, you'll be sick."

"Ain't that silly now! Animals allus does it. Takes 'em days t' stalk another beast for killin', 'n then they gorge. Stummicks is made for shrinkin' 'n stretchin'."

"And you've made your kill?" Her words startled and hurt her. Why, she didn't think that! Surely she didn't think that! With shame she pled, "Oh, Hank, please—" She meant to add, "forgive me," but he interrupted.

"That's right, kinda," he grinned. "I was shore days a-stalkin' the idea that'd fetch 'em. 'N now I'm a-gorgin'," he said contentedly.

"Hank," she was very earnest, "they worshiped you. Literally worshiped . . ."

"Ain't that the truth, though! Sweetface, y' got any notion a' how much is a actual dollar t' them folks? Y' got any notion how much back-breakin' work, how much doin' without a dollar means? Why, a feller like Picayune Potter don't see more 'n thirty-forty dollars actual cash money in a whole year. Some a' 'em don't see that. Some a' 'em sees mebbe two hundred."

"That's what I mean. Can you live up to what they are expecting of you, Hank?"

"All they're a-askin' for right now's a mite a' hope, liken Swith said. 'N God'lmighty, iffen I can make them feel that-a-way, I can make hundreds—thousands—feel the same way. I can do it, Sweetface, I can do it!" His voice rose.

"But you said today something about making people divide the riches. That's just silly. You said if all the riches were divided maybe these people could own their own land. Things just aren't done that way. It wouldn't even be good for people." She hesitated. "I hate to say it, Hank, but lots of your friends are shiftless. They think they work, and I guess they do. But my goodness! They don't mend their porches. Some of them are fine, like Tim. All I've met are kind-hearted. But, Hank, they are shiftless."

"Hell, Sweetface, I know most a' 'em ain't worth a dang. But then agin, they been plumb discouraged for generations. 'N folks like them don't get no learnin'. They just kinda foller their instincts 'n does the best they can. Just kinda smellin' 'n a-feelin' their way through the days."

"Yes." It seemed almost hopeless to her. "Even paint and nails cost something."

"Ain't it so!" He grinned and looked appreciatively at the white walls. "But when I think of it—that most everybody I know or am like to know can't read a letter! How'll I ever get 'em learnt enough so's t' pick out my name from lotsa other names? Even if I lick that law, how'll they learn my name? Like you said, Sweetface, most a' 'em is plain shiftless. That there school you think you're a-goin' to run—there'll only be a passel comin' after a time 'r two. 'N then there's the whole state t' be a-coverin'!"

"Too bad," she said casually, "that they don't have men's pictures on the ballots!"

He raised his head in that startled, ready-to-jump, hearing way he had when an idea shot at him from out of her words.

"That's it!" he exclaimed. "I'll have cards made, thousands 'n thousands. Big ones, with m' pitcher on 'em. 'N under my pitcher HANK MARTIN, big 'n clear. 'N I'll have m' pitcher 'n my name on m' wagon. Like in a first-grade reader for babies. Here's a pitcher of a animal that's plumb familiar 'n under it in big letters is C-A-T."

"Why, Hank—why, Hank! That might really do it!"

A swell of love pushed at her ribs, love made bigger, sweeter, with something lofty, something proud. Oh, she thought, I was so silly this afternoon to be afraid for him! I worship him, too.

"That's wonderful, Hank, it's so simple."

"Everything's simple. All the right answers is simple, seems 's though." He grinned. "Right now I'm a-knowin' I gotta be a-goin' t' the city t' get goods for m' wagon 'n get on with my peddlin'. 'N I purely hate t' leave y'. But the answer's simple. How 'bout you goin' along?"

"I'd love it, Hank! I've hated the idea of six, even eight weeks here alone."

"Roarin' thunderbolts, sometimes I gotta be gone that many months mebbe! You shouldn't oughta be here alone. Gotta do somethin' 'bout that." He stretched. "Gotta do somethin' 'bout learnin' the ins 'n outs a' what Jules was a-meanin' 'bout money systems 'n rediscounts, 'n such. He like 's not can gimme the name a' some books I should oughta buy in the city. Let's go over t' Jules's house."

"Oh, no. Not looking like this. Not through the wet fields."

"Aw, he's seen me barefoot afore 'n muddy. I got things t' say t' Jules. I'm a-goin'. Anyways, you should oughta be a-restin' for yore ridin' tomorra."

She followed him to the door, wanting to beg him to stay home and knowing it would do no good. She wished she had the courage to try to lure him into staying home. He hesitated, looked down at her, and knew her longing.

"I jus' plumb gotta have this somethin' 'bout money tolt t' me, Sweet-

face." He was almost apologizing. "We should oughta be a-honeymoonin'."
Bending, he looked into her eyes with a slightly upward, teasing slant.
" 'N you was the one," he taunted, "as was feared you wasn't a-goin' t'
get nothin' but lovin' in this here marriage!"

He jumped over the steps and strode into the bluing twilight, singing
lustily:

> "The 'gator slithered t'ward the shore
>   To find a spot t' sun in,
>   His belly on a tussock scraped . . ."

Lightning bugs twinkled like earth-bound stars and tiny mosquitoes,
newborn in the day's damp heat, buzzed their bewilderment. A frog
grated noisily out near the live-oak tree and the first evening cool stirred
in from the west. A feeling of the greatness of life, of the privilege of living,
held her in a thrall of content. To live, just to live, was splendor enough.
All the little things of the earth were content with themselves and so was
she. She was Verity, Hank Martin's wife. She went inside, lighted the coal-
oil lamp, picked up the checkered material which was to become curtains
for the cupboard, and began sewing.

The little house was still and empty without Hank, and Verity had a
foretaste of the loneliness of waiting months and months when he would
be gone. After a few hours of sewing she busied herself with packing a
small bag to take with her on the morrow, prepared herself for bed, and
then sat again beside the table waiting.

It was late when Hank came in with his light, lithe step that was yet a
tread. The little swell of lovely expectancy came in her throat as she
heard his step on the porch. He opened the door and the yellow lamplight
blued his hair and brought out the planes of his dew-damp face. His
whole expression was of reverent pleasure as he looked at her. She leaned
over the table, both hands stretched toward him in intimate, wordless
greeting.

"A joy past believin' it is t' find you here a-waitin'." He tiptoed toward
her as if entering a sacred place.

"I'm so lonely without you," she said. "How can I stand months of waiting? The world is just empty when you're gone."

"It shouldn't oughta be. 'N I wish you'd 'a been with me this night."
His voice took on a tone of reflective wonder. "Y' know what, Verity?
That there Jules, he said some right interestin' things 'bout me, he did."

"What, darling?"

"He's a strange 'un, but we kinda understand each other, seems as
though. He was a-tellin' me t'night 'bout him a-goin' t' war. He was just
a ordinary soldier 'n for the first time in his whole dang life he hadda
chancet t' know common folks, 'n he says he found 'em good in battle—
even great, he says. It seems Jules was full 'n runnin' over withen pride

in the common American fellers when they're doin' battle, 'cause they fight like as if they're inspired—like as if they plumb understand the meanin' a' democracy 'n see its greatness, he says. That's while they're a-facin' the enemy, y' understand. 'N Jules, he says he hopes for great things from common folks when he comes back—'n then y' know what he says, Verity?"

Hank looked at her with pride. "Jules says, 'That's what's remarkable about you, Hank.' 'N then he tells me in a sorta way a' his own that I'm a feller as lives every day t' do battle 'n that likely I can do great things. Yeah, he said that. He actual spoke some such words, he did."

He shook his head, finding it hard to believe Jules Bolduc would speak thus. Verity was proud and pleased. She patted Hank's hand.

"Jules's great-grandpappy owned all this whole section—all a' Cypress Bend—'n the old feller gave this place its name t' sorta honor the bald cypress as grows in our swamps. I get t' thinkin' 'bout that whilst Jules is a-talkin', 'n I think on them tales a' how his great-grandpappy made his first big money offen the cypress. You'll see lotsa cypress in the swamps on this here trip we're a-takin'. They're like t' be draped withen moss, they are, 'n their roots double up 'n push big knobby knees up through the swamp for t' draw in air. Big 'n tall like t' old kings they stand, 'n their heartwood is just plumb immune t' decay 'n termites. It'll allus stand strong 'n smooth agin the weather 'n the years. It'll plumb resist acids 'n such, the lumber cutters tell me. Fine-grained it is 'n of a rich color."

His eyes looked off into nowhere and he went on softly, "Whilst Jules is a-tellin' me in his own way just what Maw tolt me in her way—that I'm a feller as can mebbe get back t' Zion—I'm a-settin' there a-catchin' the feel a' that Jules. But I don't plumb catch it till I'm most home."

He struck the table with his fist. "God'lmighty! A feller like t' him a-lettin' hisself be what he calls a 'spectator'! Helluva note. 'Cause d'y' know what? I gotta feelin' he's some'at like t' the cypress hisself. Yeah, strung withen some old dead moss, he is. But still 'n all, I gotta feelin' he's like t' have the same kind a' heartwood."

She was enchanted. Music and rhythm were in his speech.

"Why, Hank," she said, "that's beautiful. I love to hear you talk."

He grinned. "I'm a describin' man." He leaned over the table, put his warm hard hands over her ears, and pulled her gently toward him until their lips met. "I ain't yet got words enough for t' be a-describin' of all yore wonders," he whispered. He kissed her again. "That's kissin' afore lovin'," he said huskily.

She stood in their little yard, holding her smallest suitcase, enjoying the coming of day while waiting for Hank to drive up from the barn. The first golden feelers of the sun paled the strong last stars of morning, turning the trees from black etchings into living things of green. The sky, seeming conscious of its dignity, had vaulted its ceiling aloofly from low little clouds. From over Tim's way a cow lowed her morning news of a full udder. Wood smoke from Jules's kitchens mingled dryly with the night-damp smell of fields. Jules's hunting hounds began to bark a greeting to their feeder, and the wide country mellowed the sounds and spread them out thinly.

Hank's big black gelding, Beauty, neighed joyously as he came out of the dark barn, his mane tossing prettily as he threw his head within the limits of his reins. The appearance of Hank's wagon shocked Verity, so different it was from the day of their wedding. No longer was it modestly wearing its tarpaulin cover. It flaunted its wares shamelessly. No wonder Hank had been so long getting the thing ready! A high centerboard reared up from its middle on which were displayed shiny cheap pots and pans, catching the light in their surfaces and tinkling tinnily as they jiggled and swung. Samples of bright oilcloth gleamed here and there like brazen flowers, among samples of less bright calicoes, laces, and cheap ribbons. In the exact center, above the other displayed goods, a very pink life-size cardboard baby, clad in real diapers and real bootees, reached a fat dimpled hand for a lace-edged hood. An old buggy top lay folded back against the glass case which glistened back of the seat, the iron arms bolted securely to the seat's sides. In the glass-fronted case were patented cure-alls, the joint and muscle liniments, powder and rouge, needles, threads, and tapes. Strips of leather with slits buttonholed over the heads of nails driven in the wooden back of the case held all these things in place. In the bottom of the wagon were piled the bolts of material, the boxes, and crates.

She hadn't minded the wagon on their wedding day and she resolved that she would not mind it now. Hank grinned down at her before jumping to the ground.

"Ain't m' wagon a daisy, though!" he exclaimed with pride. "Better'n any store window I most ever saw. Lordy me, some a' m' customers is plumb a-goin' t' spend their last cent. Mebbe go in debt."

She couldn't take her eyes off the cardboard baby.

"Ain't that little ol' baby somethin'!" he declared.

"Funny expression," she said. "I guess it looks startled."

"Huh! Lemme tell y', iffen ever a baby a' one a' my customers gets its feet in shoes, that child's plumb gonna have reason t' be startled."

She laughed up at him. "If it's as bad as that," she teased, "considering 'how beautiful are thy feet with shoes, O prince's daughter' maybe you'd better give away a pair of bootees now and then. Since mothers vote."

She laughed at his amazement, thinking him surprised at her teasing.

"Why ain't I never thought a' that afore! One a' them whole sets a' clothes! One t' any woman minute I see her a-bulgin'! Wed 'r unwed, she gets one! 'Specially will she please me iffen she gets herself 'n all her kin so's they c'n read 'n write my name." He backed away from the wagon and looked at it critically. "Yeah, 'n under that there baby I'm a-goin' t' have wrote 'If y' got one a' these a-comin', y' got his clothes a-comin', too!' "

He took her hands in his with a kind of reverence, looked at her admiringly.

"So young 'n peart, 'n still so knowin'. Lord God Almighty allus gives me His best." He touched her hair above her ear, ran a finger along the brim of her small blue hat. "Come, my beloved," he quoted softly, "let us go forth into the field. Let us lodge in the villages. The mandrakes give a smell, and at our gates are all manner a' pleasant fruits, new and old, which I have laid up for thee, O my beloved."

He picked her up in his arms and held her tightly, possessively, for a second before putting her into the wagon.

"Mandrakes," she said dreamily, "I wonder what they smell like."

He climbed in and took the reins.

"You ain't a-honin' t' smell 'em, are y'?"

"Oh, I just wonder whether they'd smell sweet like apple blossoms or spicy like cloves."

"Cloves! Well, what th' hell is mandrakes?"

"Some kind of an herb, I guess."

"Roarin' thunderbolts!" he exclaimed. " 'N me a-thinkin' they was heducks!"

Her laughter broke free and sweet. She put her arm under his, her cheek against his shoulder.

"Oh, Hank," she laughed, "I love you!"

"Y' got the kindlin' power, Sweetface. Yeah, y' shore got it. Plumb hate t' go off from our house. Purty, all white, ain't it?" He sighed lightly. "Dang that there Jules. Plumb cheated me outen days a' honeymoonin', he did. Funny, the things a man thinks he has gotta do."

The reins slapped Beauty's rump smartly and the horse rippled his shiny skin, lowered his head, and tautened himself for the starting pull in the mud.

"Damn mud," Hank muttered. "Been trompin' through six inches a' dust 'r twelve a' mud all m' life, seems 's though."

"Where are we going now?"

"Into Caziyoux swamp. Gonna see Spurge McMenimee. Best trapper 'n 'gator man in the state. Spurge is a somebody extry special. Lotsa these here settlements got just one boss-man. That is, iffen there's one man as is stronger 'n wiser'n the others. Spurge now, he's such a feller. He's judge 'n jury. He's the law. He banishes men from the settlement for stealin'. Or mebbe has 'em whipped till clost t' dyin'. Or iffen it's something plumb terrible they draw lots 'mongst the menfolks 'n two 'r three take the sinner into the swamp. Spurge, he's one a' my favorite folks."

Negro children called excitedly when they saw Hank's gorgeous wagon. "Looky dere, looky dere! Hit's Mistuh Hank!"

He called each child, handed each a thin stick of peppermint candy, beaming and talking while they dug their bare toes into the mud, shy and anxious. Mostly they were wide-eyed, skinny-legged, knobby-kneed young things.

Taking a tin whistle from his shirt pocket, Hank would blow three shrill blasts at spots along the road where no sign of human habitation could be discerned, open his big tin candy box, and wait, perhaps grunt to Verity, "Have the damdest time a-keepin' the ants outen this candy." After a few minutes some ragged children, sometimes black, sometimes white, came running, then came their mother puffing from her hurrying, and, if their father worked his own fields, he also came after a bit. Sometimes his sale was a few yards of calico, sometimes only a single row of pins which he tore from a full paper and for which he received four pennies. To each he introduced Verity with a glowing pride, and introduced each customer by name to Verity. She was amazed at his memory. It was late in the afternoon when she met the Cajun Ribidoux family.

"You heard I been married? You ain't? Well, this is m' wife. Yes, sirree, she's Miz Hank Martin. Sweetface, this here's Miz Ribidoux 'n her brood." Pointing out each child, "Emmeline, she's twelve; Reuben, he's 'leven; Sidney, he's gettin' t' be a fine big feller, too, he's most ten now; Josephine, she's eight; Alois, he's seven; Halley, he's six; Philip, he's four; 'n them two little butterballs is Gracie 'n Jacqueline, they two'n three. Where's the baby, Miz Ribidoux? He sleepin'?"

She thought, Somehow Hank manages to make me feel like a queen. Giggling within herself, she added, Queen of one of those silly countries where rulers manage to look dignified on the back of the camels or jackasses.

She began to see Hank's wagon as the countryfolk saw it, an exciting thing of beauty and plenty. Amazement grew in her as she thought how Hank had developed this rich friendliness since he started walking the hills and swamps peddling the pretties his first fourteen dollars had bought. Men greeted him with love as a kinsman who always brought laughter and pleasure; women greeted him with a love sweetened with an anxious yearning to serve him. Older women mothered him and young women from fourteen up adored him.

They spent the night in the Ribidoux home, a shamble of splintery boards, opened here and there in inch-wide cracks to the weather.

While Mrs. Ribidoux and the older girls worked at stove and table, Hank and Verity sat with the rest of the family on the flappy, unnailed boards of the low porch with their feet resting on the ground. Hank looked out at the fields.

"Ain't y' got no cotton, Hilbert?" he asked. Mr. Ribidoux threw out his hands and shrugged his shoulders.

"Boll weevil got him las' year, yes."

"And this year?" Hank asked.

"No money. No seed. We jus' about go hongry, thees winter, Hank. Jus' about, yes. We got our sweetenin', though. Cane good. Corn good. Got coupla hogs. But no cotton, no money. Can't kill the sow, so we ain't got much thees winter, no." A thick weariness clouded his voice.

"Too late t' plant cotton, ain't it?"

"Uh-uhh! I like for try!" he cried.

"I ain't seen yore mule," said Hank.

"I sell him, Hank. Fi' dollar, I get. But if seed I had Mamma and the childrens can follow me an' walk it into de groun'."

"You come with me." Hank headed for his cart, followed by Mr. Ribidoux and most of the brood. Digging under the tarpaulin which shielded the wagon's treasures from the heavy dew, he located a big can.

"Gimme a hand," he said.

Together they lifted the can to the ground. Removing the lid, Hank reached in, lifted out a handful of the fuzzy whitish-gray seeds.

"Y' can take m' word for it, Hilbert. This here's the best damn seed I could find. How much you need for yore patch?"

Mr. Ribidoux wrung his hands.

"No money, Hank," he wailed. "No money."

"Roarin' thunderbolts! Did I say anything 'bout money, Hilbert? I'm a-givin' it to y' now. Iffen yore crop's good, you pay me come pickin'. Iffen it ain't no good then you send one a' the young'uns down t' my house next spring. Send him in time for the plantin'. Iffen I ain't t' home, my wife'll dole it. By God, a man should ought have his cotton patch."

Mr. Ribidoux crossed himself, and the children, watching their father, crossed themselves.

"Go on, now, one a' you young'uns, 'n get a pail t' put some into," commanded Hank, "a great big pail," he called after the screaming, running children.

Mrs. Ribidoux hurried onto the porch.

"What does?" she called. "Papa, what does?"

Mr. Ribidoux waved his arms excitedly, jumped up and down.

"Mamma," his black eyes gleamed with a showing of tears, "Hank, he's give to us cotton seed. Bucket cotton seed. No money, Mamma, but Hank, he's give to us!"

Mrs. Ribidoux clasped her hands, lifted her eyes to heaven.

"Blessed Saint Mary," she said fervently. Lumbering down the rickety steps, she scurried to Hank and embraced him. "Blessed Hank. A saint you are!" She laughed and cried. "Come now, we eat. I send all the childrens early this morning fishing. The scacalait we have got for supper."

After supper was eaten the stacked-up pallets were pulled down and spread for sleeping upon the floor of the one-room shack. But one pallet was dragged up a wobbly ladder and laid on the planks which were nailed to the cross rafters at one end of the house. Mrs. Ribidoux opened a cypress box and brought forth some good old patch quilts with great pride.

As Verity climbed up the ladder, a wave of sick terror flashed through her. The poverty of all these people struck her suddenly like a fever. Sitting on their pallet in the tiny balcony-like loft, Hank took off his clothes with complete unconcern for the staring eyes of the children below, but Verity sat there, stiff and miserable. He rolled over to her, put his head in her lap, and started unbuttoning the collar of her dress. She contorted her face into a fierce command to stop. He chuckled.

"Ain't you feelin' lovin'?" he teased, whispering.

Tears of embarrassment and utter misery came in her eyes, and Hank was contrite. He sat up and put his arm about her protectingly.

"Shush, now, Sweetface," he whispered. "Shush, now. You should oughta know me well enough by now t' know I love lovin' you too much t' snatch it quick 'n secret agin pryin'. Lovin' you's a ceremony, Sweetface. Just slip outen yore dress 'n let them kids see that purty petticoat a' yourn. They ain't never seen the like." He kissed her cheek gently. "Then you lay down 'n put yore head in the holler 'tween m' shoulder 'n m' neck. I'll hold y' all still 'n solemn. When we lay that-a-way it plumb gives me the same fine feelin' I get in church."

It was midmorning and the mist was finally surrendering to the sun which filtered down through the thick-leafed trees. The air had almost the tangible softness of river water and carried in waves and ripples the varying smells. Sunlight dappled Beauty's back, and when he walked into a spiraling column of gnats he snorted them out of his nostrils, with patient endurance.

"Ain't the woods beautiful?" said Hank softly. "There's a freshness a-comin' from the lake way yonder, 'n the rottin' logs 'n stumps give a richness like a good, clean manure. 'N over that-a-way where the water stands one 'n two foot high little old insects is a-hatchin', 'n them smart little things is a-flutterin' 'crost the water to find a tree to crawl up till they get plumb uset t' the world. 'N out 'long the edges the water lilies 'n hyacinths is a-growin' s' thick 'n heavy a man nigh'bout can lay on 'em t' dry out 'n study 'r sleep in the sun." He looked up. "'N then I like the smell the sun sends down—the smell a' the tree's top leaves a-bakin'. Som'at like bread when it's just a-gettin' t' the crustin' stage in a oven, ain't it?"

How strange, she thought, that all my senses should be sharpened because of Hank. She had always been intensely aware of people and things, and yet life now was brighter, more hurting, more soothing, vaster.

Their road was just a corkscrew path hewn through this jungle, and she tried to look deep into the woods and classify the various shades of green.

"Makes one wonder if there really is a life after death," she said, thinking of her mother. Her mother would have liked to grow things in this country.

"Wonder!" he exclaimed, "I'm s'prised at you, Sweetface. Why, 'course there's life after death! A-course there is. Nature don't waste nothin'. The animals eat 'n what don't go into their flesh they throw outen theirselves for the earth t' take in. Trees like the pecans 'n such as shed their leaves in fall needs for t' have them leaves left t' rot t' feed their crops a' nuts 'n leaves. There's somethin' in leaves 'n stalks that feeds the earth." He waved an arm outward. "Take the sugar cane. We need it for sweetenin' but after we grind them stalks dry a' their juice we pile up them stalks to rot, 'n then spread 'em out to give the earth a meal."

He turned toward her. "Naw, sir, nature don't waste nothin'. Neither did Jesus. He could do miracles 'n He done one with the loaves 'n fishes, 'n then He said 'gather up the fragments that nothin' be wasted.' Well, I allow that when the Lord made the earth, 'n the fish, 'n the animals, 'n give man dominion, He didn't aim that His best work, which was humans, should be wasted. I feel plumb certain shore there's a way for the souls a' folks t' be used after we give our bodies t' the earth."

"Very few folks have dominion, it seems."

"Ain't no fault a' the Lord's, I don't reckon. Sometimes I get a-thinkin' most folks let theirselves get took captives like in Maw's psalm, 'n they just stay took for whole generations. Letting theirselves get wasted liken the psalm says, 'n liken Grammaw Kelts 'n Maw, fair honin' for Zion." The narrow road came to an abrupt end. "Far 's we can go by wagon," he said.

He blew his tin whistle three long clear blasts, waited a few seconds, then blew again and waited.

"It's gonna take Spurge some little spell to get home t' his whistle iffen he's out."

The whistle roused some of the birds from their noontime quiet, and a little cheeping chatter came from the trees. Hank blew again, but scarcely had he finished when his answer came. Three long, clear blasts from a whistle like his own. Hank blew one long blast to say that he had heard, then came two short staccato notes from the distant whistle.

"Them two means Spurge is a-comin'," he explained and jumped to the ground. "We gotta meet him at the edge a' the swamp. You should oughta have boots over them shoes a' yoren. But we ain't got none."

He put a tarpaulin over the high display board, took the pack he had carried on his back before he possessed Beauty and the wagon, climbed into the body of the wagon, and filled his pack with the things he thought he might sell at this settlement. Then he removed his shoes and socks, took off his coat, and stuffed all into his pack. He took from the wagon a steel-pronged stick of cane length.

"For snakes, iffen we need it," he said, stuck a long knife into his belt, and lifted his gun from the wagon.

"Good gracious!" Verity exclaimed. "This must be a terrible place. And it feels so peaceful."

"Shore, it's peaceful. It's got the onliest kind of peace there is in this world. Everything livin' on everything else 'n what ain't used in somethin's belly goin' back t' God, 'r mebbe just t' the earth, liken I said." He grinned up at her. "The worms has t' burrow into the ground to hide from the birds, 'n whilst they're a-burrowin' they're a-makin' holes that lets the roots a' plants 'n trees get air. The roots pulls in air 'n juices from the ground 'n shoots it up into leaves 'n flowers. 'N the birds fly high t' keep outen reach a' ground animals; the insects 'n flies eats the disease lumps offen trees, 'n the birds keeps the insects from gettin' to be too many, 'n the butterflies 'n the bees carries the pollen a' rooted things. Things as can't walk to each other 'n look out for their own pollenizin' like you 'n me can." He waved his hands. "'N the little fish eats insects, 'n the big fish eats the little ones, 'n the gulls 'n pelicans eats both. The animals all eat other kinds of animals 'n fish too sometimes, 'n the 'gators eats anything. 'N all this makes peace for us humans, 'cause we eats 'em all." He adjusted his pack and added, "Plumb generous a' the Lord givin' us dominion over the likes a' this."

Looking up at her, he said, waving his hands at the jungle, "'N all a' this ain't got the beauty you got. Yore hair's a fine spreadin' top bloom, yore eyes is sky withen a stormy ocean in 'em, 'n just a little green a-peekin' through like to young buds—" he held out his arms and she went into them happily—"'n yore lips! You got lips to make—"

"And I have teeth to bite you with," she said, and bit him on the ear.

"Lord save us," he said huskily, "Lord save us," and held her close against him. "You got the kindlin' power. You shore got it. You make the flames t' burn bright in m' brain, 'r the flames to bust out hot through m' body liken a mighty fire as is plumb tired a' bein' kept a-smolderin' 'neath a bankin' a' old ashes." He let her slip to the ground. "It's like you was plumb full a' the fly-upinest pepper. 'N I purely love every ornery grain a' it, I shore do."

"Darling," she murmured, "darling."

"Well, we gotta get a-goin'." He tied the horse to a tree. "Kinda hate t' be a-leavin' him here. I should mebbe oughta cut back the underbrush so's the animals won't get closet enough t' scare him. Oh, well, Spurge'll send som'un' t' look out for him, I reckon."

When they reached the edge of the still swamp water he carried out his pack to a cypress stump, carried her to another, then whistled shrilly and yowled, "Spurge! Spu-urge!"

"I'm a-comin'." The rich voice sounded quite near.

"He's clear in 'mongst the trees," said Hank.

"Who you got with y', Hank?" yelled Spurge McMenimee.

"Hang onto yoreself, man, I a-s'prisin' you-all with m' wife."

They heard a long whistle indicating surprise.

"Heah you tellin', man," yelled Spurge.

Hank laughed. "He ain't believin' a word," he whispered to Verity.

Standing in his pirogue Spurge poled his way between the stumps and trees, his eyes fastened in amazement upon Verity. His only garment, a pair of almost legless bib overalls, gave full glory to his wide shoulders, to the splendid muscles of his back and arms and to his fine slim legs with muscles which stood out as though sculptured in bronze. He trailed a flat-bottomed rowboat, and his pole was about fifteen feet in length, having on its skyward end a vicious steel hook. Pumping Verity's hand up and down in a crushing grasp, he balanced the pirogue with an astonishing exactness, keeping the water from shipping over its low sides.

"I declare," said Spurge, "I do declare. Law now, everybody in the settlement done gonna be powerful pleasured." He hesitated, " 'Ceptin' mebbe Sunny Lou."

"Sunny Lou?" she asked.

"Sunny Lou!" exclaimed Hank heartily. "How is my little sweetheart, huh? Lordy me, bet that child has growed a-plenty since last I seen her." Turning to Verity he said, "That child's the purtiest thing y' ever did see. She's thirteen years, now. Reddest hair ever growed on a head. Hangs in waves, it does. 'N not airy freckle on her nose liken most redheads. I call her the Little Flamingo."

"Plumb spoils her, he does, Miz Martin." Spurge grinned. "No livin' withen that young'un fer days arter he's gone. Moons 'round liken a eighteen-year-old arter a gone sweetheart. I swan t' goodness it troubles her maw 'n me som'at."

They settled in the rowboat and Spurge in the pirogue poled them expertly through the swamp and through what seemed to be little boat paths in the marshes. When they reached clear deep water Hank took up the oars of the rowboat and Spurge trailed. Again at the marshes on the other side Spurge poled them.

She saw a settlement of houses built on stilts all on the swamping edge. Some were only tiny shacks, some, like Spurge's, with little added shacks attached by covered runways. Tiny docks ran out into the water like narrow plank sidewalks elevated on pilings.

Everyone in the settlement was out to greet Hank. They whistled and called and yelled at him. Most of them seemed to be screaming questions about money. "You bringin' us money?" "You bring us dollars?" Hank yelled back, "You're dam tootin' I brought y' money, Whitney." And "Gotta roll t' choke a 'gator." She was puzzled, thinking that he had come here to sell goods.

Spurge slowed up and pulled alongside a rather better kept dock than most. And there, jumping up and down screaming excitedly, "Hank! Hank!" was one of the loveliest children she had ever seen. Sunny Lou's brilliant hair lay in ripples below her shoulder blades, a soft golden bloom was on her skin—skin of the thick, soft texture of a sturdy rose. Back of her were her mother, Lula May McMenimee, two younger sisters, and three little brothers. But Sunny Lou shone forth like a hothouse flower in a mustard patch.

Suddenly she saw Verity. "Who's that?" she cried. Hank got up on the dock and Sunny Lou threw her arms around him and hugged and kissed him with all her might.

"Kiss me, Hank," she commanded.

"You bet," said Hank and kissed her, but the child kissed him with such fervor that his face reddened. Pulling her arms loose from his neck, he said playfully, "Lordy me, Flamingo, you're shore clingin'."

Putting the child aside, he spoke to the other children and to Lula May. "Got a s'prise for you-all. Most knocked Spurge outen his boat. I done brought m' wife with me. Yes sirree, I'm married! This is Verity, friends."

Sunny Lou whirled and stared again at Verity. Light hazel eyes that were almost topaz stared while her mother greeted and exclaimed over Verity. Lou let out a long shriek of pain, whirled on Hank, and beat his chest with her slim young fists.

"You allus said I was yore sweetheart! You allus said you'd wait for me! You did! You did!"

Her father and mother pulled her away from Hank. Spurge's face was white with embarrassment and shame. Lula May tried to cushion Sunny Lou against her soft bosom and soothe her, but the child beat her off.

"You done it," she screamed at Verity. "You done it! Y' ketched him when he wasn't lookin'. Y' ketched him like—like a muskrat, I betcha! You ketched him in a trap, I betcha, I betcha!" She sobbed hysterically.

Spurge grabbed her and shook her violently.

"I aimed t' marry him, someday, Paw," she chattered.

"'N I aim t' lay the worst whuppin' on you that y' ever got!" said Spurge fiercely between his teeth. "B'God, I aim t' break a 'gator pole 'crost yore rump. A-shamin' us all afore the whole settlement. A-carryin' on liken a strollop twicet yore age. Now you git—git on into the house. I aim t' blister yore rump 'tillst it won't set y' fer a whole moon."

Released, Flamingo ran up the narrow dock and into the house crying uncontrollably. Her father wiped the sweat from his face with his bare arm, her mother wiped the tears from her own cheeks with her apron. Hank stood staring after the child, utterly dumbfounded, muttering, "God-'lmighty. God'lmighty!" Misery wearied Verity, loading her heart and her arms and legs with dead weights.

"Spurge—Lula May—" Hank implored the girl's parents, "God-'lmighty, I'm purely sorry the Little Flamingo feels liken that. I got a love for her. I shore have. She's got a fire in her, bright as her hair. I allus knowed she wasn't no lunk, 'n I should oughta knowed not t' tell her she was my onliest sweetheart. Not t' tease her t' hurry up 'n grow up for me."

"You ain't never done her nothin' but good, Hank," said Lula May. "Ain't no fault t' you, Hank. She jus' one a' them fightin' fools, liken Spurge. Spurge, he taken it out on 'gators, is all. 'N then, Sunny Lou, she's thirteen. I was only jus' pushin' fifteen when he swep' me up t' a preacher."

"You lyin', woman," accused Spurge.

"No," Lula May replied blandly. "I was lyin' then. Tolt him I was seventeen, I did, 'n all these years he ain't knowed no differunce." She half laughed.

Hank chuckled. "It purely looks like Sunny Lou is some'at like both her parents. I ain't a-aimin' t' butt in on yore rights, Spurge, but I shore hope y' won't beat the young'un."

Spurge scratched his head.

"I hope you won't either," Verity managed to say.

"That's right kindly of y', ma'am," Lula May said gratefully.

Inside the little house the sobs of Sunny Lou, who was in the girls' bedroom, could still be heard. Verity sat primly in a splintery rocker while Lula May prepared fish and rice for dinner.

"You got the lists a' the skins you-all gimme?" Hank said. "Done swell, I think," and he opened his shirt, unpinned a large, thick envelope, tore its flap, and spilled out greenbacks on the table. He counted them carefully into Spurge's hand.

"Well, what'cha know!" exclaimed Spurge. "Looky here, Lula May, looky here!"

"Law, law!" said Lula May.

"Got ten cents more a foot for them 'gator skins than that thievin' trader was a-givin' y'. 'N right smart more for the muskrats, too."

Turning to his sons, Spurge said, "Git in yore boat 'n run tell all the folks we're a-handin' out money for their catchin's in 'bout a hour over t' the church."

As they ate, Hank and Spurge figured out just how much was coming to each man who had sent skins out with Hank. Verity sat quietly, making no effort to talk, unable to eat.

"You comin' t' the meetin', Maw?" asked Spurge of his wife.

She shook her head. "I stayin' with Sunny Lou." He nodded.

A feeling of distaste for the meeting came over Verity. She could not hear Hank talk about Lincoln again, and she knew he would get everyone in this village pledged to give a dollar a year and to spell his name. She hated to stay in this house, but Sunny Lou's sobs were no longer heard, and perhaps she could sit out on the funny old porch and let the sun and water strengthen her.

"May I stay here with you?" she asked Lula May.

"A-course, ma'am, a-course."

Hank was about to protest. She knew he was about to say she should oughta meet all these people. But seeing Lula May's pleased expression, he only nodded.

After the men left, she went outside. She leaned against the pine-board post beside the steps and didn't care that the sap was oozing from it, making the back of her dress gummy. She sat there for what seemed like hours, sometimes feeling completely blank, sometimes remembering the scene with Sunny Lou, sometimes imagining the scene at the church with Hank making his pleas and the excitement when the people learned he had made a good deal for them.

The sun was less than an hour from setting when the screen door behind her opened and closed gently. Looking up she saw Sunny Lou in a fresh little cotton dress, a really lovely shade of muted pink. Lula May stood back of her, smiling and pleased. The child's eyes were only slightly swollen and she was indeed beautiful to look upon.

"Hank gimme this," Sunny Lou said and touched her skirt.

Verity thought again that Hank had an eye for color, and usually in remarkably good taste in everything except his own clothes. Then the realization came to her that men's clothes were awfully patterned and Hank's love of color couldn't be satisfied within the boundaries set for gentlemen. The pink dress completed the picture that was Sunny Lou, the Flamingo, and her yellowish-hazel eyes looked oddly at Verity.

"I should oughta be shamed," the child said, " 'n I am too, I reckon."

And I reckon you don't look the least bit ashamed, Verity thought, but she said, "It's all right, Sunny Lou."

"I didn't mean it when I said you ketched him in a trap liken a muskrat. Liken Maw says, I should oughta have sense enough to know Hank's a man growed 'n when he called me his little sweetheart he called it to me liken Paw does."

Verity's heart softened to her and she said more gently and with more meaning, "It's all right, Sunny Lou. It's all over and forgotten."

"Yes, ma'am," replied Sunny Lou, and she smiled at Verity. "I'd shore like to be a-doin' somethin' fer you. Could I mebbe pole y' 'round the marshes?"

"No, thanks, Sunny Lou. You can't handle a boat in waters like these, can you?"

"Oh, yes, ma'am! Can't I, Maw?"

"She shore can, Miz Martin. She knows where it's safe 'n she knows all the fine purty places, too."

"That's splendid," said Verity.

"You're a-comin', then?" Sunny Lou asked eagerly.

Almost too eagerly, Verity thought.

"No, thank you, my dear."

Sunny Lou's arm flew up to cover her eyes.

"You ain't forgive me! You jus' a-sayin' so. You won't go with me, 'n I know it ain't all right."

"It was only that I am so comfortable here, Sunny Lou," Verity was a little distressed. "But I'd like to go out on the water, too. Does she really know how to handle the pirogue and keep out of danger?" she asked Lula May.

"She shore does. Spurge trained her good. Now you take good care a' Miz Martin," she said, settling the matter.

Sunny Lou poled the pirogue expertly around the water hyacinths and through the trees, all the while looking at Verity in a secret, studying way. The water twinkled with the uncertain light of sun through the thick growth and the shadow of a gaunt, dead cypress draped in its mourning moss was mirrored in the still brown water. The undergrowth was rich and rank, the living trees spread their branches and their moss like feather-dripping wings, the dead cypress stumps stood like jagged monuments, and the brown still water guarded its secret as to why it gave both life and death.

"Looky back a' you at yonder hummock," said Sunny Lou sharply.

Verity turned rather gingerly, feeling it to be unsafe to move in the tiny pirogue unless one was expert. A huge alligator lay drying himself in a spot of sun.

"Good heavens!" she cried, "an alligator!"

"Yup," said Sunny Lou, and added, "You scairt, ain'tcha?"

"Yes, yes, I am," Verity admitted. "Pole away from here. Let's go home. I've never seen an alligator before," she added nervously.

"You seen one now," said Sunny Lou significantly. "There's a-plenty a' 'gators right 'round here."

Verity stared at the child. "Why," she said, almost unable to believe it, "you headed straight for this place!"

"Yup," said Sunny Lou, " 'n yore plumb scairt." She pulled her lips into a hard downward line, tears welled up in her eyes, and she poled toward the 'gator.

Verity stared at Sunny Lou. The intent which she sensed in the child couldn't possibly be! Numbly Verity's mind repeated over and over, She's only thirteen, she's only thirteen.

Then a resounding splash as the 'gator slithered off his hummock and slapped his tail on the top of the water penetrated her mind and shot fear from her stomach to her brain like a scourging fire. She looked back wildly. The huge thing was only eight or ten feet from the pirogue. With the smooth end of the pole Sunny Lou prodded at the beast's snout to anger him, to make him fierce, to make him open his mouth wide, as she had seen her father do. The beast opened his mammoth jaws and snapped at the pole, but Sunny Lou jerked it back too quickly for him. His jaws made a reverberating and horrible sound, and he came closer.

"Stand up, you outlander," screamed Sunny Lou.

Then Verity shrieked with all her might.

"Hank! Hank! Hank!"

Sunny Lou kept prodding the beast, which snapped again and again in his rage. And then Verity heard Hank's whistle sounding with frantic urgency and she knew Lula May had heard her.

The whistle pierced through Sunny Lou and impaled her, terrified and immobile, her magnificent eyes filling with terror.

"Paw!" Sunny Lou uttered the word with a strange, almost stupefied horror.

"Pole away from here!" screamed Verity.

"Yup," said Sunny Lou dully, and she poled automatically, unseeingly, straight into a cypress knee. The boat tipped and sent them floundering into the water that came almost to Sunny Lou's shoulders. The soft mucky bottom of the swamp sucked at their feet.

"Swim!" screamed Verity.

"Can't nobody outswim a 'gator," said Sunny Lou almost dully. Then, as they heard the 'gator beating the boat with his tail, trying to reach them, Sunny Lou stood as though her legs were paralyzed and shrieked and shrieked. She still held the pole, and Verity jerked her forward and took the pole from her, heading for the cypress knee, the stump of which stood about four feet out of water. She pulled and jerked Sunny Lou after her, the 'gator getting nearer, nearer. They scrambled up on the stump and stood on its jagged uneven top.

"Is that hook to catch them with?" Verity demanded fiercely.

Sunny Lou only nodded.

"Answer, damn you," hissed Verity.

"Poke it in his throat! Poke it in his throat!" and she kept repeating it as though a spring were broken and she couldn't stop.

The great beast found the same knee of the cypress as they had found and came at them, mouth open hungrily. As though hypnotized, Verity plunged the vicious hook down his throat and let go of the pole. The wild thing flounced and flailed with the fifteen-foot pole stuck in his throat. The pole struck at them and around them.

"Dodge!" cried Verity.

"Poke it in his throat! poke it in his throat! poke it in his throat. . . ." and Sunny Lou slumped in a faint onto the jagged points of the stump and began slipping off into the water. Verity knelt, then lay on her stomach, put her arms around Sunny Lou's waist and held her up. The stump's points cut in on her stomach and breasts, and then the pole struck her just above the waist and she went numb all over. She heard the pole strike the edge of the stump as it also struck her, and her brain told her clearly but for that she would now be dead. She heard Hank yell in terror for her, and she heard the single well-placed bullet with which Spurge killed the enemy.

Their cuts and bruises had been washed and bandaged by Lula May and the old black midwife, Granny Dazy, who was the only doctor in the settlement. And now they sat, Verity and the child, wrapped in clean old patch quilts, their feet in pans of hot water, trying not to look at each other.

"But God-damit, Maw," raved Spurge for perhaps the twentieth time, "why'd y' let 'em go?"

And this time Lula May tried to answer, for the anxiety was over.

"Sunny Lou been out lotsa times. She knowed how t' keer fer herself." In spite of her best intentions she let an accusing glance run out toward Verity.

Hank sat in complete silence now, his eyes never leaving her face. He's studying me, Verity thought. She knew he was trying to decide whether it had happened because of her carelessness, or because she was just green. He couldn't think she meant harm to the child. He saw me trying to protect the little devil, she thought fiercely, and twisted in her chair. The stabbing pain in her back above her waistline made her sick with nausea. She was about to speak of it, but Spurge was talking.

"'N I'm a-thinkin' there's more t' this than is to be seen with jus' a-lookin'."

"Whyn't y' tell on me?" Sunny Lou burbled hysterically, her face contorted with the fresh-coming sobs. "Whyn't y' tell on me? Whyn't y' tell?"

Verity turned her head. Spurge ran to Sunny Lou and jerked her to her feet.

"Tell what?" he demanded.

"I was a-goin' t' let the 'gator git her," she sobbed, "I was—I was—"

Spurge's hand fell from his daughter limply. Lula May dropped a pan; the gasps of her brothers and sisters could be heard through the open door. Hank jumped to his feet and stared down at the child curiously. Granny Dazy groaned, "A chile a' de debbil, I'se a-gittin' de preacher." She took her string of nutmegs from her neck and whirled them around herself to ward off the evil spirits and ran out the door.

Many of the villagers had gone to the rescue, making a frenzied exit from the meeting hall, and now they sat quiet and waiting in their pirogues near the McMenimee dock.

"Preacher! Preacher!" the old black granny yelled, swinging her nutmeg string violently. "Come-y hyah! Come-y hyah!"

A sympathetic murmur rose from the crowd, for they thought someone was dying. The preacher was too old to join in the hunt and had come to the house to wait with Lula May. He now came up the dock and into the house.

"You meant to do *murder?*" the shocked, hollow voice of Spurge Mc-Menimee, leader of this settlement and the only judge and jury in the community, was demanding of his child. "You meant to do *murder?*"

A great terror came into Sunny Lou's face as she began to realize the enormity of the thing.

"No, no, I jus' meant t' let the 'gators git her," she sobbed, shrinking down into her bundling quilt.

Sobs jerked Spurge's huge frame.

"Y' know, Sunny Lou, I gotta treat y' liken any other bad person. I cain't bias t' y' causen you're mine. I cain't. It ain't justice. Oh, God," he cried. "Oh, God!"

"God'lmighty, Spurge. What you a-sayin'?" Hank demanded sternly. "Go careful, man. She's yore young'un, 'n she's a wonderful young'un. Think, man!"

"It's her hair, Paw," said Lula May pleadingly, clutching at the old superstition. "It's the witch's hair. It keeps her vain past goodness."

"Pray, preacher," commanded Hank, and Verity knew he was needing time to think this out. She wanted desperately to help this father and mother, and perhaps even this child.

"Oh, Lord," moaned the preacher, "looky down here on us. We-uns got a young'un here as got killin' in her heart. . . ."

Hank grimaced. He tipped up the terrified little face and gave her a reassuring wink and nod. Turning, he studied Spurge's proud and bitter face. Whatever the answer, it must meet Spurge's sense of justice, for his word had been law for everyone else and it must be a righteous law for his own as well.

". . . 'N bless us with yore wisdom, Lord, Aaa-men."

The preacher rose and hacked his throat and looked at the others uncertainly.

"God'lmighty," said Hank softly. "It come t' me whilst he was a-prayin'. Liken a vision it was, like to the words spoke to Moses from the fiery bush. 'She needs learnin',' the voice said. 'She needs learnin', she does. She's liken to the captives in a strange land. She's a-cryin' t' get back t' Zion. She's liken t' the captives that wanted t' get back t' Zion.' 'N I see plain that it's a right good answer." He put his hands on Spurge's shoulders, stopped, thinking out his words carefully. "Banish her to a Catholic convent, Spurge. They'll take young'uns in some places for nothin'. God, man, iffen she was mine I'd fair be bustin' with pride for her. She's got guts. B'God, she's one as has the guts t' get back t' Zion. Banish her to a Catholic convent, Spurge. That's justice."

"We-uns ain't Catholics." said Spurge, looking a little bitter.

"Well, what of it!" exclaimed Hank. "The Methodists ain't got no schools. They all too dang pore."

The preacher cleared his throat ostentatiously. "That's a right fine idee," he said, trying to sound authoritative. "Give her to the Catholics."

Spurge looked from one face to the other, then stood before his daughter to pronounce judgment.

"Please, Spurge," said Verity gently, "please . . ." But Hank motioned her to silence.

"Sunny Lou, I'm a-sentencin' y'," he choked. "Sunny Lou, we gotta give y' t' the Catholics. 'N yore hair is t' be cut clost t' yore head 'n what's left on yore head is t' be blackened with yore Sunday shoe polish."

The child clutched at her hair wildly. "No! Oh, please, no!"

Turning from her, Spurge walked out of his house to tell of his judgment on his beloved daughter as he would tell them about any other miscreant.

"Shush yore cryin', Little Flamingo," whispered Hank. "Shush now. This here's purely yore lucky day. Yore hair'll grow in jus' liken it is now. 'N you'll have learnin' 'n be a somebody."

The child looked at him and believed every word. And the child's mother looked at him and worshiped him. And Verity thought, He's a great man, and wanting to touch him, she leaned forward and gasped in pain.

Lula May looked at her sharply and helped her to rise.

"I'm a-takin' y' t' bed," she said.

Verity nodded.

Verity sat on the edge of the bed and Lula May plumped the pillows.

"Vision, he says he's got," she said softly. "But I knowed he ain't. I knowed he's m' onliest hope 'n I kep' my eyes on him. I seen him a-thinkin' 'n a-schemin' it out."

"How right you are," Verity whispered, and stifled a groan.

"I'll fetch some a' Hank's linament 'n rub that there bruise the pole give y'."

"No, no," said Verity. "My ribs are broken, I think."

Gently Lula May pressed around the spot. Convinced, she stood back and looked at Verity with something of worship.

" 'N y' never tolt!"

"We can't let Spurge know," said Verity.

Lula May nodded thoughtfully.

"Granny Dazy'll know what t' do fer them ribs." Her eyes glowed with a dangerous resolution. "I'll steal some a' Spurge's skins . . . I'll steal 'em from somebody else, even—'n I'll bribe a shet mouth in Granny Dazy."

The picture of Spurge having to deal out justice to another member of his family terrified Verity.

"Good God!" she gasped, tortured with pain and beginning to feel as fierce as the rest of these wild people. "You will not! Send Hank to me," she commanded; "I'll have Hank bribe a shut mouth in old Granny Dazy."

Lula May stood before her, struggling for words, and finally they came.

"You're mebbe good 'nuff for t' marry up with Hank, after all," she said and turned to leave, hesitated, and came back to defend her child. "Y' shouldn't oughta think there's a somethin' wrong with m' pritty one— m' Sunny Lou, 'n God! I'm gonna miss her—jus' cause she loves Hank don't mean she got somethin' wrong with her. There's a-plenty got their hearts busted 'count a' you. A-plenty, I c'n tell y'. Sunny Lou, she's jus' the younges', that's all. 'N she ain't old 'nuff fer t' hide it."

"A-plenty?" Verity repeated foolishly—

"Oh, it ain't Hank's fault," said Lula May hastily. "He's got th' kindlin' power, that's all."

"The kindlin' power!" She was amazed, since it was what Hank had said of her.

"The kindlin' power," said Lula May firmly. "Some got it little, but Hank, he's got it great big 'n special. Hank, he's one a' them as has got the power t' kindle the fire as dreams is made of. He purely has," she said softly.

She stood a second trying to study it out, then went on, "He c'n kindle a dream in men, he can. They borry a stoutness from him, 'n they wants t' do big things fer him. 'N he c'n kindle a dream in the hearts a' women-folks, too. He c'n kindle the same dream in them as he can kindle in the menfolks 'bout money 'n schools. But women is made fer bringin' into the world more a' them things as they thinks is worth their lovin'. God only give us one way t' do it," she said simply, " 'n so women lusts fer a man liken Hank."

Lula May's wisdom beat at her with the fierceness of the 'gator pole. It struck at her from every direction and she couldn't dodge it. I've got it little. Just for Hank's warmth, perhaps. But Hank, he's got it great big 'n special. 'N women lusts fer a man liken Hank; he c'n kindle a dream. He c'n kindle a dream. . . .

"I'll fetch Granny Dazy," said Lula May.

6

Hank's first big battle was well organized and well executed, and it should have proved the man's caliber to the entire state. But editors ignored the most dramatic, the most indicative event since the emancipation of the Negro.

Yes, in my opinion, Hank Martin's manning of the gin mills indicated the things to come. Men who had never worn shoes, men who had never hoped for anything, whose only treasure was the shotgun or the rifle by which they killed the only meat they ever ate—except, perhaps, an occasional home-butchered pig—came into the towns and villages and took over the gin mills.

And men were killed, two dying right in Hank's own dooryard, but. . . .

THE DAY the Little Flamingo was turned into a clipped and terrified black crow by the ugly magic of scissors and shoe blackening and taken by her father in his pirogue, via lake, lagoons, and river, to the good Sisters of St. Joseph, was also marked by being the first and only day in Hank's life when he was grateful for the still muddy roads.

He carried Verity from the boat to the wagon, trailed by three men from the settlement who carried Hank's pack, and the great bundles of pelts which were the winter catch. The guard Spurge had sent to care for Hank's treasures had done his job well but had sprinkled his hair and his fishy clothes with Cologne and perfumes.

"Goddam, boy," Hank swore at him genially. "You got the stinkin'est carcass ever walked a swamp on its own legs."

"I got them stinks fum outen back a' thet glass thar," said the grinning boy.

"Not all a' them, you didn't," exclaimed Hank. "Not by a damsite." And as they started home, he called back to the men, "Troll that young'un back a' yore boats. Wash the smell a' his paw back int' him else'n his maw's gonna think she's drawed one outen another flock."

Their laughter was full-timbered and hardy like the forest in which they stood waving their farewells.

"Thank God the road's still some'at muddy," said Hank. "Iffen this blackjack was dried in ruts harder'n buckshot y' couldn't 'a rode it with them ribs. How you feelin', Sweetface?"

"If I could forget Sunny Lou, I'd be all right. Granny Dazy did a good job, I guess. I'm pretty comfortable." The terror of that experience would live in her to her dying day. She shuddered and drew close to Hank.

"Forget Sunny Lou," he advised. "It was plumb her lucky day." He laughed softly, teasingly. "Here I married me a lady. A lady, mind. A lady t' guide me right. A lady what should oughta be above the low, mean dirt a' politics. 'N dang if she ain't the very one as forces me t' pay out the first bribe ever I paid in m' long 'n successful career in politics!"

He added with mock piety, "Ain't you plumb shamed? Here I gotta take you home 'stead a' t' th' city. 'N here y' are with ribs busted in y', 'n with a bribe a-weightin' yore soul." Mimicking the preacher he rolled out, "Lord, looky down on us. We-uns got a sinner here."

"Hank Martin, if I didn't have these broken ribs, I'd lay Beauty's whip across you until you couldn't sit for a whole moon." Realizing then that she had copied the angry Spurge's words, she blushed.

Laughing at her, Hank said, "I swan iffen I don't think you're a-soundin' plumb fierce."

"Well, I feel fierce. Such a country! Such people! I really think I should take Picayune Potter's advice and start using a crowbar."

He roared with laughter. "Why, you dang little pepper pod! You're shore goin' t' be a somethin' t' see iffen ever you ripen t' red hotness."

"You subject me to a few more Flamingos," she said scathingly, "and I'll ripen fast! And you can believe that!" she added with great emphasis.

" 'N I do believe it! I declare I do." And his rich zestful laugh meagered the many small songs of the forest.

"How much did you have to pay that black old rascal?" Verity asked.

"Couldn't pay but the first half a' her bribe yesterday."

"Well, how much did she ask?"

"One dollar cash money 'n I was t' deliver int' her gran'daughter's hand this here packet." He took a small folded paper from his pocket. " 'N I was to say t' her that her Granny Dazy send it 'n that it's a new-life charm. 'N I'm t' tell her she's t' wear it atween her breasts."

"How perfectly silly!"

"Mebbe," said Hank. "Mebbe not. Granny Dazy does a right lively little bizness in gris-gris. Most a' the niggers hereabouts is some touched withen a bit a' voodoo 'n mebbe a bit a' them French-talkin' niggers. Gris-gris," he explained, "is a voodoo charm for t' cast a spell. But this 'n is gonna cast a good spell," he said comfortably. "Granny Dazy says this here black gal done went t' a plumb splendiferous revival where there was a no-'count, travelin' spell-castin' preacher. 'N this here preacher-man's so good the gal—her name's Selah Marie—just follered him. But somehow she got herself a young'un. 'N the preacher-man run off 'n now the young'un is terrible sick with the miseries 'n Selah's still a-mournin' for the preacher-man. So I gotta give her this new-life charm. Some bribe you got me a-payin', ain't it?" He laughed.

Verity looked at the little package.

"What's in it?"

"Open it up 'n we'll see."

Carefully she unfolded the paper, and two tiny wings glistened their green-black iridescence through a sprinkle of dirt.

"Huh! Hummin'bird wings 'n goofer dust, most likely," said Hank.

"What's that?"

"Goofer dust? It's dust offen a grave."

Carefully Verity folded the paper over the charm and handed it back to Hank.

"I shore don't see where that nigger's a-stayin'. I'd 'a swore I knowed every person that lives offen this road. But old Granny says to start watchin' in about what would be eight hours' easy walkin' from the swamp. Says there's four pecan trees on one side a' the path 'n two magnolias on t'other side 'n a cottonwood."

The sun was high and stirring a boiling heat which struck them like puffs of hot, steamy air from a passing engine whenever they moved from shade into sun. All the little creatures of the grasses and the trees lulled into their noonday quiet.

"There's a right fine hush in the world this time a' day. The critters gives the world t' man 'n lets the poor fools sweat at their work in the sun. Long 'bout now we oughta be findin' that Selah."

It was about an hour later when Hank said, "Lissen." At first the sound was like a throb, something felt rather than heard.

"Yonder's the trees we're a-lookin' for," said Hank softly. "It must be that Selah a-singin'. She shore sounds mournful. A body c'n plumb hear the pulse a' heartbreak. I'd like t' hear her in a right joyful jump-up song."

There was only a slither-through space between the bushes to indicate a path. They sat quietly listening:

"Dey nailed His hands 'n dey nailed His feet,
An' de hammers wuz heard in Jerusalem street,
An' dey nailed alongside Him two thievin' snakes
Dat dey foun' a-hidin' in de high canebrakes.
O Angel, roll away dat stone,
Wing dis'un home,
Wing dis'un home."

"Lift me down, Hank," said Verity; "I'm going, too."

He hesitated a second, then lifted her from the wagon and carried her through the brush. Reaching the clearing they saw a fat young colored woman seated on the ground swaying from side to side as she sang her hymns. With fierce tenderness she held a bundled baby against her bosom. Her wide face uplifted to the sun was wet with her tears and wet with the sweat which seeped out from the edges of her woolly hair. She squatted before a three-sided slattern shelter which had once been built for some farm animal, probably a mule. But the inside of the shelter, Verity noted, had been brushed clean of dirt and cobwebs and the "floor" was thickly laid with fresh green branches.

"Selah," Hank called, "Selah Marie!"

Selah Marie's singing stopped and she jerked her head around, startled.

"Yore granny sent us," Hank hastened to add, "Old Granny Dazy sent us." He held out the packet. "Old Granny asked me t' give this t' you. She said I was t' tell you it's a new-life charm 'n you're t' wear it atween yore bosoms. It'll bring y'all new life, yore Granny says."

But as Hank held out the charm Selah shook her head and did not reach for it.

"Ol' Granny too late," she said, and swaying from her hips she rocked her child and wept.

Sympathy tightened Verity's throat. She put a hand on Selah Marie's shoulder.

"It is never too late for new life, Selah. You and your baby come to Cypress Bend with us. We have a wagon and you can ride with us. Is something wrong with the baby? He isn't crying."

"He daid."

Softly Verity said, "I'm sorry, Selah. But you can't stay here. Wouldn't you like to come with us to Cypress Bend and have a funeral for him in the Colored Methodist Church?"

"Dey wouldn't," Selah choked. "He bo'n in sin." And she rocked in her suffering.

Verity didn't know what to do. She looked pleadingly at Hank. Hank winked at her.

"Born in sin!" he exclaimed. "Hear you talkin', woman! Why, that there pickaninny a' yoren was borned just liken everybody else in this world was borned. Jesus said, 'Let little childern come unto me.' Jesus shore didn't bother t' say their folks hadda be married up. Now a young'un's paw can mebbe be a sinner. But a young'un's maw just purely can't be a sinner. No, sirree! Them long nine months a' uncomfort 'n pain plumb washes t' nothin' all the pleasure times y' got with his paw. I'm a-tellin' y' that baby wasn't borned in sin." He held out Granny Dazy's new-life charm.

Selah's eyes looked up at Hank, not quite daring to hope.

"Is you tellin' de Lawd's truf?"

"I shore am!" he replied firmly.

One of Selah's black hands took the charm and stuffed it down her dress front.

"Now, raise up, woman," commanded Hank, " 'n claim that there new life. 'Cause you been washed whiter'n snow."

"Whiter'n snow," she murmured, "whiter'n snow!"

"Come on now, woman. That congregation gonna be plumb proud to give yore baby a fine funeral 'n proud to have y' 'mongst 'em."

Selah stood. She looked at Verity. "You wants me, Mizzes?" she asked politely, hopefully.

"Very much," said Verity, sincerely, simply.

"I is comin', den," and she followed them to the road. Seeing the wagon, she gasped over its gay colors.

"Is you Mistuh Hank Martin?" she asked.

"That's me, Hank Martin."

She shook her head in wonder. "Ol' Granny shu' fix up fine chawms," she said with awe. Then she climbed into the back of the wagon and began to sing softly.

The sun poured down on them and little soapy flecks of lather began to show on Beauty's hide.

"Purely looks like I'm a-goin' t' be a-payin' Granny's bribe the rest a' m' life, mebbe," Hank whispered. "Iffen I know niggers, that husky darky's done took us for her white folks. 'N it's a compliment, too, seein' we ain't what niggers calls quality."

Verity slipped her hand under Hank's arm. Her ribs hurt some, but the stabs of pain seemed only exclamation marks emphasizing an inward peace.

"Ain't it great," said Hank, "us here a-ridin', content 'n sweatin' in the sun!"

A little content crept into Selah, too, for she crooned a go-to-sleep song:

> "Lil' Lawd Jesus got a moon round His haid,
> Um-uum, um-uum, rockaby,
> But lil' Lawd Jesus a babe liken yo',
> Um-uum, um-uum, rockaby. . . ."

Content rode home with them and lived with them much of the time. Selah took to the ways of polishing a house and was a genius at making an oven do right by her food. But her early training in the field stayed with her and she was proud of it. The following year, when the cold rains of early spring were drawn back up by the sun, making clouds of earth mist, she held her strong black hand, fingers outspread, before Verity's face, and said, "I'se got a green hand, I has. An' I is a-plantin' wid it, Miz Verity. Turnips an' cabbage an' beans an' all dem t'ings. An' a veg'table pear vine usn should have fo' ourse'ves. An' a cane patch, too. Usn make our own surrup, then."

"You can't do all that, can you, Selah?" Verity asked.

"Yassum, I can. An' keep dis lil' ol' house, too. You is busy wid teachin' folkses t' spell an' such. An' wid yo' prettifyin' de yawd wid flowers." At this point a cloud passed over her face. "Usn oughta have us a baby. Usn ain't got nothin' t' count on 'ceptin' Mistuh Hank, his comin's an' goin's. Mens is fine and usn got a need fo' 'em, I reckons. Nothin' lak de way mens needs womens, though, don' seem lak. Mistuh Hank, now, how you know what he doin' all de time he gone?"

"That will do, Selah!" Verity exclaimed. "Don't you ever say such a thing again." But the blood ran fiercely to her face, for she knew what Selah was thinking and she knew, too, that Selah wished to protect her against any hurt.

"Mens is mens," Selah said firmly and turned away still talking. "Usn oughta have us a baby. Cain't count on no man. But one you raises up yo'sef, he come de closes'."

Yes, Verity guessed what troubled Selah and later she knew. One warm evening she sat leaning against her oak tree feeling a need for Hank when she heard the voices of Selah and "Brother" Tape Dilton, who was escorting her home from prayer meeting.

"You know dat floozy woman whut jus' jine our chu'ch?" Selah asked.

Tape was as thin as Selah was wide and his voice was deep as a bull-frog's.

"Y'all means dat one fum Mentoola where de lumber camp at?" he croaked, low and musically.

"Uh-huh. Dat one. You know whut she say w'en I say I is with Mistuh Hank?"

"Huh-uh. Whut?"

"She say she cooks at dat camp. An' she say folkses pow'rful crazy 'bout Mistuh Hank. Mens an' womens. She say mens jumps an' hollers an' womens hollers an' follers. She say de womens jes' plumb git dat lolly-gag look. She say de woman she work fo' t'ink he good's St. John or St. Peter, or certain shu' he good's Elijah. She say her boss-woman say Mistuh Hank purely got hissef a chariot a' fire, too, she say. Uum-uump!" Selah groaned. "How a man lak dat gwine stay pure true an' good 'nuff fo' Miz Verity? You reckon he pure true an' him gone t'ree, fo', mebbe five mont's at a time, huh?"

Brother Tape cleared his throat with profoundness.

"Sister Selah, I disliken de way yo' speaks. A-co'se a man stay true w'en he find his own true love. A-co'se he do. Cullered an' w'ite, dey stays true."

Giggles burbled from Selah as she jabbed Brother Tape's thin ribs with a powerful elbow.

"Go long wid you," she said coyly. "You is declarin' dat 'cause you is courtin' me."

Verity rose and walked through the night to the top of the knoll near Jules's house. But walk as fast as she could, she couldn't lose the words of Lula May McMenimee. She told herself she was unfair, that it was the same quality which might take Hank to success. Didn't his charm lie in his driving power? She loved him as he was. Still, always to hear your husband discussed, always to see that others, many others, felt they had an almost personal life with him, was sometimes hard to endure. But Hank was Hank.

The front door of Cypress Manor opened and Jules stood there, his fine long lines darkly sculptured by the light within. Loneliness grasped her and wrung out a cry for a friend.

"Jules!" she called, and she had never addressed him by his given name before.

"Verity?" Then he saw her. "Ah, Verity, my dear . . ." Quick life came to him and he ran across the gallery and under the magnolias across the dewy meadow.

Always before she had been a politely spoken "Mrs. Martin."

"Seeing you there," she said, "I suddenly felt that you were my friend and I called 'Jules' before I thought."

"And I answered 'Verity, my dear,' because that is how I always speak to you in imagination." He laughed, a little confused, a little apologetic.

Startled, she exclaimed, "Oh!"

"It's quite all right. Quite all right. Why, Hank has called me a damned onlooker, a blasted celibate. I am civilized, you know. Often I think I'm too civilized. Else I would catch into my own existence a little of the fierce under-throb of this country in which I was born. Perhaps I was too long away. Will you walk with me?"

"Fierce under-throb," she said, "I'm half afraid I'm catching it a little."

"Perhaps." He smiled. "But you are directly exposed to it."

"You mean Hank, of course," she said rather resentfully.

"Certainly," he said. Admiration came into his voice. "He has a remarkable mind. Amazing memory. Have you noticed that he remembers everything he reads in those books of his? In no time at all I am starting him on law."

"That's wonderful, Jules," she said, feeling comfortable and snug again.

"When Hank calls me an onlooker, he is only repeating what I have called myself. I should not resent it. But Hank makes me sound so useless." He laughed a little.

"But what would Hank do without you? You're wonderful, Jules. Just wonderful. So kind and helpful. I always feel better when I look out my window at the big oak and knoll because I know you're just beyond."

"Just beyond," he repeated, his voice hardly louder than the thought.

"What, Jules?"

"Beautiful night," he said. "Wonderful to be a part of it with you."

She studied him, then said with the abrupt frankness of a child, "I like you, Jules."

Pleased surprise wiped out the cynic and for an instant gave him the fine eagerness of one who has only to reach out and pluck his slice of life. Then slowly his old one-sided grin came back.

"Thank you, my dear. I often think about the emotion we call 'like.' I like you, too, which means that I enjoy your company, enjoy your mind, have a fine respect for you, approve of all you are and of all you show signs of becoming." He shrugged. "Odd, is it not, that we can love someone whom we do not like? And yet completely, thoroughly like someone whom we do not love? Only the very fortunate are blessed by loving whom they thoroughly like, whom they thoroughly approve. And yet—that, too, can be unhappy."

"How perfectly ridiculous," she laughed. "No one with any sense at all would marry without approving of the one he loved."

"According to that, ninety-nine per cent of all adults would have to be classed as moronic. No, I prefer to believe they are so blinded by some bright need of nature that they cannot read the signs right."

"Oh, you!" she exclaimed impatiently. "Why do you always have to put people in classes? Don't you ever see anyone as an individual?"

"A very few."

"Everyone is an individual to Hank. He sees everyone's problems as different. You know, it's really wonderful."

"Indeed? I thought they were all voters."

The taunt hurt her, pushed at her throat, and shoved the fine sense of friendship outside her. The feeling of aloneness pressed in on her and she turned from him.

"Good night, Mr. Bolduc," she said, then thinking the words stiff and foolish, she repeated, "Good night—Jules," and ran toward home.

"Verity—Verity, my dear—" he called, and his words touched her with a soothing softness, like the air she stirred with her running. The hurt of aloneness lifted and she became a part of the universe, loving the feel of feet wet with dew—dew that made the earthy growths send up their perfumes—loving the feel of her body moving through air and space, loving the feel of stars about her head as the lightning bugs turned themselves on and off for her like carefree comets off their orbits.

Over toward home one bug stayed lighted with a strange steadfastness, and then it moved, not jumpily, but swinging slightly and low to the ground. A lantern being carried from the barn!

"Hank! Hank!" she called.

The lantern lifted high and swung wide.

"Hank! Hank!" and still no answer. Her being forgot the dew and the air and the stars and prayed, Let it be Hank.

But the lantern light was small and the barn shadow deep, and her eyes grew misted as she ran. Then the light went out.

"Hank," she cried, "answer me!"

"Lord save us," he said reverently. "Lord save us!"

She stopped, waiting to see his outline detach itself from the blackness. "If I'm not dreaming you, come here quick."

"You ain't a-dreamin' me—'n stand right where y' are. Don't move for a minute. I been a-dreamin' you, though, all these weeks. But like allus, you're finer'n I can dream, a-standin' there in yore white dress with yore hair a-managin' t' glitter with nothin' but starlight 'n bugs for it to reflect."

He sighed and came slowly out of the shadows.

"Sh! Don't move," he said. "Lord, it's like givin' a man a chance t' walk soft 'n sure right through the gate a' heaven, 'thouten even rousin' Saint Pete t' give a body the grillin' he should oughta have afore enterin'."

"Why didn't you answer me the first time I called?" she demanded, but stood still in her pose.

"Lord, Sweetface, there was so much joy in yore voice it plumb stunned me. So much joy, I dassn't think it's meant just for me. It purely turned me humble, 'n I think on how thirst is the world for joy. So I didn't grab it. I let it go by for the world t' lap up, like the generous feller I am. But I ain't too generous. I says t' myself, I says, 'Iffen it's meant for you, there'll be another gourdful a' joy for you t' quench yore thirst on.' Yes, sir, that's what I told myself."

Standing before her now, he reached out a hand and ran a finger down the line of her cheek. Catching his hand she held it against her breast.

"Darling, darling," she whispered, "I feel all the things you say but I can't put them in words the way you can. Oh, I wish I could!"

"I'm content iffen you just do the feelin'," and laughing softly he pulled her to him. She lifted her face, but he said, "I ain't fitten. Got two weeks' sweat 'n dirt a-scalin' me liken a scurf. There's times when the sweat 'n dirt a' roads 'n fields mixes right 'n fitten with lovin'. But there's somethin' diff'rent 'bout tonight—with you a-comin', runnin' to me through the night, a-callin' m' name. I could purely feel the throb a' God a-beatin' in the world. I purely could."

Listening to Hank she half expected to hear a great heartbeat. But she heard the frogs gargling and the katydids rubbing their wings to make songs for their ladies, and saw the fireflies darting swiftly about as though hunting their wingless mates.

"What you a-thinkin', Sweetface?"

"That it's unfair that only male katydids can sing, and only male lightning bugs fly—and wondering if I was a wingless mate."

"Hank's little glowworm," he chuckled. "It shore pleasures a male critter mightily to get near home 'n see his mate a-glowin' for him in the dark. Great feelin', it is!"

They laughed and she felt precious and silly.

"Don't like this here dirt, but there's nothin' like too much preparation to dull the sharp edge of a man's honin'." Looking about, his eyes rested on the trough beside the pump. "That's the stuff!"

Running to it he started peeling off his clothes.

"That there trough makes a plumb perfect bath tub."

"Selah's in her house. She might see you."

"Well, I ain't nothin' but a growed-up baby. She's seen lotsa babies." Leaning toward her, he whispered. "Toss me some soap outen the kitchen door, Sweetface, 'n go to yore bed 'n wait, a-glowin'."

Verity knew the very next morning that she was different. Within her was an odd content with herself, a feeling of cleanness of spirit, a feeling which reminded her of Hank's churchy hymn words "washed whiter'n snow." Smiling at her foolishness, she still could not cease to be aware of it. And with the content was a sense of fulfillment, a quiet willingness to wait on time for another season.

Walking toward the village with Hank at her side, watching the play of shadows and light upon the earth, and feeling the quick heat of the sun when a cloud rolled from it, she toyed with the idea of telling Hank that she believed she was a mother. But his thoughts were all of seeing the village folk and telling them of his plans for thwarting Mr. Robert Castleberry, come picking. She thought perhaps it was nature's rule that a woman should have this secret from her mate for a month or two. A few weeks in which to make her child her very own. Perhaps it was the only time given a woman to possess her child before sharing it with another, before giving it to the world. Yes, she would wait. And anyway, perhaps she was only imagining.

Hank had sent Selah into the village to tell Tim of his arrival and to have as many on hand as could come. He was excited.

"I'm a-tellin' y', Verity, I got a way to plumb fix all the Black Skimmers as are short-weightin'. Just wait'll you hear what I done at the Capitol. By God'lmighty, I'm gonna fix that thievin' Castleberry crowd 'n them Newtons, too."

"But are you sure they are short-weighting?"

"A-course I'm sure. Hell, you can't get the same story from everybody for years on end 'thout there being some truth in it. 'N I've stood 'n watched 'em weigh light after we weighed the stuff on small scales bag by bag." His face glowed with purpose. "God'lmighty, Verity, you realize I got nigh to four thousand followers in my Hank Martin Organization in just this here one year?"

"Four thousand!"

"Four thousand! Yes sirree, 'n most 'f 'em ain't never voted. When they git to the polls they're plumb gonna be a s'prise vote t' every ol'-timey politician in the state iffen I can find a way. But you just wait'll you hear!"

His stride quickened.

"Not so fast, Hank."

"Looky there. There's some mules 'n wagons tied. Must be they sent for some folks in the country. Hurry up, Sweetface, I don't wanta be leavin' you behind!"

There were quite a few wagons tied in front of Tim's shop, and two more were driving up; folks afoot were heading toward the place. Smoke rolled up from the shop and as they drew nearer, the sweet smell of baking rolls greeted them.

"Sophy's a-bakin' 'n a-orderin' folks about to beat hell, I betcha," Hank laughed. "Ain't it a marvel to be me 'n have folks love me this-a-way! God'lmighty, it's purely a marvel!"

"Hank," she laughed, "you're so utterly lacking in modesty . . . in every way."

"Modesty, hell!" he howled. "That there dictionary I been a-studyin' words in says modesty is puttin' a low estimate on yore own capabilities, bein' bashful 'n shy. 'N then another definition it gives is observin' the proprieties a' sex." He grinned down at her. "Now, I'm a-askin' you straight—you ever seen anybody get someplace in this here world a-goin' 'round shy, liken he has gotta hide hisself? A-sayin' he ain't no good? Why, accordin' t' that, Jesus Christ was the most unmodest man there ever was, 'cause He said, 'I and my Father are one.' I feel a greatness in me 'n by God'lmighty, I don't care wno knows it!"

She only laughed and he half shook her.

"And what about the proprieties of sex?" she teased.

"Why, there ain't no such things. Only proprieties there can be is to be a man liken God made you. 'N welcome the consequences a' yore pleasures." He laughed chummily and squeezed her arm. "Mebbe a feller oughta even go so far as to be grateful he don't just have them consequences come on him 'thouten no pleasures a-tall."

His words gave her an almost smug feeling of well-being and confidence, and she laughed gaily. He sniffed the air.

"Now there's Sophy's cakes 'n rolls. M' belly needs fillin' again. Ain't it wonderful that I got a taster that makes eatin' a pleasure?"

He stopped and bellowed: "Sophy! So-o-phy! Tim!"

The wagon-wide doorway filled with people.

"Howdy, friends!" Hank howled.

They shouted their greetings and some came to meet him, among them Tim and Swith. Tim, so mighty in body; Swith, so frail, so wishful.

"I can't leave m' bakin', Hank," Sophy screamed and waved a batter-dripping spoon at him.

"Hank, Hank, my boy!" said Tim, embracing him. "Air y' fine? A-course y' are. By the Lord-Harry, we're shore plumb glad to be a-seein' of y'! Been gone nigh onto five months this time, ain't y'?"

"I shore have, Tim. Too dang long." Turning to Swith he took the bony, birdlike hand in his own and looked down on the little man fondly. "How're y', Swith? How's the treasurer of my home organization?"

"Ask him instead, how is the treasury," Picayune suggested, puffing and wheezing.

"Well, how is the treasury of my home parish?"

Swith's eyes grew watery, and pride made him hesitate on his words almost to the point of stuttering.

"I—it's a-bulgin', Hank. We're in our second year now 'n we got one thousand six hundred 'n forty-eight dollars, we have!"

"What d'y know," said Hank slowly, "what d'y know! Does that mean a even eight hundred 'n twenty-four members has paid for two years?"

"Nope," said Swith, "it means a lotta folks ain't paid for this year yet. But they will," he added hastily. "They will. We got nine hundred 'n sixty-three members. They live all through the parish."

Hank stared at Swith with respect. "God'lmighty!" he said chokily, "God'lmighty! Who's been a-gettin' all them members?"

"Swith," replied Tim. "That man's been a-troddin' the roads some'at like you uster."

"But god damn, he ain't got a body liken mine. He should oughta have a horse." Turning to Swith he placed his hands on Swith's shoulders and asked, "How you been a-livin' 'n eatin', Swith? How you managin' yore keep?"

"Oh, I ain't tetched a penny a' the organization money! Not a picayune, I ain't," he declared quickly.

"But you should oughta done just that," declared Hank. "The laborer is worthy of his hire. You're plumb worth it, Swith."

The great blue eyes looked up worshipfully at Hank, his frail body shaking with emotion.

"No! No!" Frantic denial rang in his voice. "No, I couldn't. Not a picayune. Every penny of it has gotta go fer that hope to git the riches divided. That'd make it a right purty world." Tears came into his eyes.

"But you gotta eat!" Hank exclaimed. "You're plumb valu'ble. I declare you are. You gotta eat."

"I eat." Swith's voice was full of pride and determination. "You looky here, Hank." Wiping his eyes on the back of his hands he looked around. "See yonder blackbird in the pecan tree far side a' Tim's house? He's a-settin' way out to the right."

They scanned the tree.

"Nope," said Hank, "can't spot him."

"He's there," said Swith, and picking up his gun, which had been propped against him, butt on the ground, he swung it to place in a flash. "You'll see him drop," he said, and fired.

A little black speck fluttered to the ground.

"See?" Swith asked.

The men whistled in admiration.

"I shore did, Swith. Dang if I didn't allus think you had weak eyes."

"Nope. I got eyes for seein' far-off things, I reckon." Swith smiled up at Hank. "You see, I eat when I need to."

"Well, you rate a horse, Swith. Dang if y' don't. Come on, now, I got lotsa things to say."

The news of the treasury of the "home" organization meant a lot to Hank. It meant, as he told his friends, that there was money to do the first job he planned to do. Verity sat on a rough plank seat listening in amazement.

"Now, here's m' plan," said Hank as he warmed to his subject. "Throughout these five parishes, all the local gin mills is owned by Castleberry 'n his crowd or by the Newtons. Liken I've said afore, friends, they're Black Skimmers. The world is full a' Black Skimmers; but this here Hank Martin Organization is pledged t' help the little fellers as the Black Skimmers can swaller up 'thouten even lessenin' their speed a' flight." He paused dramatically. " 'N here's our first step t'ward gettin' the little fellers their rightful share—t'ward keepin' the little fellers outen their gullets a piece longer."

His voice hung in air, suspended there with hopes. Sophy's tin cups were no longer rattling. Only the fire in the forge and Jenny's twins dared make a sound.

"We're a-goin' to have hundreds of weights made. Weights of iron for t' test all the gin scales hereabouts. Tim here," turning, he pointed at Tim, "he's a-goin' t' cast them weights in molds. We're a-goin' t' watch 'em made honest right here. We're a-goin' t' pay Tim for the work outen the treasury—you see he gets paid, Swith—then we're a-goin' to send weights enough for every cotton scales there is. 'N then we're a-goin' to have our own members a-standin' guard at every gin. Iffen the scales is crooked there's gonna be hell t' pay. Get yore shotguns oiled 'n ready 'cause this is war for a just 'n righteous cause."

Stunned at all this plan implied, his people stared and shifted uneasily, then, as his spell lessened, they looked at each other questioningly. Up through Verity's breast a cold sharpness formed like a pointed icicle stopping her windpipe. Trying to protest she could make no sound come from her. Looking frantically at the faces of his hearers, her eyes locked with Tim's and read in them a troubled question. From her eyes, he seemed to form that question into words.

"Guns, you said, Hank?" he asked.

Sophy rose and waved a clenched fist. "Yes, guns, he said, Tim. 'N I say so too! Iffen Hank says guns, he means guns!"

"That's right. That's shore right!" The conviction of rightness in Hank's voice stirred the people like a call to colors. "This is war! This is war, friends! War for the freedom of men. We got a right to what's ourn. For generations people like to us has been lost like to the captives in a strange land. Which same we read about in the psalms a' David. But for generations people like to us—the poor white trash they call us—has just let ourselves stay captives when we should oughta been fightin' t' get back t' Zion. The psalm says the captives complained and cried, 'How shall we sing in a strange land?' " He tore at his collar till it burst open, smacked one palm into the other, jumped up and down, and cursed. "Why, goddamit! I say t' you that we should oughta fight first for our rights 'n sing afterwards! I feel I got a mission, friends. A mission! An' that's to do all I can in a human way—all the time a-askin' the Lord's help 'n guidance—t' free the slaves. Are you free? Are you? No! But, b'God'lmighty, iffen y' do yore duty now that you got a somebody—'n that's me—t' lead you-all, 'n stand the burden a' all that leadership means—iffen y' do yore duty, iffen you yoreselves don't never know that freedom, b'God'lmighty, yore childern'll know it!"

"We're with y', Hank, iffen the Lord'll let us!" It was Swith's voice, piping and quavery with excitement.

"Iffen the sonsabitches ain't got crooked scales they can't object," said Harry Disbro almost reasonably.

Verity began to breathe again. Of course! If they aren't crooked they can't object and if they are they should be stopped.

"All right. All right." Hank waved his hands quieting the crowd. "Now the local mill here is run by Mr. Roy L. Saucier 'n y' all know he come into this settlement a-representin' Castleberry the fourth. Don't never overlook he's the fourth in his line!" His voice scorched the Castleberry lineage. "Now when I was at the Capitol I looked up some things 'n I found out that lotsa states has a department that's called the Department a' Weights 'n Measures, 'n their bizness is t' check all scales 'n such. Now this here state ain't got one. Now lissen close—five years ago the Governor wanted to have such a outfit. 'N who bucked him? Why, Castleberry's crowd 'n them Newtons 'n others liken to 'em in other parts a' the state. We'll purely fix 'em all in time. Ain't that enough? Ain't it, friends?"

Yes, it was enough. It was a great plenty. These men and women were no longer just grubworms with no expectations beyond making their little furrows in the ground. They were human beings with a purpose and a cause.

As Hank pulled from his pocket a paper containing the list of gins in the five parishes where they had members, and began to lay specific plans for the manning, Verity rose and went out into the sunshine.

Jenny, bone thin, crumpled, and soiled, ran toward the hitching posts after an escaped twin. As she caught him up and turned, holding him tight to her scrawny breast, she looked tenderly on the red, protesting little face and said softly: "Y' got reason fer squallin'. But someday y'll have things better, y' will."

Yes, Verity thought, someday our babies will have things better.

The following months of Hank's absence were filled with whispers concerning the activities of the Hank Martin Organization, with whispers about Mr. Roy L. Saucier's unease. Verity could not feel a deep interest in it all. A peculiar, perhaps a divine immunity surrounded her. When she walked in the village, talked with the villagers, or even with Jules, she felt apart from all their interests. She walked with a fence around her, barricaded from all worldly things except sudden hunger and occasionally a faint, watery nausea. These brought an ever-surprising realization that childbearing was, after all, a physical process. Sometimes she laughed at herself for feeling so superior because of pregnancy. But mostly she did just what must be done because her brain still recognized the daily tasks, the daily friends; but all the rest of her absorbed the sun and the rains and waited for the first little shooting kick of life.

She wanted to keep this knowledge from Selah, but Selah's eyes searched hers and the rich voice seemed always to be singing lullabies these days.

One bright morning when all living things shone and dripped with leftover rain drops from a dawn-time shower, Verity walked along the roadside absorbing the splendor. Her starched blue gingham hung limp and clinging, for she chose to walk through the tall weeds of late summer. She heard the rhythm of horses' hoofs making muffled beats in the mud, like dashers churning butter. She knew it was Jules and turning, stood with her hand shielding her eyes from the straight rays of the sun, still low against its earth bed in the east. Looking into the sun eye to eye, she felt energetic and tall. It is something to feel as tall as the sun, even if the sun is sitting down at breakfast.

Jules reined his horse to a walk, and the up-thrown mud no longer struck the animal's belly nor Jules's boots and trousers. The two spotted dogs ran to Verity.

"Down! Down!" Jules commanded, and the dogs stood before her, restricting their greeting to the joyous wriggling of everything back of forelegs. "I knew you'd be out. Such a wonderful morning! If we hadn't met I'd have come to your house."

"Why?" she asked.

"I have just returned from Loder City. Robert—Robert Castleberry—tells me there are rumors everywhere that the white trash—forgive me, Verity—are planning to do something drastic. Picking time begins in only a few weeks. He tells me the men have banded together. Call themselves the Hank Martin Organization." He looked down on her earnestly. "This morning Moses assured me that it is known everywhere. Can this possibly be true?"

She hesitated only a second.

"I see no reason why you should not know. Yes, it is true. There is some such plan."

"But," Jules almost gasped, "surely Hank can be made to see that it simply will not do!"

"Why not, Jules?"

"It's fantastic! It is the most gigantic insult! The Castleberrys and the Newtons would not be parties to thievery. And what is more, they will not endure the insult of being told they are suspected of thievery. They are gentlemen. You are from the North, Verity, my dear." He dismounted and stood beside her. "You do not understand exactly. But if Hank's men come with guns and some are killed," he shrugged, "the Castleberrys and the Newtons could not be convicted in any court in the state."

"And if one of the Castleberrys or the Newtons is killed?" She asked it coolly, seeming only to want information.

"The killer would hang, of course."

"But suppose Hank is right—that they *are* thieves—that they are Black Skimmers?"

"Black Skimmers!" Disgust was in his voice. "Hank's dramatics! He is—"

"Please, Jules—"

The one-sided grin played over his face.

"Believe me, I mean this well. For a moment—that evening at the house —Hank even had me thinking in terms of Black Skimmers."

"I know," she said slowly. "But just suppose that Hank is right?"

"Hank cannot possibly be right. I have known these men and their families all my life. All my cotton, ever since I first went away from home, has been handled by Robert." He laughed. "Hank would point out that I have grown poorer and poorer." Serious again, he said, almost pleadingly, "Verity, you must realize what this means. You must be sure Hank realizes. He dare not accuse such men lightly."

"Judging from the preparations I wouldn't say he is accusing them lightly, Jules." Then, like a rocket, some of the new fierceness flared. The fierceness which she always felt dated back to her meeting with the Little Flamingo. "Dead moss!" she cried. "Hank was right—you're literally covered with dead moss! Can't anyone in your rich upper class be wrong!"

He was startled. "I'm not championing one class against another class. I know those men well. And from all I hear, Hank's plans have all the earmarks of gangsterism. Sounds like something that bootlegger, Capone, up North, would do. Or that ghastly Guy Polli in Crescent City."

"Do you mean to stand there and tell me that your friends, the Castleberrys and the Newtons, have never ganged up on the poor people around here?"

She could endure no more, and turning she ran from him. Anger beat in upon her. She had been content for months. Content like the earth to wait another season, to wait for her baby, to do nothing but wait and nurture life; and now all her content was shattered.

Worry and unease harried her for the next weeks, making her retch with nausea.

"Y'all shoulda done dat pukin' de firs' mont's," said Selah.

"You have to know everything, don't you?"

"Yas'm." Selah was undisturbed by her sarcasm. "Y'all cain't keep no securts fum me." She laughed. "Lawsy, Miz Ver'ty, I bet I knowed it near 'bout sooner'n y'all did. Dere's a look comes in de eye. Yas'm, dere is. A kinda wide an' watery look, it is. Lawsy, eva'body in de town suspicion it. W'en I in Mistuh Squeeze-nickel Noady's sto', a-buyin' usn some vittles, Miz Peck she whispuh is you dat-a-way? 'N I says I reckon so."

"Get out of here, Selah. Go to your own shack." Tears streamed down Verity's face. "Oh, damn it! Oh, damn it!"

The door had opened and Hank stared at them.

"What th' hell! Sweetface, how come I find you liken this?" Glaring at Selah, he demanded, "You been abusin' her? What for's she a-bawlin'?"

"Don' pay her no mind, Mistuh Hank," Selah grinned. "She goin' to have us a baby."

"A baby?" Hank seemed not to understand at first, then, "God'lmighty," he said softly, "God'lmighty! Is that a fact, Sweetface?"

Verity nodded dumbly. Hank stared at her, puzzling.

"You ain't got no common attitude 'bout this, have y'? You ain't a-sayin' them damits 'cause y' don't want it?"

She couldn't speak, just shook her head denying.

"Lawsy, no, Mistuh Hank. She mad at me 'cause I knowed. Mad 'cause near 'bout eva'body know it. An' her a-tryin' fo' to keep it securt so's you be firstes t' know." Selah laughed comfortably.

"Ain't God good t' me!" said Hank reverently. Then, turning on Selah, he bellowed, "Well, get t' hell outa here, y' black skinful a' sin. Ain't y' got sense enough at a time liken this t' get out? Go on, now, hurry up! Pick up them size twelves a' yours 'n set one in front a' the other double time." Selah hurried toward the door, laughing. "God'lmighty, here I am gonna have me a baby! Here I come home 'n find white women 'n black women a-bawlin' 'cause I'm gonna have a baby. Why, God'lmighty, I been gonna have a baby for months 'n I never even knowed it! Ain't that a helluva note!"

"I thought it was," said Verity, new tears rolling.

"Here, here," said Hank softly, "ain't I allus told you—don't never salten yore eyes for what's done 'n over?"

99

"It's not done and over," she sniffled.

"It shore is. Can't be undone. 'N I'm purely thankful, Lord. That young'un's gonna have a pappy to be proud of. That's a promise, Sweet-face." He kissed her. "Me, gonna have a baby! What d'you know!"

A few days later strange men whom Verity had never seen came to her door. Most of them were marked with the same awkwardness, the same odd eagerness, an eagerness that lay like transparent tinsel over dull hopelessness. They stood on her little porch in overalls and bare feet, or with hideous store clothes and heavy boots, their shining guns the only well-cared-for thing about them. When Hank was home they came in and listened carefully to directions, and one from each group was picked for leader of his crowd. Some of them came from water huts and grew no cotton. They came to help the cotton men because they were one in Hank's big dream. With maps spread out on the kitchen table, and with Verity and Selah cooking and serving, Hank planned his campaign.

The day Spurge McMenimee and his forty-two followers arrived was a great day. Hank, answering the knock, bellowed at Spurge, "God-'lmighty, Spurge! I knowed y'd come! I'm gonna have a baby! Ain't that wonderful? I'm purely a-prayin' I don't bust myself under the strain."

The two men greeted each other with such enthusiasm, such great pleasure, that all present caught the feel that here were brothers. Spurge was as fine a figure in trouser-cut blue jeans and white shirt as he had been in the short-legged bib overalls. About his waist gleamed the fine, well-rubbed leather of wide belt and two holsters, deep-cut, so that re-volvers could be pulled fast and quick with no snagging catch on the cylinders. And in his hands a long and lovely rifle glinted bluely like his eyes.

"I reckon y'll survive that strain, Hank," he said. Taking Verity's hand he bowed with his great natural courtesy. "It pleasures me mightily t' be a-seein' of y' again, ma'am. 'N the news a' yore expectin'll pleasure near 'bout everybody."

"Thank you, Spurge," she said and thought how swiftly she had ad-justed to having this news shouted at top-lung strength. "How are Lula May and all the children?"

"They're all peart," he said and looked away from her.

"'N my Little Flamingo?" asked Hank, his voice soft with concern.

Pain passed over Spurge's face. He answered stonily.

"We got a letter. I ain't never opened it."

Hank studied him a second. "Hell, ain't it, the way fightin' goes on in a man liken love, an' the things he has gotta do whilst answerin' some in-sistence in him on duty 'r justice?"

"Yeah," said Spurge stoically.

"She's yore first-borned, Spurge. I got tenderness in me for first-borns right now. I hope mine'll have the guts Sunny Lou's got." Putting an arm around Spurge's shoulders, he added, "Hope you'll be a-readin' that there letter first chancet y' get."

God forbid, thought Verity, that my first-born should have the same type of guts. The Little Flamingo! Every time Verity thought of her she felt a memory fear, a memory pain of that 'gator pole. And yet there was in her a sympathy for the child; she was only a fierce wild thing like a baby bear.

The time for cash money and backaches had begun. It was picking time. Colored folks, men, women, and children, were reporting to the great plantations. But throughout five parishes on share-crop farms and on the owned-and-mortgaged farms, there was a noticeable lack of adult men. The picking there was left for the time being to the women and the young'uns. A good percentage of the men were in Cypress Bend, sleeping nights on Hank's little porch, in his barn, in Tim Peck's smithy shop, on the Disbro porch, in barns with mules, and most anywhere they could drop.

Each night Hank walked out among the men, like a general worrying about morale, and each night he returned to report to Verity.

"It's wonderful! By God'lmighty, it's purely wonderful. They ain't a-goin' t' be licked. They got a hope for the first time in generations!"

Selah's beau, Tape, came to Hank one day and stood before him bashfully, first on one foot and then on the other, like a thin and overworked crane.

"Mistuh Hank, suh, please." His voice went into such a deep croak that it broke off in a confused gurgle.

"Who're you?"

"He Tape, Mistuh Hank," Selah beamed. "He kind uv settin' t' me, Tape is."

"Is that so!" Hank exclaimed amiably in the midst of all his work and plans. Grinning at Tape he said, "One thing you allus wanta remember, Tape—don't never court her too earnest. You're li'ble to wake up hitched. She's a good cook but I sometimes think she's schemin'."

Selah laughed, but Tape shifted feet, twisted his old hat, and hawked his throat clear of frogs.

"I ain't come fo' funnin', Mistuh Hank."

"No?" Hank asked. "For what, then?"

"I'se come fo' askin' y'all—I owns m' own lan'—two acre. I'se got me a cotton patch. Does you git hones' prices outen dem gin mills—well, does usn—de culla'd folks git hones' price, too?"

"You're dang tootin' they do, Tape. Honest price for all men, white 'r black." Hank's voice rang with honest assurance.

A wide toothy grin shone from the black face.

"Usn thanks y'all, suh," he said. "Yessuh, shu' do. Cain't usn he'p?"

Hank jumped up as if electrified.

"God'lmighty! You niggers gotta stay outa this. Iffen you niggers takes a part, I'm ruint." Turning to Swith and four other men he called them by names and howled, "You know where all the gins are. Get a-goin'! For Christ's sake, see to it not ary nigger raises a hand. Iffen there's fightin' the niggers is to back theirselves 'n their cotton down the road. They ain't never t' see nothin', nor know nothin'. Get a-goin', take horses, take anything. Get a-goin'!"

He dashed out of the house with them and hurried them on their ways. When he returned he clapped Selah on the back and grinned, "You're a great big life-size good-luck charm! Iffen it wasn't for you a-havin' so much lure for the men so's they come a-settin' t' y', I might never 'a thought what a defeat yore race might 'a brung me!"

From Tape to Selah a message flashed which said this was like all else, there was no equality for them. Hank's face sobered.

"Y' got me all wrong. Y' know well's I do that yore people'd be lynched. Iffen y' got the brains God give a shrimp, y' know too—'n y' know it well—that the rich, the kind as has had yore kind in slavery, thinks less 'a' my kind than they do a' yoren. Yes, in lotsa ways they do. 'N to my kind yore people is almost a worse threat."

Pacing back and forth, waving his hands, he delivered what seemed to Verity to be one of the most enlightening speeches he ever made. For her it made clear some of the odd subtleties.

"I want no enemies amongst yore people. You should oughta have a country a' yore own. You're a-feelin' sorry for yoreselves 'cause you was slaves. White men fought one war to free yore people, 'n you was only slaves a few hundred years. But folks like to me 'n my kind has been slaves since the world begun." Shaking his fist at the heavens and at Selah and Tape, he orated roundly, " 'N you take it from me, there ain't no more freedom for yore people tillst my kind a' people is freed—'n that's the God's truth! We gotta get freed by some changes as is all linked up withen money 'n law."

The white men present sat tense and quiet. Tape forgot his embarrassment and stared at Hank, completely caught in a spell. Selah swiped the tears from her eyes with the back of her hand, pulled a large blue kerchief from her apron pocket, and blew her nose long and loud.

Tape jumped at the sound. "Gawd, Selah!" he said. "Nigh 'bout made me think yo' nose de trumpet uv Gabri'l." Some of the white men laughed. But not black Tape. "Fo' Gawd," he said earnestly, "you done make me feel better den I'se felt since I pulled on m' mammy's black breas'. I wants ter go tell de deacons. Selah, she plumb right, Mistuh Hank. You got a chariot uv fiah." As in a dream he turned and opened the door, chanting emotionally, "Elijah got a chariot uv fiah; Mistuh Hank got a chariot uv fiah; all us chilluns got a chariot—" But as Tape reached the door he came out of his dream, and Hank's lounging men in the yard came sharply to their feet, snapped their guns into position to be swung quickly to shoulders.

Turning as if on a fast-spinning swivel, Tape cried, "De law's a-comin'! De law's a-comin'!" and he came back in, slamming the door.

In the yard Hank's men stood watchful and silent, parting to let the enemy pass.

"Leastways thirty deputies," said Hank softly as he looked through the window. "'N God'lmighty! The Black Skimmer! The Black Skimmer, men! Castleberry hisself, 'n Saucier, too! Why, they must be crookeder'n a body dare believe!" Turning to his men, he whispered hoarsely, "Such opposition's purely a compliment, men! A confession, too, was y' t' ask me. 'N them deputies is every one strangers. He's brung 'em from Loder City!"

A revolver handle pounded thunderously on the door. The knob turned. The door was kicked open. Strangers, belted and holstered, guns in hands, stood in the opening, glaring at Hank's men.

"Where's Hank Martin?" an officer demanded.

Jumping forward, Hank yelled with the fierce bellow of an animal attacking, "I'm Hank Martin! 'N what the hell d'y mean walkin' into my house? This ain't no public place! That there ain't no public door! What the hell d'y mean?"

"Got a warrant for you." The deputy took a folded paper from his pocket.

"What's the charge?" Hank demanded as a murmur ran through the crowd.

"Inciting a crowd with intent to disturb the peace."

"Incitin' a crowd with intent to disturb the peace!" Hank bellowed. "A crowd? Just one crowd? Why, I got leastways fifty crowds in five parishes! Intent to disturb the peace," he sneered. "Why, that's purely a insult t' my capacities! Does my men 'n their guns look like we're a-fixin' for some clownish brawl? 'R does it look like war?" His head went up and back in a great laugh. His men echoed him faintly in relief.

The deputies were being motioned aside, and Robert Castleberry entered Hank Martin's house. Long and taut like a drawn sword he stood, his green eyes gleaming like the jade he loved.

"Serve that paper," he commanded the officer.

Hank held out his hand for the paper and the officer laid it in his palm. Slowly, and with great ostentation, Hank took it and read it. After a few seconds he looked up. As he did so, all Verity's fears for him took wings and flew away, for a teasing mischievousness glinted in Hank's eyes.

"Well, well," he said elaborately. "Well, well. A disturb-the-peace warrant. Ain't I heard yore lawyer is a real blue-blood, Castleberry?"

The green glare did not waver, nor did Mr. Castleberry lower himself to answer.

"Well, his blood's too blue. His brain ain't gettin' no sustenance. None whatsomever." Slapping the refolded paper into the deputy's hand, Hank sneered, "That was issued in Loder City. Ain't no such warrant good un-lessen it's issued in the parish it's served in."

The deputies looked confused. The one with the paper said, "I supposed it was issued here. I didn't look at it—"

"Shut up!" Castleberry snapped. Then to Hank, "You are mistaken. You know nothing of law."

"I know a damsite more'n you 'n yore blue-blood lawyer put together. I just proved that. Now you back outa my house, you Black Skimmer. Go on, get a-backin' there."

Castleberry stood still and drawn. Hank's men lifted their guns. The deputies crowding the doorway lifted their revolvers.

"None a' that, men," said Hank. "We don't wanta disturb the peace. Not 'less we're forced t' stoop to such. Back out, now, Castleberry. Lemme see what a Black Skimmer can take into his innards in a backward flight."

From out Castleberry's green eyes, from out his whitening face, there shot the purest hate. There was no hint of defeat; no hint of chagrin. He turned. Taut and straight, like good steel walking, he passed between the deputies, seeming above and beyond such ugly knowledge as the need for drawn firearms, and on, superb, magnificent, through the little yard.

From mouth to mouth ran the whisper, "Black Skimmer," "Black Skimmer." Hank's men followed him out the door, guns up, the deputies backed in two lines alongside the forward-facing Castleberry. In Roy L. Saucier fear for his boss geysered up like the old faithful he was, as he screamed, "Run, Mr. Castleberry, run!" And in a panic Saucier pushed through Hank's men, going toward his employer.

It struck Verity as funny: a mouse instructing a lance. She understood the saucy, jeering impulse which moved Picayune Potter to lift his gun high above his head and let go a shot toward the bayou.

But another shot sounded just a split beat later, and then another. Everything happened so fast, yet she saw it all, heard it all. She heard Roy L. Saucier's scream of pain as the first shot that was fired by a deputy got him. She knew the deputy was confused, had thought Saucier one of Hank's men. She heard the deputy utter one small moan as the bullet from Harry Disbro's gun went through his heart. The deputy lay dead at the foot of the steps, right at her very feet, his own gun still smoking from the shot that killed Saucier. She was suddenly racked with pain and fear. Her hands flew protectingly to her stomach. She looked wildly about as Hank bellowed to the men.

"Stop! Stop! Quiet! I got somethin' t' say!" As the crowd quieted, Hank said, loud and scathingly, "Every person here seen that nervous fool of a deputy shoot Castleberry's own man, thinkin' he was one a' us." He looked over the crowd, giving Harry and every one of his followers confidence. "You done right, Harry. Nothin' else you could do—a nervous fool shootin' into our men, a-threatenin' the life a' any one a' us."

Castleberry fastened his cold green stare on Harry Disbro. "You will hang for this!" The hate-filled, incisive words acted as a bracer on Hank.

"Never!" said Hank in a hoarse, fervent whisper. "Never!" Verity saw him breathe deep, thin his belly, and knew he was pushing out fear. "Worse'n the killin' of yore nervous, pulin' men is the insult you give us a-comin' here withen a no-'count paper." He shook his fist at the taut Castleberry. "You'll never condemn Harry. The day's past when you can get us down yore gullet, 'cause we're one big body now!" Like a general to his army, Hank commanded, "On to the gin, men!" He took Harry's arm, "You too, Harry."

Then, with great show of disdain, he said to Castleberry, "By the time you manage to figger out the right paper as will put Harry in jail a spell, you'll be proved t' be a thief. 'N carry yore dead outa my yard . . . Onward, men!"

Sinking to the gallery steps, Verity shut her eyes against the milling men, shut her ears to sounds, and put every ounce of herself into the one job of clinging to consciousness in the midst of pain, into waiting for strength to come to her again. For with the killing of two men, Hank's child gave its first kick of life.

7

Hank Martin had the beginnings of a kingdom by the time his first child was born—a kingdom of dreams for the lowly and poor. And when his peddler's whistle shrilled the news of her birth, the lowly and the poor—Hank's people—brought tributes of wild geese and ducks, of fox and deer, of chickens and diapers and gingham. They came barefoot through the gum-tar mud. . . .

SELAH and Tape lifted her and carried her to bed. She was a furnace of pain in body and mind, aware of just one sweet thing—Selah, her strong and ministering hands, her scolding, loving voice.

"Dat man a-walkin' out a-talkin' big 'bout otha men's young'uns an' his own near 'bout neva gittin' t' take a breaf. Um-m-ump! Ain' mens a somepin'!" Turning on Tape, she screamed, "Git out, you nothin'-but-man! Fotch me pail cold wata'. Yo' feetses ain' nail ter de flo'."

As she put cold cloths on Verity's head, loosened her clothes, and propped her with pillows, she said over and over, "Whut fo' y'all so upset, Miz Verity? You ain' gwine ter lose usn dat baby is you, jus' 'cause dere's hullabaloo in yo' ya'd, is you? You gwine hafter git accustomated ter hullabaloo, you is. Um-hum, you shu' is. Plumb accustomated. Yas'm, you is. Now, you ain' gwine ter lose usn dat baby, is you?"

When Verity finally managed to shake her head in weak denial the tears came, slow at first like the first meltings of a northern spring and then in a flood as if the topmost peaks of her being had lost their white coverings in an avalanche.

Selah sat quietly by the bed watching, wiping the tears and laying on cool cloths. After a long while she spoke.

"Heah-heah, heah-heah, honey, dat ain' gwine do no good. Naw, sir, no good a-tall. But Selah knows whut fo' you is cryin'. I shu' does. Don' be breakin' yo' heart, honey, 'cause yo' man ain' perfeck. Why, lawsy, honey," she cackled with broad, forced humor, "Gawd done made man fu'st. Gawd done practice on man. Den Gawd, He look man over an' study on His mistakes. An' den Gawd make a perfeck critter. Yas'm, Gawd make woman after He git practiced up a bit."

Selah nodded solemnly. "I knows whut you is feelin', y'all cain't keep no securts fum me. You'se got a purty heart in you an' you keeps it in you. Selah done seed de worry in yo' face w'en Mistuh Hank show his heart to eva'body." Laughing almost to herself, she added, "An' lawsy, ain' it a han'some sight w'en he gits it all granded up fo' struttin'! Um-ummp! W'en he take his heart out fo' showin' it plumb ready ter cakewalk!"

Selah chuckled and chuckled, unaware that her words hurt. Verity turned her face toward the wall.

"You gittin' sleepy, chile? Dat shu' good. Iffen you sleeps, you be fine."

Verity lay in a state of willing inactivity for three days. Slowly the inner forces mended as her strength returned. The baby still moved within her and this was good. Hank had not been home since he left with the men. The third morning Verity got up feeling new and almost strong again.

"Mr. Hank hasn't been home? Nor sent any word?" Verity asked as Selah put her breakfast on the table.

"No'm, he ain't. Tape, he say mens still watching at de gin. Tape, he say mens gwine stan' watch ter see eva load weighed t'rough de whole pickin' season. He say it shu' make a 'citin' sight all de wagons down de road, all de mens wid guns. He say eva'body know now Mistuh Hank right. Dem owners bin a-thievin' eva'body. Tape, he say Moses say Mistuh Jules downrigh' shocked wid de scandalization."

"Which scandal? That Mr. Hank is right? Or the shooting? Or that Mr. Castleberry has been stealing him poor?" When she thought of Jules's attitude, she went completely over to Hank's side.

"I reckons he jus' mean de whole mess, Miz Verity."

All day she longed for news of Hank, longed to know what Jules was thinking. Sitting in her low rocker sewing, her fingers idled time after time as she tried to analyze the depressing sense of a need for endurance and tolerance which knocked lightly at her consciousness. Was it simply because she was pregnant or was it some prescience she could not name, perhaps did not want to know?

Hank came in the late afternoon, unshaven, disheveled, and furious, clutching a copy of the Loder City *Courier*.

"Lookit this!" he cried. Coming to Verity he handed her the paper and indicated the item. "I'm a 'peddler a' pins, pots, 'n potions,'" he howled. "That's what they call me! 'N m' name 'is said t' be Hank Martin.' 'N I led my people t' believe the cotton prices was unfair! Not a word 'bout them blue-blooded bastards that's been a-thievin' for years! Oh, no, not one word 'bout that! Why, them fools on that there paper ain't sure a' nothin'. Everything's alleged—alleged—alleged! B'God-'lmighty, I ain't alleged them Black Skimmers is a thievin' lot. I proved it. 'N still this here spineless sheet don't print it!"

It was a little story of only four paragraphs, telling of "an uprising of the poor whites," throughout five parishes, of the killings in Cypress Bend, one Harry Disbro's arrest for shooting an officer, and of the deaths of two others who were Hank's followers, Jedidiah Haskins and Hoke Marsh. The last paragraph said, "The uprising was allegedly led by a peddler who goes through the state peddling pins, pots, and potions. His name is said to be Hank Martin." No mention of the Castleberrys or the Newtons.

Hank walked back and forth and raved, but Verity couldn't answer. She had been haunted by the thought of Jenny and Mrs. Saucier and that deputy's family, and now, two more.

"Those men—Haskins and Marsh—have they wives and families?"

"Shore," he tossed off the answer almost absently. "Imagine that paper! Ignorin' the greatest thing that's happened in these parts in years on end. 'N me—a peddler a' pins, pots, 'n potions! My name is *said* t' be Hank Martin! Why, m' picture should oughta been on the front page. Someday I'll cram them words down their choking throats!" Hank dropped into a chair at the table and stared at the paper.

She stared at him, not wanting to think public recognition meant more to him than the deaths and jailing of his followers. Crossing to the table she stood before him, her hands in protective gesture across her stomach.

"Hank," she said softly, "Hank—you almost frighten me. You're sitting here mad and worried because a newspaper ignores you in a way. But you're ignoring the suffering you've brought on some individuals. Oh, yes, you've been proved right and a good many people got more money for their cotton. That's fine as far as it goes. But Jenny's our friend. And those two men, Haskins and Marsh, they were your friends too."

"Shore, Verity, but you don' think for a instant the men didn't know they was li'ble to get popped off iffen there was trouble, do y'?"

"Perhaps not," she said, feeling oddly driven. "But, Hank, I'm standing here pregnant with your child. If the tables were turned and you were sent to jail because you'd followed an idea, a cause, that Harry started—well, I'd hate Harry with all my heart. You are my husband; you are safe; you are the leader of these men. But, Hank—even to me it's not worth it. All this killing. Four men dead and one jailed. And you say this is only the beginning of your campaigns, as you call them. Four widows, and heaven only knows how many fatherless children." Sobs broke from her and her hands flew up to cover her face. "Hank," she pleaded, "what's the sense of my having your child when you seem to have so little regard for life?"

He drew back sharply as if she had struck him.

"Me—little regard for life? Are you crazy, woman? My heart plumb aches for them as die. Ain't nobody hates the notion a' death more'n I do. I think God gathers in the fragments so's nothin' is wasted. But I love this here earth. I only just wanta make it more near to a paradise."

Drawing her to him he said, "Sweetface, lookit—iffen men as is capable a' leadin' was t' quit with the first shots, this world'd be purely a mess, seems as though. Take George Washington. He was a traitor. Why, shore he was. This country had English rule and Washington was a traitor to it. Lotsa men died follering Washington. And ain't you glad they did?" Handing her his huge blue handkerchief, he said gently, "Here, blow. Then lookit Lincoln. Widows wrote him, women pleaded, men stormed 'n threatened. But he prayed 'n fought. I gotta do the same!"

Tilting her face up and looking into her eyes, he said, "I ain't never heard nothin' that seemed acc'rate 'bout how the wives of them there men felt. Nor whether their women tried t' argufy 'em outen their convictions. But," he grinned, "I shore got a conviction that no man can't get great a-shushin' his woman. I want you should allus speak out. Time 'n agin it's done me good a'ready. There's sometimes a kinda whetstone in yore scoldin' 'n yore argufying as hones me quick 'n sharp."

She dried her eyes and tried to smile.

"'N don't you be a-worryin' 'bout Jedidiah Haskins 'n Hoke Marsh. Iffen ever I saw two men as is weary a' livin' 'n producin' young'uns, it's them two. Too dang weary to dodge iffen they seen the bullets a-comin'. 'N you know yoreself Harry's a natural-borned sluggard. More'n likely he'll plumb love settin' in jail."

"Well, Harry may sit in jail and love you for bringing him ease," she bridled. "But the women of this state are going to be influenced by what women like Jenny and Mrs. Marsh and that other widow endure. These people are ignorant and superstitious. It seems to me they're divided into two kinds—Swith's kind, the fanatics who need a dream desperately, and the others who say simply 'iffen the Lord'll let us.'" Her voice rolled out the last words like a voodoo chant. "It seems too bad your followers can't take out insurance against the perils of Hank Martin." She sank weakly into a chair.

"Insurance," he said slowly, "against the perils of Hank Martin. That's just what they should oughta have, seems 's though! God'lmighty! Would that pay me big dividends! Be the first evidence folks'd see a' Hank Martin gettin' the riches divided!" He beamed on her and said softly, lovingly, "Hank's little whetstone. Dang if you ain't."

Chuckling, he took a pencil from his pocket, scribbled figures on the pine boards of the table.

"Let's see—Harry didn't never get more'n a hunderd 'n sixty cash money a year, 'n others a' the organization c'n help tend his acres tillst we get him out. Allottin' the same sums to the widow Haskins 'n the widow Marsh—'n they got boys most growed that'll soon be a-earnin'—'n soon be a-payin' their dollar into the organization. That's four hunderd 'n eighty a year for the three a' them—that's thirteen dollars 'n forty cents just about, first a' ev'ry month to each a' them." Looking up he grinned happily. "Hell, I c'n give 'em that outen my own pocket iffen I gotta. 'N then I'll start a-collectin' one dollar 'n ten cents a year. The ten centses to 'cumu-late to benefit folks as need it."

A load lifted from Verity's heart. Hank wanted to do what was right. He had only to see it. But the idea of paying out thirteen dollars every month to several widows amazed her.

"Can we afford that, Hank?" she asked. "Why, we don't spend much more than that ourselves—cash money, as you say."

"Well," he grinned, "that ain't 'cause I don't make it. 'N it ain't 'cause you can't have what you want. Just figger a little, Sweetface—all over the lakes 'n lagoons 'n rivers there's settlements a' trappers 'n I'm a-handlin' their pelts. I don't never pay lodgin' 'n board. In thousands a' homes Hank Martin is more welcome than sunshine. I don't never feed m' own horse, even, 'cept when he's in m' own barn. 'N all over the state, 'ceptin' in a few parishes up t' the north," an in-seeing look clouded his eyes, "folks is a-payin' to belong to m' organization. I'm a-goin' to order all the funds transferred into one place, into one lump. All that money I can use some-day when I see a fit cause."

"The parishes up north— Do you mean near your home? Your moth-er's home?"

"Yeah." Pain flashed across his face. "Yeah. Allus promised myself I'd get back t' see Maw. Someday—when I could walk in 'n say, 'Maw, I found the road t' Zion.' " He rose and looked out the window. "Well, I went north this last trip. Maw 'n old Grammaw is both dead. Hurt me some, it did, Sweetface. Still, I got confidence she's somewheres better, 'n so it ain't bad. It's just—oh, I reckon I just sorta wanta to say it to her personal."

How great a thing it is to be a mother, Verity thought. But how sacri-ficial. Looking at Hank, thinking of him as he always appeared—so self-sufficient, so boisterously sure, it was hard to realize he could feel the deep childish need to return to a mother and prove he had done well.

Hank sighed. "I didn't go to my home, Verity. Didn't have no heart to see Paw 'n my brothers. Someday, when I'm governor, I'll have to do somethin' for 'em, I reckon. Feller can't just pay no mind t' his kin after he gets t' be a somebody. I got no good feelin's for 'em, though. Fact is, they gimme the jaundice."

As he turned to face Verity, the hurt was so plain that all the mother in her wanted to help him and protect him. But she said nothing. She waited for Hank to clear his own mind of shadows.

"Pity I didn't think t' send Maw some money oncet in a while. I should plumb oughta have a barrel stave laid crost my rump." He grinned rue-fully. "It's purely hell the things a man should oughta do, 'n don't never think 'bout tillst it's too late."

Selah knocked, and Verity was glad to have her come in grumbling.

"Law, knockin' at de do' when I comes inter de onliest kitchen I'se got, to de onliest stove I'se got t' cook on," Selah mumbled. "Knockin' at de do' lak I don' live heah."

"Well, you don't live here," said Hank. "You live yonder t'other side a' them tomatoes you planted. You think I'm a-goin' t' have a big dark wench a-walkin' in on me any time she's a' mind? Cheer up, Selah, I plumb guarantee y' when I get us a house big as Bolduc's, there won't be no doors you gotta knock on 'ceptin' mebbe a few upstairs."

"Heh, heh," sighed Selah largely, "ain't he one fo' funnin', Miz Verity! Usn wid a house lak dat! Oh, dat 'minds me. Law, I nigh 'bout fergit! Mistuh Jules, he pass by w'en I'se in de fiel' a-choppin' wid de hoe. He call ter me an' he say tell y'all he stoppin' back heah on his return fum de town."

"Here!" Hank beamed. "I been a-worryin' how is Jules a-takin' it 'bout Castleberry. Been honin' t' go t' his house but reckoned it's plumb his turn for showin' his cards. It's suppertime. We ain't never returned Jules's invites. What we got for supper?"

"Usn got peppa' hash wif co'n, an' mustard greens, an' cowpeas. An' I'se fixin' de fines' biscuits Mistuh Jules eva' et. Usn got de fines' clabba' fer t' make dem biscuits eva' you see. Um-um, dat shu' a fine cow usn got now. Fines' milk eva' I see. Sours up int' de bestes' clabba'. Um-um! Even de whey betta' dan some cows' cream."

Thinking of Jules at her table flustered Verity and she hastened to her linen shelf. Nice tablecloths were things she cherished. Whenever she laid one she felt a little rise of gratitude that she could have a pretty table after the years of oilcloth in the orphanage. She chose a soft yellow cloth and after spreading it she went into the yard with her kitchen shears. As she cut lavender and purple asters she wondered about Jules. He had been so sure Castleberry could not be dishonest. Jules was a puzzle. Such a cynic, in a way, thinking of people in classes. How, then, would he react to these recent events?

"Hank," she asked as she entered the house, "what makes you think Jules will stay for supper? He was very angry about your accusations, you know."

"Yeah, I know," Hank replied. "Iffen he holds I shouldn't oughta done it just 'cause they was blue-bloods, I'm gonna be plumb disappointed in Jules. But no matter what he says, I gotta have Jules's friendship up to a point, I have. I can't tend m' business, earn a livin', 'n take time out for goin' to reg'lar schoolin' for law. 'N law I gotta have. 'N Jules I gotta have for a kinda private teacher liken you been up to now."

"Mistuh Jules, he look plumb peaked dis ev'nin'," said Selah.

"What time did he pass?"

"Long 'bout t'ree 'clock, I reckon."

"I never will get accustomed to evening beginning in the afternoon," commented Verity. "I've worried about Jules. He's been a good friend."

"He's a-comin' now," said Hank from the doorway. "He shore rides somethin' handsome, don't he?"

Watching him coming toward them through the day's last paleness, Verity felt as she had that night months ago, felt an urge to call to a friend. She wanted to call, "Jules, be my friend! Be Hank's friend! Cypress Bend would be unbearable without you." She waited, feeling he must not be urged, feeling his decision must be entirely his. But she hoped. Had he not called today? Was he not coming back? He needn't have come.

As he dismounted, Hank started forward to greet him, but Verity stood waiting in the door.

"Ev'nin', Jules," Hank called.

"Good evening, Hank," said Jules. He tied his horse to the gatepost, then came forward, hand extended.

His gesture toward Hank thrilled Verity and she steepled her fingers in the childish gesture of prayer and happiness.

"You were right and I was wrong," said Jules clearly. "It's been a shock to me, Hank. I cannot imagine Robert stooping to such a thing. Nor the Newtons, either. But there's no denying it now." He hesitated but seemed to have more to say.

Sensing this, Hank prompted, "'N so . . . ?"

"I do not see eye to eye with you in your method of exposing this fact, since your method has all the elements of lawlessness. But I do thank you for opening my eyes. There are things about it to regret. Men have died and enemies have been made."

"Enemies, huh? Yores 'r mine?"

"I was thinking of mine. For the first time in generations Cypress Manor is not open to the Castleberrys."

"Well, roarin' thunderbolts, Jules, I never suspicioned you was one a' them there sentimentalist fellers as cries to have back a yesterday!"

Coming down the steps of her tiny porch Verity held out her hand to Jules, saying, "It's not that, Hank. Jules cries for the fine trust of the yesterdays."

"Thank you, Verity, my dear," said Jules and kissed her hand.

"Fine trust!" Hank exploded. "I ain't seen no evidence a' nothin' like that in the hist'ry I been a-readin'. Hell, Jules, them forebears you're a-talkin' 'bout bought 'n sold humans. They was niggers, t' be sure. But them niggers had a right t' be left in their own lands. 'N them forebears you're a-talkin' 'bout didn't do nothin' 'bout dividin' the riches. They left that for you t' write a cynical paper 'bout, 'n for me to do somethin' 'bout."

Jules seemed puzzled. Hank roared with laughter.

"That's right, Jules. You 'member that first night we et at yore house? Minute I saw Castleberry, I knowed he was a Black Skimmer 'n I tolt you some a' what I was a-thinkin' 'n I asked y' for that there paper y' wrote.

You gimme it, 'n I been a-thinkin' ever since." He thumped Jules's chest. "There, y' see," he crowed, "you're a partner in m' crime whether y' knowed it 'r not."

"Your reasoning is unique." Jules shook his head slowly.

"Goin' back refutingly, like them philosopher fellers say, t' first causes," said Hank. "We was hopin' you'd stay 'n eat supper with us."

"It will give me much pleasure," said Jules.

"You been a-ridin', so 'spect you'll wanta wash. You gotta wash out back. This is one a' them horrible share-crop places owned by a feller named Jules Bolduc, y' know."

"Selah will bring you warm water and towels," said Verity.

As Jules reentered through the back door he stood still a second looking at the room.

"Make yoreself t' home," said Hank; "I'll go tend yore horse."

"You have made this place charming, Verity. I would not have thought it possible." He looked about with frank interest.

As he stood near the back door, the coal-oil reflector lamp on a high shelf caught him full in its halo, giving his smile a tenderness Verity had never seen before. Standing between the little wood stove and the old white-painted cupboard with its stiffly starched curtains of green checkered gingham, his eyes seemed to encompass everything and yet to be saying something special to her. Selah looked up from the oven before which she knelt, having peered in at her biscuits, and grinned broadly at him.

"You ain't a-lookin' so peaked lak you did w'en you heah earlier dis ev'nin', Mistuh Jules," she said. "An' w'en you eats dese biscuits you ain't goin' t' look peaked a-tall."

"I am sure of that, Selah," he said sincerely. "Green floors—I have seen them in only one other house. A maharajah's palace. It is very pleasant."

"It was Hank's idea," said Verity.

"Was it?" Walking toward the shelves of books, he looked at the titles which varied from the fifth-grade reader to biographies of Lincoln and Saint-Simon. "I have underestimated Hank." His voice was very low and earnest. "Quite as you accused the first time we met."

She knew it to be an apology for the times he had given her unhappiness by making her defend Hank. A need rose in her to sit somewhere alone with this man and discuss her husband, a need to tell him how she felt about those men who were dead because they believed in Hank. She wanted to tell him that her father's people had been Quakers, wanted to tell him about her mother and her mother's belief in American opportunity. She wanted to tell him about Hank's childhood and how he felt about his mother. She wanted to tell him about the Little Flamingo, and the new thrusts of fierceness she felt flame within her. Oh, yes, and about the Ribidoux family and the way Hank helped them and many others. She wanted to see him take all these pictures and place them in some different way—

the way he saw them, and let her look at them then. Perhaps the struggle of these many thoughts showed upon her face, for he seemed so still, so waiting.

Hank bounded up on the little porch and into the room, the screen door slamming behind him.

"Say, Jules, you seen the Loder City papers?"

Jules nodded.

"Well, what the hell you make a' that? I prove them Black Skimmer's guilty 'n not a word 'bout them. But the leader a' the white-trash uprisin' is 'alleged' t' be me."

"Suppah's ready," announced Selah.

They sat down. Hank bowed his head and rattled off grace.

"Lord bless this food 'n Yore earth as yields it t' us, 'n thanks t' You, Lord, for the suns 'n rains that guarantees us a-plenty more. Amen." Without stopping an instant he raised his head and said, "Why, them blue-blooded, yellow-bellied, kowtowin' dim-wits as print that there paper ain't got sense enough t' know the biggest thing that's happened in these here parts in years has been a-goin' on. 'R is it that they're just a-feared t' print the truth when it's agin the likes a' Castleberry?"

"It could be either," replied Jules, smiling. "But when you are running for governor and really need to have the voters know about you, why, then, you will probably get a publicity manager."

"What's that?"

"A man who sees to it that the things people should know about you are told to the papers. A man who helps plan the kind of events which a paper will almost have to print."

"Y' mean t' tell me, Jules, there's men as makes a business a' the likes a' that?" Hank was dumbfounded. "You mean t' set there 'n tell me there's men I c'n hire that'd be like reporters kinda workin' hind-side-to?"

"An almost perfect description of their function," said Jules.

A long low whistle came from Hank's pursed lips. "Now how come I could live this long 'thout knowin' that!"

"With your sense of organization, you would have created such a job if there had never been one before. I am convinced of that."

"Publicity manager, you called it, huh? I shore gotta have me one a' them someday. I hadda notion to raise hell with that there paper. 'A peddler a' pins, pots, 'n potions' they called me. I'll push them words down their throats someday."

"Oh, dear," said Verity, "let's talk about the weather!"

Hank winked at Jules.

"Beginnin' t' act liken a wife, ain't she? Well, the weather is purely elegant. Now that settles the weather. Let's get back to me." Pointing his fork at Jules, he said seriously, "You was a long time a-comin' here. You been all these days a-makin' up yore mind 'bout me. Now what you a-thinkin'?"

"Hank," Verity protested.

"Oh, I know he's a-eatin' m' vittles at my invite. 'N he knows it. Now that's settled liken the weather. 'N iffen I remember rightly he took a poke at me when I was a-settin' at his table."

"My apologies," laughed Jules.

"All right, all right. Now let's put our cards face up on the barrel head. You're a-goin' t' make money on yore cotton this year. You looked down yore nose on me when first I mentioned law. Now I wanta know—you gonna learn me law 'r ain't you?"

Leaning over the table, he looked into Jules's face earnestly, and Jules looked back, soberly, sincerely.

"I am. And what is more, I expect to see you win your first case when you plead in behalf of your friend Disbro."

Studying Jules a second, wondering if this was sincere, Verity concluded it was.

"But, Jules," she cried, "you surely don't mean poor Harry has to sit in jail for—"

"Ain't that a wonderful notion!" cried Hank. "Me, personal, Hank Martin, in a court a' law, a-freein' ol' Harry! Now there's somethin' one a' them publicity fellers should oughta work on!"

"But you can't mean you'd let Harry sit in jail for four years?"

"Four years!" Hank repeated. "What d'you mean, four years?"

"Doesn't it take four years to become a lawyer?" she asked.

"In one a' them colleges, mebbe. Where they slow a fast one down for the dummies' sakes. I aim t' cut that in half."

"But even two years! Why, good heavens, Harry's your friend! Do you mean to tell me, Hank Martin, that you'd let poor little Jenny's husband sit in jail for two years just so you can show off?" She felt ashamed of him, outraged.

"Ain't I a-payin' Jenny outen m' own pocket as much as Harry ever made?" he demanded. " 'N as for Harry—why, he'd purely love t' have calluses on his rump 'stead a' his hands."

But Verity seemed not to hear him. Turning on Jules she glared at him.

"And I'm surprised at you, too. Egging Hank on while poor Harry—Oh, why is it that whenever we three are together I have to get mad at both of you!"

"Now wait," laughed Jules. "Disbro did shoot the deputy and they are holding him without bail. I assure you his case will not come into court before six or eight months. My idea was quite different. I do not expect Hank to be admitted to the bar by the time he pleads for his friend. I will gladly offer my services as Disbro's attorney, but my idea was this—Disbro can ask for you, Hank. If you are willing you cannot be refused. Courts being, presumably, to establish justice, anyone may plead. He does not have to be an attorney."

Watching Jules's face like one hypnotized, Hank studied him for a long minute.

"Jules," he said, "I don't know should I oughta swaller that whole 'r not. How come you got a mind to see it done that-a-way?"

The old cynical smile, the sardonic gleam played over Jules's face.

"I shall be frank," he said, almost musingly. "I hear from Loder City that Robert burns with shame for trying to stop you with a worthless disorderly-conduct warrant." Laughter broke from him, free and unrestrained. A natural laughter heaped with roguery and glee.

Verity had never heard him laugh so before. It was a handsome laugh. Like circus music, she thought, an invitation to wonders and fun. Hank's laugh rose from chuckle to roll and she sat restraining her own laughter so she could hear and remember.

"I got you," said Hank. "You shore are a smart feller, Jules. It'd humiliate Castleberry more t' lose the case t' me than t' lose it t' you. 'N that'd pleasure you, Jules?"

Jules flushed. "You put me on the defensive again, Hank."

"Well, now," said Hank largely, "I'm purely sorry. I purely am. But I gotta think on that a spell. Supposin' I lose? Supposin' the judge is one a' these here blue-blood cronies a' hisn? I gotta think on that a spell."

His expansive tone annoyed Verity. The free, open moment was gone. Jules was again the satirical observer.

"You interpret my suggestion as an intention to use you to bring greater humiliation to Robert? In a way, that is true." Turning to Verity, he smiled. "Does Hank ever see anything as it is presented to him? He seems to have chosen the inverted view." Dismissing the subject, he touched the flowers and said, "They are fine and hardy. You have a way of planting flowers to get the very best results in gradation of heights and colors. One seems to blend into another in your borders."

"T' hell with the flowers," said Hank before Verity could speak.

Verity was puzzled. There was some strange subtlety here that she did not understand.

"We will not let you dismiss the flowers as you did the weather," said Jules smoothly.

"I ain't a-dismissin' 'em." Hank grinned broadly at Jules. "I was just fixin' t' take the inverted view. Yeah, I was goin' t' remark that them flowers take a helluva lot a' manure."

Jules laughed. But not as he had laughed before. It was a polite company laugh. Not an invitation to wonders and fun.

After Jules had gone, Verity sat quietly in her low rocker, eyes fastened on the high lamp in the kitchen end of the room, seeming still to see Jules's softened smile, so different it was from the familiar, usual one, which drew his lips sidewise and downward as he said good night. What was fundamentally wrong that Hank and Jules, who had so much respect for each other, could not really get together in anything?

Hank strode back and forth, hands jammed in his pockets, head forward. Save for the creak of the old floor boards his steps were almost soundless. His walk always fascinated Verity. So upright, yet with such a forward tenseness, knees always flexed as for a spring, tread so light and so sure. Treading back and forth in the small room, he looked caged. Verity rose and opened the bedroom door, feeling the need for space.

"Hank," she tried to make her voice light, merely curious, "why did you take the attitude that it would give Jules more pleasure to see Mr. Castleberry lose than it would to see you win?"

She had spoken to his back. Three more strides took him to the end of the room and he turned, grinning.

"'Cause it's a fact. Inverted viewpoint!" He chuckled. "Pore Jules. Us a-movin' here has sure changed things for pore Jules. Here he was a-settin' in the sun not even a-pleasurin' hisself mightily in it. Just a-settin', doin' some fancy thinkin'. Bein' one a' life's spectators!"

He made another round of the room.

"'N then we come along 'n here I am just nigh to makin' him take a part. 'Cause d'y know what, Sweetface?" He came to her, touched her cheek with a finger in that sweet gesture which implied wonder at her reality. "That feller Jules is half in love with you. Mebbe more'n half."

A blaze of fierce heat flared over her. Jumping up from her chair she faced Hank, so fiercely attacking that he stepped back from her.

"Hank Martin," she cried, "I've got a good notion to slap you!"

"Roarin' thunderbolts!" he howled, "I ain't a-layin' you no blame. Nor Jules neither." He grinned. "You dang little pepper pod. You're a-bulgin' with a young'un 'n that young'un is mine. 'N iffen you was to have fifty I'd know they was all mine." Grasping her arms he held her from him, looking into her eyes. His voice went into the husky, passionate tenderness she so loved. "I'm plumb a expert at smellin' out love. But I'm plumb a expert at recognizin' a virgin, too. 'N you're one, 'n you will be till the day you die iffen you was to bear fifty young'uns."

Pulling her stiff, unyielding body to him, he put his arms about her waist and held her possessively against him. Within her the baby protested against its mother's sudden disturbing movements and kicked her violently.

"God'lmighty!" exclaimed Hank in a prayerful exultancy, "God'lmighty! I feel my young'un a-kickin' agin my own stummick. I feel him!" he rejoiced triumphantly. "I feel him! How knowin' of God t' let us feel the little feller a-knockin' t' come into the world."

As he looked down upon her she marveled at the strange, strong beauty of his face. In the soft yellow lamplight his hair had the blues and greens of a blackbird's wings, his flesh warmly rosy with sun and wind and his eyes wide from coming upon a miracle.

She wanted to lean sweetly against him and gather some of this strength and beauty for herself and child, wanted to tell him that for the days he was at the gin she lay quiet and ill. But a thin steel rod stayed unbending in her back, prodding up through her brain, reminding her that she was very angry with him.

"Come to bed, Sweetface," he whispered. "I'll curve myself around yore bulgin' just snug 'n comfortin' to you. 'N we'll lay quiet 'n prayerful whilst I catch yore fine feelin' a' bein' a parent."

Tears pooled and ran down her face.

"I want to, Hank," she said, "but I'm still mad at you."

The smallest of tender smiles flickered in his lips and eyes. He felt his pockets for a handkerchief and found none; so he pulled out his shirttail, lifted the edge to her face, blotted a tear gently as ink is pulled up into a blotter.

"That's just what I mean," he said softly. " 'N I admire for t' see it in you. You're like them azaleas. You ain't depravin' yore honey. Allus yore heart 'n yore mind has gotta sing a duet to yore body. They got to sing 'this is it.' 'N that makes a virgin. And," he added firmly, "I don't believe they'll ever sing that duet for nobody but me."

"But, Hank, you have no right to say Jules is half in love with me. Jules is your friend and he's my friend. You shouldn't say things that will make me so self-conscious. You have no right to say such a thing."

"Lookit here, Sweetface, Jules is a gentleman. He would be one iffen he didn't have a picayune. Like Tim—he's a gentleman, Tim is. But Jules, he's one a' them idealist fellers, too. Up to now he's been a feller, seems as though, as was a dreamer who is careful to keep his dreams just dreams. You know, so's they wouldn't disappoint him none. But I'm a-goin' to make him defend Harry, 'n d' you know why? 'Cause it'll do me more good for it be known that Jules Bolduc is with me than it'll do me t' win Harry outen jail myself."

"I don't understand. And what has that to do—"

"Just this. My own people are for me. I need to be thinkin' a' spreadin' my influence so's to take in the middle class. 'N the middle class a' folks are snobs. They like to be sure they're associatin' with a few topnotchers. So here's where I'm gonna snag my first topnotcher—Jules, last of the Bolducs."

It sounded like a trap—a trap set for Jules, and her dying anger flared again.

"It sounds like a trap. You'll have to explain that better, Hank."

He grinned.

"Do you think I'm a kind a' poison? D'you?"

"Of course not. But—"

"Then there ain't no buts. Jules is willin'. He said he'd take the case, didn't he?"

"Well, yes—"

"O.K. He's gonna take it. I'm gonna get a publicity man. 'N lotsa folks as would mebbe sneered at me for years is gonna sneer not so big nor so long. They're gonna say, 'Iffen that Hank Martin can have Jules Bolduc for him . . .' "

It couldn't do Jules any harm to take Harry's case. Why should Hank make such a point of it? Could it possibly do Hank as much good as he thought?

"And what has all this got to do with—"

"With me sayin' he's half in love? Sweetface, don't you see iffen I shove that feller Jules into the field, iffen I make him play ball instead a' spectatin'—iffen he finds he likes action—well, I'm askin' you—is he gonna stay a dang dreamin' celibate? Is he gonna still keep his dreams just dreams? So far, Jules Bolduc ain't never give this world a idea. All he's ever give is just thoughts he's got outen books, books wrote by other brains in other ages. Is he gonna like action? Is he just goin' to sleepwalk a spell for me during Harry's trial? Or is he gonna come outen them dreams 'n run into the field for more action?"

Run into the field! She saw him again standing lazily in the manorhouse door, leanly silhouetted by the soft hall light. Saw him come to eager life as she called. Saw him run into the field, no, the meadow, run into the meadow to reach her.

"You see, Sweetface," Hank's voice was soft but, oh, so firm. "You see, I want you should hear it first from me. All my pore people need a mite a' backin' such as Jules can give mebbe. After this one turn in court for us, after he gives me just that much public recognition a' my rightness in this here cause, I can then get some other feller from good family. Like Varick Kirkendall, mebbe. I can buy him, but the middle-class folks won't think so." He sighed, said almost hopefully, "Jules'll likely slip back to his dreamin'—mebbe."

Throughout Hank's words she relived that evening walk and talk with Jules. What had he said about loving someone you also liked? It was just good talk. It meant nothing. She had been annoyed with Jules and, oh, how happy, how wondrously, gloriously happy when she had found Hank and his lantern by the barn! I'm just Hank's glowworm, she thought.

"How silly you're being, Hank," she whispered. "How very silly."

"That's good," said Hank huskily and ran a finger lightly over her cheek.

When Hank took off again, a sturdy bookrest had been added to his wagon. It rose awkwardly but efficiently from the dashboard. Tim took great pride in fashioning its folding back, and immense pride in the spring clamps to hold the pages of heavy lawbooks, despite the gusty winds of early fall. This time a crowd of the villagers gathered at Hank's house to see him take off. They came singly and in groups. Tim and Sophy and their boys. Jenny and her twins, Jenny wearing a brand-new blue calico which flaunted a very full gathered skirt. Her thin little fingers constantly pinched a fold at each side and spread the skirt into outward wings for her own admiring eyes. A pang of tender understanding hurt Verity. She knew the feel of luxury which extra yardage, not needed for duty as covering, could give after years of skimpiness. Coarse, cheap insertion lay in a tidy square at the neck and Jenny's hair was wound in slick braids. It was evident the twins had been starched and spotless when they left home. Only a few smears of grease from the fried hog rinds they sucked were in evidence now.

Jenny advanced shyly to Hank as he adjusted the heavy book on the new rack. Spreading her full skirt childishly, she looked up at him, worship in her eyes.

"It pleasures me somethin' powerful, this dress," she said. "Mebbe I shouldn't oughta bought it withen some a' the money y'all paid me for Harry."

The gesture filled Verity with painful memory. It was so like the Little Flamingo in her dress of muted pink, and the words, "Hank gimme this," ran through her head like a chorus.

"A-course you should oughta bought it, Jenny." Hank beamed on her. Seeing a self-doubt still in her eyes he leaned down from the wagon seat and spoke confidentially. "You can more'n earn that there dress iffen you was to persuade Swith to get hisself a horse. He could move faster 'n get more members. We gotta have members, Jenny."

Both looked over at Swith.

"Swith can tell folks how I fixed up you 'n them others. Nobody should oughta be a-feared then."

"That's shore the truth, Hank," she said, and her eyes grew bright as she realized she held a bright new sword with which to fight for Hank.

Tim, Sophy, and others crowded around him. Verity felt almost left out. She desperately wanted to push them all away, climb into the wagon beside him and go, and go, and go.

"Mr. Bolduc's a-comin' yonder," said Tim, pointing toward the knoll.

Against the morning sun Jules and his horse seemed one in dignity of breeding and color. Jules's highly polished brown boots glistened with the same high gleam as the horse's bay flanks. About animal and man there was a valiant correctness. Jules sat so straight and easy, with his free right arm about a square, bulky bundle which Verity knew to be books. The horse held his head so high and arched that his checkrein slacked. Watching them, Verity knew a sense of solidity, staunch and sweet. "That's what Hank meant," she thought, "about him being a gentleman." Maybe it was the indefinable quality which can come only to descendants of blooded, registered lines, whether animal or man. But instantly something in her rose to resentment of this idea. There must always be a first champion to start every line.

In answer to Hank's welcome, Jules pulled up beside the cart, spoke graciously to Tim and Sophy, nodded to Squeeze-nickel and several others. Only Tim spoke his "Good morning, Mr. Bolduc," with no hint of servility.

Handing Hank the heavy package, he seemed hesitant about speaking further. Verity knew he didn't want to risk hurting Hank before his followers by directing his studies in their hearing.

Hank grinned at him. "Talk right out loud, Jules. These here folks're all my friends. They know you're a-learnin' me law 'n they know I aim to learn it in record time." Hank pointed to his reading rack. "Roarin' thunderbolts, Jules!" he said as he took the books, "you was gonna bring me a whole year's readin'. Why, I'll have these here books learnt in a few months—likely by the time I get back!"

"If you do you will be performing a miracle," said Jules.

"Well, performin' miracles is my specialty," said Hank.

"In some of these books," replied Jules quietly, "are some cases which I have marked. Cases having a bearing on the Disbro trial."

Verity caught her breath. Hank had been twice to Jules's house. She had assumed that of course Hank had asked him to take Harry's case. She saw Jenny stiffen and lean forward eagerly, was aware of the crowd's tenseness, aware of Hank's change of expression.

"Well, now, Jules," he said loudly, "I shore appreciate this. I purely do. 'N powerful glad I am to be a-gettin' a chancet to be a-readin' of it. But—my friends here, 'n little Jenny here—she's Harry's wife'—'n yonder there's his twins—my friends here mightn't feel I was yet capable a' winnin' a case of law. 'N so, Jules, I'm acceptin' yore fine offer to take his case yoreself." Turning to the crowd, he said, "Mr. Bolduc's offered to take Harry's case. Now how about givin' him a rousin' hallelujah!"

He led the cheer himself with a loud and hearty hallelujah. The others came out of their amaze to cheer with an awed unbelief.

A slow pink crept over Jules's face and the upward jerk of the horse's head told Verity that Jules's hand had not kept its lax hold. Sometimes she felt that Hank held few surprises for Jules. But what kind of surprises might Jules hold for Hank? The horse tossed his fine head, champed at his bit, pranced with a fine nervousness to be off. Would the horse, Verity wondered, without his checkrein and with the flick of a whip, stretch out his neck and go flying down a track like his racing sires?

Among the villagers were whispers of surprise, words and looks implying that it was impossible a Bolduc would ally himself with them even in a court of law.

"Yes, sir," Hank was saying, "Jules Bolduc, hisself personal, is a-goin' to take Harry's case. Yes, sir, he tolt us, Verity 'n me, when he was a-eatin' dinner in our house just t'other night."

To Verity's ears came a soft chuckle. Looking back she saw Selah standing by the gate, eyes dancing with merriment, and Verity heard again her words, "An' lawsy, ain't it a handsome sight w'en he gits it all granded up fo' struttin'!" Looking quickly back at Jules she saw in his eyes a touch of the same brand of merriment.

It was "struttin'," perhaps, she thought resentfully, but obviously it was effective. Hank had made his point. Furthermore, the effect would reach into another class of people, according to Hank. Sending an encouraging smile to Hank, she found his eyes studying her.

As their eyes met he jumped from the cart and came to her, took her hands in both of his, and held them warm and claiming.

"You're my wife." His eyes grew soft as his voice. "My wife, Sweetface, 'n I gotta get a-goin'. I aim to be returnin' afore my son is borned."

Holding his lips so near that the words were felt as much as heard, he whispered, "I ain't one for habit pecks, liken I've tolt you afore, 'n I want you should know this ain't one a' them. I want this kiss should live forever right where I'm gonna leave it, 'n I want it to whisper to you these here words, 'Hank plumb loves you, Sweetface.'" Then just where cheek and ear join, he pressed his lips, gently, sweetly, turned and hurried through the little crowd and climbed into the cart.

Taking the whip from its socket, he flicked Beauty lightly. "Giddap," he clucked. As the horse started, Hank raised his voice in song:

"Work for the night's a-comin',
Work through the sunny noon . . ."

The crowd took up his song, singing with him as long as his strong, clear voice could be heard. Tears shut out the picture of him but she knew he would sing and be gay as long as he was in view, and that as soon as he could no longer be seen, he would open the lawbook on the new rack, strain his eyes to read the small print as Beauty pulled the jogging cart over the rutted roads; knew he would read a paragraph, lift his eyes to see trees and flowers and birds, while his mind readjusted into something meaningful the just-read paragraph. Perhaps he would reach for his dictionary and reframe the law's meaning in some of his own simple but showy words.

She had meant to ask Hank's friends to have some coffee, but they started off for their homes while singing. Only Jenny and Swith and Jules remained, Jules still sitting his horse, his eyes looking down the road where Hank had gone.

A great sigh swelled up from Swith's narrow chest. "Well," he said in a pathetic imitation of Hank, "I gotta git a-goin'."

"No, you ain't," said Jenny flatly. "You gotta git a horse afore you git a-goin'."

"Oh, no!" Swith declared almost frantically. "Why, Jenny, can't you see I can't spend a picayune a' that there money? Not on me! Not for nothin' but the—Cause. I wouldn't spend that money fer a horse!"

"My soul," exclaimed Jules pleasantly, "what money could possibly be too sacred to be spent on a horse?"

"The organization money, sir," said Swith and his big blue eyes and bony face burned with fervor.

"But, Swith," said Jenny, "Hank he said you should oughta travel faster. Hank he said fer you to tell folks how he's a-payin' me just as much cash money as Harry ever made. Hank he said, too, you should oughta tell how he is a-payin' them widows in yonder parishes, too."

"I'll shore tell," said Swith. "I shore will."

"I have a hor . . ." Jules began, then stopped abruptly.

"Mr. Bolduc, sir," said Swith, "was you aimin' to mebbe join up with our organization?"

No hint of a smile was on Jules's face as he answered Swith.

"No," he said, "I never join anything. But thank you just the same, Mr. Dupree."

Flushing with pleasure at being Mr. Dupree to Mr. Jules Bolduc, the little fellow bowed almost formally to Verity, said, "Good-by to you, ma'am," shouldered his gun and started away—with Jenny running after him.

A perverse curiosity prodded Verity.

"Weren't you about to offer Swith a horse?" she asked Jules.

"Yes," he shrugged. "I almost made that mistake."

A grin spread over his face, roguish and merry, then slowly, with a gathering freedom, chuckles rose into splendid laughter. She loved this laugh. It made her feel free; made her feel she could fly through space in one of those airplanes she too rarely saw in the sky. This laugh took her on a swift high flight into pure fun. Fun that had no dark underside.

As his laugh came to a soft, slow landing he leaned from his saddle and said, "For the first time in my life I see that a natural fastidiousness is no hindrance to making strange bedfellows in politics. Do you realize, Verity, my dear," he grinned, "if I had donated a horse, the fanatical and honest Mr. Hannibal Swithers Dupree would have decided it entitled me to a life membership in Hank's organization?"

Sitting erect again on his prancing horse, he lifted his hat to her.

"Well," he laughed, "I have to get going. It seems to be the mode, you know."

His crop flicked a shining bay haunch. The horse stretched his neck forward against his checkrein and took off in a cross-country gallop into the field.

The months passed, not so much in loneliness as in remoteness. Tim and Sophy came often when the sun was out and the roads not too deep in mud. The mud also controlled Jenny's comings, but she came often. Usually she stayed for supper, carefully watching Verity's use of her knife and fork, carefully copying Verity's ways.

"You look purty when you're a-eatin'," she said simply. "Most folks don't. Some looks like hawgs a-rootin', 'n some looks like turkeys a-gobblin'."

She often slapped the twins' hands when at the table and uttered large threats. "Iffen y' don't learn to shovel up yore vittles withen spoons—"

Swith always came straight to her to report whenever he returned home, but he came back only when he felt he had so much money he had to get it in an iron box " 'n bury it good liken the rest."

Jules spent much of his time in Delamore getting acquainted with Harry. Often she wondered just what Jules did to prepare for his first case in court. Word came through Squeeze-nickel, who made trips to Delamore for store supplies, that Harry was fat and happy and swelling with pride over having so grand an attorney.

These days Verity spent much time just sitting by the window looking out on the road. She sat now in the big pillowed chair. The child no longer permitted her to sink into her little low rocker. She even found it hard to sew, and the picture of the pink cardboard baby on the center-board of Hank's cart sometimes floated before her eyes. A little resentment lived in her as she thought of Hank handing out layettes "the min-ute I see a woman a-bulgin'," and not one diaper had he brought into the house. But she quieted this feeling as best she could, thinking she should be grateful to have the freedom to get what she could. And she could have asked for all she wished. She and Selah spent rainy days pad-ding a big clothesbasket with soft new cotton and lining it with blue sateen. Often Verity watched Selah as she built a roaring fire in the stove or moved about cooking and washing and knew with gratitude that in the big black woman she had a real and true friend.

Verity's time drew near and she longed for Hank's strength, longed for a word from him, watched all day from the window for Hank, for Beauty and the cart with the cardboard baby. She began to hate the rains, for her child stirred constantly and Hank could not get over roads with a loaded cart that would sink hub-deep.

Selah eyed her anxiously.

"I is thinkin', Miz Verity," she said as she stared out at the rain, "I is thinkin' usn got ter make sartain shu' usn got all de fixin's fo' pullin' dat baby inter de world. Usn countin' on Miz Peck fo' ter he'p. But, Miz Verity," she hesitated, "las' time I done seed her, she got a misery lak de croup. But iffen she don' git heah, Selah can birth dat baby."

She felt trapped. She should have gone to Delamore where she could have a doctor. But Sophy had midwifed for every birth in the community and she blamed herself for not having the initiative to do what was best. It was the rain and the mud that trapped her. The terrible roads. Black-jack was right. Why hadn't Hank warned her about his wretched coun-try? But she knew she was being unfair. A doctor was just not considered a necessity here.

These uncertain nights Selah slept on the narrow sofa in the kitchen-living room and Verity's bedroom door stayed open, for the stove roared all night, fighting the damp cold. And then one night the world went still, for the rain quit after pouring for thirteen days. In the quiet Verity cried out with the sure knowledge that this was it. As Selah scurried from stove to bed, clucking soothingly and anxiously, fixing hot water, bring-ing Verity a big cork to bite on, saying, "Bite it, honey-chile, 'stead uv yo' lips so's you won't scream. You mak yo'se'f plumb nervous was you ter lay an' listen ter yo' own screamin'." Between other duties she scur-ried into the bedroom with a carefully held little packet.

"Dis heah Granny's new-life chawm. New-life chawm whut usn need now," and with a big safety pin she pinned it inside Verity's gown. "Soon's dat baby holler I takin' dat chawm back, I is."

The baby hollered just as the welcome sun pearled the wetness of the purple morning. She gasped for her first breath and screamed her shiver-ing protest as Selah held her by her feet like a chicken and gave her a slap to let her know she was in the world.

"Ain' it a shame," grinned Selah happily, "usn got ter take a lickin' fo' we can even eat or git a didy. I declah to goodness, baby chile, Selah shu' hates fo' ter smack you down dis-a-way. I declah I does."

Anger flooded Verity and weak tears flooded her pillow. She held her child, a girl, poor little thing. Someday she would go through this and there was no dignity in it at all. Just none at all.

"Anyway," she said half bitterly to Selah, "at last I'm convinced God is a man."

When Verity waked the sun was high and Selah, the crying baby in her arms, was high-stepping and full of song. She sang with a pure delight over having a baby and the choice of song suggested she was more than happy to have a girl, for she sang:

> "Oh, Delilah wuz a woman, fine an' fair,
> Wid a figger sweet, an' dat sartain air;
> Samson wuz a man big an' strong,
> But he don' stay dat way long."

The anger was gone from Verity, leaving only a spent content and an in-tense longing for Hank. She lay on her pillows feeling wispily thin and glad to see Selah's pleasure, but so tired, so tired. As in a dream she watched the big woman dance.

"Yes, Samson wuz a man big an' strong,
But Samson ain' strong very long . . ."

Did she hear footsteps on the porch? Raising herself on an elbow she tried to listen beyond Selah's rhythms.

"No, Samson don' stay big an' strong;
He can't even keep his strong hair long . . ."

The door pushed open softly and Hank and a stranger stood there watching Selah. The trousers of both men were rolled above their knees, their bare legs heavy and black with mud. On Hank's back was his old tarpaulin pack and in his bearded face was that special miracle look. The stranger beside him wore a rain-beaten but still jaunty Fedora which he removed to show thick, taffy hair, straight and sleek. His Oxfords were slung round his neck and his swagger camel's-hair coat was mud covered and limply wet. His eyes took in Selah, then went back to studying Hank's face, intently, as a scientist studies the whirlings of a new germ. Watching him Verity thought him different from all others. Not like Jules, not like Hank, not like anyone she had ever seen. There was something gleaming and sharp about him, something daring, something dizened yet real.

"Snap out of it, man," the stranger said in a voice full and rich but clear as organ tones. "There's your son. There's the son-of-a-Hank that made me walk nineteen miles in the damdest mud in the whole wide world. There he is, already old enough to be out dancing."

As he began to speak, Selah turned. Still grinning, she swayed the baby possessively and tapped a foot.

"Fine time fo' y'all ter be a-comin'," she scolded.

Dropping his pack gently on a chair, Hank held out his arms for the child.

"Gimme my son," he said softly.

"Can't do dat, Mistuh Hank," she laughed, "usn got us a girl."

"Hank," Verity called weakly. He didn't hear. He stood staring down at the crying baby now in his arms. But the stranger heard. The stranger took a gingerly step forward, conscious of muddied feet upon a clean floor. As their eyes met, his red-brown ones opened wide for a fractioned second, and she was grateful for the immaculate whiteness of her bedspread, for the fluffy pinkness of her knit bed jacket, for the loving brushing that Selah had given her hair. The stranger's hand flew up to his own whiskered jaw, his eyes to Hank's face again.

"A girl," Hank repeated over and over. "A girl."

He seemed suddenly to remember his wife's part in this and he turned toward the bedroom. "Sweetface," he said huskily, near tears, "Sweetface, a girl." Walking into Verity's room he stood beside her bed, holding his child and looking down on his wife. A big man filled with wonder and tenderness and great strength. Resentment and weariness and bitterness left her and in their place came a conscious sense of healing and coming wellness.

"You're not disappointed, Hank?" she asked.

"No, sir!" he exclaimed. "Lord God'lmighty allus gives me His best! When was she borned?"

"This morning about five-thirty. Selah was wonderful."

"Sophy not here?"

"Nawsir," said Selah from the doorway, "Miz Peck, she sick."

"Nobody knows yet I got me a daughter?"

"Nawsir, Mistuh Hank, don't nobudy know nuffin' yet."

"Roarin' thunderbolts! I'll blow for 'em!" He started for the outside door, the baby in one arm and with the other hand pulling out his whistle.

"Heah, you," cried Selah, "y'all cain't take dat baby inter de sun. Her eyes ain' ready fo' dat."

"No?" he asked. "Like kittens, huh?"

"No, dey ain' lak no li'l ol' kittens," Selah scolded. "Law, fine baby lak her wid a pappy whut thinks she lak ol' cats! Shame ter y'all, Mistuh Hank."

"Why, you black skinful a' sin," he said happily, "iffen she'd quit squallin' mebbe I could tell was they open." Handing the whistle to the stranger, who stood leaning against the doorjamb absorbing everything, Hank said, "Here, you've seen me blow that there whistle. Go out into the road and see can you blow it long enough 'n loud enough t' be heard yonder."

The whistle sounded shrilly.

At the outer door Hank put a hand over the baby's eyes to shield them.

"Louder," he shouted to the stranger. "Hell, feller, my new-borned girl-child's got better lungs than that."

But a faint shrill sound came back on the cool breeze.

"That's Tim," Hank said. "Blow her some more 'n then you can quit. There'll be folks a-comin' now. Mebbe quite a few." Slipping one of his soiled fingers under the tiny curled fingers of the baby's hand, he looked at it with wonder. "Little girl," he whispered as he walked with her back to Verity's room, "open them eyes a' yoren 'n lookit yore paw. Lookit me, girl, I'm the feller as is gonna do everything in the world for you. Lookit me, girl, I'm the feller as is gonna learn you to fight. I'm the feller as is gonna learn you to pleasure yoreself in the world."

Standing before the bedroom window, he looked out and upward. "I'm purely grateful to You, Lord," he said roundly. With both hands under the child he held her out from him as though for inspection by someone outside. "Here she is, Lord, the girl-child we done helped You to give to this world."

Then in the straightforward tone of one asking a reasonable thing of a trusted friend, he said, "But, Lord, I'm a-askin' You straight for a blessin' on this here girl-child a' mine. I'm a-askin' it, Lord, 'n You allus give me better'n I ask for. Lissen careful, Lord," he raised the baby high like an offering to God, "here she is, Lord, red-faced 'n squallin', 'n I'm a-askin' You, Lord, to show her the pinnacles in this here world, 'n then, Lord, give her strength to get up 'em. 'N don't stint on the strength, Lord, make it enough 'n plenty so's she can have joy in her whilst she a-climbin'. You know, Lord," his tone was reminding and confident, "liken it says in Yore book, 'I lift up m' eyes unto the hills from whence comes m' help.' I'm a-askin' it, Lord, 'n I'm a-thankin' You. I purely am."

Lowering the baby to cuddle her against his breast he whispered to her huskily, "Don' never let the world take the holler outen you. Yore pappy purely loves yore gutty squall. No, sir, baby, don't never let nothin' mute you."

He stood so a second. In the other room, Selah sniffled, the stranger sat by the stove in a painted pine chair, attaining somehow, in spite of its unyielding, straight hardness, an attitude of lounging. But his eyes held the squinted tenseness of seeing a strange and moving sight. As Hank laid the baby in Verity's arm he pulled out his handkerchief, turned his head, and made dabbing motions against his eyes.

"Who is he?" Verity whispered. "Why is a stranger with you?"

"Oh, him! I plumb forgot him. Hey, come here, friend," he called.

The stranger made a helpless motion at his bare, mud-covered feet.

"Don't pay the mud no mind," said Hank. "Come here, 'n get introduced proper t' my wife. Him 'n me," he explained to Verity, "we walked nineteen miles t' get here. I got plumb feared my s—my daughter would get borned afore I could make it. Thirteen days a' rain! Them goddam roads! Beauty was like to pull his heart outen him. So I left him 'n the cart in the barn a' friends. I wanted this here feller t' stay 'n drive Beauty here when the roads dried some'at. But he's a stubborn damn Yankee clear from New York City. A writing fool, he is. Worked his way through a college called Columbia, which he says is a good college. He took journalism, which he says is a high-grade way to get to wash dishes 'n wait tables for a livin'." He grinned and slapped the smiling stranger on the back. "Which is what he was a-doin' when I met him in Loder City."

The stranger took Verity's hand and bowed.

"Verity," said Hank, "meet S. G. Milady."

Hank stepped back and viewed S. G. Milady with the blatant pride of a discoverer.

"I'm a-tellin' you, Sweetface, the feller's a stubborn dang fool but I like him, Sweetface, 'cause he don't see nothin' drab. Iffen it's ugly, b'God it's black; iffen it's pretty, b'God it's pink 'n blue 'n purple."

"Mr. Milady," said Verity, "we're delighted to have you." She looked questioningly at Hank.

"He's workin' for me," cried Hank, delighted with his surprise. "I hired me a college feller for a dollar a day 'n found."

This meant something special. This man was not here to sell pins, pots, and potions. "To—to do what?"

"I'm a recorder of truth, Mrs. Martin," grinned S. G. Milady.

"The hell you say," said Hank, "he's my publicity manager, Verity. Ain't that a somethin'! You know, Sweetface, one a' them there news fellers as works hind-side-to."

A knock on the door sent Selah flying. Moses handed her a handsomely wrapped large, flat package.

"I wuz speakin' over de telephone to de sto' an' Mr. Noady say he guess de baby done come. Mr. Jules in de city but he 'struct me careful fo' ter bring dis soon's I hear. Boy?" he asked.

"Nawsir," Selah replied vehemently. "What usn want wif a nothin' but boy? Usn got us a girl!"

"Das fine," said Moses.

The present from Jules was a magnificently hand-tooled white leather baby book. Verity fingered it with reverence. She knew by its looks that Jules had had it specially made.

Taking his pen from his pocket, S. G. Milady said, "I am a recorder of truth, Mrs. Martin—may I?"

Doubtfully she handed it to him.

"I see some folks a-comin'," Selah called.

The young man opened the book and wrote on the flyleaf. As he finished, Hank picked it up and read:

"A princess is born. The whistles shrill the glad tidings
and the loyal subjects come bearing gifts."

He looked at his new employee and his head side-jerked in a quick cross slant of approval.

"That's shore fine," he beamed. "A princess is born. That's shore fine. Purely makes me a king, don't it?" He grinned.

Young Milady laughed and with mock courtliness swung his hand to his heart and bowed low.

"Your humble recorder of truth, sire," he said.

8

As a result of that trial, Robert Castleberry the Fourth, and Hank Martin, the nobody, became known enemies, for the short-weighing scandal was bared to the public.

But the trial was not held for that cause. No, indeed! It was, perhaps, the strangest trial in the history of our courts; for it tried a dead man for murder and found him not guilty!

The look on Judge Esterbrook's face as he watched Hank's followers pour in was. . . .

"Her name's Azalea," said Hank firmly.

"Her name is Nancy," said Verity. "Nancy—it's a pretty name. So light and happy sounding."

"Nancy—bah! It ain't got no meanin'," replied Hank.

"Name her for her mother," suggested S. G. Milady. He looked up from the pad of paper on which he was writing his eternal notes, his taffy hair taking a deeper shade from the lamp's yellow flame. "There's a name with meaning."

"No." Verity was prepared to be stubborn about it. "It sounds like a responsibility. I just want her to be beautiful and happy."

"Lawsy, Lawsy," grumbled Selah, putting a pile of dishes in the cupboard with much noise and impatience. "W'y you don't name dat chile fo' her pappy? Ev'budy stare in her face w'en she squallin' an' dey says, 'My, my, spit'n image uv her paw!' She ain't. Not 'zactly. Dem cloudy eyes uv hern gon' be lak you, Mistuh Hank, but her haid gon' grow red shines to its black, 'stead uv mos'ly blue, lak you." Wiping her sudsy hands on the dish towel, she walked over to Verity's low chair and looked down at the sleeping baby. "Dat chile's bones is laid some diffrunt fum you, Mistuh Hank, but a'ready she stick out her jaw lak to you w'en she screamin' her wants." She shook her head with decision. "Name her fo' her pappy."

"Well, how you gonna do that!" exclaimed Hank. "Ain't nothin' you can make outen Hank as is fitten for a girl."

"Isn't it true," said S. G. Milady. "No one knows better than I the gruesome suffering which the wrong name can cause."

"Is that a fact?" asked Hank. "Initials ain't no proper way for a writin' feller to sign hisself. What's that S. G. stand for?"

"I squirm as I answer," he grinned ruefully, "but I shall tell the truth, the whole truth, and nothing but the truth. It's Salbert Gregory Milady. So in school the fellows made me answer to Sally Milady."

"God'lmighty," said Hank. "Was yore maw in the throes a' delirium?"

"Nope. It was Father who was delirious. Named me for a proud forebear, one Joaquim Salbert."

"French, huh?"

"French and ghastly," grinned Salbert Milady. "Imagine the effect on me. I, who dreamed of a pen mightier than the sword. A pen that would cut through to the truth to bare to the world the hypocrisies of men."

"Spell that there name," said Hank.

Hank wrote it as it was spelled out for him. "Helluva name," he muttered and studied it. Then suddenly he beamed. "There's yore new name," he crowed. "There it is. With just two strokes a' my pen I done made you a name as is fitten for a writin' man t' live up to."

Turning the paper toward his new friend, Hank gloated, "Cut through, you says. A sword, you says. 'N that's what I made you into. Ain't the meanin' a' that there word a sword?"

Curious, Verity leaned over the table and looked. Hank had struck out the l and the t, then rewritten the name below without them.

"Saber," she read softly. "Saber . . . Saber Milady. Why, that's a wonderful name!"

"Damned if it isn't," the newly christened said. "Hank, you're a genius. Imagine a syndicated column on politics with a copyrighted lead reading CUT OF THE TRUTH BY SABER MILADY." Jumping up he grabbed Hank's hand and slapped him on the back. "Hank, that's great," he grinned. "You can't know what it means to find a name at long last. Darned if I'm not actually going to call it mine, too. Saber, a curved and shining sword!" And to the laughter of Hank and Verity he postured with prancing outward slashings.

"Tch! Tch!" Selah clucked and came to Verity and took the child. "Tch! Tch! Shame to y'all, Mistuh Hank. Namin' a full-growed nothin'-but-man an' dis yere honey-girl 'thout no name a-tall. Nigh 'bout two week ol' an' Selah still hafter say, 'No, ma'am, no, suh, she ain' got no name yit.' An' it nigh 'bout Christmas. Law, law, w'en dem fiahcrackers start dere shootin' fo' ter glorify de Lawd, dis chile gon' have a name. Yes, Lawd." Cuddling the baby, she continued her scolding. "Y'all wuss put ter namin' her dan Mammy wuz namin' me, an' I is de nineteent' chile she done bus' herse'f fer. She feelin' powe'ful bad an' de preacher-man, he read de psalms. 'Whut dat dere Selah you keeps a-sayin'?' Mammy asks. 'Dat lak amen, to de lastes' uv de prayah. It lak sayin' dis am de end,' preacher-man say. An' m' mammy look square at Pappy an' say, 'Dis one am de end, man, an' I ain' funnin'. Selah, man, Selah.' "

Hank roared with laughter and Saber Milady threw back his head and laughed till the tears ran.

"For Selah's sake, Hank, name that female offspring of yours," he laughed.

"I is naming her now," said Selah with dignity. She dipped her free hand in the drinking bucket. "Hit a plumb pity y'all lak yo' pappy, but you is, so I names you Hancy. Hancy. Miz Hancy, das you, honey-girl," and she dripped a few drops from her fingers upon the baby's head.

"Hancy!" Verity exclaimed. "That's hideous."

"No, ma'am, it ain' no wuss 'n Nancy, an' hit got some sense ter it, seem lak," Selah replied.

"Hancy Martin," said Hank softly. "Folks'd shore know she's mine."

"Hancy," repeated Saber, "that's an O.K. name."

"You black skinful a' sin," said Hank, "gimme m' young'un 'n get outen here. You're a-gettin' fresher 'n the mornin' dew."

"Yes, suh, Mistuh Hank," she smiled broadly, "I gives y'all Miz Hancy." Turning to the visitor, she said sternly, "An' you, Mistuh Sabah—don' you be fixin' fo' ter glue yo'se'f inter de chair fo' no big conversationin' wid Mistuh Hank dis night. Miz Verity she lak ter wilt."

She hurried out the back door.

"Correct," said Saber and stood.

"I'll walk a piece with you," said Hank. "Sophy's a-makin' you easy in the shop, ain't she?"

"I live like a medieval prince," he grinned. "A fire in the forge, a bed in the stall, corn pone and chitterlings for breakfast."

But Verity scarcely said good night. She looked at her child. Hancy! The name would stick. She knew it would and she disliked it. Why hadn't she thought to name her a good Quaker name like Prudence? Why hadn't she known that if she wanted it her way she should have said to Hank the instant he came home, "It's a girl and her name is . . ." She sighed. "Her name is Hancy and it's perfectly hideous."

Hank had fixed himself a spot in the barn where he could study his lawbooks undisturbed by the activities of Selah as she cared for Verity and the baby, and after Verity was up he still stayed all hours at the barn, for the baby seemed to keep the house in a turmoil of feeding and crying and washing. There he sat day in and day out reading, reading. Sometimes he rose and strode the barn length reciting in his own words what he learned; sometimes he walked over the meadows, through the stubbled cane fields, and on toward the bayou, waving his arms in gestures as he recited or made fancied speeches to the jury. Sometimes he walked to the manor house to ask once more of Moses if he knew when Jules would return, or where Jules was. Sometimes Saber Milady sat with him and checked on him as he recited, Saber turning page after page, marveling at the accuracy of Hank's memory.

Sometimes they talked all day long. Hank liked to hear the stories Saber told of the political men of the North. There was the fabulous organization, or place, in New York City called Tammany Hall, and he loved the secret plottings about President Harding of which Saber told and Saber lamented his recent death, saying that if all the news hawks whispered was true he should have had to live and face the scandal and if it was not, he should have lived to clear himself.

When the baby slept, Verity longed for Hank's company and so she sometimes sat in the manger or on the haymow ladder listening to all this fine talk. The winter sun came in through the cobwebbed western window high-lighting the right side of Hank's dark face, the left side of Saber's taffy-colored head. Beauty, whom Papa Ribidoux had driven home, munched and whinnied, switched his tail at an occasional winter blowfly. The tarpaulin-covered cart stood loaded and waiting. A little oilstove glowed and sputtered, heating a pot of strong black chicory-coffee and giving out its candlelike odor to blend with the sweetness of hay and the pungency of coffee.

"You know all this here stuff you're a-tellin', Saber, 'r are you makin' up stories?" Hank asked.

"There's a columnist in Washington—a friend of mine—who has the nosiest nose for news ever a reporter was blest with," replied Saber. "He swears he positively has the low-down on it and when he gets proof in the shape of papers he'll spill to right parties." He gulped from his tin cup. "This accidental president we have now, Cal Coolidge, is going to have the nasty job of cleaning up a mess that was made during his own vice-presidency, I guess. Feel sorry for him if he does."

"What kinda feller's this here President Cal Coolidge, anyhow? I can't seem to recollec' nothin' 'bout him."

"Oh, he was raised on a farm in the granite hills of Vermont," Saber replied.

"The hell you say," exclaimed Hank. "Just a hillbilly like to me!" Turning to Verity, enthusiasm burning in his eyes, he said, "You hear that? Mebbe I should oughta decide t' be President. We got a hillbilly in there now 'n Abe Lincoln, he didn't have no better start 'n me."

"One step at a time," laughed Saber. "You're doing all right, Hank. You've done wonders, in fact. You ought to have a radio."

"Yeah," said Hank thoughtfully, "mebbe I oughta. They got a new station down to Crescent City. Stuck now for want a' more money. Reckon it'll be runnin' someday, though."

"Man!" cried Saber, "if I was heading for politics that's what I'd want to own! Think of the power—a radio station! Someday men will talk around the world!"

The look of pouncing came into Hank. His nostrils dilated, his muscles tensed. Leaning forward, he asked softly, "You think it's good as a newspaper—do you?"

"Not quite yet, perhaps," said Saber. "But, after all, usually a paper is only local. A radio broadcast can be taken into a hookup. A man's own voice can be heard over a whole state, over a whole nation."

"Isn't that wonderful!" exclaimed Verity. "Imagine sitting home and hearing a president speak. I wish we had a radio, Hank. It would help a lot when you're gone to have news of the world and music."

"You could have a crystal set," said Saber. "But mostly they're building big sets now that work electrically."

"'N this state ain't got no electricity t' mention outside a' the towns. Rate so goddam high can't nobody have it 'ceptin' the rich. Makes m' blood to boil, b'God, it shore does."

He rose and paced the stall, then turned on Saber, asking intently, "Tell me the truth, feller—is this here state the most backward state in the whole dang country?"

"As I live and breathe, Hank," laughed Saber, "if I hadn't seen this back country I'd never have believed it. The cities and towns look normal. But ten miles out of the cities and the highways are mud ruts. A few are rich and most are—" He shrugged.

"You think folks'd feel they knowed a man jus' from his talkin' on one a' these here radios? 'Thout never even seein' him, I mean. How's these here radios gonna make money?"

Sensing his eagerness, sensing some intent behind his questions, Verity waited.

"Advertising. Nothing like it. And, yes, I think people feel they know a man just by his voice. They feel they know him when they read what he has to say."

"God'lmighty!" Hank's voice rose with excitement. "This is it! This is what I'm gonna do with all that there money."

"What money?" asked Saber.

"The organization's money, a' course," and he slapped Saber on the back. "I'll go get Swith t' dig it all up 'n gimme it."

"But, Hank, it takes more than a few dollars," said Saber as though reasoning with a child.

"Hell, we got some thousands," said Hank proudly. "'N they can all gimme a extry dollar, or mebbe turn in a good part a' their extry cotton money."

A long, low whistle came from Saber and he looked at Hank with the same look he had on the day of his arrival, as a scientist studying the whirlings of a new bug.

The next day Swith brought the money in a wheelbarrow. Not pushing it ahead, but pulling it. He had made himself a beast of burden by means of a crude rope harness about his shoulders and stomach, thus leaving his hands free for his ever-ready rifle. Through the still gummy mud he came, the handles of the wheelbarrow serving as shafts, his sparrow body straining, for the mud made heavy hauling and the money was in numerous boxes of iron and tin, still black with the wet earth out of which he had just dug his treasure. The fund was in one-dollar bills, in silver change, and coppers. It was the exact same money he had received from the rough, calloused hands of the members. Not once had he set foot in a bank to change his sacred treasure into bills of larger denomination.

Through the early morning mist he came like a symbol in Revelations, a little man insisting on keeping his treasure burdensome when it could be light and no less rich. Into the barn he came panting and gasping, but with the worshiping dream in his eyes glowing steady and clear.

Shaking his head in wonder, Saber walked forward and stared down at the boxes.

"Is this the money?"

"Shore is," answered Hank.

Reaching for one of the boxes to heft it, Saber was brought up sharply by Swith's gun.

"Keep yore hands offen that, outlander!" Swith's voice was high and piercing.

"God'lmighty, Swith," exclaimed Hank, "don't be so fiesty. Put that there gun down. Roarin' thunderbolts, you know Saber's a friend a' mine! Why, dang it, Swith, he's my publicity manager, 'n well you know it. Now how much is in them boxes?"

"Seven thousand 'n six hunderd 'n forty-eight dollars there is," he answered with meek pride. Hesitating, he asked pleadingly, "Hank, you shore—you plumb shore you should oughta put that there money where you're a-puttin' it? You was a-sayin' you're a-puttin' the money in a high tower as will send words 'n music into the air. It don't seem t' make no sense." Tears came to his eyes.

"It'd make sense t' you iffen you was to hear my voice a-comin' to you from miles away, wouldn't it, Swith? It'd make sense was you t' hear my voice a-tellin' millions a' people someday t' go to the polls 'n vote for me, wouldn't it? I'll bring you a little box 'bout so big," Hank's hand measured the size in the air, "'n that there little box'll bring the voices a' strange men into yore shack. 'N someday it'll bring mine!"

The little man stared up at Hank, wanting to believe this amazing tale but quite unable to comprehend.

"Aw, hell," said Hank affably, "come on along. Then you'll be a-seein' of yore own sight. We're a-drivin' t' Loder City 'n takin' the train from there."

"A train," Swith said wistfully. "My! But I should oughta be out a-gettin' more members 'n money." He stared at his boxes, torn between two duties; but as he looked at Saber, a stranger and an outlander, decision came. "I'm a-goin'," he said.

"That's the stuff, Swith!" said Hank. "When y' get back you'll be a-tellin' such tall stories you should oughta land me a million members—'r land yoreself in the hoosegow." He laughed. "Saber, lift them there boxes in, 'n lets get a-goin'."

"Not on your tintype, Hank, old boy. That's Swith's job. He puts them and he sits on them all the way." Smiling at Swith, he added, "I can't risk your suspicion, Swith."

Swith looked solemnly at Saber and then after a second he broke into his wide, almost softly sweet smile and Verity knew he was accepting Saber.

"I wish you'd wait until after Christmas—the baby's first Christmas," she said, feeling already lonely.

"Now don't be a-tellin' me," Hank chided, "you're a-thinkin' she's a-goin' t' miss me. Wouldn't s'prise me helluva lot, at that. You'n Hancy comfort yoreselves best y' can, a-knowin' I'm a-layin' a foundation, I am. Well," he turned to Saber and Swith, "hop in, you sloe-foots. God'lmighty, I gotta get a-goin'."

"I've spoken my bread-and-butter pieces before this," said Saber to Verity as he took her hand. "I hope this is the right thing for Hank to do. Thank you for everything, and—" he hesitated, ". . . always remember I am your friend."

"But you're coming back," she exclaimed. "You sound so final."

"I may return, and I may not. It seems to me that I could serve Hank quite as well if I was on a paper. After all, Hank is ten or twelve years from active politics."

"Hah!" snorted Hank. "Ten 'r twelve years! Why, I'm plumb a-goin' t' be governor in half that time!" He picked up the reins and slapped Beauty's rump. "Take care a' yoreself, Sweetface." Turning to Saber who sat in the seat beside him, he said, "Now, talk, Saber. You was a-goin' t' tell me why you felt s' bad when that there Franklin Roosevelt feller got his legs paralyzed lately."

Even as he lifted his hat in farewell salute to Verity, Saber began. "Well, I liked him. I voted for Cox last election. Among other reasons, I thought if Cox died Roosevelt would make a fair president. I always think of those things, but it happened to Harding instead."

"Why would he make a good president?" asked Hank.

"When he was Assistant Secretary of the Navy under Wilson he was largely responsible for the 11-foot subchaser with which we fought enemy submarines so successfully. Also for the remarkable North Sea mine barrage. Now most naval experts thought it a foolish idea. But Roosevelt stuck to it."

"What's that got to do with the makin' a' presidents, for God's sake?"

"Why, hell, Hank, he had an original idea and he stuck to it. He took that idea someplace, someplace where it benefited the people. Now he's done for." His voice came back to Verity above the low moan of the wagon wheels.

"Well, cheer up. Feller ain' never done for 'less his brain quits him. Like's not it don't make no diffrunce t' the world. Nothin' he can do 'at I can't do." Hank's certainty came back to her clear and loud and a tear fell just as Saber howled with glee.

"I believe to heaven you mean it," Saber laughed. "Now listen, Hank, do you honestly think . . ."

She wheeled about and ran into her little house.

"Law, law, Miz Verity, whut de mattah now!" exclaimed Selah.

"Oh, I'm so sick of big words, and big dreams—and big loneliness," she sobbed.

"Dat man goin' off an' it Chris'mus time! But," Selah consoled, "he done lef' usn some fiahcrackers."

"Firecrackers! Wretched heathen notion," she wept. "I want mountains and pine trees and sleds and snow."

"Tch! Tch!" Selah made her comforting sounds but Verity went into her bedroom and wept.

The days went by with a dull aching loneliness, far worse than the days before the baby was born. Then she had waited with nature's own patience, but now she was filled with desires for full living. She longed for new clothes, to go someplace, and she thought with envy of Hank in Crescent City. Her whole being cried for Hank, Hank. Christmas morning she stood on her little porch bogged with loneliness. The distant sounds of firecrackers, the bright warm sun, all were out of keeping with Christmas for her. Only the bare branches of the pecan trees stretched blackly against the sky's green-blue seemed right. So forlorn she was that Selah skittered around with extra hurry simulating excitement, and her voice slid up to a false high.

"Ain' fitten usn not take dat chile t' de house uv de Lawd first Chris'mus she heah. Do y'all good fo' t' go 'mongst folkses." Verity smiled at Selah's decision and accepted it. "I ca'y my honey-Hancy to town, den y'all go ter yo' chu'ch an' I goes ter mine. Usn go heah 'bout peace on dis earf."

All through breakfast preparations Selah muttered her scoldings of the absent Hank.

"Womans bust derese'ves birthin' babies an de mens hides in barns fum de squallin' an' runs away ter mak derese'ves full uv big impo'tance. Um-

ummh! Dat preacher-man I got fo' li'l while, he same way, seem lak. Ain' no man good 'nuf fo' no woman. I knows it. Yas'm, I knows it well. So I askses y'all, Miz Verity, wha' fo' is I eatin' de honey which dat Tape hand me? Huh? I knows dat honey likely got specks in it right now, but I swallers it an' likes it. Um-ummh! I knows dat honey gwine have flies in it bigger'n cows someday. All dat man-handed honey do have." But she was far from depressed by the prospect. She grinned her widest grin. "Yas'm, all dat man-handed honey do have," she giggled. "Tape, he gwine be ter chu'ch dis mo'nin'. An' I is wearin' m' black calico wid de heaps uv red rickrack. All dat wiggly red on black look naughty lak a voodoo dance, it do. I gwine mak dat skinny man's eyes jump right outer his haid w'en I swishes down de aisle."

As Selah danced out the back door to go to her little house Verity's spirits rose. She looked over her own dresses wishing she had something just slightly naughty herself.

They started out feeling rather gay. Selah's dress with the heaps of red rickrack braid was indeed a magnificent sight and her big hips swung with pagan rhythm, making the rich-sounding swishes she so loved. Her many violent-colored cotton petticoats, starched to a paper stiffness, crackled and flounced their clean beauty on the world, for Selah lifted her top skirt high from the dusty road. Carrying the baby she kept a few steps behind Verity as was fitting, chattering amiably most of the time.

Standing on the corner in front of Squeeze-nickel's store, Selah laid the baby in Verity's arms for Verity now must go one way to her church and Selah the other.

"Now you's got de baby's bottle, ain' you?" Selah asked.

As Verity answered, a loud derisive call came from around the store.

"Caw! Caw! White trash! White trash! Caw! Caw!"

Looking about, Verity saw that the little street was empty of people save for themselves, saw anger flare in Selah's face.

"Who dat givin' you de blackbird?" Selah asked.

Verity shrugged and turned with the baby.

"Caw—caw—caw—" The raucous derision was in a young voice. "Caw —caw—you killin' white trash."

A young boy's head and arm flew up from behind Squeeze-nickel's steps and a string of sizzling crackers, their wicks woven together, landed on the baby's woolly blue blanket. Selah screamed as Verity frantically brushed the firecrackers off, frantically beat out the small circular flame in the little blanket. The crackers fell to her feet and she stood, seared by one actual small burn on her ankle, seared by one great burn of fury and defiant humiliation throughout body and brain.

"I gwine kill you fo' shu', white boy!" screamed Selah, and moving with an impossible swiftness for one so big, she leaped to the store steps.

"Selah! Selah! Stop!" cried Verity.

But Selah grabbed the boy and shook him as a dog shakes a rat. He was probably twelve years old, neatly dressed in his Sunday best. Hate looked out of his eyes and between his teeth he managed to utter his derisive "Caw—caw—"

The crackers finished their popping around Verity's feet and grimly she walked to the boy.

"Why did you do it?" she asked coldly. "Answer me. Why?"

"You killed my paw." His screaming answer sounded hiccuppy, for Selah still shook him viciously.

"She ain' never kilt nobudy, you no-'count white boy. I gwine bash you one fo' dat!"

"No, no!" commanded Verity, looking down at the yelling Hancy.

"Your old man killed my paw," screamed the boy.

"What's your name?" Verity asked.

"Saucier," he cried. "Saucier. And you know it. Your horrid old Hank Martin killed my paw."

"He did no such thing. A deputy killed your father," said Verity. "Do you hear me? A deputy killed your father."

"Hank Martin killed him. Mr. Castleberry said so."

"Mr. Castleberry lies," said Verity scathingly. "Come, Selah."

Reluctantly Selah released her hold on the boy. The boy glared at Verity and Selah. "White trash," he hissed. "White trash. Nigger-consortin' white trash."

Grabbing the baby's bottle from Verity's hand Selah made an effort to hit him with it. The nipple came off in her hand and the milk spilled down her dress front.

"Nigger-consortin'!" she muttered furiously. "You is de po' white trash," she called after him. "I gwine fix you. You see. I gwine fix it so's you and yo' widder-maw cain't live in dis town. Iffen yo' maw cain't raise you up no better'n dat she don' git no sorry fum me."

Holding her dress from her she looked down at it angrily. "Dat Saucier fambly gwine be right oncomfo'table time I gits t'rough talkin' come termorra. Cain't nobudy live in dis here town whut so uppity dey can call you white trash, Miz Verity. Naw, sir, not nobudy. Mistuh Squeeze-nickel won't sell 'em nothin', Mistuh Tim won't shod fer 'em. Not airy culla'd man in de whole parish won't plow fer nor hoe fer 'em, time I gets t'rough! Naw, sir," she nodded emphatically, "dem Sauciers—whut's lef' uv dem, is gwine hafter move ter Mistuh Castleberry's town. Dey shu' is. Selah fixin' dat termorra!"

Verity made no answer. Stoically she walked back home. Peace on earth! Where was it? Hank was right. There was much in the world to fight for. But, oh, this killing, this terrible killing! In a way she didn't blame the boy; she had some notion of how he felt. The scathing hate, the derision in his voice! All taken from his elders, of course. Mr. Castleberry said so, did he! Well, if Mr. Castleberry had been honest, Hank would never have had to march on his mills.

Back home, Selah still muttering, Verity rocked Hancy and thought in a cold terror of all the awful things that might have happened. Selah knelt before her, removed the stocking from her burned leg, and ministered to her lovingly. As Selah talked constantly, mentioning the name of almost every villager who would never do "nothin'" for the Saucier family, a great aching lump of hurt settled in Verity's heart.

"Onery mean, onmannerly young'un," Selah stormed. "White trash, dat's whut he is. Law, he wuss dan de turrible po' white folkses. He wuss 'cause he ain' haf ter work hard 'nuf fo' ter git no humbleness an' he ain' rich 'nuf fo' ter have no culla'd mammy ter learn him good manners. De rich quality folkses got good manners. Us culla'd folkses done learn dem propah."

Leaning forward, Verity wanted to thank Selah, to tell her how wonderful she was, how much she thought of her, but she couldn't speak.

It came to her that one of the shocking things about it was to discover that not everyone loved Hank. Mr. Castleberry had seemed a remote sort of enemy, almost like the embodiment of something rather than a man. But in the following days she began to think of him as the Black Skimmer. She had seen a black skimmer in the bayou. Sleek and beautiful he was, swift and sure. And as he beaked the water skimming the small things into himself, his flight was no less fast.

Swith returned a few days after Christmas. He knocked his timid knock, and when Verity answered he asked, "Air y' feelin' all right, Verity? I heered in the town. We plumb gonna blackbird them Sauciers outen town."

"Don't do that, Swith. It wouldn't be right or fair." She was a little appalled. "Probably that poor woman is distracted with worry now."

"Yes, ma'am, she is," said Swith. " 'Cause that there Black Skimmer he ain't done nothin' fer her. Whyn't he keer fer his men's widders liken Hank? Well, it plumb look like he's gonna hafta look out fer her 'cause she ain't gonna find no way t' make no livin' fer that young'un here, she ain't."

"But it's not fair," she protested.

"Yes, ma'am, it is fair," the little man spoke with absolute decision. "Can't nobudy shoot nothin' at Hank's young'un, not even jus' crackers, 'n git away with it." He patted his shiny rifle and put it beside the door. A blissfully happy smile came on his face. "Hank put our money in the tower of words," he said, "an' he needs still more'n we got. My goodness, it's wonderful! It's purely wonderful. Why, I heerd a man talk in Chicagy. That's a town away off from here. The snow is two feet high there he said. My!"

"And where is Hank?" she asked.

"I hadda git back 'n git workin'. Like I said, Hank's gotta have more dollars fer the tower a' words. I come back to Loder City on the train alone," he said, seeming to expect praise for this feat when he expected no praise for tramping through the country alone. "But Hank made me leave my gun in Loder City. It was turrible, 'thouten m' gun."

"I envy you, Swith," she said.

He smiled, very pleased. "You do?"

"Yes. Where's Hank?"

"Him 'n that Saber feller, they stayed fer somethin' 'bout contracts. Hank, he said fer me t' be a-tellin' y'all he's a-makin' a stop fer t' see Spurge, so's t' git some a' the winter catch. 'N then he'll be home. Oughta be here few days arter New Year." Then bracing himself and doing his imitation of Hank, he said, "Well, I gotta git a-goin'." Picking up his gun he went out the door saying, "Don't you be a-feered. Folks here'bouts'll tak right good keer a' you." He smiled his sweet smile and left to search for the dollars Hank needed for his tower of words.

On New Year's day Moses brought word that Jules was in Delamore.

"Mistuh Jules say," said Moses, bowing before her with his fine courtesy, "I is ter tell you an' Mistuh Hank 'at he got evathin' tied up fine fo' ter free dat Disbro."

"Oh, that's wonderful, Moses!" she cried. "That's wonderful!"

"Yes'm, Miz Verity," he smiled. "Mistuh Jules, he telephone me up fum Delamore an' he say special car'ful, he say, 'Tell dem ter be lookin' fo' de papahs fo' ter mak y'all witnesses,' he say."

"When does the case come up?"

"Well, now," Moses was stalled. "Well, now, he say somepin' 'bout calendahs—but—lan' sakes, Miz Verity, I jus' cain't rightly say."

"The subpoenas will say."

"De whut?"

"The papers we have to expect," she replied.

"Yas'm, yas'm. Well, good mornin' t' y'all," and Moses bowed himself out.

The day before the trial and still no Hank. The papers came but Hank did not. Excitement ran high and throughout the parish preparations were made for a gala exodus to Delamore. Lunch baskets were packed, best cotton shirts and best cotton dresses and sunbonnets were washed and ready for donning. Verity went to the manor to telephone Jules in Delamore. His voice came to her smooth and reassuring. As she talked she felt her taut nerves calming.

"We will choose the jury and begin without Hank. It may even prove an asset, Verity, my dear," he said. "If I feel I am losing I can demand a recess until my chief witness is located. Really, it is quite all right. You have no idea where to start looking for him, of course."

"No, I haven't," she said. "I never do have. He went to Crescent City. But that was weeks and weeks ago."

"Hank did not expect the trial quite so soon. You may remember that I first said it would probably be eight months. But I got it set forward. How is the baby? Moses told me it was a girl."

"She's wonderful, Jules."

"And what is her name?"

"Hancy," she said.

"Did you say Nancy?"

"No. I wanted to name her Nancy," she sighed, "but it turned out to be Hancy. H—you know—H as in Hank."

A silence, then, "Yes, yes, of course, H as in Hank."

It was suddenly funny to her. She giggled. "Hideous name, isn't it, Jules?"

"Ah, well, a rose, et cetera. Is she like you, Verity?"

"No, like Hank." And for the first time this fact came to her with a little pang of regret. She thought, she might have been a little like me.

"A feminine version of Hank!" Jules exclaimed and laughed. "I tremble for the next generation! You are starting early?"

"We are all starting in wagons at three in the morning."

"But suppose it rains?"

"Tim and the other weather experts say it will not. Something about smoke and birds, and rings around the moon."

"Very well, my dear. I shall be expecting you."

She hung up the receiver, feeling very excited. At last, something to do, someplace to go. At last she understood how country women could make social gatherings of funerals and births. It was simply a desperate need to eat and laugh with someone for whom you didn't cook every day, someone whose every idea was not known and by familiarity grown dull.

The night was still and black when Tim came for her in the big old wagon. Standing in the doorway of her little home, dressed in her plain blue coat and plain felt hat, a nostalgic memory came to her. She felt again as she had when she left the North to come to this country. Perhaps it was because she wore the same clothes, even the white collar on the blue wool dress was the same. Perhaps it was because she was leaving her baby behind with Selah, as in the North she had left the familiar and dear. Perhaps it was going somewhere without Hank.

"Go 'long wid yer," commanded Selah. "Law, you ain' nussin' dat chile. Selah been stickin' dem bottles inter dat honey-girl's mouf w'en you home. Go 'long now. Miz Jenny should oughta lef' dem boys wid me. Law, dey boun' ter be dre'ful nuisancin', dey is."

She huddled in the wagon bed with the others, chilled by the damp winter night in spite of the blanket Selah tucked around her. As Jenny readjusted herself beside Verity, she noticed Jenny's ragged old dress.

Jenny smiled. "I got my purty dress on underneath for t' keep it clean for Harry t' see."

"Of course," said Verity and patted Jenny's hand.

"Y' think he'll git freed?" Jenny asked quaveringly.

"Of course." But now that the day had come she found she lacked confidence without Hank.

Jenny began to cry. "Oh, why'd'n't Hank come!" she wailed.

"Pshaw," said Sophy comfortably. "Pshaw, now, Jenny, Hank'd be here iffen he knowed. Hank's a-plannin' great things fer us all. Why pshaw, mebbe Hank's heerd somehow, 'n mebbe he's on his way there."

Verity's spirits lifted. News about Hank had a way of traveling grapevine throughout his organization. Almost anybody was likely to tell Hank.

The string of wagons, mostly mule-drawn, jogged over the road, making a queer medley of creaks and groans. When finally the sun came up, so came the spirits. Picayune was the first to feel truly gay. He sang in his pitched, crackly voice:

> "Oh, I got a gal that's big 'n tall,
> 'N her big lips flaps like a red parasol—"

"Here, here," reprimanded Tim, "that ain't fitten. We're a-goin' t' save a man. Bust yore lungs on a righteous song." Tim hawked his throat and began:

> "Onward, Christian soldiers . . ."

The whole line took it up and the singing continued until it was time to open the lunch boxes.

It was nearly eight in the morning and the wagons had just left the rough dirt roads for the one strip of pavement which ran through Delamore's main street. Mule and horse hoofs and iron wagon rims on cement made such sharply different noises that excitement rose in Verity. These were noises of a different world—she hadn't seen a town for so long! She rose and stood back of the wagon seat.

Far ahead and coming toward them at breakneck speed was a smart gray roadster.

"Just lookit that autymobile!" exclaimed Tim, and tightened the reins.

But as the car came to the wagon in the lead it slowed, and the driver looked at the people and came on.

"It's Jules!" cried Verity. She waved and called.

Tim halted his mules, waiting.

"Is Hank in town?" Verity called.

"No. No, he isn't," replied Jules. His face was set in a queer anger. "Is— is Disbro's wife in your wagon, Verity?"

"Yes, here." She took Jenny's hand.

"What's happened? Somethin's happened!" Jenny whispered.

"Yes," said Jules. His fists clenched and his lips looked white and furious. "Mrs. Disbro—your husband has been shot."

"Shot"—"Shot"—"Hey, Harry's been shot!" The words ran from wagon to wagon.

"Kilt?" asked Jenny in an echoy whisper. "You mean kilt?"

As Jules nodded Verity's heart pounded with a frantic demanding—is my life to be made up of killings? Shot—shot—shot! And then her fainting weakness hardened into iciness.

"How?" she demanded harshly.

"The jailer found him just a short while ago. He was sitting in his chair by his cell window. He was shot through the neck by someone outside." Jules turned his head to spare himself the sight of Jenny's great eyes, of Jenny's small body shuddering uncontrollably.

"And no one knows who did it?" Verity asked.

"No." Jules turned to Tim. "Let someone else drive, Tim. You and your wife—can you get in the rumble seat? Verity, you and Mrs. Disbro get in the front seat with me."

"No," said Sophy, "I'll drive 'n keer for the twins. You go, Tim. Where's Harry now, Mr. Bolduc?"

"Madden Brothers, undertaking parlor," he answered. "We'll see you there, Mrs. Peck."

They rode in silence save for Jenny's moans, and as Verity viewed Harry's dead body and his mutilated throat, held Jenny's convulsive body, heard Jenny repeating over and over, " 'N he died in jail just like 's if he was guilty. 'N he only wanted t' keep that deputy from killin' his friends. Mebbe Hank—" The icy thing in her began prodding her brain. Even if Harry's killer was found it still might not clear Harry's name. In a way she knew this wasn't important to the future of Jenny and the twins. They would suffer no stigma in their community. But it was justice. It was justice that Harry should have had a trial and been proved not guilty of malicious murder.

The wagons pulled up outside the funeral parlor and Harry's friends and neighbors came softly in. When Jenny finally wept on Sophy's broad bosom, Verity asked Jules to go into the office and talk with her.

Looking up into his stern, set face, she asked, "Jules, why did this thing happen? I can't understand it! I just can't understand it."

"I'm afraid I do." He walked to the window and stared out at the waiting wagons. When he spoke, a deep sadness was in him. "Who could possibly be back of this save someone connected with Robert? Surely not Robert himself. I refuse to believe it of him—and yet, Hank proved beyond question that his gins were run crookedly. Consistent and perpetual thievery! I can still scarcely credit it. Can a man of Robert's pride, of Robert's understanding, let that be aired?" He mopped his brow. "My taking the case made him more nervous, I suppose. My name also has some weight with the news. And you know, Verity, evidence presented in court can be published without fear of libel." A bitter sardonic grin played on his lips. "You remember the many 'allegeds' that so angered Hank? A paper would not have to allege with court evidence."

"The Black Skimmer," she murmured. She studied Jules intently while the hard icy something in her prodded her brain. It poked and prodded and stirred with a tormenting sharpness and then finally it molded an idea.

"Then we must have the trial just as if Harry were there," she said as though speaking an obvious truth.

Jules's head came up as though jerked by a bit.

"It's impossible! You don't know what you are saying. The man is dead!"

"The court's job is to establish justice," she cried. "Is it justice that he be robbed of his honor just because he is dead? Why can't Harry's honor be tried? Why? That's justice!"

Into Jules's eyes came a soft, almost tear-filled look and he lifted a shaking hand to cover them for an instant.

"Verity," he said softly, "Verity, my dear. If justice, just pure justice, means this much to you—" His hand fell limply to his side. "Poor little girl."

"Oh, where is Hank! And where is that Saber Milady! I'll bet if Hank was here he'd get that trial! I'll bet Hank could talk the judge into holding it!" She glared through tears at Jules. "Are the Black Skimmer's lawyers in town?" Her voice burned the title.

Jules nodded.

"Oh, if Hank was here he'd talk that judge into this trial." Her voice was a low, intense cry for the right and just.

"Perhaps I, too, can talk him into it," said Jules softly. He took her clenched fist in his hand and kissed it. "It may not even be difficult." He smiled crookedly. "I have just remembered that Judge Esterbrook himself has acres and acres of cotton. And Robert owns the nearest gin mill." Dropping her hand as if it were a hot little stone, he turned and hurried to the door. There, he hesitated, and when he faced her he was again the smooth sophisticated man she first had met. "The dear old judge will hem and haw, and say, 'But, Bolduc, my dear sir, it is unheard of! Completely irregular, sir!' But I shall take your point, Verity, my dear. I shall say, 'Quite the contrary, Your Honor. Since when has it been irregular for the courts to determine theft? To restore stolen goods? He who steals my good name, you know. And this man's good name was all he had.' " Suddenly Jules's real laugh, the merry one, broke out. "You are a very dangerous woman. Justice, here I come!" And he was gone with a most un-Jules-like slamming of the door.

She sat in the mortuary office waiting, her body filled with a lax numbness, her mind filled with the words, "Make the judge do it, Jules. Make the judge do it." She was still there sending her plea out to Jules when the door opened.

"Jules?" Her voice was a question and a hope.

"Jules, hell," said Hank. "What for you a-speakin' out 'Jules' liken that?"

"Oh, Hank! Hank!" she cried, and with his coming came the tears. They rolled down her face in a torrent. "Oh, Hank, Harry's dead!"

"Yeah," he answered, almost cautiously, trying to decide whether Harry or Jules was the important subject of the moment. "I heerd a' the trial in Loder City so I hired me a autymobile 'n come here 'n then I heerd 'bout his killin'. Helluva note."

Leaning over the office desk he tipped up her face with one hand, studied her eyes a second, then smiled. "Sweetface," he said softly and touched her cheek. "What for you a-callin' out 'Jules'?" he asked again.

"I'm expecting Jules," she sobbed. "Jules has gone to make the judge hold Harry's trial just the same."

Hank pursed his lips and looked at her quizzically.

"Come agin," he chided. "Harry's dead. Y' said so yoreself."

"That's no reason his honor should die," she flared at him. "In war lots of dead men are awarded medals. I don't see anything strange about it."

"Here, here, Verity," he commanded, "slow down a mite. Slow down, 'n then back up, 'n start plumb at the beginnin'. What you a-meanin'—a trial?"

"Is Saber with you?"

"No, he ain't. He got hisself a job in Crescent City. Stubborn dam Yankee."

"Oh, dear," she wailed, "if we get this trial I want it in the papers without any allegeds."

"God'lmighty, Verity, I'm nigh t' losin' m' patience. Now what you a-talkin' 'bout? A trial for Harry!"

"Just that, Hank. A trial to clear Harry. They had no right to hold him for straight murder in the first place. Jules has gone to persuade the judge."

As she talked, there came into Hank's face that intent, fixed, preying look. His tongue tip moistened his lips.

"God'lmighty," he said softly, "God'lmighty." Then the intent look was slowly replaced by a doubtful, studying look.

"You think Jules can sell the judge on this here notion?"

She nodded.

"So it's old Jules in the field, huh?" and he sighed.

For an instant his words had no meaning for her and she was about to answer when Hank continued. "But I shore didn't think he had it in him, not like to this! Well, Sweetface, it's a great thing anyway y' lookit. This here's one a' them there golden oppertunities! B'God'lmighty, this'll put Hank Martin 'n his organization on the front pages all right, all right. 'N my picture too, 'n the crowd's picture, 'n—yeah, me 'n Jules together. 'N that'll be good—for the organization."

Grabbing the desk telephone he put in his call to Saber. As he replaced the receiver to wait for his ring, he leaned toward her and whispered, "You b'long t' me." Then came his husky, passionate, "Lord save us. Lord save us."

The familiar thrill ran through her. The lovely, familiar thrill, followed by stabbing distaste for herself. Here, in a funeral parlor, with Jenny wracked and sick, and Harry dead and Jules arguing somewhere with a judge. She turned her face from Hank just as the phone rang. As through a fog she heard Hank's monologue.

"Yeah—yeah— Hey, that you, Saber? Lissen, feller, you 'member 'bout Harry Disbro who was in jail? . . . Yeah, well, he's been kilt. . . . Yeah, shot through the neck whilst he's a-settin' by the window in his own goddam jail cell. . . . Yeah, that's right. Now lissen, Saber, Harry's trial was set for t'day. All the folks from Cypress Bend is here 'n lotsa others. . . . No, now lissen careful . . . I'm a-tryin' t' get a trial for Harry anyhow. . . . Why, God'lmighty, his name's got a right t' be cleared, ain't it? Don't the army send medals t' honor the dead? . . . You're dam tootin' it's a story! . . . Hey, Saber, hang on a minute. Be sure 'n hang on, now. . . ." for Hank had just become aware of Jules, who had been standing in the doorway some seconds.

Verity had seen him the instant the door pushed open a crack, seen his glowing, excited eyes take on a blanketed look as he listened to Hank. Now his eyes looked back into Hank's eager ones and told Hank nothing.

"Well," Hank demanded, his hand over the phone's mouthpiece, "do we have that there trial, 'r don't we?"

With eyes still blanketed, his lips smiled sardonically and, Verity thought, with just a hint of ridicule.

The hint of ridicule stung Verity as it had on their wedding day, and yet—and yet— Oh, Hank was obvious with his publicity. Jules had done this thing for her in answer to her cry for some kind of justice and now, somehow, the whole thing would become a morbid carnival for Hank's organization.

"I'm a-askin' you—do we have that there trial 'r don't we?" Hank's voice came out with a tight tenseness.

"We do," replied Jules quietly. "Court convenes and the choosing of the jury begins in exactly forty minutes."

Slowly Hank relaxed. "Ain't that a-somethin'!" he exulted. Then into the telephone he howled to Saber. "Lissen, that there trial's beginnin' in exactly forty minutes. . . . Yeah, start pickin' the jury in forty minutes. . . . Well, likely there'll be some argufyin' amongst the lawyers. Now

lissen, you get a airplane, see. I'll get somebody t' go out to the big
meadow as lays d'rectly north a' the town t' bring you in. . . ."

As Hank went on talking she sat looking first at Hank and then at
Jules, whose clear-cut face now seemed chiseled in stone. Hank slammed
the receiver on its hook, jumped to the door, and down the mortuary
halls he howled to his friends.

"Hey, Tim! Sophy! Jenny! You-all come in here, you hear?"

Their answers came back clearly to Verity.

"It's Hank!"

"Praise the Lord, Hank's come!"

"Glory be t' God, Hank's here!"

They rushed down the hall and jammed into the little office.

"Now lissen, friends," Hank's voice rolled in fine vibrato, "here's what
I'm a-goin' t' do. It ain't fitten that Harry shouldn't have a trial—dead
'r alive. Harry's killin' plumb looks t' be the work a' the Black Skimmer.
Now here's what we're a-goin' t' do. . . ."

But drawn by Jules's eyes, he stopped his big speech for a second. Yes,
it was a full and heavy second before he continued. And in that second
Jules Bolduc and Hank Martin measured each other with the harsh, chill
rule of distrust.

Judge Esterbrook pounded his gavel furiously for quiet, and the clerk
of the court bellowed, "Quiet! The judge wants it quiet!"

In her seat beside Hank, Verity felt Hank's tenseness, felt his discom-
fiture. But she could not tear her eyes from this scene and from Jules to
look at Hank. Jules stood relaxed and at ease before the judge's bench
and had stood so during all the howled objections of the other attorneys.

"Your Honor," cried an attorney for the prosecution, "how can the
trial of Harry Disbro proceed, when the man is admittedly dead? How
can a jury be picked to try a dead man for murder? Why, sir, it is a farce
—a farce. It would make a joke of the law. It would make of this court
a lewd jest, inviting the scorn of the intelligent and the laughter of fools.
Who shall be tried here?"

"Your Honor!" cried Jules, suddenly taut.

Judge Esterbrook looked very doubtful of this whole procedure. His
eyes told clearly that he had no wish to be scorned and laughed at; and
certainly not in behalf of the people who crowded his court right now.
His eyes swept over the crowd and in them Verity saw a definite distaste
for this whole business.

"Your Honor!" Jules's voice commanded Judge Esterbrook's attention.

But as Judge Esterbrook turned to give his attention to Jules, Verity saw
in the judge's face a determination to put an end to this. He opened his
lips to speak, but Jules swept into words of his own.

"Who shall be tried here, you ask, when a man lies already dead?" Jules's voice was low and to Verity it was as if emotion and intellect were yoked and pulling evenly together. "Is it intended that a court of justice shall try the flesh of man? Or is it intended that justice weigh those qualities and acts which make the man? The flesh of the man we still have—it lies out yonder in a coffin. It may still be hung from a gibbet. But the qualities which made the man have been poured into the world for good or for evil. . . .

"Is it then the flesh which justice must weigh? No, it is the validity of honor, of intent, of spirit, and of thought which justice must weigh!

"Was this man valid? Did he pour into the world that which is honorable and meant in his heart for good?

"These are the questions."

The stillness was a tribute to greatness, like the hush one knows on a high mountain when a vastness is seen and felt, and after the awe-bound minute Judge Esterbrook spoke softly and firmly.

"The trial of The People versus Harry Disbro will proceed as scheduled."

9

For a while it looked as if Hank would start as have many poli-
ticians—by raving and ranting against the utility companies
—for he made large threats against Southern Light and Power.
He declared he was bringing suit to force Southern Light and
Power to service all small towns and settlements. And then
suddenly he dropped the entire matter, it seemed. However
. . . .

THE LINE of wagons, now a funeral cortege, began its return trip to the Bend that same night. The trial had proceeded with unbelievable swiftness. The facts about the short-weight scales of the Castleberry gin mills went into the records with quick sureness under the smooth guidance of Jules, while old Judge Esterbrook sucked in on his drooping white mustache and forecast to the worried, frantic prosecutors their defeat with his constant "objection overruled."

Now Harry, in his cheap pine box, murdered, but not guilty of murder by reason of self-defense, rode at the head of the line through the damp, cold night. In the second wagon Verity huddled in her blanket, Jenny's twins on her lap and Jenny's small and shaking body pressed against her.

As the line of wagons started from the mortuary, with the photographer who had accompanied Saber taking his amazing flash shots, Hank took Jenny in his arms and spoke to her earnestly.

"You gotta remember, Jenny, it's a powerful pore heart that don't find nothin' for t' be rejoicin' about. You got lots to be a-rejoicin' for, Jenny girl. Lots." Waving his arms at the crowd and at the staring townspeople he said, "Lookit . . . them's yore friends. Yore young'uns' friends. I'm yore friend, Jenny."

"I'm a-feered," said Jenny simply. "Mebbe someday they'll git you liken Harry. Then what'll me 'n the boys do?"

His eyes opened wide, his nostrils flared with an angry fighting fear.

"Don' you never say that agin, you hear?" he commanded. Straightening, he said tensely and perhaps too loudly, "I got a big job t' do. Harry done his job. Done it good, too. Stands t' reason I should oughta live t' do mine. Liken the Bible says, 'He that hath begun a good work in my name shall see it unto the end.' " He relaxed, for with those words he had reassured himself. "Yeah," he said, turning to Saber, "yeah, that's a good one for y' t' print, Saber, 'cause, b'God'lmighty, it's purely a promise a' the Lord. I'm a-goin' t' divide the riches 'cause there ain't no freedom for the pore now. 'N that's a good work. It purely is."

Jumping up on a wagon, he shouted to his people, "Come on, sing!" And throwing out his arms, he began:

"Must Jesus bear the cross alone,
And all the world go free?"

And as the mule-drawn wagons moved groaningly, the others joined their voices with Hank's in a great and homely chorus:

"No, there's a cross fer everyone,
'N there's a cross fer me. . . ."

Running beside the moving wagon, Saber yelled, "Hey, Hank, thanks a million. It's my first scoop, you know. Papers with my first telephoned story about the Black Skimmer's thievery have probably been on the streets for hours. Morning extras will carry the pictures. I'll send you some copies."

"Send me a thousand copies, Saber," yelled Hank. "You'd be a man withouten a name iffen it wasn't for me." He waved wildly. Turning to his friends in the wagon Hank gloated, "You hear that, Tim? You hear that, Verity? Did y' hear that, Jenny? Harry's shore done a big job in this world, he has. Borned pore 'n dies a-makin' the world know for the first time 'at there's a fight agin the likes a' the Black Skimmers in this world. B'God'lmighty, someday mebbe the whole wide world will raise up 'n wipe out the Black Skimmers."

A thrill of hope ran through Verity. She was electrified for the moment, as were the others. But only for a moment. Then the thoughts that nagged at her all through the trial came back; the thoughts that minimized Jules's performance; the thoughts that minimized the entire procedure. She had scarcely heard the trial for looking first at Jules and then at the judge and thinking, Yes, it is just that Harry be tried. But would there be justice if the attorney was not a Bolduc and the judge did not own cotton? She wished she didn't know about the judge owning cotton, for then she could have believed in justice for justice's sake. She wished Hank had not had Saber fly up. Yet she herself had wanted the story in every paper. How dare she believe there was some big, though subtle, difference between Hank's desire for publicity and her own?

The dam of daze suddenly broke in Jenny and she crumpled under her flood of grief. Verity put an arm around her and held her tight.

"Jenny," said Hank, "Jenny—lissen, Jenny. Don't never salten yore eyes for what's done 'n over. Y' gotta find strength in y' t' fasten onto somethin' that's worth some rejoicin'."

"Later, Hank," said Verity quietly.

"It'll do her good iffen she bawls good 'n long," said Sophy comfortingly. "Ain't she lost her man? She ain't got nothin' but two li'l fellers 'n they shore ain't growed old 'nuf to be no comfort. Let her bawl, Hank."

Hank looked down on Jenny with troubled, studying eyes and Verity knew he was trying to figure out something for Jenny. Holding the sobbing Jenny, Verity seemed again to hear the derisive blackbird, the "ca-aw, ca-aw," of the young Saucier boy. Had Hank begun good work or had he started in the hearts of men a stream of hate? Or was Hank right when he spoke of men like Lincoln? That killing goes with progress, with any kind of war?

The pale winter moon and the pearling banks of clouds rode serenely high, and a wind came from the southwest bearing the smells of river and bayou, and in the chill the people huddled deeper in their wagons and ceased their singing.

They entered Cypress Bend just as the morning dressed the world again in its rich vestments of light and color, and Harry Disbro lay in state in the hitched wagon in front of Tim's shop. The women hustled and the men grouped around Hank listening to his tale about the tower of words. Voices were muted to a proper church hush. Smoke from the forge rose like incense and the air became laden with the fragrances of the living as the chicory brewed and the pone baked.

Jenny sat on an upturned box, little and pale, obediently drinking her hot drink and nibbling at the pone, her eyes constantly upon the twins.

"Now, Jenny, honey, you just gotta eat," Sophy scolded softly. "You ain't put scarce a mouthful int' y' since yestiddy mornin'."

"I'm a-thinkin', Sophy," said Jenny dully, "Harry should oughta mebbe be buried now. Now's a fine time fer his funeral. The deacon's here. Everybudy's here. Ain't many men," some pride came into her, "as has a funeral percession from Delamore t' the Bend."

"There shore ain't, Jenny," Sophy replied. "Sensible, too, it is. He ain't been proper embalmed 'n iffen it was t' turn warm—well, now, whoever could want a finer funeral? I'll tend everythin', honey. I'll send some a' the men off t' fix him a restin' place."

When stomachs were full and they felt able to face another ordeal, Brother Dal Dady climbed into the wagon beside the pine box and spoke the last rites for Harry Disbro. To Brother Dady length and piety were inseparable and when the sun climbed high Sophy whispered irritably to Verity.

"The long-winded say-nothin's plumb a-goin' t' make me cook 'em dinner!" And she hawked her throat loudly to let Deacon Dady know his congregation felt some unrest. Others hawked and coughed and blew, stealthily, as though they regretted these necessities. Brother Dady hesitated, cleared his throat, finished his sentence, and intoned, "Let us pray. . . ."

Verity had been thinking about her baby, wishing she was free to go home to Selah and Hancy and start the business of forgetting. But as she realized everyone present felt the same way, a mingling of guilt and sadness came on her. Not heavily, but inescapably, like some race sin she shared with all men, it was—this need to forget the dead and pick up one's own little round of duties, to scrub a floor, to change a crying baby, to hoe the beans and mix the bread, to love and laugh again.

At home Hank was silent. Verity had expected a glowing recapitulation of the trial, of the trip to Crescent City, but he took his lawbooks and his little oilstove and went to the barn. As he fondled the baby's hand a second and spoke to Selah, his eyes scarcely left Verity's. Was there something hurt and haunted in them? Was it Jenny's words "Mebbe they'll get you liken Harry"? A wave of fear and nausea swept over her. There would be no life at all without Hank. To calm herself she took the baby after Hank left the house. She sat in her little rocker, kissing and cuddling the baby and telling Selah of the trial and the burial, of Mr. Saber's coming in an airplane. At Verity's invitation to sit down Selah went properly to the kitchen end of the room and sat in a straight chair by her worktable. Verity smiled and wondered at the foolish ways of people with their servants. It was quite all right for Selah to hold her baby, to put her strong black arms about her when she was ill, but Selah saw to it that the proprieties were kept. She would not sit in the same "room" with Verity and "look to be a-visitin'."

"Po' li'l Miz Jenny," said Selah, shaking her head in deep sympathy. "Whut she gon' do now, huh? Dat husbin uv hers, he wasn't a-nothin' much, but he de onliest one she got." Then looking sharply at Verity she asked, "An' whut de matta' wid yo' husbin? Mistuh Hank he ain' natcheral. Seem lak he oughta be heah a-struttin' an' a-givin' us a big conversation, it do."

Looking up quickly at Selah, Verity thought, She doesn't miss anything. So she hadn't been imagining. Something was troubling Hank. What to do about Jenny? No, she felt that couldn't be it. Planning to find some way to trace Harry's murderer? But she knew the Delamore police were doing their best. After all, Harry had been shot while under their care. And it wasn't like Hank not to think out loud when home. She hated to admit it, but it looked as if it must be something about Jules.

There was that instant in the mortuary when Hank and Jules had seemed to be measuring each other. What had it meant? During the trial she had decided she must have imagined that look. They had been so friendly. No hint of rift showed in their faces or actions. What had Hank said on their wedding day? "Laugh it off. Allus remember you can kiss their ass today 'cause you're a-plannin' t' kick it tomorrow." A tiny ripple of distaste went through her. Why was she more affected by these words now than she had been then? Had she then thought them just words, spoken defensively, while now she knew them to be a part of his working philosophy?

Rising, she put the baby in her basket and donned her coat while Selah politely busied herself with stove and pans.

Hesitating a second at the door she looked about her little house, at the baby, at Selah, and knew a deep and healing sense of anchorage. It needed only Hank, smiling and talking. She turned toward the barn.

Low clouds made a prism for the setting sun. She breathed deep and looked at the spread of land clothed in lovely lights of lavender and co-balt, of sea blues and purples and reds. The pecans had changed their silhouette since Christmas. Little lumps showed on their branches, prom-ising leaf before long. The fertile stretch of earth was singing its bright green song of spring. From the harrowed fields came the faint reek of ripe manure newly spread, and the yard held the moldy sweetness of last year's leaves dissolving themselves into the earth. The strange earth never wearied of its job of absorbing and making over the old and worn into the new and sweet. Yes, she thought, the ground is the wife of the world. It is the one concerned with saving, with economy, with the bring-ing forth out of the near-nothingness of seed, with the constant renew-ing.

Ruddled by the sun the path to the barn stretched its invitation to her to run down it and do her job of renewing some faith, some sweetness. Oh, yes, she thought, this is wrong. Suppose Hank needed her now. Was it those words of Jenny's? Or was it Jules? She ran down the path.

Pausing at the barn she heard no sound. She tried to open the door softly, but the hinges creaked. Hank lifted his head from his hands and looked at her with eyes that held something of despair, something of fear, and over his face was a shadow of a net. A sharp piercing went through her, a queer terror. Like some fine caught animal he looked. Her eyes flew to the window and she laughed nervously. For there was the net—the sun shining through the cobwebbed window put that net over his head. Running to the window she swiped at the webs with her hand, tearing them down and wiping her hand on her coat. How could such gossamer threads make such coarse shadows? Turning, she faced him and smiled with relief to see him unshadowed in the light.

"They—they made a net over you," she said, feeling a little foolish.

"A net?" he repeated absently. Then, "That's how I'm a-feelin'. Caught."

She slipped her hand into his curled and listless one.

"Caught, darling?" she asked softly. "Caught by what? Oh, Hank—Hank darling—you should have been in the house with me telling me all about the trip to Crescent City."

"Yeah," he said, not moving.

Clasping his hand tightly she said, "Hank, I love you so—I want you to be the finest, most honest man in the world. Be honest with me now, Hank. I'm your wife, your partner. I wait here for you month after month—long, lonely months, Hank." With a soft wistfulness she repeated, "Long, lonely months waiting. Waiting. Please, Hank, don't keep me lonely when you are home."

Lifting her hand he kissed its palm and curled her fingers over the warm spot, and held it tightly, sweetly closed.

"Sweetface," he murmured.

"Was it what Jenny said?"

He shook his head. "No, 'cause there's allus that. I see that after t'day there'll allus be that. I knowed when the men tolt me 'bout the fire-crackers throwed at you 'n Hancy. I'm a-hopin' you ain't a-feared, Sweet-face, 'cause there's a somethin' in me that's gotta go on. Makes no differ-ence what. There's a somethin' drivin' me. Somethin' inside me as whips me all the time, there is."

"But that's good, Hank. That's ambition," she comforted.

"Yeah, but—"

"But what? Tell me."

"It's that dam Jules," he exploded and looked at her searchingly.

She was not surprised. She sat down and waited quietly.

"It's that dam Jules," he repeated. "I knowed he might wake from his sleepwalkin', but, b'God'lmighty, I never knowed he was so good as to argufy a judge into somethin' so diffrunt as a trial liken t' that. I got a dam good notion t' lay off peddlin' 'n learn me all the law there is." Anguish came into his voice, into his whole attitude as he rose and strode back and forth with fists clenched. "There was Jules—him as allus called hisself a spectator a' life tillst I come along. Tillst I come along withen m' bride t' my side. There he was a-struttin' in front a' the jury box, a-makin' a plea—'n a dam fine plea it was, too. Full a' almost hidden sounds 'n almost hidden words. Words y' knowed he meant 'thouten him a-speakin' 'em. Words like such as Lincoln might 'a spoke. Words as was sparse 'n all reined in 'n harnessed. Beautiful 'n movin' they was, 'n me—Hank Martin—a-settin' in the congregation. Me, a-settin' there wordless. Me, a spectator, liken he used t' say he was. I ain't never a-goin' t' be in that there spot agin—never!"

She sat confounded and silent. What a perfect description of Jules's ways and speech—full of almost hidden sounds and almost hidden words.

Hank stopped his pacing and looked at her intently.

"Yeah, reined in 'n harnessed," he said. "Liken you, he is in that."
Then softly, with a heavy cadence of worry or foreboding, he whispered,
placing his hand over his heart, "There's a knowin' somethin' in me. A
knowin' somethin' as my brain won't speak t' me clear 'n plain. I keep
a-fossickin' around for t' find it exactly. It's purely a pity I got such a
need for Jules. In that there funeral parlor Jules looked at me for a
minute liken other rich 'ristocrats do. Like as if I'm a clown, like the Black
Skimmer said. Like as if I ain't fitten for y', Sweetface. Like as if he's
a-studyin' on givin' me a race." He watched her closely. "I'd purely like
t' be shed a' him. I purely would."

"Why, Hank Martin," she cried, "Jules Bolduc has done more for you
than any other one person."

"Yeah," said Hank. "Yeah, 'n I like t' be the one as does the doin'. I
got no complaint agin him bein' full a' learnin'. That's a right smart help
t' me. 'N it's why we come t' Cypress Bend. But a-gettin' a trial for t' try
a dead man! Why, god-damit! Verity, that's purely the kind a' thing as
comes t' my mind. How come Jules t' get such a idea? That's the kind a'
thing as I would be a-thinkin' out."

A queer feeling as if something was going out of her, hissed a message,
It was my idea. No, Hank, you wouldn't have thought of it, but you
could have done it. She suddenly realized that Hank garnered from her
and Saber and Jules and perhaps many others—but was that a fault?
One's ideas went into Hank but came out executed so differently. Jules
had executed her idea of the trial exactly. It was Hank's coming that
made it into a show. Looking at Hank she saw a reflection of the look he
gave Jules. She thought, He may never be really friendly to Jules unless
I set him straight. He'll just use Jules and then . . .

"Why," she said in a small voice, "it was my idea. And Jules laughed
and said, 'Why not? I have just remembered the judge owns acres and
acres of cotton.' "

A vast relief showed in his face.

"What!" he howled. "Owned cotton, huh? Ain't that purely a somethin'! So Jules ain't got that extry-plus git-up-'n-git I was a-thinkin'," he
mused. "So the old judge owns cotton, does he? That purely makes him in
m' debt, it does. Enriched, he is, because a' me. God'lmighty, don't it
beat hell 'at no matter what y' do t' help the pore a feller seems bound t'
be a-helpin' some a' the rich too!" He rubbed his hands together in glee.
"I'll mebbe be a-needin' the judge agin."

He threw back his head and roared with laughter. A dull dislike for
herself set in on Verity's mind, gnawing and mean. She had belittled
Jules to Hank. And yet, it meant so much to Hank. Hank could receive
Jules now with no consciousness of self-doubt. She was miserable.

"Sweetface," said Hank, looking at her with admiration, "Sweetface,
allus you're a-bringin' of gifts as make me more joyous than a young'un

with shoes. Dang if you ain't. I'm fair honin' t' see them papers. There'll be my picture 'n Jules's. Together, more'n likely. 'N that'll be good. That'll make folks set up. 'N what d' you reckon goes on 'bout now in the Castleberry house? B'God'lmighty, ain't I give that Black Skimmer a lickin'!"

Needing to get off the subject now that Hank no longer felt inferior to Jules, she asked, "Where were you all the time? Swith said you went to see Spurge to get their winter catch, that you'd be home soon. But you were weeks."

"I was with Spurge. When I got there Spurge had just got word from the good sisters that the Little Flamingo'd done run off from them. We was some worried. So Spurge 'n me tried t' trail her, startin' from the convent."

"Did you find her?" she asked coldly.

"We heard tell a' her red hair here 'n there but we didn't find her."

"That's good," she said.

"Good!" he exclaimed. "God'lmighty, Verity, Sunny Lou's round fifteen 'n runnin' loose. It shouldn't oughta be. What ails y'? Iffen Hancy was fifteen 'n took int' her head to go a-wanderin', wouldn't y' be a mite upset?"

Somehow, thinking of her as a young thing in relation to her parents put a different light on Sunny Lou, and yet . . .

"What ails y', Verity?"

As he asked the question she flared in anger.

"What ails me, you ask. It's quite all right for you to moan over some slight, or fancied hurt from Jules and make me miserable worrying about you. But if I don't show affectionate concern for that—that little devil who tried to kill me, you ask what ails me! Not that it really matters, I suppose. But have you ever stopped to think how I feel always hearing echoes of how the women fall for you? Like hearing that some woman in some lumber camp thinks you have your own chariot of fire!" Shame blended in her anger. She wished with all her heart to have the words back, unspoken.

But Hank looked at her with a deep amusement and delight.

"Y' dang little pepper pod," he said huskily. "Just when I'm a-thinkin' you're bland 'n sweet as mush 'n 'lasses, y' go peppery. Ain't nothin' pleasures me more 'n t' bite unexpected into pepper." He pulled her to him, ran his lips up her neck to her ear.

"Don't!" she said, wanting to command, but the word came forth only a whisper.

"Jealous, b'God'lmighty!" he gloated. "You're the prettiest blend a' glowworm 'n pepper pod as ever a man was blest with in a wife."

Feeling his lips against her ear, feeling the pulsing warmth of his body brought a longing for love and forgetting. But the knowing little cell in her brain stood aside and talked to her. Yes, it told her, sex is the great narcotic, the universal drug. To know its roseate release we lie, we betray. Against all the rest of her the one little cell fought and she tightened her will and pulled away from him.

"Don't you never pull away from me, Sweetface," he said softly. Then teasingly he quoted, " 'Turn away thine eyes from me for they have overcome me: thy hair is as a flock of goats that appear from Gilead. Thy teeth are as a flock of sheep which go up from the washing, whereof every one . . .' "

"Idiot!" she said, half laughing, half mad. "Solomon was singing of the glory of the church."

"With five hunderd wives he was a-singin' t' the church! Roarin' thunderbolts, I been plumb deceived 'bout that feller's wisdom iffen that's a fact."

He was so sincere in his amazement that laughter came to her, and with it a sort of self-forgiveness.

"It's a fact," she laughed.

"Couldn't nothin' make me believe it," he declared.

She giggled. "It says so, right at the head of the chapters."

"Aw, mudlarks," said Hank disgustedly. "You shouldn't oughta believe them chapter headin's. Some scaredy-calf set out for t' whitewash Solomon. Or mebbe," he grinned, "mebbe the feller had wisdom, after all. The ol' feller was a king. Probably knowed his politics. Probably had hisself a publicity manager 'n they got his words all fixed up for the people. You know, all hottened up for them as like it that-a-way 'n all holied up for others. Well, now I got that figgered out," he sighed with great exaggeration, "I can be a-believin' in his wisdom agin." Placing both his hands at his waist, he folded his flesh inward. "Emptier 'n a hibernatin' bear, I am. What we goin' t' have for supper, y' know?"

"Spice cake," she said.

"Ain't we purely lucky, Sweetface?" he asked. "Think what's afore us just now—spice cake 'n a whole long night!" Taking her hand in his he urged her to hurry up the path, chanting, "Make haste, my beloved, and be thou like to a roe or to a young hart upon the mountains of spices." Sweeping her up into his arms he hurried toward the house. "One thing certain sure I c'n plumb rely on that Selah a-makin' me a cake a' some size. One as could plumb be took for a mountain a' spices."

In his arms she felt almost content. But his very next words filled her with a wretched unease. He exclaimed, "Dang if that ain't Jules a-lookin' out our window. I don't see his horse. He shore didn't just walk over here, did he?"

"Let me down, Hank."

"He should oughta see y' in m' arms, mebbe. I'd like t' be a-carryin' of y' on one a' them silver salvers folks is allus a-talkin' of."

"Yes, roasted, just to your liking, I suppose," she said.

He laughed. "You was concocted just t' my likin' from the beginnin'. Mebbe from the beginnin' a' time."

"From the beginning, maybe," she said, "but life with you is changing me."

"Well, roarin' thunderbolts, you think life with you ain't changin' me?" Then looking into her eyes earnestly, he said, "No—that was just in jest, it was. Ain't nothin' in me t'day I ain't felt a hint of afore. Nothin'! Some things in me is a-growin' 'n some is a-dwindlin'. The one thing as is shore a-growin' is the plumb fine feel I got for you, Sweetface." His pace halted as he spoke, then she felt his fine muscles coil for speed. " 'N now for Jules," he said, trotted to the house, and kicked on the door.

Jules opened it to them. Looking up at him from Hank's arms, she thought again how smooth he was. Like the fine old pieces in his house, carefully wrought and polished to satin finish, instead of to a high bright shine of a lacquer or a speeded-up mechanical buffing.

"Howdy, Jules," said Hank genially. "Shore s'prised us a-seein' you in the window. No horse nor nothin'."

"I was returning from Delamore in the new gray car which cotton bought," he grinned and bowed slightly, "and for which I am, therefore, indebted to you. But something broke just as I reached the village. So I walked."

"Well, so y' got a autymobile now. What the hell good 's it goin' t' do you withen roads liken we got?" He let Verity slip to her feet.

Holding her hand out to Jules, she said, "Thank you for coming, Jules. You'll stay and have supper with us, of course?"

He touched his lips to her hand. "Yes, I will. And thank you, Verity, my dear."

In Hank's eyes there was a laughing acceptance of this rite, and she was grateful that Hank could receive Jules naturally and cordially, but the unease weighed in her heavily as she heard Hank's next words.

"I gotta hand it t' y', Jules, y' shore pulled one as was purely a-somethin.' I didn't never give you yore proper due a' respect, don't seem's though. B'God'lmighty, Jules," he said largely and Verity knew he was baiting Jules, "I didn't never think y' had it in y' to turn such a sizable trick as to argufy a court into doin' a plumb unprecedented thing."

"It was no trick at all," said Jules promptly. "The idea was Verity's and the judge owned cotton." Bending over the baby who lay sleeping in her basket, he lifted a blanket edge and looked at the little face. "This, however, is quite a trick. In fact, I venture to predict she will one day be declared remarkable. Perhaps even unprecedented."

"Oh, Jules, thank you," said Verity huskily. But she wasn't thanking him for the compliment to Hancy. With all her heart she was thanking him for his complete lack of posturing. She realized she had become so used to Hank's taking to himself every little shine, every little glory, that she had thought of it as an attribute of all men. A common trait for women to coddle in them. Jules turned toward her and smiled with a complete knowingness. In the twilight dim, with the fire in the stove showing its bright flickers through the stove-lid rings, like lightning bugs, she knew a memory feel of the night on the knoll and the sweet beauty of meeting a friend.

"Well, let's have some light," said Hank, the wind out of him for the moment. "How the hell c'n y' cook in the dark, Selah? Why'n't y' light a lamp?"

"I ain' a-doin' nuffin 'cep' stirrin', an thinkin', and seein'," said Selah in a musing, singsong chant.

"Hell, you ain't no owl," said Hank and held a fagot to the wick.

"All womans sees some things in de da'k." Her soft rich voice was feathered with laughter. "An' I is lookin' right at fire, I is."

Verity looked at her sharply and Selah began a bustling busyness.

"And a darky woman sees more and farther than any other. Someday I shall add one more legend to the collection about your race," said Jules easily, smiling at Selah. "It will tell the story of the tribe of colored folk who were punished for going to extremes in their ability to see far through the dark. So they have eyes like owls. Eyes which cannot move in their sockets as do human eyes. They must turn their heads to look. No breadth to their vision. It is a very sad affliction."

"Yas suh," mumbled Selah, "yas suh, dat shu' tur'ble. Shu' is."

Verity leaned over the baby to hide her smiles. Hank, lighting the high reflector lamp, said, "I didn't have no notion y' knowed anything 'bout animals 'n birds. 'N I still don't think y' know a helluva lot 'r you'd be a-pointin' out in that there story y' say you're a-goin' t' write that owls hear extry well, which kinda balances their bein' dull-sighted in the daytime 'n havin' no roll to their eyes. Lord God Almighty allus gives a balance."

Jules laughed. It was his true laugh and Verity grew very still enjoying some strange, new inner glow, feeling washed in varicolored lights. Like standing small and awed before a Christmas tree, seeing the reds merging softly with the blues and whites.

"No," said Jules, "I have not your feel for the poetry of nature. The poetry I know is all man-made."

"Y' like poetry, huh?"

"Very much. Certain types, that is. By the way, your friend Saber Milady is almost a poet himself. It is a great art to combine news events with accuracy of description and yet to make it read with beauty."

"Y' mean you've seen the papers! Well, why didn't y' say so? Where are they?" Hank looked eagerly about.

"Over there," said Jules, "under my coat. I thought you would like to see them."

As Hank excitedly unrolled them Jules went on.

"There is one disappointment, however. The Loder City papers carry no story at all about the trial. Saber's employers, though, have done you proud. And the story in the Delamore paper is also rather good. The Sherman papers carry a small story but a good one. You will note Robert announces to the world that he is deeply concerned to find his managers have, apparently, plotted together to cheat both him and the growers throughout the countryside. He is firing each and every one of his managers." He sighed. "Poor devils. Unless Robert finds a way to use them in some capacity where they do not deal with the public, what will become of them? No one will hire them."

"Well, that's their funeral," said Hank, lifting his head from the papers for a second. "Say, ain't that a swell picture a' you 'n me, Jules? This one, here. Lookit, Verity, ain't that a piparoo?"

It was a very good picture and she studied it. The two men stood, hands clasped in congratulation, and clustered around them were the folk of Cypress Bend. An arresting picture. A picture no reader would overlook. And there was a fine picture of Mr. Castleberry, taken, no doubt, from the paper's files. Beneath it was the caption: "Robert J. Castleberry, to whom the witnesses persistently referred as the 'Black Skimmer.'"

In spite of herself, Verity felt a little sorry for him and his beautiful, proud wife. Then she corrected herself, told herself firmly she felt sorry only for his wife. Learning that one's husband is dishonest—that was a blow no woman should have to sustain.

Throughout supper, while Hank talked of the trial and told Jules in unstinted words of praise how great a job he'd done, Verity sat thinking of Mavis Castleberry. For the most part Jules sat silent, not needing to speak, for Hank was in one of "his big conversations," as Selah called them.

And then her attention became sharply focused.

"But you are wrong, Hank. Absolutely wrong," Jules was saying. "You are building in your followers a hope that is foolish to the point of being disastrous."

"What's disastrous about it?" demanded Hank. Then, grinning, he jibed, "It's just what you said. You said, 'What folks want is for the riches to be divided with 'em.'"

"Great God, man," exclaimed Jules, "that was in satire! My contention was that reformers fail because, though they may know what the world needs, they do not offer the people what they want."

"Exactly," shouted Hank. "The people want the riches divided 'n I'm a-offerin' 'em just exactly that."

Jules sat very quiet for a second, then in a reasoning voice he said, "Hank, truly, I have never met any man with a larger degree of potentiality for greatness. You can be a great man. A great leader, Hank."

"Y' hear that, Verity?" Hank beamed. "Ain't I allus tolt y'!" Turning back to Jules, Hank said earnestly, "I'm a-thankin' y' for them words, Jules. I purely am. A-comin' from you, they got banks a' meanin' in 'em. 'N I'm a-thankin' y' 'n I'm a-sayin' t' you, Jules, that I'm appreciatin' of yore aid."

Seeing that Jules was a little taken aback by the sincerity of Hank's speech, she thought how few times he'd seen Hank at his best. They were always sparring. In her heart she thanked Hank for that speech, as she had thanked Jules earlier in the evening.

Again, Jules was silent for a second. He was touched by Hank's acknowledgment.

"I have done you very little good, Hank." Jules's voice held a touch of regret. "And when I think that you have turned my satire into the chief plank of your platform, I have a deep conviction that I have done you great harm."

"Harm!" cried Hank outraged. "Why, I'm a-turnin' that there satire, as you call it, into the greatest, stoutest goddam plank ever a politician put into a platform! Lookit what I done in just over two years! 'N why? Why, 'cause the idea a' makin' the rich divide is the perfect mortar for t' make the poor stick together in a organization! Lookit the money the poorest people on earth is willin' to dig up for t' give t' me. They gotta fossick 'round for t' find them pennies t' make them dollars, 'n don't you never forget it!" His pounding fist made the dishes jump like tiddlywinks.

Is that it? Verity wondered. Is it possible that he doesn't believe in the idea himself, but sees it only as a way to get a following that will take him to power? She dared not think this! She dared not!

"I do not forget it," said Jules after Hank's thumping stopped. "I assure you, I do not forget it. I hear you were able to invest over seven thousand in a radio station."

"I shore as hell did," said Hank. "'N someday you're plumb a-goin' t' hear my voice tellin' thousands 'n thousands that we gotta divide the riches. Just you tell me," Hank demanded pointedly, "what d' you know 'bout being pore? What d' you, Jules Bolduc, care 'bout the pore? You, what's had everythin' this world can give! What d' you know 'bout the feelin'—the sick 'n terrible feelin' that fair comes t' a man's soul when he feels hisself a-shrinkin' t' be a pulin' critter just for the want a' money?"

"Many of the rich have done much to help the poor. It is not impossible to feel compassion. Many a man has cried with Moody, 'Who has given me this sweet, And given my brother dust to eat.'"

Listening to him, feeling the restraint in the man, Verity heard again Hank's description of him. "Full of almost hidden sounds and almost hidden words."

"Aw, mudlarks!" said Hank. "Poetry! Hell, when a people has been

hopeless pore for generations, 'r even strugglin' withen a mite for generations, they want more'n words."

"Quite." Jules's voice became suddenly incisive, and leaning forward
he looked intently at Hank. "I trust you are prepared to give them more?"

Glaring at Jules, Hank jumped to his feet.

"I'll be a-findin' of a way when the time is come," he shouted. "Liken
the Bible says, there's a time 'n season for all things."

Feeling some great drama, some great turning point in her life, Verity
sat with hands clasped tightly, waiting. She felt so bound by ignorance.
She wanted desperately to know enough to help guide Hank.

"Quite right," Jules was saying, pleasantly. "And this is unquestionably
the season for planting the seed of economic unrest. Already the agricultural sections of the country are feeling the result of the war. Already
industry is finding it difficult to give work to labor. It will be far worse
before it is better. There may even be another war before it is better. You
may be the right man to plant that seed. Why, then, Hank, do you not
plant good seed?"

"You ain't a-tellin' me, are y'," asked Hank sarcastically, "that there is
tested, proved, 'n guaranteed seed for the growin' of a perfect economic
plant?"

"No, indeed!" Jules smiled. "But you surely realize, Hank, that if all
riches were divided it would be only a short time until the poor in ability
would again be poor in pocket. You, yourself, are demonstrating this
every day. You are finding a way right now to take from those poorer than
yourself, although you were as poor as the poorest a few years ago." Jules
sighed. "I fear you are planting seed that will grow only unrest, perhaps
even revolution or war. Or perhaps only a nation of perpetual infants."
Looking away from Hank, his eyes met Verity's. There was a sadness in
them. "Or perhaps," he continued softly, "forgive me, Hank—but perhaps
it will only grow the Judas in you—or perhaps in many."

Hank's blenching face tautened, the nostrils flared, making deep lines
to the corners of his narrowed lips.

"Watch yore words, Jules. Not no man calls me the betrayer a' my
Lord."

The rich comity of Jules remained unruffled, save by concern to be
understood. He put a hand on Hank's arm.

"I mean nothing personal. You must believe me. All of us have a little
Judas in us. All of us betray the good in ourselves at times. And every so
often someone makes a spectacular betrayal." Jules was almost pleading.
"This is not easy for me, Hank. I see great things in you—I want you to
have a sound theory to carry you to greatness. Or at least as sound as we
can think out."

Hank sat stonily, tensely quiet. With heart aching, with mind crying for
a right balance, Verity leaned forward and laid her hand on his.

"You are saying to these people, Hank, that we should have a division of the riches," Jules went on, quietly, sincerely. "You have given me the right to speak by saying it is I who am guilty of the idea. I have, therefore, the right to prove myself a fool by falling into the error of all reformers—by saying what I think the world needs." He smiled crookedly. "But you—Hank, you could really be a reformer. A current runs through you that pulls as naturally as gravity. This is a great gift. With this and a theory that, when practiced, would lessen the burdens of men, you can be the greatest man of your generation."

With conscious effort Hank relaxed and pushed back resentment, looked at Jules a long moment, studying him.

"I dunno," said Hank softly, "should I oughta swaller that whole 'r not." As Jules did not answer, Hank asked, "What the hell you tryin' t' say, anyhow, Jules?"

"That you are, perhaps, the right person to set in motion the idea that the time has come for a change in the rules of the money game. A change which will stop this obstructed consumption of goods; make an equalized distribution of opportunity for all classes and therefore a more equalized distribution of money."

"Well, God'lmighty," howled Hank, "what d' y' think I'm a-yellin' for! I'm a-yellin' for exactly that."

"No," said Jules. "You are yelling for division of money."

"And what's the diffrunce? You're plumb turnin' out t' be nothin' but a splitter a' hairs."

"The difference is that one changes the rules so that all must play a fairer game, and the other simply takes—chiefly from the poor themselves. The best that could come from it would be a governmental paternalism which would make us into a nation of weaklings, with leaders thinking only of power and place. Leaders, whose integrity dies little by little with every election, every vote."

Hank strode back and forth in the little room, hands behind him, head forward. Verity could see the steam rising in him, feel the swell of his emotions. She knew he was working up to some high emotional show that would turn things about. Whirling to Jules with the suddenness of an animal springing, Hank said scathingly, "B'God'lmighty, Jules, you come here t' my house in a cloud 'n with a rainbow 'round yore head. For a fact, y' do. Right down t' the part 'bout the little book." He grinned, "But I ain't a-swallerin' y' whole liken as if you was a vision, I ain't." Waving his arms heavenward, and with the tones of a great organ, the natural vibrato of his splendid voice throbbed and pushed at the walls of the little house. "Y' handed me a bunch a' papers one night, 'n I walked the floor, a-tryin' for to understand the meanin'. 'N when I made it into somethin' good I done used it and only good has come a' it, so far 's I can see. You're a-ridin' in a autymobile as is bought withen profits account me.

Black Skimmers was a-swallerin' the cotton 'n the cane, 'n my people was a-grievin' a-thinkin' they lived in the years a' the locust. . . ."

Verity sat spellbound. What was his great quality—this current, as Jules called it?

" 'N now, Jules, you come t' my house liken I said. 'N y' say t' me 'bout the book y' done handed me—you say, 'Take it and eat it up: it shall be in thy mouth sweet as honey but it shall make thy belly bitter.' "

Pausing with the drama of the natural orator, Hank then lowered his voice to a husky whisper.

"But I ain't a-swallerin' y' whole, liken no angel clothed in a cloud, I ain't," he said, and shook his head, emphasizing his wariness. "No, sir. 'N what's more, ain't nobody gonna tell me what's t' be sweet in m' mouth 'n bitter in m' belly."

Finishing, he held his pose and held his audience. After a long minute Jules sighed and rose, holding out his hand to Hank.

"You are not swallowing me whole, Hank," he said, as Hank took his hand. "And, of course, I must reserve the same privilege." Jules smiled cynically. "How are you coming along with your law studies? When I can be of any help along that line, let me know."

Hank beamed, seeming to feel he had won some victory, but Verity thought only that these two were still at variance, that something was wrong.

"I'll be a-seein' of y', Jules, 'n purely grateful I'll be for yore help withen the lawbooks."

Verity was unable to speak. She felt imprisoned, in a strange role of inactive onlooker, impotent. With great effort she rose and walked to the door with Jules, saying no word of good night, only giving him her hand.

Jules looked into her eyes and spoke earnestly.

"I was aware, Verity, of your slight disappointment in Disbro's trial. It would be well," Jules continued, "to remember that in this world there is no such thing as true justice. Usually the best we can procure is a less imperfect justice."

Raising her hand to his lips, he bowed.

"Good night," he said, "and thank you, Hank, for a most interesting evening."

When he was well away from the house, Hank shut the door, clenched his fists. "Goddam that there Jules. Iffen only I didn't need him so dang bad I'd purely be shed a' him! A-comin' here liken the seventh angel . . ."

"Oh, stop!" cried Verity. "That seventh-angel business was your idea! Jules came here because he is your friend. You should listen to his ideas on money. I think Jules was right in lots he said."

"Not no man's gonna tell me what's t' be honey in my mouth 'n bitter in m' belly." He pounded the table. "No, nor call me Judas, neither."

"Oh, Hank!" Her cry held a plea, a despairing plea. "He didn't call you a Judas. Be reasonable. He simply said that each and every one of us have some Judas in us. And we have."

Leaning toward her he asked huskily, almost fearfully, "You feel you got some in you?"

"Yes," she said earnestly. "I have." The odd paleness of shock seeped into Hank's face. Seeming a little weak he put his hand on a chair back and stared at her. "Yes," she said very low, "I guess I have. For instance, right now I'd like to forget your political planks, forget everything and just be in your arms. But I'm your wife and I have to try to make you see the truth. At least I have to be truthful with you. I can't know the truth in the sense of what's good for all men. But I have to tell you what I think is right. And, Hank, I think you're wrong about this money thing and that Jules is right. I see clearly what Jules means. . . ."

"God'lmighty!" said Hank, and throwing his head in that upward and back gesture he howled with laughter. "God'lmighty, Sweetface—y' plumb had me scared, y' did." Then the look of wonder and passion came into him, and touching her cheek with a finger tip, he whispered, "Iffen all the sweet givin' from you t' me is the Judas in y', I'm plumb gonna greet that there Judas withen love 'n kisses. Yes, sir, that's a plumb new picture a' Judas—bein' the sugar 'n spice 'n everythin' nice." Still laughing he picked her up in his arms and sat down with her in the big pillow chair.

Struggling against him she said, "Hank—please—let me say what I want to say. A wife who doesn't try to make her husband see the truth is no wife at all. Now listen to me, Hank—"

" 'N should a wife be all the time a wife?" he grinned. "I plumb crave the Judas in you, Sweetface."

Tears came to her eyes and rolled down her cheeks.

Kissing her wet cheeks he said huskily, "Don't never salten yore eyes . . ."

"This is not done and over with!" she cried. "It's something we'll have to live with all our lives."

Kissing her neck, Hank murmured, "Yeah, ain't it wonderful! Aw, I dunno as Judas is the right name for the givin' in y', after all." Swiping away the tears with his hard, warm hand, he said, his voice almost breaking, "You bet it ain't done 'n over. You bet we're a-goin' t' live withen the likes a' this all our whole lives."

Holding her head against his shoulder, snuggling her and nuzzling his lips against her hair and temple, he gave her the feel of being precious; but her tears would not stop. She had wanted to make a point—make it clear and lucid. But Hank heard only what he wanted to hear. She wished she could be free of this thing that prodded her, wished she could hear only what she wanted to hear. With this wish, she smiled wryly, and silently said to it, "Hello, Judas," and wept anew.

"Can you be a-rememberin' what kind a' kissin' I like long 'bout now?" Hank whispered. "Can y', Sweetface? Spite a' them tears, which is likely only from the strain a' these days. Can y', Sweetface? Could y' long 'bout now be rememberin' 'at I like kissin' with meanin' afore lovin'?"

Oh, the sweetness of this! He gives out warmth like the sun. She rubbed her wet face against his collarless throat, loving the fragrance of his skin, vital and oddly sweet like a handful of springtime earth, like a blend of cypress bark and leaves. Raising her head she put a hand on his cheek and urged his lips to hers. Oh, the sweetness of this. . . .

The sun was high next day when Jenny came. As she entered the house Verity thought, as she looked up from her sewing, that Jenny was almost beautiful. Too terribly thin and worn, haggard from sleeplessness, and yet, there shone in her eyes a new fire. Her body had none of the old look of drooping. The squared erectness of a soldier was in her. She closed the door and stood against it looking at Verity.

Hurrying to her Verity put her arms about her.

"Where are the boys?" she asked.

"I done left Pete 'n Perk to Sophy's house," she said. Then drawing a long breath, she looked squarely at Verity. "I been a-grapplin' withen m'self the whole night. 'N I ain't a-feered no more. I got a notion a' how I c'n earn my keep. Mine 'n the twins'. You're m' friend, ain't y', please, ma'am?"

Knowing this was some great moment for Jenny, some inner triumph, Verity answered, "I am indeed your friend. How can I help you, Jenny?"

Jenny swallowed and said desperately, "Don't you think I be near 'bout 's good 's Swith?"

"Why, of course!"

"Well, there!" She was triumphant. "I c'n do liken Swith does. I c'n git members. I c'n go 'bout the country 'n tell 'bout Hank 'n them Black Skimmers. I c'n do liken Swith does, I tell y'!"

Looking at her, Verity choked up with a tenderness. So little and thin. Underfed her whole life, she had the gaunt look of so many of these people. With many even the eternal sowbelly was a luxury.

"But, Jenny," she said gently, "it would be too hard for you. I don't think Hank would let you."

"I know he won't lessen you help me argy. There should oughta be a way fer me t' do somepin' t' take m' thought offen Harry. To help Hank, who has allus done right by me." She grew almost fiery in her eagerness. "Hank he needs more money for that there radio place. Hank he wants fer t' study the law. 'N he should oughta do it, seems 's though. Hank he'll pay me them dollars, 'n payin' all them there dollars makes it longer 'n longer tillst he c'n get them things. It shouldn't oughta be."

"Jenny, Jenny," Verity said softly. "How fortunate Hank is to have people love him so!"

"Oh," exclaimed Jenny quickly, "I got a heap a' feelin' fer you, too."

"Yes, yes, of course," said Verity. And then she smiled sincerely. "Hank gives you a dream—an object in living."

"That's shore how it is!" cried Jenny. " 'N I gotta earn my keep. I ain't a-feered no more. I'm plumb a-goin' t' fight, I am. Hank's in the barn. I heered him recitin' loud 'n powerful."

"Yes, yes, I know," Verity replied thoughtfully. "I'll go to the barn and talk with Hank about this, Jenny." Opening the door she added, "Fix yourself some coffee, Jenny. Selah's working in her garden."

As she neared the barn, she stopped, listening. Hank was making a plea to an imaginary jury. His voice rolled out emotionally, and Verity smiled with pleasure. She hated to interrupt him, but she opened the door and called out, "Hank."

"Hi, Sweetface," he greeted her, "come on in. Set over there 'n be the jury. You'd shore vote my way, wouldn't y'?" He grinned.

"I sure would," said Verity. "But I came to get you to vote Jenny's way."

"Jenny's way?"

"Jenny's here. And, Hank, she wants to do something for you and I think you should let her do it."

"I ain't a feller as objects t' folks doin' for me," he grinned.

"She wants to travel around like Swith and get members."

"Roarin' thunderbolts! That puny little muffet can't stand that! You crazy? Why, folks'd plumb get the wrong view a' me, they would. Hank Martin a-sendin' out a puny little muffet for t' work for him!"

"Are you through steaming, Hank?" She smiled at him. "You want to get on with your law study, don't you? And I want you to study. I want you to have sound knowledge. Maybe," she became very earnest, "maybe you will find time to study finance. Maybe you'll find time to study many things you should know if you could send out a cartload of wares, by someone you can trust. You could have a cart traveling every parish. You would be entitled to a percentage of their sales and you could have money enough to get through law in double-quick time." She knew she was making some impression on him for the intent look, the about-to-jump look came into his eyes.

"Ain't that a somethin'," he said softly. "Ain't that a somethin'! Jenny, she could do the city a' Delamore. Jenny, she could go to the houses in the town. Delamore's plumb ripe for t' hear more 'bout Hank Martin now. Yes, sir, Jenny could be a-doin' that now 'n some time soon I'll have them wagons in every parish, I will. They'll sort a' be my travelin' representatives. 'N a-makin' their own way withen the wares, too." Glowing with pleasure over the idea, he beamed and rolled out his words like a song of thanks. "Little ol' Jenny a-wantin' t' serve me! Why, there ain't hardly nobody low enough t' be mean t' the little wren! Lord, ain't it wonderful t' be me 'n have folks a-lovin' 'n a-servin' me! Lord, ain't it wonderful t' be me!"

Walking back to the house with Hank expanding on the virtues of this plan, a captain in every parish someday soon, selling goods for him, extolling his virtues when he should run for office, getting members, making money for him to invest in things that would promote the great idea—her heart grew stout with faith in him, faith in all he would do, in all he would learn. For, as he said, it was truly wonderful to be Hank Martin and have people serving and loving him.

As he opened the door, Jenny turned facing him, her shoulders squared, a little fighty look overlaying her lifetime of meek acceptance.

"Jenny, Jenny!" cried Hank jubilantly.

But seeming to misinterpret him, Jenny shook a measuring spoon in the air and her voice cracked with determination. "I'm a-goin' t' do it, Hank! I'm a-goin' t' earn m' keep! Mine 'n the boys'! 'N please don't you say me no."

"Why, hell, Jenny, I ain't a-sayin' y' no. Verity gimme yore plea 'n I'm a-sayin' you yes. Why, b'God'lmighty, I'm plumb a-makin' you a organizer for me. A political organizer, you are, Jenny, from this minute on." He looked surprised by his own words. "Why, roarin' thunderbolts, I betcha you're the first damn female political organizer in the whole United States, I betcha!"

"Oh," gasped Jenny. "Oh—oh—" and she threw herself into Hank's arms and sobbed convulsively.

"There, there," Hank soothed, "there, there, Jenny, girl. I'll shore try t' make up for Harry. There, there."

Verity turned her back on them. Poor little Jenny, she thought, she worships him. Hank is her god. Crossing to the window she looked out at her oak tree and at the knoll. Oh, Jules, just over there, beyond the screening knoll, do you see what Hank is? What Hank has? Do you see that it is wonderful to be Hank? He has the kindling power, great big and special—he can kindle a dream, he can.

Eighteen months slipped by, eighteen months filled with a fine sense of progress and a dear security, for Hank was home more than he had ever been. For four months now he had been home constantly save for short trips to Delamore to help Jenny or to speak to a group. Hank liked Verity to go with him, but she was again pregnant and the wagon ride sickened her.

Hank studied constantly, long hours that were a miracle of concentration, and he was a little thin, a little haggard. In him burned a fire, a hot, wild urgency to be done with this studying of law, to take his examinations and be on with the business of acquiring some greatness, some money to put in the "right places." Time after time, as Jules reviewed him on the law, he proved his amazing memory, and Verity took especial pride and delight in seeing the admiration on Jules's face.

Along with law Hank studied all he could about utilities, concentrating on electricity. Dozens of times she had sat patiently listening to his "big conversations" about the radios, the kind that plugged into electric sockets, and how were his people to hear him if they had no electricity? He wasn't thinking especially about the real countryfolk. They who knew him would vote right if they could get to the polls—if it didn't rain. But the poor in the towns and the small cities—how would they be swayed? He hadn't had the time to put in years on developing their friendship. But the rates —the terrible electric rates. The small townsfolk felt they could put up with the inconvenience of lamps for quite a spell.

"Yes, sir, Verity," Hank had said time and again, "I'm purely gonna hafta arrange for some friend in one a' the towns to bring suit agin the electric company. Somethin' as will make all my members notice electricity. Why, that goddam Southern Light 'n Power Company has got a franchise, they have. A franchise, mind you, what gives 'em the right to be the only 'lectric company in these here parts. That there franchise plumb guarantees 'em immunity, it does, from any competition whatsoever. Can't nobody else have a 'lectric company! Ain't that a helluva note! 'N here's Cypress Bend withouten no 'lectric plant, nor no wires from some other town nor nothin'. Town after town ain't got no 'lectricity whatsomever! 'N me withen a part ownership in a radio station! Iffen that ain't somethin' for t' make my blood boil! Why, God'lmighty, iffen there was 'lectricity them radios is bound t' be sold—who ain't a-goin' t' do withouten his sowbelly t' bring the world into his parlor? Iffen there was 'lectricity in all these here little towns 'n settlements likely we could be a-gettin' higher pay for the advertisin' time on my radio station, too. Yes, sir, that there company ain't a-givin' the right service t' the country settlements, they ain't. I gotta get hold a' that there company's franchise 'n see what they guarantee the people in exchange for such a great privilege. No competition! Helluva note!"

He spent most of his time in the barn studying, for when Hancy was awake he could do little. The toddler clung constantly to his knees, and if she brought him one of her toys to admire, a string of spools, a can lid, her tobacco-box wagon, and he did not give her instant attention, she lifted her dark curly head, glared resentfully, jutted her baby jaw, and jumped up and down in a demand for his attention. Always vastly amused by this he exclaimed, "You're purely yore Hank's young'un, you are!" He refused to curb her, but he kept himself out of the house, refusing also to be annoyed when he was not in the mood for it.

When he got copies of the Southern Light and Power franchise, he studied them and restudied them. Walking the barn in the daytime, walking the house at night. For weeks he had read the articles of franchise over and over, looking up in his books the complete meaning of each and every phrase, hunting a hidden snag. For weeks Verity lay alone in her bed until almost morning, often wakened by the second baby's kicking, or by the tread of Hank's feet, by the thump of fist on table, by the sound of stove lids as he put wood on the fire. One such night in early fall she was wakened by a loud exultant yowl, and Hank bounced into the bedroom.

"Verity, Verity, get up 'n fetch that black skinful a' sin for t' fix breakfast! I gotta get a-goin'. I got it, Verity!" He spoke through his teeth in a sort of sizzle of anticipation and raised a clenched fist in triumphant gesture. "I got it! I tell y' I got it!"

"What?" asked Verity, a little foggily, pulling on a warm robe. "Got what?"

"Lookit, Verity, lookit." He waved a sheaf of papers at her. "Right here in these here franchise papers it says plain 'n clear that the company guarantees t' service the communities accordin' t' the laws a' the state 'n the needs a' the people 'n industries. That's the guarantee the goddam corporation hadda give the state."

As she looked blankly at him, he roared with self-delight and ran back to the table on which were spread many huge books. Pounding one he cried, "It's right here—it's right here what the laws a' the state are," pounding another book, "and there's the precedent for it! God'lmighty, I purely got them rich bastards withen their britches down! I'm purely gonna give all the folks in the country 'lectricity 'r, b'God'lmighty, there ain't gonna be no more company!"

"What?" she cried, half frightened by the wild glee in him. "What? Explain it to me, Hank."

Grinning with appreciation of his own cunning, he said, "There's a old law, Verity, one as was made in the time when gaslights was brand new. It ain't never been repealed, nor nothin'. It still stands, b'God'lmighty! It still stands. 'N the law governin' a 'company givin' light to a town, countryside, or community must, in order to keep their franchise, supply light to any community within the territory serviced by them should one-tenth of the population petition the servicing company or corporation for light.' " Throwing back his head, he roared with laughter. "I got them bastards. Surer'n all hell, I got 'em." Picking up another book, he went on, " 'N right here is a case agin the gaslight company. Ten per cent a' the folks a' Beulah, a little settlement just outside Crescent City, done asked for gaslights. 'N since they was in the territory included in the franchise the law ruled the company hadda give it! Oh, Lord, ain't You good t' me!" he cried jubilantly, "ain't it wonderful how Y' allus gimme Yore best!" Turning on Verity, he demanded, "Rejoice with me, Sweetface. Rejoice with me!"

The full meaning of all this was slowly dawning on her. "I think I understand," she said. "You're going to get ten per cent of the people in each settlement and town to sign a petition asking for light, agreeing to pay their rates, and the company will have to do it. Is that right?"

"Good girl," he beamed, "good girl! Y' bet yore life that's right. 'N I'm a-startin' this mornin' for to get them petitions. After I eat I'll plumb catch Jules afore he takes off for his mornin' ride, afore he goes out t' look at the cotton 'n cane. Jules'll make sure the petition is drawed perfect. B'God'lmighty, I bet y' I surprise old Jules with my findin' a' this. Goddam, I knowed I could find one a' them there loopholes a' the law, was I t' look long enough 'n hard enough. I'll sign ten per cent a' the households too, just t' be sure it can't be interpreted that-a-way. Get Selah now, get everythin' ready for me whilst I harness up. That Light 'n Power Company's purely gonna get the s'prise a' their lives when I bring suit. They purely are. Been a-chargin' such damn high rates 'at only the most prosperous a' folks c'n pleasure theirselves by a-playin' God, by a-pushin' of a button, 'n a-sayin', 'Let there be light.' " And laughing, with no sign of weariness from the many long nights and days of study, he left the house for the barn, chuckling, "I'm purely gonna change that. The pore shall say along withen the rich, 'Let there be light.' A mite more liken to gods they'll be!"

She stood on the little porch watching him as he strode to the barn, loving the great vitality of him, adoring his love of the people. He would make them a little more like gods! Suddenly she needed a last moment with him before Selah should be with them in the kitchen, needed to touch him, to tell him how wonderful he was to her, how sweet had been these months with him at home. Knowing that when he "hadda get a-goin' " it might be a long, long time before he would be home again. She ran clumsily after him, for the child was heavy within her.

"Hank," she called, "Hank."

Turning, he stood still, watching her. Not coming to her, but just seeming to like the sight of her. A softness came into his face to blend with the jubilant scheming.

"Sweetface," he said, "ain't nothin' more beautiful than you in that there long yeller wool thing y' got on, withen yore yeller hair a-streamin', withen the bulge a' my young'un in y'. Stand still, Sweetface."

She stopped and stood still in the early morning light.

"Hank," she said softly, "don't stay away from home too long. Not even to make people a mite more like gods. The baby will be coming and—oh—"

"I know," he said. "Allus when I'm a-leavin' I plumb hate m'self for the hours I ain't spent alongside a' you, when I could 'a. A-seein' you there, the sky behind y', withen you so golden yeller, 'n the sun a-shovin' a streak a' gold into the sky—purely a golden image y' look t' be. 'N yore idolater I'd like t' be this minute." He shook his head and a whimsical smile came to his lips. "Purely gulled I am by a thing as lives inside me. A thing as is all time caterwaulin' that I gotta get a-goin'; that I gotta hurry 'n get t' be a somebody." He sighed. "A golden image, 'n plumb pinioned t' the sky, y' look t' be. 'N I'll be a-rememberin' of you just that-a-way." Then, as if impelled by honest insight, he added heavily, "Least-ways, I'll be a-rememberin' when I ain't a-hearin' the caterwaulin'."

After another second he turned, his head went forward; into his whole body came the eager, forward bend of a woods creature on the scent, and swiftly, lightly, he trotted to the barn.

10

It was about this time that Hank Martin developed into a great orator. No orator ever drew crowds who traveled such distances, under such adverse conditions. They came on mules, wagons, and on foot. They poured out of the back remote sections of hill country and swamplands.

Yes, it was about this time that Hank toured his state setting up a huge old circus tent—a circus tent, but with a high platform in one end from which he spoke with the emotional and passional fervor of the evangelist, exhorting his hearers to come forward to sign a card of membership, to leave a dollar with Jenny Disbro.

He went through the land, a one-man circus, crying like a prophet of old, "There is a generation. . . ."

So GREAT was her loneliness after Hank's departure that her heart seemed as heavy as her child-burdened body. Her spirits did not lift and soar in fanciful thinking as before Hancy was born. Only the great patience of nature saved her, the patient waiting combined with the feel of remoteness. For months she lived in the barricade with no word, no message from Hank. As her time for deliverance drew near she longed for him, longed for his strength, grew weak and pale knowing a strange need for his strength, the touch of his hand, the warmth of him. Night after night she waked to tears, and after Selah took to sleeping in the outer room, she suffered trying to restrain her sobs. Her friends worried over her, and Sophy came each day to see whether she would be needed. Selah rolled her great eyes and watched Verity closely, never leaving Hancy in the house when she worked in the garden, for Hancy wore her mother out.

One hot day as Verity sat in the big chair by the open window which looked out on the road and the garden, she saw Selah take one of Hancy's hands and slap it smartly.

"Selah done tell you no. Y'all done pull up a plant. Y'all got ter learn ter mind, chile."

As Hancy screamed and wept with anger, Verity smiled. Bless Selah. Just then Selah looked back at the house and seeing Verity, she took up the screaming, kicking child in her arms and came to the house.

Verity knew something was going to be settled here and now. Wondering what was bothering her, Verity said, "You look as though something were worrying you."

"Yas'm. Dere is."

"Well, before we go into anything else, spank that child. She has a terrible temper."

"Dat's what I got on m' min'," beamed Selah, vastly relieved. "I was gwine ast y'all wuz usn nevah gwine correck dis chile lak Mistuh Hank."

"Mister Hank doesn't have to deal with her all the time. He just goes away," said Verity.

"Yas'm, he shu' do. You shu' speaks de truf, sugar," said Selah. She put the screaming Hancy over her knee and paddled her, talking all the while. "You near'bout two year ol' now, Hancy-honey. Y'all cain't go on lak dis! Law, time you ten you be debbil 'n sulphur ter live wid. I declah you a somepin'!"

Squirming off Selah's lap, Hancy ran out the open door, calling, "Hank! Hank! Hank!"

The two women looked at each other in surprise and amusement.

"Law, dat chile's firs' word a-callin' her pappy!" laughed Selah.

Verity watched the chubby baby figure toddling down the steps, her little pink dress standing straight out from her shoulders, and as Hancy looked back at her mother something about her expression was so like Hank that Verity's heart was wrung. It was then the sharp ripping pain came. Crying out, she looked at Selah, feeling terror and weakness.

"Lawd a-mercy!" exclaimed Selah, "heah we is agin. I is blowin' de whistle dis time." And grabbing the whistle from its nail by the door she ran out to the road and blew blast after blast. Small and thin the answer came, and Selah blew again and again, then listened. Hearing the second answer she ran back into the house.

"Miz Peck be comin' soon now," she said breathlessly. "Come on, now, honey, we git you in yo' bed, den I git dat Hancy penned up, so's she won' be a-trippin' me up. Law, dat chile de most in-de-wayest chile evah I did see. Dat chile jes' certain shu' de whole worl' done been made jes' fo' her." Laughing with a nervous robustness, she added, "Whut us gwine do w'en us got two lak dat, huh? Um-uummph! Ain't dat gwine be a somepin'."

But Selah's constant chatter could not take Verity's attention. Hearing her, she still did not seem actually to hear. She was in a nightmare of pain. This was not as it should be. The second baby was supposed to be easier. She told herself that it was all because she now knew what a mess she was in for. Why, then, this weakness? Why could she not muster her courage and fight? But some dreadful inertia was in her.

She lay in her bed responding only to pain and to longing for Hank. A queer near-unconsciousness came on her. She heard everything, felt the tearing pains, felt as if she could not speak if she really wanted to. But her mind seemed to float above her body, held by some invisible string, like a floating kite tied to a post. She knew when Sophy came, heard Selah's tear-choked voice, felt Sophy's sure and practiced hands, heard Sophy command Selah to blow the whistle again and to blow it frantically, again and again, so that Tim would come and some others, perhaps. Lying there in her chains of torture and weakness, she knew when the first answer to the whistle came. The kite of her mind knew it was Jules and tried to say "Thank you, Jules," but no words traveled down the kite string to her lips.

"Mistuh Jules, Mistuh Jules!" cried Selah, "Miz Verity's baby, it ain' a-comin' right!"

"I'll bring my doctor from Delamore." Jules's voice trembled and Verity wanted to speak. "Thank God for that car! What word from Mister Hank, Selah? Where is he? Can I send for him?"

"Who know where-at dat man is!" Selah exclaimed in disgust.

"But—" Jules hesitated, "surely he will be here any minute— Or is this child before its time?"

"Nawsir! Dis chile right on time. Mistuh Hank, he know, he do. Mistuh Hank, he likely habin' a big conversation with folkses. Ain' neva heah w'en usn needs him."

Without comment Jules hurried away.

Verity's kite mind was ashamed and hurt and appreciated Sophy's scolding of Selah.

"My land, Selah, y'all plumb got a heap a' nerve t' be a-sayin' of things liken t' that to Mister Bolduc. Hank'd be here iffen he could."

"Yas'm, might be. Mebbe so. Seem mo' lak mebbe not." Then exploding fiercely as she laid a hand on Verity's brow, "Dat man ain' neva 'round w'en she cain't be no woman-use, seem lak. Fo' Gawd, dat man done time his visits lak de moon."

The delicate kite mind cringed and she made a valiant effort to cry out in shame and protest, but no part of her stirred.

"I plumb got a notion t' slap you down," stormed Sophy. "Don't you never let me ner nobody else ketch you a-sayin' the likes a' that agin."

"Slide me ovah dat basin col' watah, please, ma'am," said Selah, giving no sign of having heard Sophy.

"The very idea," Sophy continued scolding, "the very idea. Bitin' the hand that feeds y'. Why, Hank Martin's purely the lovin'est husband ever I seed. Ain't scarce airy woman in the state but what'd—" She stopped abruptly.

"Uh-huh," said Selah, "das whut I means. Dat man shu' speaks some purty words. He shu' do."

Into the kite mind came a queer mixture of knowledge. It was knowledge but it was so mixed. Someday she would remember to sort it out and look at it, and she would remember to give Selah the dressing down of her life. Yes, she was very angry with Selah. Maybe she was mad enough to be a Simon Legree. Maybe she would whip Selah because Selah had owl eyes. Yes, that was why she would whip Selah. Selah had owl eyes. Selah saw too far in the dark. It was a very sad affliction, just as Jules said.

A loud knock at the door startled her floaty mind like some warning that it must be very acute now, and so it was gratified by its own smartness when it heard Saber's voice.

Selah rose and looked through the doorway at him.

"Mistuh Sabah," called Selah, and Sophy said, "Why, Mister Milady!"

"Mistuh Sabah," Selah called again. "Come in heah, please, suh. Usn gittin' 'nother baby, but Miz Verity, she dyin' seem lak. Dat baby don't kick no mo'. She don' kick no mo'. Jes' lay heah."

How funny, the kite mind thought, how very funny. Dying? Why, I was never so smart in my life, never so free. Why, I know everything, I feel everything, and my heavy body doesn't matter any more.

"Isn't Hank home, Selah?" asked Saber, and his voice rang so clear and yet so full, like lightning full of thunder.

"No, sir, he ain't. How come you heah?"

"I heard you were expecting a new baby here. And remembering Hancy's birth—well, I'll wait in the village. Hank will surely come soon."

"Yes, yes," said Verity's kite mind. "Hank will come soon," and she wouldn't whip Selah because she had owl eyes, for Selah's owl eyes were crying the biggest tears in the whole world.

"My baby heah, she plumb want dat man," Selah wept; "cain't nobody mak her ter hear 'em. But I bet she heah Mistuh Hank. Oh, Mistuh Sabah, why you didn' bring him wid y'all dis time? Whut dat nuthin'-but-man doin' so big 'n long, I wantses ter know!"

"He's doing something remarkable to get electricity."

"'Lectricity, is it?" sobbed Selah. "De light uv life gittin' blowed out uv her 'n dat man chasin' 'lectricity. Fo' Gawd, Mistuh Sabah, Miz Verity ain' gwine live iffen somepin' don't happen. Mistuh Jules, he gone fo' de doctah."

Her wonderful kite mind flew out the window to see if Hank was coming down the road. Hank was doing something wonderful about electricity; Hank was catching all the lightning bugs in the world and hanging them from tree to tree in Cypress Bend and when Hank kissed her they all turned on their lights. But when Hank lifted his lips from hers they all went out and Cypress Bend was in the dark again, and Hank threw back his head and laughed and laughed and laughed. It was the gayest time she'd ever had! It was so gay—so gay—

Opening her eyes she looked on a world of beauty. Her little white room was dimmed to the sun, but though the shade was low she saw it was early morning, for the flowers and grass and leaves all doubled their splendor with dew and the sun gave a light of magnificent whiteness throwing shadows of deep, deep shade. Life pulsed in her faintly and she remembered she had been sick. Why, she'd had a baby! She was thin, thin, light-feeling and thin. But there was another cot in her room. A strange cot and a strange woman on it.

"Selah," she called, but her voice was very small.

"Glory be ter Gawd," came Selah's voice, and Selah, in a voluminous nightgown of outing flannel, came running in from the next room, and the strange woman sat up in the cot and smiled at her.

"Miz Verity! Glory be ter Gawd!" Tears brimmed out on Selah's cheeks.

"Well, we've done it," said the strange woman.

"Yas'm, glory be ter Gawd!" Selah repeated.

"Where's the baby?" the small voice asked. It struck Verity as funny. She felt so strong and sure until she moved or until she spoke, then everything turned out to be weak and small.

"Baby!" exclaimed Selah, as if she had never heard the word before.

"Boy or girl?" It took great effort to ask it.

The strange woman held Verity's wrist, taking her pulse. Selah gave the woman a scared look.

"I think we better tell her," said the woman. "I'm your nurse, Mrs. Martin. You've been very sick. Your baby—didn't live."

"No!" said Verity, feeling stubborn about it. "No, I won't have it!" But the look in Selah's face told her it was true. A year of her life wasted and no little son to show for it. A weight of self-blame settled on her. She should have known she hadn't been feeling right. A child should come into the world with its mother knowing the glory of giving of herself, her body, and her time. She had failed this child as Hank had failed her when she needed his strength. But she should not have needed his strength so much. It was wrong. Her job had been to think of the child, not give herself to moods, to need of Hank's strength. Shuddering with the bitterness of her loss and failure, she turned her head to the wall as the tears came. I am not well now, she told herself, but I will be better. I must be better. And when I am well I will be strong—strong. I will be strong of heart and strong of spirit. I will never again—so help me God—I will never again fail another because I am crying for strength from Hank. Never.

Her fists clenched feebly, but she knew her mind clenched this thought with determination. I will never fail another because I am sunk in my own need. Though the tears rolled uncontrollably, she knew she would, sometime later, try to think this thing out.

She had lain unconscious for four days, and through the weeks of convalescence her mind churned with the emotions about her lost son—for it had been a son—a delicate blond-haired boy, Selah said. She felt she had sacrificed something of herself, something of her mother, by not bringing this child to life.

And where was Hank now? It wasn't like him not to come. Why, when Hancy was born he had come in spite of everything. Had something dreadful happened to Hank? Was he dead—like Harry? Sometimes she concluded he must be and the fever would burn again, terrifying Selah and the nurse. If she hadn't been having a baby she wouldn't have worried about his absence. Hank had been gone from home for longer periods than this. Oh, Hank, where are you? What's happened to you? Are you dead, like my son?

But under Selah's loving scoldings she improved and as she grew stronger she remembered her determination never to fail another because of her own need. Daily she braced herself to chat with friends, to put on a brave front when Jules came, to remind Selah to correct or spank Hancy. Hancy was so cute with her Hanklike ways, for Hancy could be beguiling and demanding. Each new word of Hancy's gave her a small, sweet pleasure and Verity reminded herself anew that she had much to live for.

Now, five weeks later, she sat dressed in the same old blue coat and the same blue wool dress with the trim white collar. She was waiting for Jules, who had asked her to attend the syruping which was to be that evening in the plant that he had just built. It was a sort of dedication, he told her. A community project. Everyone was welcome to use it and he had the equipment with which to can the syrup for sale.

It had taken some insistence on Selah's part to make Verity go. "It do you good, Miz Verity," Selah insisted. "Law, how dis Bend gwine hab a pa'ty an' y'all not dere! It ain' gwine feel lak no pa'ty iffen you not dere. Mistuh Jules depend on you. Evabody depend on you. I is dependin' on you. I plumb lookin' fo'ward t' seein' dis yere pa'ty. An' I ain' gwine go unlessen you is gwine, too," she added, cunningly.

So Verity had promised, and Selah left with Hancy.

Now, alone in the house, Verity heard a car. She rose, breathed deep, brought a smile to her lips, and went to the door, tensing each muscle of body and face. This, she thought, was what was meant by girding the loins for strength. Every atom of her wanted to collapse into weeping.

"Jules?" she called out to the man who was getting out of the car.

"It's I, Saber," the voice answered. As he came out of the car's shadow she saw his rakish silhouette, the hat at a dashing angle, loose-swinging swagger coat. Vaulting up on the little porch, he took both her hands in his. "You are well, again," he said in his ringing, incisive voice.

"Yes," she said, forcing herself to smile.

"I know," he said softly. "Hard to believe your baby—and Hank's—didn't live."

"Yes," she said. This talk of death struck cold terror to her heart. Bracing herself, she asked, "Hank? Oh, Saber, where is Hank? Do you know?"

"You mean you haven't seen nor heard from Hank since the baby— Well, something truly amazing must have happened to him!" He shook his head.

"Oh— Oh—" she moaned.

Putting his hands on her shoulders, he shook her gently. "Hank's well," he said. "At least he was yesterday. He has been in Crescent City and avoided me. But—" He stopped abruptly as Verity sank into a chair, weeping with weak relief.

"Oh, Saber," she sobbed, "I've thought him dead—like Harry."

"Far from it!" He was almost contemptuous but checked himself. "Don't cry, Verity. Please don't cry."

"What brings you here, Saber?" She dried her eyes and tried to remember her resolve to be strong.

"I have to see Hank. I'll never know until I see Hank."

"Know what? What's Hank been doing? What's happened?"

"I'm not sure," he said. "Hank went all through six parishes, village by village, settlement by settlement, getting folks to sign for electricity. He also went to Sherman, took the bar exams. He passed the highest grade they have seen in Sherman in years on end. Then he drew up his papers to sue the Southern Light and Power for service in all those villages. The company was petrified. They invited Hank to talk the matter over. He came to Crescent City. He left Crescent City. The suit is dropped." Leaning forward, he asked tensely, "What do you make of that, Verity?"

"That's not like Hank," she cried. "Hank's a fighter. They couldn't scare him off!"

"Exactly," said Saber, dropping into a chair. "They couldn't *scare* him off." The emphasis on scare startled her. She looked at him sharply but he lounged wearily. Looking sleepy and bland, he asked, "May I wait here for him, Verity? Those roads! They are all Hank says and more. Buckshot, they call this dried earth. Cannon ball would be nearer the truth. I'm tired out, Verity. I swear I don't see how Hank stands it. A wagon is worse than a car. A wagon's slower but a car's springs and tires should make up for that. Where were you going?"

"Jules—Jules Bolduc, you know—has built a small syrup plant for the use of the community. Everyone for miles around will be there tonight. A sort of dedication. Jules is coming for me. But if Hank is coming—"

Saber sat up straight and looked at her in surprise.

"Good Lord, you wouldn't stay home from the only shindig that has come off in ages just in case—just in case, mind—that the great attorney, Hank Martin, may deign to come home for a few hours?"

"What makes you so sarcastic tonight?" she asked, taking off her coat.

"Lord God'lmighty always gives Hank the best," said Saber in a good imitation of Hank at his largest. Then, shaking his head, "You're most frightfully thin, Verity."

"I'll fix you some coffee and eggs. I know you're hungry. There's no place to eat between here and Loder City, is there?" She was so happy! Hank was coming home! Hank was well—Hank was well. The stove sang it and the lamps sang it. The fat in the skillet sang it and the teakettle took up the song.

Saber jumped to the door when footsteps sounded, but his face fell when he saw it was Jules.

"Good evening, Mr. Milady," said Jules.

"Happy to see you again, Mr. Bolduc," said Saber as they shook hands.

"I would have sworn you were disappointed," laughed Jules.

"He's waiting for Hank," said Verity happily. "He says Hank will be home any minute."

"Yes. Yes, he will. I came loaded with that news myself. I am late, due to a phone call from Crescent City, and . . ." He hesitated, seeming troubled, looked anxiously at Saber, then, forcing a smile, he said to Verity, "The moon is very bright tonight. And I would swear I saw the outline of Hank's wagon down the road. That high centerboard, you know."

"Oh," she cried softly, "oh, Jules—"

Saber started for the door but Jules stayed him. Holding Verity's coat for her, he said, "Meet him at the gate, my dear."

Dear Jules, he gives me my moment alone with Hank, and clutching the coat about her shoulders she walked slowly out and down the path to the gate. Two wagons came down the road, but the centerboard with its pink baby stood high in the moonlight. Clearly she heard Hank's voice talking to some folk from the Bend who were hauling their cane to the syruping.

"God'lmighty." Hank's voice held startled concern. "God'lmighty! 'N my wife?"

"She's might' nigh well, I hear tell, Hank," a man's voice drawled.

"God'lmighty," and this time it was a prayer of thanks.

Standing in the shadows, she waited until the other wagon went on as Hank called out, "Tell everybody they'll be a-seein' of me this night iffen my wife is fine agin. Tell 'em all howdy."

"I'll shore be a-doin' that," the man answered and cracked his whip at his mules.

Looking over the two cars, Hank cursed heartily under his breath. "God-dam. Iffen it ain't that Jules agin." He did not go to the barn, but tied Beauty at the gate.

"Hank," she called softly. "Hank!" Running to him, she threw herself into his arms. "Oh, Hank, I've been so scared!"

Holding her, smoothing her hair, kissing her temples, her neck, her cheek, he said softly, "I know 'bout the boy 'n 'bout you. Perkins just tolt me. Likely y' think I failed y', Sweetface. But afore God, I had a thing t' do. I confess t' you now I was a-listenin' t' the caterwaulin'. I just couldn't deefen myself to it." He sighed heavily. "I hadda come home withen real steps made for t' git myself up the first mound toward them pinnacles. I hadda be able t' bring y' 'n the young'uns—'n Hancy, I mean —I hadda be able t' say t' you, Sweetface, that we're a-goin' up, that we're on our way. . . . You're a-shiverin'. Here." Opening the full new over-coat he wore, he wrapped it around her, folding her inside it, close against him. "There, there. The little boy's gone. Don't never salten yore eyes for what's done 'n over. It's a pore heart 'at don't find nothin' for t' be re-joicin' over. 'N we ain't pore, b'God'lmighty!"

The security of his arms, the warmth of his hard body, the earth-sweet smell of him was tonic to her after the weeks of fear for him.

"I'm rejoicing," she whispered. "I'm rejoicing. Because, you see, I thought you might be dead. I thought sure you'd come when the baby w—" She stopped, not wanting to speak of that again.

"I had a thing t' do," he said. "I just couldn't deefen myself to the callin' 'n the drivin' inside a' me, seems 's though. Purely gulled I was tillst I was a-comin' home 'n then happiness come on me. 'N now," he whispered huskily, "now I got a plumb rare happiness. A happiness I sometimes get withen you, Sweetface, 'n no place else. A happiness as is plumb shot full a' churchy peace, it is."

A silence came on them, a natural and unifying silence, and her grate-ful heart sent out its thanks into the still, bright night.

After a few moments he asked, "Jules is here, I see. 'N who else?"

"Saber," she said.

"Saber?" He seemed suddenly wary, lifting his head, looking toward the house like a hound scenting up wind.

"He came just a few minutes ago."

"Come on," he said, and loosening his arms started for the house.

Nearing the porch, Jules's voice came to them clearly.

"But what good will it do you to know?" he asked.

"What good!" cried Saber. "What good! What good are freedom of speech and freedom of the press if no one speaks or writes the truth?" Outrage rang in his every word. "It is the business of newspapers to print the truth."

"I fear you are idealistic," said Jules with smooth cynicism. "The busi-ness of newspapers is to print the facts. There is a great difference between the facts and the truth."

Bounding up the steps, Hank entered, saying, "Good old Jules, allus a-argufyin'. Howdy, Saber." Shaking hands with the men, he went on, "Now go ahead, Jules. For oncet I'm likely t' be agreein' with y'."

"Yes, go on, Bolduc," said Saber, and the sharp glittering quality was in him. "It's a difference which, as a newspaperman, I should know."

"Glad to see you home, Hank," said Jules, then, turning to Saber who was studying Hank through narrowed eyes, he went on. "Applied to people a fact is the obvious or known act. A truth is sometimes the unknown act combined with the motive or the qualities of the heart and mind." Verity's mind came to attention. Turning from the stove, she looked at Jules. He seemed interested only in the abstract idea. But at just that instant he looked into Verity's eyes and continued, "As in music, so in man, the hidden consecutives must be taken into account if you are to know the worth of the score."

"Hidden consecutives—" she murmured.

"You're not clear, Bolduc," said Saber.

Hank removed his new overcoat and caressed its soft wool as he laid it over a chair. Verity became astonishingly aware that he wore a new suit of bright blue hue, a shirt of lavender silk, a tie of blended purples and blues and yellows.

"He shore ain't clear," said Hank. "You bein' deep, Jules, or just muddy?"

Jules smiled slightly, his eyes still on Verity's. "The hidden consecutives in music are the notes which are not apparent, not written. You do not see them and they are not played. They are the unheard notes between chords which show to the knowing musician the connection or transition from one chord to another." A hint of earnestness came into his voice, and still looking directly in Verity's eyes he said, "I repeat, it is the hidden consecutives that tell the truth."

It is the hidden consecutives that tell the truth. She mulled this thought a second. How true, she thought. Oh, how terribly true. There was a second of silence, silence filled with an apprehensive waiting for fate.

"Then I want both the truth and the facts of this case," Saber's voice snapped like a cracking whip. "Hank—"

Hank whirled. "You a-talkin' t' me in that there tone a' voice?" he demanded.

"I'm asking you, Hank, for the truth—and also the facts—about this Southern Light and Power deal you've just pulled," said Saber in a voice somewhat softer. "You went all over the country. You had those robbers by the seat of the pants. You could have put electricity through all these towns. You could have done your followers a service. You went to see the executives, you called off the suit. Why?"

"Why?" repeated Hank innocently. Too innocently, Verity thought. "Because it would 'a ruint the company 'n what the hell would a lotta them folks want withen 'lectricity anyways? I got t' figurin' I'd plumb sold my people a raw bill a' goods. They signed them there papers 'cause I asked 'em to, not 'cause they wanted t' pay for 'lectricity."

"But you didn't think of that angle until fifty thousand dollars rested in your hand," said Saber softly, almost musingly.

"What you a-sayin'?" demanded Hank tensely. "Why, Goddam the snoopin', condemnin' reporter 'at y' are! You're plumb jumpin' t' that there notion 'thouten ary shred a' proof. Not ary shred. You prove that damit, afore y' put any a' your rumors 'n allegeds in yore paper. You prove that there accusation." Shaking his fists toward both Saber and heaven, he said, "I got a good notion t' sue you for defamin' me afore my family 'n best friend."

In her terrified realization of this accusation, Verity, feeling in a whirl between three strange forces, turned from Hank to Saber to Jules. A smile of admiration played lightly on Jules's lips. Not a smile of approbation but of admiration for a performance.

"Do that, Hank," said Saber. "I dare you. That would be the perfect way to air the matter. And anyway, your wife should know it and your friend already knew it. I happen to know that the treasurer of the company is an old friend of Bolduc's and that Bolduc has something of his own cooking."

"Do you know this," asked Jules, "or were you only told it?"

"I know it all right, but I can't prove it in black and white." There was hard, cutting denunciation in every word of Saber's. "Hank, you stirred a real affection in me. I looked on you as a rare person. A man capable of great, almost all-inclusive love for your fellow men." Hank stopped his pacing, waiting for the next words. Jules sat unmoving, the small smile still on his lips. Seeing them all, feeling the crosscurrents of these men, looking at Hank's beloved face, aware of the new silk shirt, of the new suit, handsome despite its gaudy color, seeing his nostrils flare and whiten as they etched lines of bitterness down to his lips, she thought how dear he was. Had he really been bought? Had he really roused his people to love and dreams only to use them? To sell them out when it met his needs? When it profited him?

"Divide the riches," Saber jeered. "I had thought you a true idealist. And you are just the usual politician. And to think you stirred belief in me. You—"

As Saber's voice trailed, Verity spoke. To her own ears her voice was the voice of Lula May pleading for one she loved.

"He kindles a dream—" she said.

Hank strode to her and looked down at her intently. Jules looked at her sharply.

"Yes," said Saber, "I guess that's about it."

"B'God'lmighty," howled Hank, "iffen I kindle a dream I'll make 'em come true. Why, t' see you three a body'd think I was plumb givin' up tryin' t' do for folks." Turning fiercely on Saber, he declared, "You'll live t' see the day when all them smooth, velvet-gloved, silk-voiced dodo birds in Washington'll plumb be a-copyin' my methods."

Saber rose, his whole bearing and expression screaming disdain.

"You copied them first, Hank," he said with heavy cynicism.

Hank's doubled fist swung at Saber, but Saber dodged, his swagger coat swinging in impertinent upward flips. Then, almost slowly, he walked to the door, opened it. "Forgive me, Verity," he said. Turning toward Hank, he spoke again, the cynicism mixed this time with a wistful regret. "I suppose it is no reflection on you that you are so like the majority of politicians in your manner of accomplishing. After all, I've been a news hawk only a few years—but I'm learning. Ah, yes, Saber Milady, recorder of truth, is fast becoming Saber Milady, recorder of provable facts. All the truths seem to be off the record." His mouth pulled in a downward grin. "But, Hank, I thank you for my name. It will give me the courage to cut off a political head when the chance comes. Good night, all." And he swung through the door.

With noticeable effort Hank forced a grin. He opened the door and went out on the little porch, shouting affably, "Saber, y' dang hothead, y' ain't got no call t' be thinkin' 'bout loppin' my head. You 'n me are friends!"

Verity was startled by Saber's cynical laugh, by the words which came back mingled with the whir of the car's starter.

" 'Oh, sure, allus remember,' " Saber laughed, " 'you can kiss their ass today 'cause you're plannin' to kick it tomorra!' "

These words, in Hank's own accents, must also have stunned Hank. He stood some seconds watching Saber's car down the road while a tumult of emotions ran through Verity. One thought after another, separate yet together, like a pack of hounds after the red, red fox. The fox was the flame of her love and every other thought chased it, chased it, hounded it, hounded it, bayed its threat. Yes, her love was a fox trying cunningly to escape the pack. Raising her harried eyes to Jules, she murmured, "He says he is always gulled by something that lives inside him, driving him, whipping him to get going, to be a somebody—" Here she was pleading for him—for understanding! The concern in Jules's eyes brought her up short. I resolved I would never let anyone down because of my own need. How can I live up to that? Saber loved him, thousands love him. Can I help them to keep their belief—their dream?

As Hank entered he looked from one to the other a trifle uncertainly, then he shook his head whimsically.

"That Saber!" he exclaimed. " 'N I plumb had a feelin' for the feller. Why, I give that feller his name. Ain't that right, Sweetface? Stuck for a decent name he was, 'n I made him into a curved sword."

"Not a boomerang, Hank?" asked Jules.

Hank grinned. "Dang if it don't plumb look that-a-way. Found him a-washin' dishes, brung him home, give him his first scoop. 'N he turns on me."

Verity sat silent, wanting only to hear Hank tell the truth about this thing.

"Creating great love in others creates also great responsibilities," said Jules, as though the evening had been usual and pleasant and the talk only a discussion of generalities. As Hank poured himself coffee and cut a large hunk of cake, Jules continued, "It was well expressed by the ancients in the story of Diomed who acquired great glory in the Trojan War, became greatly loved and revered. He was capable of creating so much love and faith that he was pushed by it to power. But the sense of power went to his head. He became overzealous, so that, when he met Venus, goddess of love, in battle, he wounded her. Diomed had received great gifts and honors. Statues were erected to him all over the country, but when the first calamity befell the people, they remembered his offense against Venus and killed him."

Hank put down his cake, leaned over the table toward Jules, who appeared mild and professorial.

"The ancients had great wisdom," Jules concluded.

"Yeah," said Hank softly, "yeah. Diomed, huh? How d' y' spell that there name, Jules?"

"D-i-o-m-e-d."

Sitting back in his chair, Hank fingered a bit of cake into crumbs.

"Pore devil," said Hank huskily. "So all that there Diomed's work went for nothin'. Ain't that the way of it, though! Feller works hisself nigh 'bout t' death for folks 'n most of 'em ain't worth a dang."

After one surprised look Jules chuckled sardonically. Hank looked at him with a hurt expression.

"Think I done took the inverted view agin, don't y', Jules?" Sighing, he said, "Mebbe I have. 'N mebbe I ain't. Venus shouldn't oughta never meet a warrior in battle. Ain't no place for a goddess a' love. 'N Venus purely expected too much a' nothin' but a warrior, seem 's though. I hold that there Diomed a' yoren got a right raw deal."

"Perhaps you are right," Jules said softly. "And perhaps not. By the way, Hank, congratulations on passing the bar. I hear you made a most remarkable showing."

Hank beamed.

"Yeah, God'lmighty, I coulda done that there examination months ago, I could. D'you know, Verity, I went through that there thing just 's fast 's I could read. Roarin' thunderbolts, I didn't never even have t' stop 'n wonder out a thing!"

"That's marvelous, Hank," she said. She was pleased, and yet her voice sounded merely dutiful. As Hank told Jules some of the questions asked in the examination, just one question ran in her mind—Had he been bought?

"Shall we go over to the party?" asked Jules. "How do you feel, Verity? Has the evening been too much for you? She has been very sick."

"Yeah, I know," said Hank and put his hand over hers. Oh, the welcome warmth, the strength! "Yeah—" The fierce, tameless quality of him flared through his words of love and faith as he said, low and urgently, "I've tolt y', Verity, how I had a thing t' do. I hadda git us a good-size start t'ward bein' a somebody 'n the Lord God'lmighty allus gives me His best. 'N iffen He gives me His best He has gotta give it t' you, too. Forget the son we ain't got 'n think on the girl we have got. 'N all else we got. It's times liken t' this that we should oughta be a-rememberin' them words 'It is vain for to rise up early, to set up late, for to eat the bread a' sorrows.' "

Her fingers pressed his hand in grateful response. She smiled. "Let's go," she said. "Selah will begin to worry. She's already there with Hancy."

"What d' y' know," said Hank, "I didn't never miss 'em hardly!" As he blew out the lamp, he said, almost to himself, "Too bad we ain't goin' t' have that there 'lectricity, kinda."

"Oh, we will have it shortly, I hope," said Jules. "Something has to be done for the agricultural sections of the country. Electricity would make possible small canning and freezing factories in the country sections. And that would make new crops profitable. I sometimes think that civilization has once more reached the place where it is threatened. When there is an adverse balance of trade between agriculture and industry there has always been either war or insolvency. It behooves everyone to work toward solving this problem before it is too late."

As they left the house and seated themselves in Jules's car, Hank asked, "How's a feller to work for that?"

"Well, you're interested in seeing money redistributed," said Jules, "and so am I. Research proves—to me, at least—that one of our troubles is centralized power both of government and finance. And another is the rates of interest. Agriculture cannot afford to pay more than three per cent, while industry can afford six per cent. But all through the Middle West and the South, farmers, planters, and cattle ranchers are paying six per cent and often eight and sometimes twelve, plus bonuses, to the banks, plus all the other charges for the loan on money. During the war they did their patriotic duty, mortgaged the land they owned to buy more, to produce more. But now the buying value of the dollar is less, and that, together with interest rates, makes it impossible for the farmer to amortize his loan and pay interest." Jules sighed. "Soon, Hank, you will see that the small farmer will have to give up. Hordes of people will be homeless, will migrate to another section, broke, with nothing except their hands and their hopes."

The night was clear and cool and bright, and sitting between the two men with Hank's hand enveloping hers she was less torn than she had been. She snuggled close to Hank. It was wonderful to hear them discussing such things again.

"What the hell can a feller do 'bout that?" asked Hank, all affableness.

"Since it will be a long job to change the rules of money and interest, the most direct thing to do seems to be to bring power, electricity, and thereby industry, to the agricultural sections." Jules hesitated rather pointedly, it seemed. Then, taking his eyes off the road a second, he leaned forward and looked past Verity at Hank. "That is what I shall do with my electric company as fast as I can."

"Your company!" Hank exclaimed.

"Yes," said Jules quietly, his eyes again directly ahead. "You see, Hank, for almost two years I have tried to buy into the Southern Light and Power. When you came to me with your find of the old law, I again made them an offer. They refused." He laughed a little. "I sat by, thinking my friend Hank would bring suit and break them. I kept thinking my friend Hank would then find a way on his organization's money to make the people owners of that company. But—well, it seems you preferred not to do it by the recognized business methods."

"Goddam!" cried Hank. "Goddam! Well, b'God'lmighty, it ain't too late for me t' be a-doin' of that yet! 'N me, a-takin' a lousy fifty thousand!"

Verity jerked herself away from him, turned and stared at him, not wanting to believe her ears. But he did not notice her.

"Yes, it is too late," said Jules, unperturbed and smiling. "Much too late. Once more, I am indebted to you, Hank. You flushed the entire covey of executives and owners right past my blind. They offered to sell. I have this day raised the money for purchase. And I shall very shortly have that old law repealed so that I shall not be rushed beyond the powers of my purse."

Leaning around Verity, Hank hissed, "Why, god-damit, y' plumb double-crossed me, Jules. Is that what you're a-doin' withen this syrup plant? Double-crossin' me? You a-tryin' t' get my people t' look t' you? Well, b'God'lmighty, you're plumb goin' t' have a fight on yore hands. They love me, 'n b' all that's holy, they're a-goin' t' keep on a-lovin' me. Iffen you're a-turnin' into one a' them Black Skimmers, you're plumb gonna hafta fight me!"

"I shall never be one who can be termed a Black Skimmer," said Jules clearly and with quiet force. "Not even you, Hank, my friend, will be able to detect the slightest habit of their kind. I shall guard against such habits, believe me. And speaking of Black Skimmers," laughed Jules, "haven't you just forced quite a mouthful down your gullet?"

Suddenly Hank's head went up and back and his great full laugh rolled through the quiet night.

"I shore did! 'N what in tarnation's the matter with me!" he roared.

"You plumb done me a service, too. Dang if you ain't. You're a-bringin' the 'lectricity, 'n that's what I was a-wantin'! Dang if I ain't got that 'n the fifty thousand, too!" He laughed and laughed.

The syrup plant came into view and the great vat which was housed in a three-wall shed sent up its sweet steam and the huge fire under it sent out its red glow into the night's blue. The crowd had come out of the juicing house to hear the singing and music of Jules's darkies, who were tending the vat fires, and stood listening and sipping the raw green, foamy juice of the cane. Silhouetted by the great fire was Selah. She was singing, and her rich voice, a true blend of the Negro joyousness and lament, came to Verity with heart-breaking poignancy.

> "Fly home ter me, love, de cypress cry,
> De river calls, de cane fields sigh,
> De flowahs fold against de dew,
> We all is wiltin' fum wantin' you."

As Jules brought the car to a quiet stop, not interrupting, and Verity felt the touch of Hank's hand as he helped her from the car, she thought of Hank's words, "Venus shouldn't oughta never meet a warrior in battle." Why must her love be always a challenge? She simply wanted her love to come home. She got back into the car and let the men go forward without her.

> "Fly home ter me, love, you's my only love,
> My heart mourns lak de mournin' dove. . . ."

As the song died out, leaving its sweet heartbreak on the night, Hank called to his people.

"Friends," he howled, "friends—I'm home again. 'N it's news I've brung t' gladden yore hearts. I done made myself some money this here trip. I purely did. Now, I begin in earnest. Now, we all begin in earnest for t' get our organization into shape as will mean I can plumb get elected to a office."

Waving his hand toward Jules, he cried, "I didn't hafta bring suit liken I planned 'cause yore friend 'n my friend, Mr. Bolduc, has done bought the 'lectric plant. He plans to 'lectrify the rural districts soon as ever he can. Cry him out a hallelujah, folks!" And raising his arms like a choir director he shouted, "Hallelujah, praise the Lord for Jules Bolduc!" As they joined in the cry, Jules turned about, looking helpless and in need of shelter.

As their shouts quieted, Hank went on with the fervor of the campaigner and the conviction of the revivalist.

"I'm a-tellin' y', friends, I'm a-tellin' y'—we're livin' in a age as has purely got a prophecy t' keep for the Lord. Yes, we purely have. We're the generation as must keep the prophecy 'n clean the world a' poverty. We've been a-workin' at it, you 'n me, for some years now. But it's only a beginning. Only a beginning, friends. We're the generation as must see the riches divided 'n make the pore folks a thing a' the past. A thing as will make our grandchildern shudder when they read a' it."

Jules came back to the car and stood beside Verity, listening.

"Yes, sir, b'God'lmighty, we're the ones. Liken it says in Proverbs, 'There is a generation, that are pure in their own eyes, and yet is not washed from their filthiness.' Y' see that, friends . . . there's so many a' the high 'n mighty ones as thinks theirselves so pure, 'n yet they defile their brothers. 'There is a generation whose teeth are as swords, and their jaw teeth as knives, to devour the poor from off the earth and the needy from among men.' That's us." His voice rolled and resounded, and the great fires under the vat seemed the very flames which would burn the dross from the world.

In the dramatic long pause, Jules sighed. "He has the power, Verity. He could do wonderful things!"

"Yes, oh, yes," she answered in a soft little choke.

"And, friends . . ." Hank's organ tones billowed out. "Liken I said, I done made me some money this trip 'n I'm a-usin' it for the people. I done bought me some tents. Great big tents. 'N I'm a-takin' them tents into the country sections of all the parishes. The tents 'n the wagons for t' carry 'em will be here in a few days. Now you as can, come with me. It's a lot a' help I'm gonna need to put up them tents, 'n to let the country folks know I'm a-comin'. I aim t' be in Delamore first, 'n then on, 'n on, 'n on!"

Oh, thought Verity, oh, he'll do good with that money! Oh, he will! He must!

"Yes, I'm a-goin', friends, all through the country! Because, friends, there is a generation—'n afore God, I'm a-thinkin' it's us!"

11

*Everyone in the inner know of politics said Hank Martin could
not possibly be elected commissioner of public works and highways. They laughed him off. The vote in the country sections
had always been very light, the backwoods folk had never
bothered with voting, never been stirred from their lethargic
indifference to politics. And, pointed out the opposition, when
they gave it any thought at all, who could carry a state election
on the country vote?*

*To them Hank Martin was only a clown, a pin peddler, a
swamp angel, or a hillbilly. But they were in for the surprise of
their lives, for Hank not only pulled a country vote, so great it
could be accounted for only by the census figures, but he pulled
an amazingly big vote even in sophisticated Crescent City.
The foreign quarters, almost the entire north end of the city,
went solid for Hank.*

*How had this come about, they demanded of their ward men.
And their only answer was a tell-nothing shrug. How? How?—
But their only answer seemed to be that people just went for
Hank. . . .*

She sat in Jules's car listening to Hank, feeling the awe and hopes of the
people. The sweetness of boiling cane juice thickened the damp night air,
and the red glow from the vat fires played softly over calicoes and denims,
over the fair faces of the young, and the lined, weathered faces of their
elders. Verity felt a need for prayer. She wanted to clasp her hands and
kneel and feel certain she would be heard. She needed someone wiser, oh,
much wiser than she, to help her find herself.

And later, throughout the dancing, while the fiddles and concertina
played the old tunes, she sat quietly by, not feeling well enough to dance,
not even wanting to dance. While Hank whirled the ladies she held the
sleeping Hancy, feeling lonely—lonely, wishing she could find some way to

send the essence of herself, her soul, perhaps, on a scouting trip. A scouting trip that would show her who and what she was. But not being able to do this she would do as her mother had always done—just what she could, a step at a time.

Jules danced only with Sophy, who was almost overcome by the compliment, and then busied himself with talking to groups and coming back to Verity now and then. She thought of her brave resolve never again to fail another because she was sunk in her own needs. To do this she must find her own strength. Yes, however small compared to Hank's, her strength must be her own. Looking down at Hancy's face, so sweet in sleep, Verity whispered to herself, "Verity Wade Martin, you must find your own self, your own strength. You love Hank too much, perhaps."

Too much, perhaps—her eyes searched for Hank. He was dancing strenuously with a young woman, laughing down at her and talking, his face glistening with moisture. He had taken off his coat, and the new lavender silk shirt showed long, dark, oval stains of armpit sweat. She knew the steamy smell of him, sweet and hot like the ground mist which the sun pulled out of this land; knew the warmth that was flowing from him, even imagined she saw the heat waves, as she sometimes saw them in the summer noontimes. Catching her eye, Hank waved and laughed, and a slow current of lush weakness crept through her. She closed her eyes to shut out any chance onlooker.

In a few minutes she felt Hank beside her, could feel his nearness before he spoke. Leaning over her, he whispered, "I gotta feelin' you're a-callin' t' me t' take you home."

"Yes—yes," she replied, "I'm very tired."

"Yeah?" Hank grinned. "I woulda swore it wasn't weariness I seen. Come. Gimme Hancy. Jules is a-waitin' in the car. Selah's a-stayin'. Them niggers is a-dancin' out there liken they're voodoo wild. Every one a' Jules's niggers is there, 'n it's purely a somethin' t' see. Wanta look in on 'em?"

She shook her head and with Hank howling his good-bys, they went out into the cool fall night.

"Say, Jules," said Hank as they settled in the car, "all evenin' I been a-wonderin'. You the sole owner a' the Southern Light 'n Power now?"

"Practically," said Jules.

"Practically!" Hank snorted. "That don't tell me nothin'. Are y', or ain't y'? Or ain't y' sayin'?"

"I own seventy per cent now. A kinsman—cousin twice removed, Bruce Claibourne, owns the rest with me."

"Bruce Claibourne down in Crescent City, huh? So you're kin t' them. Claibournes 'n Bolducs—well, well, they make a right remarkable clan a' kinfolks, they do." As Jules did not answer, Hank asked, "Well, d'you wanta sell any a' yore stock t' me?"

"Why—ah—thank you, Hank, but I have decided to hold it. You see, I have mortgaged all I own to acquire it, and so I would rather have control and do things my way."

"Mortgaged everything, huh? What d' you know! Just when you was a-gettin' clear, too."

Verity's heart sank. Turning in her seat, she looked over the broad, fertile lands and sighed.

"Oh, Jules!" she exclaimed softly. "Oh, Jules, that's terrible!"

"Not at all, Verity, my dear," he said. "It will be a pull, no doubt, but —I have an idea it will be worth it. I have an idea it will do much for the people in time and make money too. It will put Cypress Bend once more among the great houses of the South. It was you, Hank, who moved me to action." He laughed softly. "Yes," he said, "something happened to me when you two came. It began in earnest when you painted your house."

"Yeah," said Hank. "I had a feelin' 'bout that myself. I shore did." His hand reached over for Verity's and, clasping it tightly, he said, scarcely aloud, "Ol' Jules in the field. You gimme a kind a' unease."

"I can't quite hear you, Hank," said Jules.

"I said you gimme a kind a' unease."

Jules's real laughter suddenly rang out. His real laugh. "I am glad to know it is mutual," he said.

"Mutual, hell!" Hank muttered.

As they parted, Hank said, "Well, that was a fine party you give for my homecomin'. Dang if it wasn't," and grinned widely at Jules.

"I shall be glad to do it every time you flush a power company my way," and Jules's laugh rang out as he turned the car for home.

Hank stood holding his daughter in his arms, looking after Jules. "Dang that feller!" he said. "Dang him anyhow." He walked slowly into the house. Verity lighted the lamp and sank exhausted into her rocker. He put the child in her lap and Verity undressed her while Hank paced the floor.

"The whole power company he's got for hisself near 'bout! Well, leastways," he comforted himself, "he couldn't 'a got it iffen he wasn't already cushioned withen lands left him by his paw 'n his grampaws. 'N he was a-losin' his holt on that tillst I come. He couldn't 'a done what I done. He couldn't 'a started withen nothin' but a few packets a' pins 'n got someplace."

"He'd be the first to admit that," said Verity. "Tonight as you were talking he said you were wonderful."

"He did, huh?" Hank beamed. "Well, b'God'lmighty, I *am* wonderful. When I think what I put over on them thievin' sonsabitches I know I'm a somethin'. Y' shoulda seen them Power Company fellers look at me—liken as if I was somethin' crawled outen a hole when first I went in their fine offices. Winks went round that shinin' big directors' table. Some pulled their grins in so hard as to make 'em look like they'd been a-eatin' of persimmons, 'n some pulled back their heads 'n narrowed their noses like as if a skunk had just give off. Them's the kind a' capitalists as just sets on their assets. 'N so cold-blooded they are they don't hatch nothin' that comes alive 'n produces more. Naw, sir! So cold-blooded they are, they near 'bout petrify the assets a' the country a-sayin' the likes a' me 'n my people ain't fitten for to enjoy the good things a' this world."

His face flashed a second with the hurt, the humiliation he had felt at being received in such manner, and her heart ached for him.

"But I'm gettin' used to that sort a' treatment. In a kind a' way I know it's good for me 'cause them kind gets such a helluva surprise time I'm through. I just stood in that there door 'n thought as I looked 'em over, I thought, Y' pewits! You ain't got brains enough to guess that I'm a-standin' here a-kissin' yore ass for the last time. 'Cause, by God'lmighty, I'm a-kickin' it afore I go back out this door! That's what I was a-thinkin' as I went in that there directors' room, Verity. 'N that's what I done."

His head went up and back, and his great laugh rolled out until the sleeping Hancy stirred. Verity thought, I can't blame him. And then she thought, I'm just a teeter-totter with a part of me standing in the balancing middle not liking whichever way I go.

"Done a better job than ever I thought. Scared 'em right into Jules's arms, I did! I'm a-tellin' y', Sweetface, it's wonderful t' be me! To get borned in the world when it's such a great battleground. Challenges everywhere y' look. Yeah, it's wonderful! D'you know what I am, Sweetface? I'm a magician!"

"Magician, Hank?"

"Yeah, a political magician. I'm a-catchin' on t' the magic a' politics all right!" He laughed, lifted his clenched right fist, and made odd little come-on motions with his left hand. "I shake my right fist at the capitalists, 'n egg on the pore with my left, 'n fifty thousand pieces a' silver rolls up my right sleeve 'n down my left sleeve right into my pants pocket. 'N like all magicians, I'm a-talkin' fast 'n loud directin' their attention to yonder outrage. 'N I ain't givin' no picayune performance."

His eyes danced with devilment and self-appreciation.

" 'N my threats at the capitalists sounds to the pore like the music a' the millennium. 'N d'you know what that makes me, Sweetface?" he demanded.

"It makes you wrong, Hank," she said quietly.

"Nope!" He came toward her, his index finger pointing upward as he shook it in emphasis. "It makes me champion of the people!"

As he held the pose she almost believed him for a second. She wanted to believe him. She realized that he both believed it himself and at the same time could laugh just a wee bit at those who believed with him. Looking calmly into his eyes, she held to some strength in her to speak the truth as she saw it.

"No," she said firmly, "you're not the champion of the people. You sold out!"

"God'lmighty," he howled, "you watch what you're a-sayin'. I'm a-playin' the game by the rules."

"Some games should have their rules changed, then."

" 'N what d'you do tillst the rules get changed? Stay outen the game?" His eyes narrowed, all laughter went from his lips. "Now, you lissen t' me, Verity. You're my wife 'n don't you never say me such a thing again."

Something in her went firm and resisting. Rising, she faced him, her eyes looking into his. "Yes, I am your wife. And I love you more than anything else in all this world. I—I love you too much, I sometimes think." She hesitated, then went on, flailing herself to make the words come. "But you just remember this—I will say to you whatever I think I must say. And I say you sold out your people because the fifty thousand was a quicker start. Because it felt good in your own pocket. Oh, Hank, please don't be mad at me. I understand how you felt when you saw those directors, I even understand that you will do good with that money. Oh, I believe that! I have to believe it! But, Hank, Hank, darling!" she pleaded desperately, "I couldn't stand it if this is the straw that shows which way the wind is blowing."

"Fifty thousand dollars ain't no straw," he roared, glaring.

Everything in her drooped and she was exhausted to the point of nausea. She sat down again, trying to tell herself she was strong and well. He was instantly concerned.

"Sweetface, you been so sick—'n me a-bellerin' here." Kneeling beside her, he took her hand and laid his face against its palm. "A-bellerin' 'bout things that don't mean nothin' beside a' you. Sometimes I think, especially when I'm a-comin' home, how mebbe you're all that saves me from a-hearin' the caterwaulin' all a' the time. 'N honest, I don't want you should shut up 'n not say your mind. Y' done me good plenty's the time." His lips nibbled up her arm, then stopping, he said carefully, studyingly, "There's a somethin' in y' that just don't give to me, seems as though. 'N sometimes I feel I kinda gotta fight t' level it down. Tonight, now, you don't seem t' be rememberin' that Jules has got the company. 'N he got it 'cause I scared that stock so low he could find the price. You been a-showin' plain that you think there's some fine difference 'twixt his 'n my operations. But we both got ours on the same scare."

"You get me so muddled sometimes. Oh, damn it!" she cried.

At her curse word he threw back his head and laughed, then with eyes twinkling he teased, " 'N who are you, that you should oughta be so snooty? Who was the first one in this family to go in for graft 'n bribin'? Huh? It was you! 'Hank!' you says to me sweet 'n pleadin', 'Hank, for God's sake, bribe a shut mouth in Granny Dazy.' "

"A dollar and a new-life charm!" she cried.

Hank shrugged. "Well, graft is graft, 'n bribin' is bribin'. One dollar or fifty thousand, the deed is the same. 'N can you be denyin' it?"

She felt helpless and frustrated and she slapped his cheek smartly. Hank chuckled, and putting his face in the curve of her neck, nuzzled and nibbled up to her ear.

"That there Venus girl shouldn't oughta never go into battle," he whispered.

For days Hank pored over a book which was his latest find and greatest pride. It was a copy he had had made in the Capitol, just after he had taken his bar examinations, listing the name of every man who had voted throughout the state before the year 1867.

Hank touched the bound pile of papers with reverence, handled it gently as a treasure should be handled.

"This here pile a' papers as ain't held together with nothin' but a mite a' chicken wire, is our fortune, Verity. It's worth more'n that fifty thousand dollars, which pleasures me, 'n troubles you." He laughed and kissed the bound papers. "First I spent a' that money was t' get this copied. The next I spent was to have one a' them fellers as knows family lines in this here state check off the 'ristocratic names so's none a' them 'ristocrats can raise a holler. I aim t' give every one a' my followers as can't read 'n write a pappy or a grandpappy as voted afore 1867."

She couldn't understand the meaning of all this and he gloated over her bafflement. Finally she pinned him down to answering her questions about it.

"It's this-a-way, Verity—there was a convention held way back in 1898. They claimed they wanted t' just disfranchise the niggers, see? But that there convention near 'bout disfranchised everybody but the rich. They passed a law which says all voters has gotta be able t' read 'n write. They gotta be able t' reckon time. They gotta be able t' remember some dates 'n places—outa histry, y' understand—or else they gotta be owners a' property worth not less than three hundred dollars. But then," Hank chortled with glee, "some smart-thinkin' feller plumb fixed everything for me— Hank Martin. Yeah, he purely did. He sneaked in a li'l ol' clause as is purely gonna make it into Hank Martin's Grandpappy Law." He chuckled with delight. "Yes, sir, that's what that there law is about to become— Hank Martin's God-blessed Grandpappy Law!"

She looked at him with amazement, completely fascinated by the way in which he could always find a law of the land which he could turn to his own use.

"But what is the clause, Hank?" she asked.

"It's purely my dish, Sweetface," he gloated. "That there clause says that a man who voted in or before 1867, his sons or his children's children cannot be deprived a' their franchise because of failure t' pass educational or property qualifications. Ain't that li'l ol' clause a beauty? Lord God-'lmighty allus gives me His best!"

She felt great admiration and great tenderness for him. "The Lord God Almighty would probably give everyone His best if everyone worked at getting it like you do, Hank," she said softly.

He came around the table to her, touched her cheek with one finger.

"Hell, Sweetface," he said gently, "ain't you caught onto me yet? I'm a feller as is like to Jacob. You know, Jacob he wrestled withen the angel, 'n Jacob said—speakin' fierce 'n determinted, I got no doubt—Jacob said, 'I will not let thee go tillst thou hast blest me.' "

She laughed and kissed his hand. How true it was. Hank wrestled with a thing until he made it come his way. Like this law, this Grandpappy Law.

"Did you say that law was passed in 1898?" she asked.

"It shore was, Sweetface."

"But why is that clause limited to men who voted before 1867? Why, that was right after the Civil War!" she exclaimed.

"But that's the point," he cried. " 'N don't call it the Civil War. A civil war implies a war within a people. 'N the South seceded. That made us two people. It was The War Between the States."

"I stand corrected," she laughed, "but I still don't get the point about having a voting grandfather before 1867."

"Well, before that there war there shore wasn't no niggers votin'. But after the war the carpetbaggin' dam Yankees come in 'n whilst the great Magnolia State is a-gaspin' for breath, her money worthless, her best men dead, her finest women a-plowin' 'n a-hoein' for t' get a bean 'n a turnip, them dam Yankees come in. They set up a kind of law in keepin' with the constitutional provisions set up by the Federal Government in the thirteenth, fourteenth 'n fifteenth amendments." He stopped for emphasis. " 'N what d'you think them sonsabitches done?"

She shook her head, knowing that she did not need to answer.

"Why, they had a convention. There was ninety-eight delegates 'n exactly half was white 'n half was niggers! 'N they give equal rights t' all male critters, so they said. But here's what they done t' disfranchise all decent southern white men—now you just harken t' this—they made a law that afore a man could vote he had to show a certificate provin' he considered the rebellion a' the South morally 'n politically wrong!"

He pulled at his collar, waved his arms, shook his fist, quite as if he had a great audience.

"Why, there wasn't a decent white man as wasn't in that there war in some way. 'N the young'uns as growed up after the war didn't see nothin' but misery 'n want t' their own folks, whilst the carpetbaggers, withen their own set a' ornery niggers, ruled. Not all niggers went wild then, y' understand, but a-plenty did. Why, white folks got so's they wisht every dam Yankee in the world hadda got kilt. Y' should oughta heard the tales my ol' Granny Kelts tolt 'bout them days. God, what folks suffered!"

She could see the remembered stories burning in his face. "But how did they get out of that condition?" she asked.

He pushed the thought of such terror from him and his voice became more conversational in tone.

"Well, 'bout 1879 the men a' this state got a new lease on life. A feller as wanted t' be governor showed 'em how. He explained careful how he was gonna play the other feller's game tillst he was in office, which he done. Then he slipped over some laws on his ignorant legislators as plumb restricted 'em." Hank laughed. "He was a smart one, he was. He slipped over a law that took heaps 'n heaps of elective offices outa the elective class 'n he made 'em appointive. Them offices from then on was appointed by the governor. 'N that's how he got control a' the local parish governments throughout the state. Wasn't he a smart one?

"Now, whilst this put the carpetbaggers 'n the niggers outa control a' the government, we still had a huge nigger vote as was growin' bigger 'n bigger. Bound t' be a somethin' someday. So in 1898 they passed me my Grandpappy Law." He kissed the wire-bound papers and laughed.

She sighed. "It makes one wonder what law is anyhow!"

"It's a somethin' for smart fellers like to yore husband t' play with, I reckon. Makes a right pleasin' toy, law does." Leaning over her, he kissed the back of her neck. "I got no blame for 'em. 'N they done a good thing. Ain't no doubt 'bout it bein' good, then. In a kinda way, that is. But it sure put pore folks in a spot. But now Hank Martin has come along. Hank Martin, as is gonna fix that up. Yeah, I'm plumb the unrisen tomorrow them fellers never thought on."

"Unrisen tomorrow," she said. "Yes, I guess there's always an unrisen tomorrow." She pressed his hand to her cheek and said earnestly, "I guess it's the unrisen tomorrows that trouble me so much. Hank, remember those words of yours—remember Hancy and her children must live in the unrisen tomorrow which you and your generation are making."

He seemed startled by this thought and looked at her searchingly. "Yeah," he said, "yeah. But what the hell! Some things a feller has just gotta do." Shaking off this thought, he said, "You see, don't you, that the Grandpappy Law made votin' in this here state purely a matter a' edgucation 'n money or a matter a' heritage? Well, d'you think when the pore whites went t' the polls as any a' them election workers had a list a' enrolled voters before the year 1867, for t' help the pore find was their pappy or their grandpappy voters? Hell, no! The rich just simply kept control 'n didn't never even vote enough money for schools, even though we had a law as says there should be public edgucation. What good was that, withouten no money voted for it?"

"But, Hank," she asked, "do you really think you can prove that even a small per cent of your followers had a forebear voting before 1867?"

"Funny part a' it is that most have lived for generations in this here country, 'n that's a fact. But them as ain't 'n them as had grandpappies as didn't vote nohow are plumb gettin' a votin' grandpappy allotted t' 'em." He threw back his head and roared with laughter. "I'm a-tellin' y', Sweet-face, it's purely a somethin' t' see them men 'n women a-memorizin' the names a' their paws 'n their grandpaws. Dang iffen it ain't! Some a' them old-time voters has got more'n five hundred votin' descendants now, male 'n female." He laughed till the tears rolled down his face. "God'lmighty, when I get t' picturin' the faces a' them election workers a-tryin' to look uppity when my people stomp up t' them polls, when they find they can't actual read, nor didn't never own a clock for t' learn t' reckon time, 'cause they didn't never have no dollars for such foolishness when a hungry belly 'n a shinin' sun was clock enough! 'N when my poll watcher comes for-'ard 'n says he's got the entire list a' all voters before the year 1867!—I'm plumb sorry I can't be all-seein' like God 'n have a look at the whole dang state come election!"

The big tent and several small ones stood in their patched and faded glory in the meadow north of Delamore, the same meadow on which Saber's plane had landed. Against Hank's bargain tent the brand-new ropes which ran tautly to the iron ground poles glistened yellowly. The countryfolk had been streaming in since four in the morning, and their mules and horses were now tied in the shade of the trees which surrounded this sun-drenched field. Everywhere people clustered together talking while they ate their cold box dinners or heated their beans and coffee over little hastily laid fires. Watching everything from the main tent entrance, Verity hunted for the realities of all this. She could not feel herself to be part of it.

Jenny, in a new pink dress and a new brown coat, came and stood be-side her. Jenny was almost overcome by the wonder and importance of it all. She looked at Verity and cried, "Ain't it wonderful! Ain't it jes' won-derful! All them folks a-comin'! 'N jes' t' think, I'll be a-goin' with Hank 'n all this here big tent, 'n all, over the whole state!" Tears welled up and she swiped them away with a childish back-of-the-hand motion. Verity's eyes fastened, however, on the open shoe box which was filled with Hank's organization cards.

"Do you think you'll get all those cards signed?" Verity asked.

"Near 'bout," said Jenny. "A-course lotsa folks is already members, but we're a-givin' them cards t' take back to folks as couldn't come. We gotta git lotsa dollars so's we can pay for the 'spenses 'n all that. 'N we'll have captains for t' cover the voters in every pollin' section, Hank says. Hank knows how t' make voters outa folks now, writin' or no writin'. He's got lists 'n after the meetin' he'll pick the captains in this here section." She sighed with long-drawn pleasure. " 'N I'm a part a' all this! I'm a political organizer, Hank says." The prideful miracle of it all was in her face. Verity's studying eyes brought her out of her dreams, and Jenny said wistfully, almost enviously, "My, but you're purty! Is them the new clothes Hank brung y' from Crescent City?"

"Yes," Verity replied, feeling self-conscious. Knowing the soft yellow wool suit and the matching coat to be most becoming, she still did not feel perfectly happy in them at times. She had exclaimed with pleasure when Hank opened the box of clothes he had brought her from Crescent City. They were truly lovely, well chosen for lines and color. Hank's good taste in choosing a woman's clothes always surprised her. She enjoyed these new things, yet she sometimes felt guilty, never quite forgetting that they celebrated the taking of fifty thousand dollars' graft.

Jenny's eyes held a strange gleam that was almost jealousy. Aware, as Verity was, of Jenny's fondness for her, she could not find a reason for the sudden, intuitional feeling that all was not as before with her and Jenny. Something was troubling Jenny. Something of which she did not feel free to speak. "You're looking very lovely these days, Jenny," she said, trying to find the old footing.

Into Jenny's eyes came a deep cloud. "It ain't enough," she said softly, regretfully.

"Enough for what?" asked Verity.

"Oh—" Her voice trailed off and her free hand waved ineffectually in the air. "Oh—" she tried again, "I wisht I was jes' like you."

"No," said Verity firmly. "No, Jenny, you don't. There's much in me that's troublesome. You're a lovely person, Jenny. Just make the most of yourself. Some philosopher, Emerson, I guess, said, 'What we are born is God's gift to us, what we become is our gift to God.' "

Jenny eyed Verity, seeming to hunt sincerity. An uneasiness swelled in Verity. She felt Jenny regarded God as Hank's special preserver and she sensed something too mighty swelling and pushing in the heart and mind of the frail Jenny.

"Huh!" Jenny's muted snort held a whole world of sarcasm. "Huh! I shore hope my gift t' Gawd'll be a heap sight better'n His t' me." She fingered the cards in her box and turned away.

Verity was bewildered. What had come over Jenny? What was hurting her now? She was pondering this when Jenny gave a startled little cry.

"I knowed she'd come! 'N here she is bright 'n early."

"Who?" asked Verity, looking at a group of young women.

"Her with all them brown furs," said Jenny bitterly. "She's kin t' the Black Skimmer, she is. Cousin, four, five times removed, I reckon." Jenny faced Verity and spoke with a flat tonelessness like a scared little girl reciting a piece. "Come out here this mornin', she did. All alone, she come. Gets one a' the men to take her to Hank, she does. I come into Hank's office tent fer t' ask him somethin'. I stops by the flap 'cause there she was a-kinda squirmin' at him, 'n a-lookin' up at him withen them big pale eyes. 'N d' y' know what she's a-sayin'?"

"No," said Verity, not caring, wondering only what was the matter with Jenny lately.

"She's a-sayin' with that voice a' hern that's had a lotta elegant schoolin', she's a-sayin' so sugary it likes to puke me, 'Oh, Mister Martin, I just had to come and see you-all. I think you must be just the most thrillin' man! Anyone who has the courage to fight my cousin! My! I thought you must be thrillin' before I met you. But, oh, my! people just haven't told me the half of it!' " Jenny managed an excellent mimicking of a well-bred young southern belle declaring with heavy coquetry that she is just overcome. Verity felt an impulse to laugh.

"And what did Hank say?" she asked.

"Hank says," continued Jenny, " 'Have I had the honor t' fight yore cousin?' 'N she says, 'Yes, indeed. And you won! I was never so thrilled!' 'N she giggles up at Hank 'n says, 'I never liked Cousin Robert, either. Our families are really not very friendly. I think Cousin Robert is just overbearin', don't you, Mister Martin?' 'N Hank, he says, 'So—you're kin t' the Black Skimmer? I'm plumb surprised he ain't swallered up so choice a tidbit as you long afore this.' "

"And then what?" asked Verity.

"I dunno," said Jenny dully. "I just hadda git outa there. She ain't no better'n them whores I seen on Bowles Street here in Delamore a-squirmin' their bellies 'n butts at strange men. Not so good. Them Bowles Street women is hungry."

"Oh, Jenny," cried Verity in distress, "don't speak that way. It sounds so —so sordid. It doesn't sound like the dreaming Jenny I knew in Cypress Bend."

Jenny stared at her with hurt in her eyes and a tight-set mouth. She batted her lids violently, fighting the tears, then turned abruptly and ran into the big tent. Verity's attention went back to the group of giggling young ladies, who were all listening to the center one in the fine furs of lustrous brown. A small toque of matching fur crowned her silvery blond hair enhancing the Persian-kitten look in the small face and the large eyes which were a startling shade of pale, lucent gray.

"Oh, Sylvia," exclaimed one young woman, "did he really? And then what did you say?"

Miss Sylvia Hylen stopped walking. She stood still, obviously enjoying her friends' admiration, obviously enjoying the drama she was creating. She squirmed her middle and nether, her lids went half shut.

"I said," Miss Sylvia Hylen's voice was a low chummy purr, " 'Oh, Mr.

Martin! You're the most th-rilling man! You're just a great big untamed lion!' "

The young ladies exclaimed over this while Sylvia held her pose.

"And then what, Sizzling Sylvia?" one asked.

Sylvia giggled. "He said, 'Yeah. I'm sure as hell king a' this jungle.' And then he laughed. Such a roar as you have never heard in all your whole lives! But really! And then he said, 'Now see here, sister, you're a right smart smooth little animal yoreself. But a little one, see? You shouldn't oughta never stalk big game.' And he made me leave. Oh, was I th-rilled!"

As if hypnotized, Verity had walked toward the group, giving no thought to the fact that she was purposely trying to hear; trying to hear because her heart was crowding her throat with fear. Watching the girl Sylvia's half-lowered lids, the lush droop of the dewy, oversized lips, the dainty, hinting swivel of her hips, Verity's brain beat at her with the 'gator pole repeating Lula May's words, " 'N God only give women one way t' do it." But when Sylvia Hylen repeated Hank's parting reprimand, Verity laughed so freely that the group noticed her, sized her up, and wondered if she could have heard. But Sylvia Hylen shrugged her shoulders, not caring, and they brushed past Verity and entered the tent. They were early, and Verity smiled as she watched them get as near the front as possible.

At Hank's insistence, Verity sat on the platform, and as she looked out over the crowd of Hank's people she spotted here and there groups of a different sort. A few of the solid middle class were there; they seemed carried away like the others. Always her eyes were drawn back to the small silver-gilt-framed face of Sylvia Hylen and her friends. Miss Hylen sat forward on the bench in a tense and thrilled attitude. All through Hank's speech her friends appeared as enthralled as Swith or Sophy or Tim. Verity was aware of the start of surprise when Hank introduced his wife, and aware of Miss Hylen's eyes each time Hank turned, and said, "Ain't I allus said that, Verity?" or pointed to her and howled, " 'N I says to my wife, I says, 'B'God'lmighty, I'm a-plannin' to devote my life to makin' folks free. Free, b'God'lmighty, in a way as means somethin'! 'N that there way is to see that folks got a chancet for to get more'n sow-belly 'n turnip greens for four, five generations.' Yes, sir, ain't I allus said that, Sweetface?" And he would turn and expect instant corroboration from her in the way of a nod. A queer suffocating misery sat lump-ishly within her, making her feel like a dull automaton, or like a ventrilo-quist's dummy.

As she listened to him tell of Abraham Lincoln, "who come of a pulin' paw, liken to a goodly number a' us. But away back he come a' solid workin' folks liken to most a' us. The first Lincoln t' come t' this country from England was a feller named Samuel Lincoln 'n he was a weaver.

He come here in 1637 'n lived in Massachusetts. But the descendants went south 'n in 1780 one Abraham Lincoln, who was our Abe's grandpappy, was a feller in the money 'cause there's a recorded sale made by him of his lands which brung him five thousand pounds. That's English money, folks, 'n one pound is equal to about five dollars. So Abe's grandpappy had twenty-five thousand dollars, folks, 'n that was a heap a' money in them days. Still a heap, iffen you was to ask me. Well, Grandpappy Abraham moved to Kentucky, and after a while he was kilt by a shot from a Indian's rifle. Well, now, Grandpappy Abe's oldest son, Mordecai, according to the law a' them times, he done inherited all the old man's wealth 'n he become a right prosperous feller. Who wouldn't? But our Abe's pappy was only ten when his paw was shot 'n his widow maw took him to another nearby county. His name was Thomas 'n he got to be a right good carpenter, but he was powerful shiftless at times. Well, now, in time Abe Lincoln got born in a hut in Kentucky. Born of folks like you 'n me was. Folks as the rich no doubt called white trash. For a whole year after they moved to Indiana, the family lived in a three-sided shed. Abe's paw was so pulin', he didn't never get the fourth side built. So you see what great things, 'n what great men can come from folks liken to us. We got it proved. Abe Lincoln done a good work, far as it went, but there ain't no freedom for nobody, black or white, tillst we gets us some changes in this money business."

As he launched into his quotations and set forth his ideas on Divide the Riches, she saw the startled looks of Miss Hylen and her young friends, the amazement and hope on the faces of the middle-class folk of Delamore who had dared come to this white-trash meeting. She pondered on Hank's very clever use of the Great Emancipator to establish the fact of his own qualifications for emancipating. Hope lived in her that he could do the great things. But she knew the hope had a little of the desperate clinging in it now. It was not the same high sureness of ignorance, the sureness that comes in a dream when only the goal on the high hill is clear and the obstacles are hidden in the ground mist.

As Hank warmed and then hottened to his subject, he jumped about the platform, mimicked the tight, unseeing capitalists of his experience and imagination. He cursed the governors of the Magnolia State because there was never enough money for schools in the country districts whether in hills or swamps, screamed the figures which told the devastating truth about the number of people—white people—who could neither read nor write, told how he himself could read because he had been suckled on the Bible, told how he'd been apprenticed out to a farmer and slaved harder'n a hill mule 'n with little more hope, told how he and all people like him—and yes, ninety-five per cent of the so-called white-collared middle class—were like the captives in the psalm whom their captors, the capitalists who just sat on their assets, commanded to sing.

He tore his collar open, ripped off his coat. His bright pink sweat-wet shirt, looking red as hibiscus flowers in the wet spots, bagged loosely around his waist, the flailing arms finally pulling the tail out. It flapped behind him like a valiant little pennant in the gale of his squattings and jumpings. It shuddered when he thinned his middle and towered on his toes, bellowing his threats at the money powers. It drooped when he covered his eyes and performed a creditable weeping for the sorrows of the poor, the generation after generation of hopelessness. It stayed still and waiting when Hank went to the front of the platform and in the hush of the big tent whispered:

"I'm aimin' to run for Commissioner of Public Works 'n Highways. Every one a' you has got to go t' the nearest pollin' place 'n help me with yore vote. 'Cause in me is yore salvation. In me is yore young'uns' salvation. 'Cause as God is a-listenin', I'll get yore children the schools they should oughta have. 'N they'll have every schoolbook free—free! No longer will a young'un not be able to go to school 'cause you can't buy his books. That buyin' a' schoolbooks is a disgrace as will be a thing a' the past when Hank Martin is runnin' this here state.

"I'm a-promisin' you roads. Thousands a' miles a' fine, reliable roads. Roads, b'God'lmighty, that'll make it possible for you to laugh at rain 'n blackjack mud! Roads that'll let you take yore cotton 'n cane 'n beans 'n strawberries out to the best market when they should be took. Roads that'll free you from the likes a' men liken to Robert Castleberry, him I call a Black Skimmer, him as was a-thievin' you outen life 'n bread for yoreselves 'n yore young'uns.

" 'N that ain't all I'm a-promisin'. Lissen close, my friends, for I'm a-tellin' you 'bout a gift I'm gonna make to every man as can acquire a home he holds title to. Are y' liss'nin'? Well, I'm gonna pass a law some-day that'll make them big bastards as own the corporations pay the taxes in this here state 'n every man jack a' you shall have his own home tax free!—'N that's a promise from Hank Martin to you. 'N I don't never make a promise I don't keep. Now you make me a promise—will you promise to vote for me so's I can do all this for you? Will you? Will you?"

Almost as one the crowd stood and roared their promise. Only a small per cent stood looking about as if amazed to find themselves here where some great force was loosed, some force they did not understand. The voices howled and screamed their allegiance, while Jenny and Swith and others scurried among them with cards and pencils and tough canvas bags for their dollars. Hank motioned Verity to get going, and as if hypnotized she picked up her shoe box, took a canvas bag, and descended the steps. People grabbed at the cards, many names she had to write herself, but everyone could drop his pennies or his dollars. As she stood writing the name of an eager sunbonneted woman, Sylvia Hylen approached.

"A card, please," she said, holding out her hand.

"Do you wish to join, Miss Hylen?" Verity managed to ask.

Miss Hylen and her friends looked a bit startled, one or two giggled, but Miss Hylen was unabashed.

"Oh, yes," she purred. "I really do. Your husband is just thr-rilling, Mrs. Martin. Why, I'd do anything for his wonderful cause. Come on, girls, you join too."

But her friends refused.

"My father'd disown me," said one.

"Mine, too."

"Mine, too," declared a plump brown-haired girl.

"Why, Janie Davol, how can you resist?" cried Sylvia Hylen. "Well, contribute, anyway. All of you. Oh, come now, you know you never saw a better show anywhere in all your whole lives! Why, he's a circus! He's si-mply marvelous!"

As they opened their purses, Verity felt sickened and without a word turned and hurried through the crowd. She went into Hank's little tent office and sank into a canvas chair.

She was embarrassed and she could see no sense in it. Every crowd has its proportion of fools of all kinds. Hank would have been amused and taken their money. Indeed, he would have told them to empty their purses, that there was no better cause. She was bewildered and it angered her. Why should she be so often bewildered by Hank and Hank's doings? Was it because she was not as big a person as Hank? She felt like a little boat tied to a great fast liner. A little boat with no course of its own, all battered and thrown from side to side in the deep, fierce wake.

No course of her own—it went back to the need to find her own strength. Her course had to run alongside Hank's. There could be no other answer to that. Perhaps she always felt confused because she had come into his activities only occasionally. Yes, that must be it. She thought on this a long while and finally decided she would not go back home. She would travel with Hank.

But that night after the evening meeting Hank insisted she return home with the other folk from Cypress Bend. While Jenny kissed and hugged and instructed the twins before they got into the wagon to return with Sophy and Tim, Hank argued with Verity.

"Now, lookit, Sweetface," he said softly, "I got a longin' for to show off my wife what's a lady t' one 'n all. But I wanta have my girl-child a somethin', too. No young'un a' Hank Martin is a-goin' to be purely nigger-raised. It ain't fitten."

"But that's silly, Hank," she protested. "Look at Jules—his family left him months at a time with his nurse."

"Huh!" he snorted, then squeezing her hand, said, "You're likely gonna be lonesome. Jules, he's gonna be powerful busy down t' Crescent City withen that new power plant a' hisn."

She let this pass.

"Hank," she pleaded, "please take me with you. My life has been very lonely. Lonely and empty. Only living when you are home. Living a few days and just waiting emptily months and months on end."

The soft, dear tenderness came into his eyes as he touched her cheek gently with a finger tip.

"Sweetface," he murmured. "Sweetface, sometimes I marvel at myself, I do. I marvel to think I can send you away. Marvel that I can leave you and be gone months on end, liken y' say. But this time I got one good reason. One I can see plain 'n clear." He stopped, seeming to consider his words, seeming to love the sight of her uplifted, pleading face. "Yeah, that's it. Y' don't rightly belong in the midst a' the caterwaulin'. Some a' it I gotta shove onto you. 'N I'm bein' purely selfish in a way t' keep you some'at apart. There's a clear, bright somethin' liken to a fast-runnin' brook in you, 'n I come to that brook 'n I spill the blackness in me, 'n I feel all clean agin." Taking her hand he placed it over his heart and sealed it there with one of his own. "'N I get all filled up agin 'n go forth." His voice dropped very low. "Sometimes I see a somethin' as plain as if it was the handwritin' for me on the wall. My beginnin's is allus with you. Liken to that brook y' got in y'. Its beginnin's is in some high place."

She was deeply touched. She stepped nearer and laid her cheek upon the heart-covering hand. She wanted to say, Oh, my love, oh, my love! But she couldn't get the words out. A melting tenderness became a foretaste of the yearning and loneliness she would know before she saw him again. Foretaste, too, of the months of nothing to do, just waiting, waiting. She felt she couldn't endure it.

"The terrible waiting, Hank. Nothing to do. And now, after the baby—"

"Well, now, there's a somethin' you should oughta change. You should oughta ride horseback mebbe. When Jules is home he can learn y'."

She shrugged. "That sort of thing isn't enough. I—I—oh, I don't know what I want. Just something to do that interests me, I guess."

"Well," he said easily, "we got us plenty a' money for you t' find somethin' as interests you, I reckon." He grinned. "Or are you a-feelin' uppity 'bout that there money?"

It was a dash of cold water. She could no longer wonder. An answer was demanded. Looking at his wide smile, studying the sureness of him, feeling so aware of his nearness, knowing how she would miss him, she gave her answer.

She spoke slowly, gropingly, and half smiling as she answered, "If I cannot change things, and cannot leave them, then I must accept them."

A flicker of unease passed over Hank's face but the sureness beamed quickly again. "You're my wife," he said softly. "Come, you gotta get a-goin'. Folks'll be a-wonderin' will they get home afore daybreak."

Touching her cheek gently, he said, "I shore got me a lady for the future governor a' this here state."

Back home again through the dull, long days of waiting, days that gave her a feeling of having become an empty thing, she thought on these last words with Hank. It was almost as if he had set her aside as being of little use now but as something of value later. Often she went to the barn and sat staring at the loaded, covered cart. Hank's peddling business was going to be missed by him. It had furnished him the personal contacts with his people, kept him in touch with their thoughts and hopes. And what was most important to her, it had furnished a business the profit from which was unquestionably theirs. She wished all their money came from the business instead of having to worry about the honesty and niceties of that fifty thousand. She wished she could drive the cart herself and go over the roads, but she knew Hank would be furious if she did. Hank had the horse with him, but she could buy another. The thought took hold on her and nagged at her mind constantly. Here was the way to legitimate profit. Not much, but whatever it was she wouldn't have to feel touchy about it. And perhaps she could someday have a cart in every parish. The wagons would be a means of keeping the people in touch with Hank. It looked like good politics, too. Hank was always afraid his people might think him "uppity." She became convinced that it would be good politics for Hank Martin's wagon to continue peddling.

Hank had been gone almost three months when she finally came to the decision to take the first step. She would buy a horse at the auction in Delamore. She wouldn't know a good horse when she saw one. But Tape would. And so that evening after Hancy was in bed she spoke to Selah.

"Do you think Tape would go to the livestock auction and buy me a good horse?" she asked.

"Co'se he will, sugah." Selah showed no surprise. "One fo' ter haul de wagon, you means. You gwine keep dat wagon at its sellin', hunh?"

"Why, how did you know!"

"I done cotched de worrysome gleam in yo' eye, honeychile." She made her little clucking sounds like a mothering hen. "You showin' good sense." She emphasized the word "good" in typical Negro fashion. "Yas'm, you showin' good sense. Down ter earf, I calls it. Lak culla'd women whut ain' th'owin' away dere washboards 'count uv honey words."

An odd, heavy feeling came on Verity. Could it be that fear had prompted this? But she shook that notion off and a little sense of anger at Selah sprouted through her words.

"I want the wagon to carry on because it's good politics."

Verity rose and headed for her bedroom. At the door she turned. "Yas'm. Shu' 'nuff," she mimicked and made a face worthy of Hancy. Selah clucked softly, broodingly.

When the big dapple-gray gelding was installed in the barn, Verity tended and admired him daily, and took him a lump of sugar each morning. She loved his soft muzzle; he was so big, so patient and gentle. Often during the days she went over the wagon's stock, counting the papers of pins, the yardage left on the bolts, the cosmetics and cheap toilet waters, and she talked to Big-Gray. She hadn't liked the horse's name when Tape told it, but as the days went on Big-Gray took on personality that gave his name meaning for her. He was almost as big as some of the brewery horses she had seen as a child in Pennsylvania; his very color, cool and cloudy and sturdy, was different from all this colorful land. Often as she rubbed his strong sleek neck she took new strength in the beginning of her venture. But who would drive this wagon, peddle this stuff? She wished she could go, but if Hank would not have her separated from Hancy in order to be with him, he certainly would not tolerate her driving alone through this country. And of course she couldn't go to half the places Hank had gone. When she thought of the nights, staying in places like the Ribidoux', she realized the utter impossibility of it. She had thought of Sophy's eldest son, Bije, but Tim wanted him to till the land while he put in his time at the forge, for Tim could fashion more than horseshoes. He loved to tinker with good steel and make thin steel plates, on which he hammered designs of flowers and strangely masculine, straight-lined, but recognizable animals. These, Verity thought, would sell for a fancy price up North if they ever found a market. She would hardly have the courage to ask for Bije, though he was a shrewd trader. The more she pondered, the more she realized her hunger for Hank. She would have to go to Loder City to buy goods and she would telephone around and locate him. He should be campaigning in some little village not more than a hundred miles from there.

Tape drove her to Delamore, where she boarded the train for Loder City. All the way she thought of Hank's surprise at what she had decided would interest her. She took her list of present stock from her purse and went over it time and time again, also the list of the items she intended to buy. She glowed with anticipation at being with Hank, caught herself smiling as she thought of his surprise. She would, of course, have to find out where he was. She knew vaguely his route and felt he should be somewhere east of Loder City and not too far. She decided to ask the conductor.

"I beg your pardon," she said as she leaned out in the train aisle, "but do you happen to have heard of Hank Martin?"

"Hank Martin?" the old man drawled. "Yes, ma'am, I have. Why do you ask, ma'am?"

"I want to find out where he is right now. He's campaigning. Has a big tent—" Her words hung unfinished as the old conductor looked at her with immense curiosity.

"Yes, ma'am," said the conductor, "I've heard of him. We had the private car of the vice-president of this road hitched to this train couple weeks back. Him and his friends were laughing about this Hank Martin. Said this Martin declares he'll get fine highways through this state."

"And," probed Verity, "didn't the vice-president think that would be fine?"

"No, ma'am, he sure did not. He said this Martin is a clown. And what's more, he's a fool if he thinks the railroad men are going to let the state put in good highways so competitors can run buses. Put the railroads in this state in a hell of a shape—" He coughed and reddened. "I beg your pardon, ma'am. Didn't aim to use strong language. But the vice-president doesn't aim to let this road be thrown into its death throes, he says, like the railroad companies up North. All due to those fine highways, he says."

"I see," said Verity. "Very interesting. And how does the vice-president think he will keep Hank Martin from building highways?"

The conductor laughed. "Well, now, ma'am, he has to be elected to something first. And surely you know as well as anyone that a man like that can never be elected."

"No? Why not?" She was annoyed.

"Well, nobody but the white trash would vote for him. He's nothing but a piney-woods hillbilly who came down to the south of the state and peddled pots and pans and pins through the swamps where no sane man'd go." He looked at her speculatively. "Excuse me, ma'am, for saying so, but Hank Martin's meetings are no place for a lady like you. Now why would you be wanting to go?"

The little imp in Verity giggled. She welcomed the little imp. Now that she thought of it, she'd missed his mischief. She looked up earnestly at the old conductor and said softly, "I'm fond of Hank Martin."

The old face reddened. He took off his stiff, hot blue cap and ran his hand across his forehead, cleared his throat. "Um—I've heard tell he's got a fetching way, but—"

"You see," said Verity, laughing up at him, "I'm Mrs. Hank Martin."

The old man's eyes popped slightly and his mouth went shut with a click of store teeth.

"And you tell your vice-president for me," Verity continued, "that he had better start thinking up ways to improve these wretched old trains, because Hank Martin will one day put roads in this state that will make the highways of Pennsylvania and New York look like sidewalks." And she finished her speech with a decisive nod.

"I declare, now! I do declare," and the old man turned strictly way-down-south, for his words sounded as thick as Selah's, almost, coming out "Ah decla'ah, naow! Ah do decla'ah."

Verity smiled at him and he bowed slightly and went on down the aisle punching the tickets of the newcomers. She turned and looked out the window. What a ghastly job it will be to build fine roads in this country, she thought. The railroad track bed was on built-up ground, and beyond the train window, not forty feet, the earth was down to its natural level, swampy and treacherous and lush, a jungle of moss-draped cypress, of high rank weeds and strange jointed grasses, wide squat palmettos. I shouldn't have embarrassed the old fellow, she thought. But she was amused.

Alighting from the train in Loder City she looked about the depot wondering of whom she could inquire as to Hank's whereabouts. She supposed the newspaper would know, though there was never anything in the paper about him. But she knew the newspaper publishers and owners had a sort of tacit understanding to keep the likes of Hank Martin in their place. Just then she saw a bewhiskered man of possibly forty years, bent from too-heavy toil of early childhood. He stood beside a dust-covered rickety Ford and he looked at her hopefully. "Taxi, ma'am?"

"Tell me," she said, walking nearer him, "do you happen to know where Hank Martin is? He's campaigning in a tent . . ."

"Yes, ma'am," he smiled, "y' shore askin' the right man. Hank Martin's in Amityville, thirty-one miles east n' north. Y' want to get took to him, I reckon."

"Yes, I do. What will you charge?"

He eyed her clothes, pursed his lips, and pondered. "Well, now, it's right smart wearin' on a car to travel that 'air road. Cars is made just for haulin' folks to hotels 'n sich." He looked up and studied the sky. "It ain't goin' to rain, though; so I reckon I can fetch you there for the same price I charged them other two women I carried out to him."

He chuckled as he named his price.

"Dollar a mile," he said and grinned.

"Agreed," said Verity stiffly and put her bag in the back.

"Better ride up front alongside me," said the driver; "rut'll like to throw you outen the back seat."

After a few miles of pavement in the city they struck the rutted dirt roads. The driver held tight to the wheel and jounced with some restraint, but Verity braced her feet against the floor slant and was miserable. Two women—two women—who could they be? She told herself she was being a fool. They could be interested in Hank's organization.

"Afternoon show'll be some time over, time we get there," said the driver. "I got me a notion to stay for the night show, seein' it's goin' to be clear weather. I been hearin' this here Hank Martin's got somethin'—somethin' for folks like me. 'Course I ain't white trash but I shore ain't rich like that Robert Castleberry. Now there's somethin' as gives me pause —I say why does Mr. Castleberry go out to hear Martin? I hear tell Castleberry kinda sneaks into some night meetin's. Hat pulled down 'n collar turned up. Is he studyin' Martin's ways for to steal his ideas or to find a way to get even? I hear Martin pulled a fast one on Castleberry. Hear tell he calls him the Black Skimmer." He laughed heartily. "That's callin' 'em, that is! Yes-sirree-bob, that's callin' 'em! Every time I think on it I can just picture that Castleberry feller flyin' high lookin' over the lakes that holds all us little fellers and see him swoopin' down to swaller us up. Dang if that Hank Martin ain't got somethin'! Yeah, I reckon this time I'll stay for the night show. Want I should haul y' back tonight?"

"I doubt it," she replied. "You see, I'm Hank Martin's wife. I don't know what the plans are."

He turned and stared at her.

"Hell," he said after a second, "don't that go to show how folks lie 'bout a man that's on his way up!"

She didn't answer. Why was the announcement of her name something that always caused some odd reaction? Would she ever understand, ever just take it in her stride? And why would Robert Castleberry be sneaking into Hank's meetings? She couldn't imagine his sneaking, as the driver said. His arrogance seemed so innate a part of him she couldn't imagine his putting it aside for a moment.

She realized she must make some conversation with the driver so he would be comfortable. She began with the fall cane crop, discussed the surrounding territory, and even told him about Hancy.

The blues of twilight were just beginning to mute the flaming reds of sunset when they sighted Hank's tent. They had driven through a winding road that seemed a veritable jungle and then suddenly came upon a great wide space. On this earth had grown huge trees which had been felled to make thousands and thousands of board feet of finest lumber. The sawed-off stumps stood, their mighty roots still firm and spreading in the earth. On the edges of this big clearing many of the stumps were still white and sap-oozing, fresh wounds of fated giants.

All around the circle small fires burned, cooking the suppers of Hank's followers. Shawled or bonneted women hovered over the fires and overalled men stood about talking excitedly. These would stay for the night meeting, she knew. She also knew that Hank could repeat word for word what he had said in the afternoon and they wouldn't mind. It would only impress them. But she also knew that Hank was not a one-speech campaigner. She knew Hank would always give a good show, repeating only those things his followers must remember.

"Yonder's a main entrance," said the driver, pointing.

Before this entrance Jenny paced back and forth, her hands clenched. From head to foot her attitude was one of tense and tearing anguish. She did not notice the car, did not seem to hear its raucous sounds. As the car stopped, Verity alighted, adjusted her hat, smoothed her hair. Sudden excitement at being near Hank swept over her. Jenny would know where Hank was. With her bag in her hand she walked forward.

"Jenny," she called, "Jenny!"

Jenny whirled. She stared at Verity then slowly walked toward her as if in a trance. Her blue eyes were big and staring and dark-circled, and her full lips bitter-tight in her too-thin face.

"What's the matter?" cried Verity.

"Gawd!" said Jenny in an echoy, hollow voice. "Gawd! I thought I was a-goin' plumb daft fer shore." She clutched the fur collar of Verity's coat with hands that had grown spidery thin. She laughed with a kind of bitter hysteria. "You shore picked the right time for to come. She's just gone in there, 'n the other one—the Flamingo—that's whut she tolt me Hank called her—" She spat the words.

A strange feel of chill went over Verity, like ice water running through her nerves. "The Flamingo?" she whispered.

"Yeah," said Jenny. "'N that 'ristercrat slut, Sylvia Hylen, she just went in too." Dry sobs wrenched Jenny in some great emotion.

"Come on," said Jenny. "You oughta fix 'em both."

She took Verity's hand and together they went toward the entrance. Half afraid, Verity hesitated before pushing back the tent flap. How silly of me, she thought. Of what can I be afraid? It's just that the name Flamingo makes me remember terror. Even if it is Flamingo, why should I be afraid? She's only a child. She can't be more than seventeen or eighteen even now. Eighteen! Why, by swamp reckoning that would make her "a woman growed" for two or three years! But she was being silly! And in that moment's self-search she also wondered fleetingly about Jenny. She pushed back the flap and stepped in.

The last blue light of the day poured into three sides of the tent from the airspace between the tent wall and the peaked ceiling. But from the west the bright glow of sunset poured in and high-lighted the platform.

Hank sat at a rough table which was on the ground just below the platform. Verity knew the membership cards were kept there. His head was bent over papers. Verity was about to speak when a girl's figure became suddenly clear on the platform. The girl had just mounted the steps on the side. In the sun's light she was so beautiful Verity gasped. Her dress was a dusty rose, a soft, form-clinging Angora knit. Her slim round waist, her high lovely breasts, were carved out in the magnificence of perfect beauty by the sun's glow, and haloed by the soft wool fuzz of her dress. Her glorious red hair in a shoulder-length shower of curls drabbed the bird for which Hank named her, and even in the careful tiptoe the easy movement of lagoon and jungle was hers. Noiselessly she went to the edge of the platform, spread her hands out toward Hank, thinned her abdomen, and lifted her breasts like a swan diver.

"Hank!" she called softly, and her voice, though soft, had the throbbing, carrying wave of a voodoo drum.

Hank's head went up. He turned toward the platform, jumped from his chair.

"God'lmighty!" he said. A kind of disbelieving awe was in the cadence of the word. He went to the platform and touched the girl's foot. "God-'lmighty, thought I was mebbe a-havin' a unearthly visitation!" He stepped back and viewed her.

"Don't call me unearthly," the girl laughed. "It ain't like you, Hank. You usually call things right."

Hank laughed. "So you're the Little Flamingo growed! I see you been a-makin' the best outen that beauty course."

"I sure have," she said softly. "Me first."

"Well, you sure are a somethin'! God'lmighty!" His voice grew tense and Verity tried to turn and run, but she couldn't move.

Hank looked up at Flamingo, his hands grasped her slim ankles, his head went back as he looked up the length of her body to look into her face.

"Thy stature is like to a palm tree . . ." he said huskily.

There was a sound like hissing steam, and from the shadowed tent wall to the right came Sylvia Hylen. She stood in the aisle and threw her scalding words at Hank. "I will go up the palm tree! And then the next line is something like this—'thy breasts are like two young roes on a mountain of spices.'"

Verity managed to turn and take the few steps necessary to get on the outside of the tent flap. Jenny followed. Verity clung to a tent rope and lowered her head. Nausea was in her stomach and fear in her throat. Plainly she heard the raised, angry voice of Hank.

"I've tolt you time 'n agin you ain't of a size to stalk me—"

Slowly Verity began walking away, Jenny holding onto her. Slowly Verity became aware that Jenny was sobbing wildly, uncontrollably. They went to a small tent inside of which were a table and several chairs and steel files. The office tent.

Sinking onto the narrow little folding chair behind the desk Verity clutched her hands together and stared at the sobbing Jenny, whose thin, almost transparent hands clenched the desk top, her white knuckles seeming to pop from the skin.

"I ain't a nothin'," Jenny sobbed. "I ain't a nothin'. That Sylvia's all silk 'n smooth. 'N that there Flamingo's more beautifuler'n any female critter oughta be. 'N you're a lady 'n beautiful enough fer anybody. But me—" she said hollowly, "I ain't a nothin'. I'm jus' poor li'l Jenny, Harry's widder. . . ."

"Stop!" cried Verity. Everything in her protested against this added shock. But Jenny did not stop. She went on and on.

"Jus' Harry's widder. I know now, a-lookin' back, that Hank allus made me to come more alive. 'N I look back 'n think, yeah, after seein' Hank 'n a-hearin' of him talk so fine, them was the times I liked Harry's love-makin'. Yeah," she seared herself in bitterness, "Hank gimme the feelin', 'n I worked it off on poor Harry. But now I ain't got a man. It's a-killin' me."

Suddenly she stared at Verity. Her last words trailed lamely. Into her eyes came the realization of what she had said and to whom she had said it. The blood of shame swept up, pinking her face.

"Oh, Gawd!" she whispered.

Verity closed her eyes. A queer feeling of sick emptiness made her weak. She felt she should say something to Jenny, Jenny who was so tortured, something to allay the humiliation she must feel. She forced herself to open her eyes and look at her friend.

"Poor Jenny," she whispered.

But her words were ill chosen.

"Yeah," said Jenny, "pore Jenny." She rose, leaned over the table and looked at Verity, a little defiantly, a little pleadingly. "I'm gonna be full a' sorrow 'bout this when I think back on it, I know. 'N likely full a' shame."

"Please, Jenny . . . I have no blame . . ."

"No, I know. 'N I'm gonna do somethin' 'bout myself." She drew a deep, shuddery breath. "We got a new man travelin' with us. Flower Higgins. He's kinda soft on me 'n I'm a-walkin' right outa this tent to ask him will he wed me."

Verity stared at her.

"Yeah," said Jenny harshly, "what Bible saint was it said 'It's better fer a man t' wed than t' burn'? Well, it goes fer women, too." And she turned, walked through the laid-back tent flap.

"Jenny!" Verity called. "Jenny! Come back! Don't do that!"

"I gotta do it," said Jenny, simply, decisively.

Verity never knew how long she sat there. It might have been minutes or hours. Just sat there in a sort of hypnotized stupor, her body numb and unfeeling, and her head a big emptiness filled only with sad and distorted pictures of Jenny and Hank and Harry, of the Flamingo and Sylvia Hylen. Hank's voice brought her to.

"Sweetface," he said huskily, "Sweetface—"

He stood in the tent opening, barely outlined against the darkening night.

"Answer," he demanded.

But she could not. He turned a flashlight full on her.

"Sweetface," he said, "it's purely wonderful t' be a-seein' you. But you're a-lookin' peaked. You're not still ailin'?"

"I have a new sickness," she said. "And turn that thing off."

He turned it off, struck a match and held it. Now she could see his eyes studying her.

"Light the lamp," she said almost commandingly.

"Shore," he said, removing the chimney and holding the match to the wick. He replaced the chimney and walked around the table, took her wrists in his hands and pulled her to her feet and to him. "What ails y'?" he asked softly, huskily, looking down at her intently, his nostrils beginning to pull down, to whiten, and with desire and hunger in his eyes. "Whyn't y' come a-lookin' for me 'stead a' settin' here?"

"I did," she said shortly, "and that's what ails me."

"Yeah?" It was a tentative question. Getting no answer, he asked, "Say, d' y' know who's here?"

"Yes," she said coldly. "The Flamingo. Also Sylvia Hylen."

"So that's what ails y'!" He chuckled and pulled her nearer. "Jealous, huh?"

"Worse than jealous. I'm sickened." She glared at him and acid dripped from her as she quoted, "Thy stature is like to a palm tree . . ."

He laughed and still held her imprisoned against him.

"Aw, hell, Verity—iffen y' seen it, then y' sure know how it was. There was me a-standin' down on the ground 'n her a-standin' on the edge a' the platform 'n me a-lookin' up at her. 'N why wouldn't I think a' that palm tree with them fine bosoms a' hern a-standin' out cuter'n a couple a' halved coconuts."

"There is still Miss Hylen." She glared at him.

"Now, lookit, can I help it iffen some—" He stopped and turned very earnest. "Lookit, that girl's made my life hell. She purely has. I tolt her 'n tolt her I don't want her a-follerin' of me. Now I guess she's gone for good. Got the Flamingo t' thank for that. The little devil. That kid tolt Sylvia Hylen—" But he stopped and started over. "'N as for the Little Flamingo—well, I ain't seen her from the day her paw took her down the river with her hair blackened. Not from that there day till just then. She wrote me 'n says what'll she do? 'N I 'member she's a beauty; so all I can think of is a beauty school 'n I send her money t' be a-goin' t' one in Crescent City. 'N that's all." He glared at her a second. "It sure pains me, Verity, to be explainin' of things like t' that." He grinned at her teasingly, and putting his lips against her throat, he nibbled and nuzzled her neck.

Her nerves came suddenly alive, hotly alive with the old sweet lushness. But at the same time something in her scorned her and jeered her for being a fool.

"Don't!" she cried.

"Y' want me 'n y' know y' want me," he whispered.

"Yes," she said with great bitterness. "And I hate myself for it sometimes." A great anger rocketed through her. Beating his chest with her fists, she cried, "Why aren't you the kind of man I thought you were! Why aren't you the kind I can want and love without this clawing conflict always inside me!" And she ran past him toward the out-of-doors.

He caught her just at the tent opening, shut the tent flap, and holding her firmly, said softly, persuasively, "Don't you never run away from me, Sweetface. You can't never make it, 'cause I won't never let you go. You're a somethin' extry special t' me. You're the sassy, fast-runnin' brook down a hillside. You're the high mountains from whence cometh my help, 'n you're the still, still glade where a feller can do his true prayin'."

Looking into his earnest, pleading eyes she wanted more than all else in the world to have done with all this conflict and inner confusion. Feeling herself giving over to him, she began to cry.

"Feller like me has gotta have one such as you, Sweetface," he murmured.

She knew he spoke words of truth, words he meant, words she would never forget; but right now there was still bitterness in her and as she thought them over the emphasis for her was on the word "one." She felt, rather than actually analyzed, that the power that was shooting him upward to prominence was the love that people felt for him. There were bound to be some for whom it was—oh, well, there were Lula May's words. With this thought, her own personal feelings diminished. A cosmic compassion, a sort of Godlike pity put her own hurt for the moment in the shadows.

"Poor little Jenny," she said softly, "poor little Jenny."

"Jenny!" roared Hank. "Jenny! Now that's a-goin' to the point a' insult! I ain't never done nothin' but just help Jenny 'cause she's pore Harry's widow!"

"I know that, Hank." She looked him over from head to foot. "You know," she said judicially, "you're not so wonderful to look at. It's the feel you throw out. It's what makes you great, and I suppose it's what makes you weak. It's why you have liked having me at home, where you can come when you choose. It's why I should be with you, building the kind of guard that only a wife can build." She nodded and almost smiled into his bewildered stare. "Yes, I can see why wives go on campaign tours."

Plainly he didn't like this kind of calm, critical weighing.

"Now, you lookit here, Verity. Don't you be a-givin' me no highfalutin' tongue lashin's that leaves me a-knowin' less 'n I knowed afore. You be a-explainin' what this's got to do with the likes of Jenny. 'N if you think you're a-goin' on this here tour, you're plumb crazy. You're a-goin' home where there's some chance a' you a-stayin' some'at liken you allus been. God'lmighty, Sweetface," he pleaded, "I need them high mountains 'n that still, still glade."

She was bewildered, full of pain. She patted his hand and tried to smile.

"Hey, boss," a big booming man, larger than Hank but with none of Hank's litheness, pushed the tent flap aside and stood there. "'Scuse me, boss, but Guy Polli is here. 'Evenin', Miz Martin."

"You met my wife?" asked Hank.

"No, boss, I ain't. Jenny tolt me she's here."

"This here's Flower Higgins, Verity."

So this is the man Jenny—she caught her thoughts and tried to smile at the big fellow. Big and powerful but gone a little soft; he was, probably, thirty-five. His eyes smiled and there was a look of awkward kindness about him that went oddly with the cauliflower ear on the left side of his head.

"Flower? Did you say Flower?" she asked, wanting to hear him talk more.

"That's account a' my ear." He had a shy, fussed manner just now, and Verity liked him. "Used t' fight with my fists. Now I don't fight at all. Just threaten with this." He clapped his hand over a holster. "'Fore y' see this big shot Polli, boss, I wanta ask you can you do without me tonight. Jenny 'n me—well, Jenny 'n me—"

"Well, what about Jenny?" asked Hank edgily.

"Well—we aim to git wed." He looked flustered. "This very night," he added, obviously amazed at his good fortune.

"So soon!" cried Verity.

"How'd you know it was soon?" asked Flower, surprised.

"Well, I'll be danged!" said Hank. "What d'you know! Little Jenny!"

"Yeah," said Flower, "hadda tell you 'fore you got talkin' with Polli. Can I go after I fetch Polli?"

"No," said Hank, "but you fetch him. I want you 'n that rod right here. Leastways tillst I take his measure. Get yoreself a chair over in that corner 'n set by 'n say nothin'. I'll tell y' when y' can go."

"O.K., boss," said Flower, and left the tent.

Turning to Verity, Hank said, "Go on, Sweetface, go on out 'n make yoreself known t' the womenfolks."

"No," she answered firmly. "I prefer to stay here. Who is this Polli?"

"Big-shot bootlegger from Crescent City 'n he ain't nobody you should oughta know. 'Sides, you get all squeamish 'bout things. You ain't got no understandin' a' politics. 'N the politics a' Crescent City is mebbe the dirtiest in the country. The dang place is controlled by Appleby, the mayor, 'n his ring. 'N they ain't nothin' but a vice ring. Hell, bootleggin' 'n gamblin' is a man's game. But them whore houses!" He spat disgustedly.

"You're against whore houses?" she mocked.

Glaring at her, he took her by the shoulders and said fiercely, "Iffen Polli wasn't a-comin' any second, I'd plumb shake sense into you. That's what I mean 'bout you a-goin' back home. I don't want you gettin' like that! 'N a-course I'm agin whore houses." A twinkle came into his eyes and a little grin played on his lips. "I hold whore houses is bad for men, account they don't build 'em up. It's better for men to hafta whet 'n hone theirselves up to bein' plumb persuadin'. Makes a man a man, 'n not just a pocketbook. Now you get a-goin'."

But she sat down. "You'll have to put me out if—"

"Here he is, boss," said Flower.

Two men were with Flower, a squat, broad man, in well-cut clothes, and a sleek, thin man whose tight coat sagged suspiciously as his right hand was kept jammed in his pocket. The square man lifted his hat from slick black hair, and his brilliant blue eyes looked affably from Hank to Verity.

Hank and Polli shook hands. "This is my wife," said Hank. She offered her hand and felt the smoothest, softest hand she'd ever touched. Except maybe Hancy's when she was absolutely brand-new, she thought. Polli's man did not accept Flower's offer of a chair, so Flower also stood. Both guards just stood, stone-still, distrust in every taut line. Looking at them, Hank grinned.

"Relax, boys, relax," he said. "Mr. Polli 'n me is gonna be friends." Turning to Polli, he continued, "Mighty nice a' you t' come here at my invite. I'd 'a come t' you, 'cept for this campaignin'. Now, I'll lay m' cards right on the barrelhead, 'n you take it from me I'm a-dealin' to you square 'n offen the top."

"That's the only safe way to sit in a game with Guy Polli," said Mr. Polli, touching his long, plump white hand to his chest.

"Only kind a' game Hank Martin sets in," declared Hank. "I ain't a-goin' to waste time a-beatin' 'round the bush, nor pretendin' there ain't a skunk 'r two a-stinkin' up yore business 'n my business. So, here's how it is—I'm gonna be the next Commissioner a' Public Works 'n Highways —that is, I will be iffen it don't rain so's the country vote can't walk through this goddam blackjack t' get t' the polls. Mebbe I don't even need no votes in yore city, but I'd shore like to make some showin' there."

"That's where I come in, of course," said Polli smoothly. "Do you know the exact extent and number of wards under my control?"

"Well, a' course I do," grinned Hank.

"You're one up on me," said Polli. "I have no idea what you control."

"You do know that just three days ago the legislature passed a bill to fill in miles 'n miles a' Lake Baudelaire. Whole south end, in fact, where it keeps a-creepin' up on rich estates on the edge a' the city?"

"Certainly."

"You know what they're a-fillin' it with?"

"Certainly. Ground rock."

"Wrong. The law states specific and plain that oyster shells discarded by the canneries in this state shall be used, but not to exceed one-third.

It further states specific and plain that the rock has gotta be bought inside the boundary lines a' this here Magnolia State."

A gleam of understanding, of vast interest, came into Polli's eyes. Hank glanced uneasily at Verity. She was sitting very still trying to look unknowing. She thought, Great God! so this is how it is done! She looked at these two men with the gleam of acquisition in their eyes. How childish, how obvious it all seemed to her. But both men looked at her with apprehension: Polli studying her, wondering if she should be entrusted with this; Hank studying her, wondering how he could get her out of here. The little imp in her came sardonically alive.

She laughed, a bit affectedly. "So Hank has optioned or bought all the rock quarries in the north hills of the state," she said almost lightly.

Hank stared, utterly dumbfounded. "How the hell did you know?"

"Oh, I've always been good at puzzles." She smiled, and Mr. Polli smiled back admiringly, showing short, even, and very white teeth against his swarthy skin.

"She is right, Mr. Martin?" he queried.

"Yeah, she's right," said Hank almost glumly. "Leastways 'bout the rock. But I also own the shell dumps a' all the canneries. Bought 'em up near 'bout a year ago. Them cannery fellers laughed at me a-plenty." His mouth grew just a little bitter. " 'N what's more, I got me iron-bound contracts that makes me owner a' the shell of every oyster that's hauled in 'n hulled for years t' come."

Mr. Polli leaned forward and asked softly, "And is there a point in that, Mr. Martin?"

Hank leaned forward. "Ain't you never heard ground oyster shells makes a most hard 'n elegant road-bed mixture?" The positive avarice that now showed in Guy Polli's face made Hank grin. He settled back in his chair and said easily, " 'N call me Hank. All my friends . . ." he hesitated and added pointedly, " 'n all my followers do."

Polli straightened, feeling the demand for allegiance to this stranger. "And my cut—?" he asked in scarcely more than a whisper.

"A full half a' all that goes into the lake. I ain't niggardly. The ownership I'm a-retainin'. Come road buildin', we'll check on the past 'n judge the future."

Mr. Polli thought this over, then suddenly beamed. "Thank you, Hank, my friend." Then added softly, "This little Cajun boy is satisfied—for the present."

Patently Mr. Polli was very well pleased with the immediate future, so Hank grinned and turned his eyes on Verity. But she looked blandly, untellingly back. Hank turned again to Polli and said ruefully, "Ain't women hell?"

"If so, I don't want heaven," said Guy Polli with a rather fetching and foreign shrug.

"Huh!" grunted Hank. "Huh! That 'minds me. Flower there, he aims to be a-gettin' married tonight. 'N it's near 'bout time for the meetin'. Better stay, Polli. You 'n me'll sign papers 'n such afterwards." He nodded to Flower. "You can go. I got no need for y' now."

"You sure, boss?" asked Flower conscientiously.

"A-course I'm sure," said Hank firmly. "Swith can be a-standin' watch at the meetin'. Go on. 'N tell Jenny to be a-thinkin' on what does she want for a weddin' present, for I'm aimin' to gift her fine 'n handsome."

Flower grinned, but he still eyed Polli's man suspiciously. Polli's man looked at his boss.

"You can go along," said Polli to his guard, "and be his best man."

Then Hank and Polli forgot their bodyguards and turned and looked at each other. They were partners. Suddenly they both chuckled.

"Politics makes strange bedfellows," said Polli tritely.

"Shore does," said Hank.

Yes, thought Verity sadly as she watched the big Flower go eagerly to Jenny. Yes, very strange bedfellows.

12

Throughout the state went Hank Martin, an evangelistlike campaigner, telling the poor that they were captives and telling them how he could free them, if they steadfastly backed him by votes.

But he knew one thing could surely lick him, and that was rain —rain which could turn the roads in the south of the state into blackjack and in the north of the state into treacherous red runners. He told everyone he'd be elected if it did not rain— if only it did not rain. And so, when election day came and the weather. . . .

VERITY felt like a tightrope walker trying to balance herself with two umbrellas. One, a huge emotional umbrella, and the other a small umbrella of good sense. The good-sense one was very small, it sometimes seemed to her. No larger than a Victorian face shade. Yes, she thought, that's probably it—just a complexion saver. One umbrella was never put wholly away while the other was relied upon. She couldn't let go of either one; so she swayed this way, then that, feeling always a little insecure, a little annoyed with herself.

She longed for Hancy during the three months she traveled with Hank, and she worried. She thought often of Big-Gray standing in the barn, and the wagon already loaded with nearly everything a peddler required. She remembered Selah's words about not throwing away one's washboard. She remembered her resolution never again to fail another because of her own needs, and certainly not because of her need for Hank. How could she keep that resolution and still do right by her husband? Hank seemed to love having her with him, but that was when he had time from planning and campaigning, in their moments alone. He liked her to mix with the voters, but there were times when he sat in conference all night long with strange men, some of whose names she would never know. Some were obviously gentlemen, the others oddly assorted.

She tried to make herself useful by redoing the files according to Hank's instructions, and Hank asked Jenny to help. The first few times Verity and Jenny worked together were hours of strain, long silences with only necessary questions and answers. Verity tried to break through this, but Jenny kept her wall up. Jenny had managed for nearly a month to avoid Verity even though the tent occupied by Jenny and Flower was usually not more than fifty yards from the larger one which Hank and Verity called home. The first day Jenny came to the office tent Verity looked up with pleased surprise. Some flesh was on Jenny's light bones, her breasts were rounding, her eyes once more fitted her face, and she had lost that burned look of the sleepless person.

"Oh, Jenny," cried Verity, "how wonderful you're looking!" Jenny looked at her defiantly. "And so smart in that black dress," Verity added, trying to be natural.

"I don't like black," said Jenny in a voice that had a reined-in sound. "But Flower does. Says it's a lady's color. But I ain't no lady."

"That's where you're wrong, Jenny." Verity was very earnest. "There's something splendid and fine in you."

Jenny looked away. "Well, let's git t' them files," she said harshly.

"Yes. Yes, of course." Verity sat down at the table. "It gets warm in this tent. Wouldn't you like to take your coat off? Spring is here and this tent makes it feel like summer."

Jenny kept her coat on, sat down opposite Verity, motioned toward a file drawer on the table. "Is them what we start on? What's Hank want done?"

"These cards signed by the members are to go into a bank vault. We're to make new cards. One file is for names in alphabetical order, another a cross file parish by parish. And wherever we have the names of the children we're to notice the children's ages. Those who will be of an age to vote this fall are to be written down on cards to be filed separately. Those who will be of an age to vote two years or four years from now are to be put in another file. Everything in duplicate, to be filed by name and also by parish."

"Lotta work," said Jenny grudgingly.

For four days they worked together with the unnamed specter forever between them, like a positive, felt presence right in the middle of their worktable. On the fifth day Hank popped in.

"Well, Jenny," he howled, "I ain't seen you since y' got wed. Been over at yore tent, 'n howled for y', too. Didn't never get no answer. Seen you kinda long-distance in the cong'gation most every night." A dull red colored Jenny's face. "But," Hank went on, "I ain't had no chancet to wish y' well in person." He beamed on her, put an arm around her shoulders. "Flower must be a better feller'n I thought, seein' as how bloomin' y' are now. Dang if you ain't a-gettin' right purty, Jenny. Li'l ol' face is plumb a flower now, atop that thin stalk." He laughed. "Why, even the stalk's a-juicin' up!" Almost tenderly he said, "Spring has come agin for you, ain't it, Jenny? 'N that's how it should oughta be."

"It's better food 'n more of it." Jenny looked miserably at Verity.

"This outfit was eatin' afore ever Flower joined up," he grinned. "Man don't live by bread alone. 'N that's the way it should oughta be, too. Say, Jenny, you ain't never said what would y' like for a weddin' present. I been a-thinkin' on that. How'd you like them twins a' yoren to be a-goin' to a good school?"

"I'd like 'em learned right," Jenny mumbled.

"There's a dang fine school for little fellers like them down t' Crescent City. Catholic, though. But what the hell! Us Methodists 'n Baptists in these here parts is the most unlearnt folks in the world, seems as though. Now, Sophy is fine withen yore kids, but they should oughta be learnin'. What say I send 'em to school? You like that?"

She gulped, stared first at Verity for a long time, then at Hank. "I shore would," she managed.

"You want I should raise Flower's wages enough so's y'all can pay it? Or you want I just say it's a present 'n do the payin'?"

Batting her eyes hard to keep back the tears, Jenny answered, "You do it. Iffen Flower don't never feel that there money in his pocket he ain't gonna have no anguish a-partin' with it for young'uns as ain't his."

Hank looked surprised. He whistled softly. "Them's purely pearls a' wisdom. They purely are. She's shore gettin' t' be one wise li'l Jenny-wren, ain't she, Sweetface?" Patting Jenny's hand, he said, "You sent word by Flower as how you wasn't a-workin' for me no more, 'n t' take you offen the pay roll. Well, ain't none a' these folks gettin' what they should oughta get. 'N here y' are, workin' for me, like allus, so I'm puttin' y' back on. Now what'd I come in here for in the first place?" He looked about. "Oh, yeah, I wanted t' tell y', Verity—in that there file in yonder corner is the names a' the key men in every district 'n every parish. Don't be a-touchin' them. I gotta look them over special."

He gave Verity a little wink and nod of affection and approval and left. Jenny's big eyes looked at Verity with welling gratitude.

"Y' never tolt him," she whispered.

"Of course not," said Verity softly.

" 'N y' never blinked even when he said he's seen me in the meetin's." She sat a long time just looking at Verity, while Verity struggled to stay calm. Jenny seemed locked in dumbness but trying to break that dumbness with the right words. At long last she said, slowly, "Mebbe I won't never git over bein' fired by Hank. Anyways, I wanta thank y' for this washed feel y' just gimme."

Deeply touched, Verity put her hand over Jenny's. She wished she had a washed feeling. She thought, I've been now with Hank a month and I've never made an issue of that episode with the Hylen girl and Flamingo.

She had known in some vague way that her lack of further action or talk with Hank was connected with Jenny. But it had remained an unworded, unsorted harassment. Now it came clear. But for Jenny's suffering she might never have seen it. Poor Hank, he needed her protection. Poor Hank—and a strange compassion filled her—he gives off heat like the sun. I've always known that and like all living things I, too, turn to it. Yes, he gives off heat—but no light. I was wrong comparing him to the sun. He's more like some earth core shoving heat up from the roots. That, she thought, is the great difference between Hank and Jules. Yes, Jules gives off light, and only a few, a very few, will get close enough to find his warmth. But Hank is sort of all-inclusive, like nature. This last perception filled her with distaste. Clearly now she saw the full meaning of Lula May's wisdom, "Women is made fer bringin' int' the world more a' the things they thinks is worth their lovin'. God gives us only one way t' do it." She could hear the flat, simple statement as plainly as if Lula May stood before her now. " 'N so women lusts fer a man liken Hank."

And she was no different from the others, she thought, except that she was married to him. But didn't the simple fact of marriage make her relationship different? Yes, it most certainly did, for it involved and colored every single thing in her life—her home, her activities, her child. Every act of Hank's redounded on her. It threatened her very soul's fiber because she was not wholly in accord with Hank. How could she keep everything whole and square and right?

"How can I guard them all?" Unknowingly, she spoke aloud in a despairing whisper. Jenny, who had been sorting membership cards, trying to act natural again, put her cards down and looked straight into Verity's eyes. A deeply intuitive look it was, throbbing and turbulent, and Verity knew Jenny felt much, knew much, which might never be spoken.

Pulling her coat over her shoulders, Verity rose to leave, for this was the day of the week when she telephoned to Jules's Moses. It was her only way of keeping in touch with home. Selah's not being able to read nor write made this necessary. But Jenny's eyes never left hers, and Verity hesitated, held by the look in them. Allegiance was there. Some strange hybrid allegiance perhaps, but allegiance. Her heart went out to this racked girl. She wanted to hover over Jenny and heal the hurts. Verity stood as in a spell. Some miracle was happening here; some swift, silent flow, warm and living, ran between her and Jenny. It was Jenny who found words for this new bond.

"We're blood kin, feels 's though," she said softly.

From the vantage point of the office tent Verity watched the growth of Hank's amazing organization. The mornings were filled with the comings and goings of new men. Sometimes, after a few words, Hank took them outside; sometimes they never came again, sometimes they stayed.

Under Hank's direction Flower was recruiting men whom he called gorillas; gorillas to man the polls district by district; gorillas who would be spread out over the state like a thousand-armed octopus. Many of these Hank had known for years, but some were new, attracted by the whispers of future pork barrels. Two of these were Jep Low, a thin, brown man, tough as barbed wire, and Vince Trullinger, big and strong and deceivingly lounging in appearance. Before Hank had accepted these two, he had sent them with Swith and Flower to the woods to test their eye and aim and quickness for shooting. Now when Flower was gone on an errand to Guy Polli or elsewhere, either Jep or Vince took up Flower's stand, or perhaps it would be Swith. Having these armed men always about bothered Verity. There was no privacy anywhere except in their home tent at night, and even then one of these men was outside in a pup tent.

At first Verity attributed this solely to Hank's love of drama, his way of attracting more attention. But as she saw more and more men of the tight-lipped gangster type come with their armed guards to call on Hank, she wondered. She had asked him about them but he had laughed her down.

"Roarin' thunderbolts, Verity, I'm just a-trainin' them men for the future. A-testin' them out, kinda like."

But Jenny told her Hank had received four anonymous letters warning him that he would never live if he ran for commissioner. Flower had told her Hank thought they came from Castleberry; and remembering Harry, the two women looked at each other and each saw fear.

Verity reached an all-important crossroads in her life the morning Hank received the party-machine men. The committee, he called them. She had been walking alone for several hours in the woods, a thing Hank strictly forbade. Hank, who had feared nothing in the world of nature, not beast, nor 'gator, nor snake, now knew a sneaking fear of man. As she came back into camp, Swith ran to her.

"Praise Gawd!" he said fervently.

"For what?" she asked flippantly. Then, half realizing, she demanded, "Has Hank detailed you to follow and guard me?"

"Yeah," he said. "There's them as threaten, seems 's though. Please don't go off alone no more," he pleaded. "Hank'd—"

She wanted to explode. She felt like giving a good imitation of Hank. She felt violence gathering within herself. Just plain violence. Not mitigated with sadness, nor the desire for better things. Just plain violence. She wanted to stand there and scream out some of Hank's choicest invectives. Clenching her fists, clenching her very innards, to keep some self-control, she turned from Swith.

She'd had no breakfast. The mess tent, with its rolled-up side walls, would give her shelter from the sun, and she could also watch for the committee's arrival. She sat on an up-ended fruit crate which served as a chair at mess table, and stared out at the camp grounds.

"Missed y'all dis mo'nin'," said the big black man who cooked for them. "Got fine ham."

"Just coffee," she said, trying not to sound short.

But he knew all was not right with her and attributed it to worry about the committee. Everyone in the camp knew this was a turning point and the whole place had that still, waiting feel that comes after all the preparations possible have been made.

"Don' y'all worry, Miz Martin," Cookie soothed, "dem big shots'll come. An' w'en dey leaves dey gwine be li'l shots, only dey ain' gwine likely know it." He gurgled with appreciation. "Yas'm, dey de onliest ones on dese groun's ain' gwine likely know it."

He placed a big tin mug on the table, then brought back two huge coffeepots, one in each hand. One contained the blackest of black coffee and the other hot milk. He tipped the pots simultaneously; the black stream and the white stream went into the cup and blended.

"Mistuh Hank shu' one fine man. You know w'at he say he gwine do w'en he guvner?"

"No. What now?" It was a struggle to keep her voice free of bitterness.

"He say he gwine make all little homes free uv tax," the man marveled. "Yas'm, he do say dat. He say all homes as ain' wuth more'n t'ree t'ousan' dollars he gwine make tax free. I askes him plain do it mean usn cain hab a li'l ol' house an' mebbe a acre 'r two tax free, same's de po' white. An' he say hit shu' 's hell do. An' den he say—I 'members his words exactly— Mistuh Hank say, 'De po' agin de rich—dat as fer 's I can go in class leg'slation, so de po' blacks benefits along wif de po' whites,' he say. Whut dat mean ex-actly—class leg'slation?" he asked.

"Oh—writing laws that take from one class of people to benefit another. Something like that," she said absently.

Cookie scratched his head and thought very hard on that but gave it up and went back to his coal-oil stove. In a few minutes he said, "I heahs ca's."

She listened. Yes, several cars. She saw Jep and Vince and Flower, who were lounging outside the office tent, come alive; saw Flower go inside to tell Hank. Several cars, all big and black and impressive, came slowly into the grounds. She saw Jep and Vince run to them, heard their questions and answers, saw the committeemen stiffen when they were told the "commissioner" was expecting them in yonder tent; saw the stifled ridicule in their attitudes and expressions as puny Swith lowered his countryman's gun somewhat and stepped aside from the tent opening to let them pass within.

It was in moments like this that she felt in accord with Hank, burned with him to make the successful and fortunate recognize men like Swith as brother beings. With all her heart she wanted to see accomplished most of the things Hank planned—freedom from tax for the small cabin and the few acres; for the present taxes on the poor were exorbitant. With all her heart she wanted to see schools, and, yes, free schoolbooks, and fine roads. Did the end justify the means? Hank declared it did. She didn't know. She only knew she hated the method.

Hank had made his bid to the minority party, knowing they had no hope of winning in any event; knowing the best they could hope for without him was to provide friction for and be an annoyance to the incumbents. But as Hank said to Verity, "I'd a heap rather have what votes they'd get from the fools as just vote reg'lar regardless, than go t' all the trouble of runnin' independent. Too much red tape, filin' 'n all. Anyways, this here United States is a two-party country. Come time when I wanta be President, mebbe, I should oughta have the name of a reg'lar party tacked onto me."

Yesterday she had seen Hank getting his figures together district by district, parish by parish. This many votes he could guarantee, "iffen it don't rain." She could imagine his laying the facts before the committee forcefully, lucidly, and declaring he would also pull a surprise vote in Crescent City. Then these men would declare, "Impossible! Mayor Appleby has that town in his palm." And Hank would say obliquely, "Yeah? You shore got a surprise comin'—'n, anyways, I don't actual need that city vote. It's just that I like t' surprise fellers like Appleby—'n you. I'll be elected anyways—iffen it don't rain."

Then he would dumbfound them with his accurate, well-compiled figures of the vote he expected parish by parish. They would roar and tell him he was crazy, that there weren't that many voters in the whole dam parish, and Hank would howl with laughter and say, "Never has been to date, gentlemen. Most of them is first voters. But total them as will vote for me against the vote of the last election, 'n you'll be a-seein' —iffen you'll compare the total with the census figures—that them people lives there someplace. Places fellers like you don't even know exists. 'N there's also a helluva lot the census takers ain't even found. 'N iffen their vote is questioned, they'll be able to take you t' their homes. Not nobody could deny them shacks has been lived in for years, mebbe for two generations, mebbe seven. You're a-overlookin', my friends, the fact that I've been walkin' to them places on my bare feet since I was thirteen years old."

And after this subject was wrestled about some, he would, she knew, appeal to their individual greed. Hank would lean forward and say in a dramatically hushed voice, " 'N, gentlemen, you ever thought much on how rich them fellers of the opposition is a-gettin'? 'N yet how much they're a-overlookin'? You ever thought much on the shrimpin' 'n the oyster concessions?"

After their ohs, and ahs, and hows, after the uneasy scrapings of chairs being drawn nearer, after the resettlings of bodies, after "the gimme-gimme look gets growed bigger'n bonfires in their eyes, I'll tell 'em"— then and only then, he'd tell them the results of his endless research, research which once before rendered him rich profit. "Everybody knows," Hank had told her, "that this here state's got control of, 'n jurisdiction over, all waterways inland. 'N also the sea out to fifteen miles offen shore. Oysterin' 'n shrimpin' is sort of concessions, therefore. But—'n here's the catch, Verity—" He grinned. "There's a li'l ol' phrase in a li'l ol' law, wrote a long time ago, as defines all waters that touch the shores as water highways, as highways and main arteries of transportation. That was wrote afore railroads 'n land haulin', when about the only inland towns was river towns. Well, as highways they belong under the jurisdiction a' the Commissioner of Public Works 'n Highways. Commissioner is a elective office, but some governor wanted more patronage to dish out 'n he just separated the waterways 'n give some friend a fat job. But the dang fool forgot to make it bindin' 'n legal. He just done it the convenient way. Well, I ain't a-wantin' it that convenient."

Yes, she knew all this and she could picture the scene; could see Hank's face as he finished with, " 'N that, gentlemen, is why you'll not only be a-lendin' yoreselves to makin' me commissioner, but it's for reasons liken to them that you'll be a-helpin' to make me governor in two years."

Leaving the mess tent, she went and sat in the shade of a cypress not far from the office, within the cadences of voices; cadences which rose at times like the roar of waves and softened again like the pleased rustle of many leaves. At times she was filled with admiration for Hank's capacity for work, the immense amount of planning, of dogged study; the tireless, constant activity, the ability to get what he was after. And at times she filled with revulsion at the way in which it was accomplished. Were such methods really necessary? Hank always said they were; that his methods were O.K.'d by long precedent. The whole picture maddened her; made her feel the kind of fury that wants to flail out at everything. She wished she'd never known about it. Yet she had to know. She'd made it a business to find out. And now she knew, she thought sickeningly. She had listened stoically when Hank told her of his plan of approaching these men, knowing she could not dissuade him; knowing that she was to Hank just what he'd said—the high mountains, the brook, and the still, still glade—things he wanted and needed, but only during the intervals between the caterwauling.

A long time she sat there, still and brooding. Finally the men came out of the tent with Hank. All was affableness and handshaking and back-slapping between them. As Hank stood looking after the departing cars, one of Hank's own men drove in with the newspapers for which he had gone, as always, to the nearest town. He brought them to her and as she took them listlessly, the Crescent City paper on the top of the pile told her in scareheads of the murder of two men. Their pictures and names stared up at her but meant nothing.

"Hank!" she called.

Turning, he waved joyously and came to her dancing an exuberant cakewalk. Flower, Jep, Vince, and Swith laughed with pleasure and fell back to give them a little privacy.

"Went smoother'n silk," he crowed, "just liken I told y'. Surprised?"

"No," she said.

"Ain't you a somethin', though! Allus expectin' the best a' yore man!" He bowed before her. "Strut with a winner?" he invited.

In bowing, his eyes fell on the paper. He snatched it, read some of it. "Back in a minute, Verity," he said, and taking the paper with him he hurried into the office tent.

She rose and followed him. Inside the tent Hank stood before the Crescent City file, a card in his hand, staring down at the pictures in the paper. The full knowledge of what this meant seared her brain. Running to him, she grabbed the card, ran her finger down the names listed under Polli, Guy, comparing them with the names of the two dead. There they were on the card.

She crumpled the card in his fist and shook it at Hank. "Killing! Killing!" she said moaningly, like a wounded thing. "By whose actual hand we'll never know, I suppose. But I'll always know where lay the beginnings of this." She struck the pictured faces of the murdered men.

Hank's mouth was set. Set with determination and some pain. His eyes were fixed on her, yet as she looked at him accusingly and with hurt, an eerie feeling came on her. His eyes, always so bright, looked so unseeing now.

"Hank! Look at me!" she demanded.

He shook his head like a pup shedding water and, sitting down, put his head in his hand.

"Don't look like that, Hank," she cried.

He grinned. Not wholeheartedly and joyously, as usual, but cynically. "I'm all right. Don't give yoreself no worry. I'm just nictitatin'. D' you understand what that is?" he asked.

"No! And I don't want to," she cried, frustrated, and furious.

"You gotta understand," he pleaded earnestly. "'Cause I'm like to have to be nictitatin' a heap in the future." At her impatience, he said, "No, now you listen t' me. Nature's wonderful 'n most kind. Birds as fly high, as have to have such sharp eyesight as to see clear 'n plain things as small as a field mouse on the ground whilst they're a-sailin' a mile up, has a nictitatin' membrane. A kinda third eyelid. A kinda filmy thing they can draw 'crost their eyes at their will. Yeah," he sighed, "birds as is built to get up high, 'n see far, 'n go a long ways, is also built so's they can nictitate at will. So's they can rest them sharp eyes whilst still a-goin'—so's they can shut out what ain't worth the seein'.''

Taking her clenched fist in both his hands, he held it firmly and went on. "Yeah, nature is kind that-a-way. She builds critters as fly high so's they can nictitate. A politician is like to be a' that breed. Yeah, I want decent roads in this here state so's the pore won't have to be takin' whatever a Black Skimmer says. I wanta see all the young'uns get a chancet at learnin'. I want lotsa things. I aim to fly high. 'N iffen a couple off-color gents is killt in the process—" He took a long breath and said firmly, "Then I'm nictitatin'. 'N that's how it's gotta be, Verity."

She felt—she almost knew—she had received a mortal blow. She could not accept this—yet it was useless to fight it.

"You can't mean that, Hank," she whispered.

"I gotta mean it," he said huskily.

Trembling, she sank onto a narrow little folding chair.

"Steady, Sweetface," said Hank firmly. "Allus remember, when you're a-feared, breathe deep, pull in. Pulled-up guts a-pushin' on lungs full a' air is right confidence-givin'."

Rising, he stood before her a second, touched her cheek with one finger, gently, in that marveling way. "That there Venus girl shouldn't oughta never go into battle," he said softly, and strode out of the tent.

She wept. She wept a long time, shudderingly, convulsively, and with a sense of hating herself for a weakling. She was sick of being forever beaten and inundated in Hank's wake. She had to chart a course for herself. She had to! She'd played around with the notion long enough. Now, she had to. And more, she had to see that Hank's child's—her child's—vast energy was directed rightly. Thank God for Selah, she thought reverently, gratefully. The monotony of the little house in Cypress Bend began to appear to Verity as peace. She had to get away from Hank for a while. She had stayed here to guard him, but she saw now she had thought to guard him against women. And women, she decided, were not his chief danger. She could understand the women. And why wouldn't she understand them? she thought bitterly. But this nictitating! What a strange and perfectly telling word it was!

She rose, consciously braced herself, took a deep breath, and with head high she walked across the grounds to the tent she had called home for these months, and began her packing.

When she had finished, she stepped outside and told the ever-present Swith to find Hank and then go for a driver to take her to Mundro.

"Tell Hank to hurry if he wants to see me. Tell him I'm leaving him. And hurry, I want to catch that afternoon train to Crescent City," she told Swith.

Hank came running. At sight of his face she remembered how she had worded the message, for bewilderment and fear were in his eyes. It was hideously hot in the tent and she sat on the edge of a cot. Everything in her was completely worn, completely exhausted, except the small, new-born iron monitor in her brain.

As Hank stood a second in the opening of the tent, the sun blazing behind him, turning his hair all purple and copper, outlining the broad, lithe strength of him, she felt, as so often before, enfolded in his gaze. Slowly he came to her, looked down at her, and then, satisfied, he swooped her up into his arms in the sudden, sure way he had.

"Swith musta misspoke hisself," he whispered. "You're just a-goin' home."

She nodded, her head against his neck, and kissed him just below the ear, loving the steamy feel of him, the tangy, rich, sweet smell of him, like pine needles and loam.

"Home is where you should oughta be," he said, "but this ain't mebbe the right time for leavin'. We should oughta have two-three days together for just a-gettin' back t' bein' man 'n wife agin."

She was very sad. Trying to smile, she said, "I've got to get going."

She wanted to stay in his arms, wanted those two or three days of being just man and wife, wanted, in fact, a lifetime of that; wanted to make some kind of bargain with fate and settle for the two or three days Hank offered, but the little iron monitor stood firm and unyielding. So, sighing heavily, she stepped back from his arms, with everything in her, except the monitor, sick with the sense of loss, and turned to leave the tent. But Hank stepped in front of her.

"I ain't a-likin' the feel a' this partin'," he said solemnly.

She could not answer. She wasn't up to finding the words she needed. The wound was too new, too sore.

Seeming to perceive in part, Hank picked her up gently. "Some things has just gotta be. 'N you gotta get strong in this world. You're my wife, the woman a' my choice. 'N I don't never go for puny critters. You ain't gotta be strong the way I am. That ain't what I'm a-needin'. You just keep the brook 'n the mountains 'n the glade in you 'n I'll allus come back." And he carried her out to the waiting wagon and put her up in the seat beside the driver. Then he motioned Swith. Hank and Swith went into the tent together and came out with her luggage. Swith climbed into the back of the wagon and, with no further word, Hank motioned them on their way. The driver clucked and slapped the horse's rump with the reins. They jolted forward.

The afternoon audience was gathering. Looking back, she saw the people grouping around him, but for once he seemed impervious to his followers. He stood, looking after her, and while her breaking heart cried within her, What now? What now? his two hands went to his lips, then his arms outspread in a beautiful all-giving gesture that promised, "I'll allus come back."

Upon the high wagon seat she sat; the wagon bumping over the rutted roads wrung her stomach muscles and tore at her back. But she held herself stony and rigid, for within she was a battleground. The little iron monitor in her brain rejoiced in her strength, while her fighting heart cried, Fool! Fool! Turn back. Hank is all that matters! Yet the little monitor fought, crying, Nictitating! Willful blindness to anything that might stop him!

Where did the monitor come from anyway? she asked herself. But she knew before she questioned. It was her heritage from her mother. The hot, humid forest around her became her mother's kitchen in the Sheltering Arm, the sound of the horse's hoofs and the dust rising from the road became the sound of many little orphans' feet on the kitchen porch stamping off the dust of the garden after their Saturday's work. Verity's mother, starched and tired, dipped the long-handled ladle into the huge earthenware jar, filled the thick, heavy glasses, and patiently responded to their demand for a story. When Mrs. Wade told the story of Abe Lincoln, she didn't say he had "a pulin' paw." No, indeed. Abe's father was very poor —but what of that? In this country every child had the right to reach out beyond, to reach for his dream. Now, George Washington was a rich man, but George Washington did not coddle himself and stay comfortable. No, indeed. George Washington had a dream of liberty for all men in this new country; so he froze and hungered at Valley Forge to give all people who came after him a better life. "And so," Verity saw her mother wave the long ladle for emphasis, "it was because a rich man, who could have stayed snug and comfortable, fought to father this kind of government that the poor boy, Abe Lincoln, could make himself into the kind of man who could expand Washington's dream to include the slaves. These men," Verity's mother added, "were good men and true. They followed the Holy Spirit which lived within them. They lived by the Inner Light."

The Inner Light—the Inner Light—Verity came out of her vision to see the little depot in Mundro. The train whistled in the distance and she was grateful she would not have a long wait. More than anything else she needed to be alone, to ponder.

"I'm a-buyin' yore ticket," said Swith importantly. So she said an automatic good-by to the driver and stooped to pick up her luggage. But Swith returned. He juggled his long gun and took her luggage.

"I'll be a-totin' 'n a-puttin' fer y'," he said, and struggled up the train steps.

She followed him down the car aisle. His gun pointed straight ahead as he held both it and a suitcase. She thought, Thank God, I won't be seeing him and his gun every time I lift my eyes, every time I turn.

"Watch your gun, Swith," she warned.

"Y' got no cause fer t' fret," he answered. He stopped beside two vacant seats. Indicating the front one with his head, he asked politely, "This meet yore pleasure?"

"Yes, yes," she said.

He placed her bags, straightened them. Verity held out her hand to say the longed-for good-by, but Swith stepped past her and sat down in the seat back of hers, propping his rifle, barrel up, beside him.

"Where do you think you're going?" she demanded.

"Along withen you," he said. "Hank, he says I gotta go clear home along withen you."

"You'll do no such thing!" she exploded. "You get off this instant!"

"I gotta pertec' y'," he said. "I gotta."

"It's insane," she hissed.

"Nope. 'Tain't," he replied stoically.

The whistle blew. The train bucked. She clutched the seat back to steady herself.

"Oh, Swith," she pleaded, "please, for God's sake, go away and leave me alone."

"I jus' plain cain't, Verity." His great eyes looked up at her with the misery of a rebuked pup.

"Oh! Oh! I'm so sick of you and your gun!" Tears filmed her eyes and, miserably aware of the curiosity of the other travelers, she sat down in the seat just in front of Swith and stared unseeingly at the passing cane fields.

The conductor did not care for Swith and his long polished firearm, either. As he stopped for Swith's proffered ticket, he asked, "That thing loaded?"

"Shore is." Swith was not meek, nor was he aggressive; just amazed that anyone would think his gun was unloaded.

"Um—well," the conductor cleared his throat, "I'll have to take that gun and keep it during your journey."

Verity realized she would have to take a hand in this. She turned to look at Swith. His right hand lay near the trigger with that caressing, expert lightness. And into Swith's face and voice came the earnest intentness which she knew so well.

"I wouldn't be a-tryin' it, iffen I was you," he said.

The conductor seemed about to speak, then changed his mind. He looked helplessly about, the near-by passengers sat in strained attention.

"It's quite all right," said Verity to the conductor. "Really. It's quite all right."

After some hesitation the conductor moved on. Verity leaned over the back of her seat and, speaking low, said, "Please get off at the next station. After all, I'm going to Crescent City, a perfectly civilized town."

"Can't be so turrible civilized," said Swith, "withen men like t' Polli a-runnin' it."

She felt the burn of tears and, turning, slunk low in her seat to avoid the stares of her fellow passengers. She could imagine herself going into a hotel with Swith trailing. And there was no train for home until morning! Would Swith expect to squat in a hotel hallway, his back against her door, rifle across his knees? She knew that was exactly his idea of careful guarding. Jules would know how to handle Swith. Jules's guarantee that she would get home safely would satisfy Swith. If she couldn't locate Jules, then Saber.

Jules was not in the city, but Saber came to the depot immediately, jaunty and quick and flashing as always. He punctuated her story with chuckles but his eyes told Verity he was weighing and appraising this tale to find its true mettle. He promised Swith that he would take over the problem of Verity's safety and added that Swith must either go back to Hank or be turned over to the police.

"You wouldn't actual do that t' me, a-course," said Swith desperately, holding to what little he could.

Saber assured him he was in earnest and tried to persuade Swith to take the next train back to Mundro. Swith had had enough of that. Humiliated and upset by the brush-off, he looked up at Saber, pathetically and stubbornly.

" 'Druther trudge it," he said. "Varmints got better sense'n most folks."

Saber grinned. "O.K., Swith. Go back your own way."

So they drove Swith to the edge of the city and turned him loose, and as he stood by the side of the car, feeling he shouldn't have let this be put over, a wave of contrite affection for him swept over Verity and she patted his hand.

"Thank you, anyway," she said. "If I ever need protection, I'll know I can depend on you."

Into Swith's eyes came the light of devotion. "I'm plumb shamed fer t' be so pesterin' t' y'," he said humbly, "but please, Verity, y' gotta be 'memberin' that Hank ain't a feller as runs when no man pursueth." He slid down the road embankment, went into the thick underbrush, and was gone.

Saber turned the car. They rode a long way in silence. As the day died in blue, the night came alive with the bright yellow glow of the many city lights. She had never been in this city, knew little of big cities anywhere, and she should have been excited. But she looked on with an unresponding detachment.

"Poor kid," said Saber, "you're worn out with all Hank's malarkey. Have you ever been here before?"

She shook her head.

"Most colorful city in America, perhaps. Here it sits, old and sophisticated, hiding behind its ancient iron-lace galleries and its hand-cut jalousies, the exciting conglomerate which is Crescent City—old France, old Spain, and, yes, old Africa. And through all, a new, raw mixture we can call young America, in itself an exciting blend of bloods and purposes."

Grateful to him, she shifted her position so she could watch him. She liked the bright scintillating quality in him, the sharp, sure flash of him. How remarkable of Hank to have christened him Saber!

"You make it sound wonderful," she said.

"I could never have appreciated this city properly if I hadn't first known Hank. If I hadn't first seen with him, and through his eyes, the country and the people which push at the very edges of this town. Sometimes, Verity, when I think of that, I see this city as a hardy old galliard, gay and fun-loving, and imbibing his bootleg liquor; a deaf and blind old galliard who cannot see that his own grandsons are becoming impotent, and who cannot hear the marching feet, the martial music of Hank's swamplanders."

They were in a park, almost at the very edge of the business section. Slowing, he said, "Look—there, all safely fenced, are a few alligators for the city folk to look upon if ever they feel the urge. And there—there are some native snakes and wild animals, all safely caged. And over there a little way is an acre, a carefully tended acre, which purports to be typical of the growths in the swamplands. And, Verity," he added significantly, "I'd bet every dollar I hope to have that there are not ten people in this whole big city who have the faintest notion of the immensity of the real things which this effete park represents!"

She looked about. How truly he spoke. Saber chuckled with a malicious glee.

"Perhaps," he said, "the ten would be the former owners and executives of the Southern Light and Power. Hank knocked those fellows into a total eclipse. I don't think they know yet how he managed to scare them into Bolduc's lap."

Becoming wary, not wanting to give away Hank's dealings, she said nothing to this.

"Oh, I know what happened," laughed Saber, "but I can't prove it. And then, I don't care."

"But," exclaimed Verity, "you seemed to care very much at the time!"

"Oh, I guess it wasn't hearing about the graft that shocked me especially. I realized that later. It was—" He hesitated. "Oh, hell, Verity, it was remembering Swith harnessed to his wheelbarrow, coming through the misty morning, like all the little men in the world pulling their hard-got cash and their dreams through the mud. It was thinking of Hank's great potentialities—a man who could so move the hopeless and the burdened." He sighed. "I guess Hank just caught me when I was a new-born cub wanting to believe in the good and true. Don't get me wrong," he added conscientiously, "I never felt any special allegiance to Hank. Like every newspaperman—perhaps every writer—I feel allegiance only to the people as a whole. You know, recording the truth so that, as Hank himself might put it, he who has ears to hear can hear."

Glancing at her, he laughed deprecatingly, "I'm awfully talky tonight."

Nodding, she said, "And a good reason for it has been kindness. Just plain kindness. Oh, I know, you felt me bursting. You've helped a lot." She was very earnest. "What would I have done without you!"

"Haven't I been an awfully good boy, though? A tops reporter not asking a question! Could you just tell me why poor little Swith was resolutely protecting you?"

"Not for the newspaper?" she asked cautiously.

"Off the record! Honest Injun—or should a Yank in this country say honest Cajun?"

"I'll take your word whatever you swear by," she declared, laughing, some joyousness bubbling in her. "Oh, Saber Milady, you've no idea how wonderfully free it feels not to be trailed! It didn't seem so bad in the camp. Swith was just one of the people I expected to see there. But on the train!"

"But why?"

"Well, Hank has had threats, letters, and—well, I don't know. And you remember Harry Disbro?"

"Of course. But—" he hesitated, then added, "Seems a little thin."

She shrugged. "Maybe it is just Hank's dramatics."

He turned off the wide main thoroughfare of the city into a narrow cobbled street lined by old brick houses with narrow wrought-iron balconies and shuttered windows, stopped before a building with handsome fan windows.

"This is Renault's," he said. "It's been serving the finest food in the world for a hundred years right on this same spot, same building, and by the same family." He stood now on the walk opening the car door for her. "And ah! *Mon amie!*" He kissed his finger tips, threw the kiss starward, lifted his shoulders, and swayed with exaggerated ecstasy. "Ah, such food! Nevair haf you taste such food! *Crevettes remoulade! Pompano en papillotte! Poulet Rochambeau!*"

"Translate!" she laughed.

"Only your palate can translate at Renault's. And then," he warned, "you will not get the conjunctives right. The little touch of this, the drop of that, the wee jigger of wine—no one else will ever get them just right. And," he whispered solemnly, "there is good wine here—old stock—for those who are favored. And I am favored. The favored are bowed to and led to a lovely back room that used to be a part of the slave quarters. But those who do not rate with Renault must sit in the front rooms."

He pushed open the old door. Entering, Verity thought at first glance that the place was completely ordinary except for the snowy whiteness of good linen and the savory fragrances. Renault himself, grandson of the first Renault, hurried forward, greeted Saber with a formal friendliness, looked over the room, remarked that perhaps he would prefer dining in a rear room? Yes, Saber would, thank you. Renault went ahead, leading the way.

Halfway down the room Verity was arrested by a dark, familiar face and a brilliant red head. Guy Polli and Flamingo! She stopped for one fleeting second. Saber, walking beside her between the widely spaced tables, felt her hesitancy, and his eyes followed hers.

Polli looked up, directly at Verity. She bowed, but Polli's eyes went blank. He did not return Verity's bow, but Flamingo said easily, "Hello, there. Long time no see. Remember me?"

The deep, lovely vibrato of her voice enriched the commonplace, flippant words.

"I most certainly do," replied Verity, trying not to feel this girl's beauty, trying not to be afraid of it, trying not to show that she had to try. But in spite of herself, she added, "But then my memory was refreshed just about three months ago."

Flamingo laughed lightly, unembarrassed. "I thought mebbe you saw me," she said.

Throughout this Polli sat looking as if he'd never seen Verity before in all his life, but as Verity started to move on, Saber spoke.

"How are you, Polli?" he asked affably.

"Just fine," said Guy Polli guardedly.

Verity realized in a flash of foreboding that Saber was not only a friend, he was a news hound. She walked on toward the waiting Renault as Saber remarked to Polli, "Pity those men got murdered with elections just a few months away. Mayor Appleby's machine will miss them, no doubt."

"No doubt," said Polli stoically.

Saber joined Verity. Renault seated them. Saber gave the hovering waiter the order, but with no fine show of the appreciation he'd had a few minutes ago. The anticipatory savoring of food was gone.

Leaning across the white-spread table, his face a puzzle, his lids half covering his eyes, he said dreamily, "She's a lambent flame, a nimbus— she's Phoebe! She's Aurora!"

"She's the Little Flamingo!" said Verity harshly.

"The Little Flamingo," he repeated, musingly. "Perfect! Far more fitting, no doubt," he grinned ruefully, "than all my goddess names. Hank named her, of course? Him bein' the most describin' man in the state, as his friends say."

She realized Flamingo and Polli had probably met that day on Hank's campgrounds, possibly even while she and Hank talked before Flower ushered the bootlegger into the office.

"Hank wouldn't name anyone for appearance alone," mused Saber. "Let's see, what are the habits of the flamingo? All I know is that their nests are mounds of mud built just high enough to keep out of water." He was being almost sadly cynical. He sighed, "Hank certainly collects remarkable playmates."

"Playmates! Why, Hank's known her all her life," she defended. "Her father is one of Hank's best friends."

Grinning, he said, "Gave yourself away with that, Verity. I was thinking of Polli and Castleberry just then." She flushed with annoyance at herself and with some apprehension. "It's funny," he went on, "how many things a man knows that he may never prove. For instance," he looked sharply at her, "I am now one of the few who will expect Hank Martin to roll up a sizable vote in this town. Isn't that right?"

"I—I don't know why he should." She was lying poorly and she knew it.

"Too bad," said Saber, "that the publishers of newspapers in this state seem to have a sort of agreement among themselves. They think he is just a howler in the wind. After that one story about Harry's trial, my editor blue-pencils everything I say about him."

After a long minute he said, "And to think that I, Saber Milady, the wise and knowing journalist, thought Hank Martin was just being dramatic when he sent an armed guard with his wife! Let me tell you just a little about this man Polli."

As he leaned across the table and lowered his voice, she felt the familiar nudge of fear and apprehension.

"Guy Polli's father," began Saber, "owned a big saloon, and when prohibition came in, young Guy was old enough and sufficiently well trained in astute business ways to be set up in a distillery. Then Guy Polli built his realm. Way down south of this city, on one of the islands in the very mouth of the river—an island used once before by an outlaw pirate—Lafitte, in fact—there is an amazing distillery. And not only that. Ships laden with good liquors have lately been boarded by supposed government revenue men, men who have what appears to be a regulation coast-guard cutter. The new pirates of the sea, they are. The modern bootleggers —Guy Polli's gang."

Stunned, she stared at him, hardly comprehending.

"But if it's known, why isn't it stopped?"

"You ask me to solve in one sentence the riddles of finance and power? Of greed versus law? And who am I to preach? For here I sit twirling a glass of wine as I talk of it. This prohibition law is ridiculous, of course. But here is the sad commentary on it—bootleg wealth has bought vast power all over America. It has demonstrated how to rule through money and fear—and of course, through the indolence of the people at large." Taking a long breath, he said, "Well, to get back to Hank. He certainly picks the playmates. Now you wouldn't think Robert Castleberry and Guy Polli had anything in common, would you?"

Not waiting for an answer, he went on. "But they have. Both are collectors of the things they think beautiful. Castleberry, who probably has never shot anything but clay pigeons for a sportsman's medal and ducks for a sportsman's outing—" he stopped a second and spoke the next phrase parenthetically, "we'll disregard Harry Disbro for lack of evidence —Castleberry collects dead, cold, polished and well-cut jades. While Polli, who has been twice held for murder and twice freed, who is known to rule by the power of the gang and the gun, collects warm, living birds. He has an aviary which covers several acres, all fenced with chicken wire. It even has a wire ceiling, Verity. Yes, it really has. A wire ceiling enclosing live-oak trees. Imagine it—a birdcage acres big and a half-mile high!"

He sipped his wine and looked at it as though seeing a vision there. She realized he had been summing up things for his own clarification as much as for her.

"I'm being fanciful—I hope." He sighed. "You never saw such a magnificent sight as that aviary. It surpasses the Arabian Nights. Brilliant. Exotic. Beautiful for a glimpse. But there's something brutal, something truly sadistic about anyone who will imprison that much beauty for himself alone. . . . And she is so beautiful," he added softly.

Trying to imagine such a place as he talked, Verity almost lost the portent. Flamingo! He was trying to tell her that if Flamingo was just a friend she might well be fenced before she could become anything more; he was trying to tell her that if she was more, then—but she dare not think beyond this! And, yes, he was trying to tell himself that he did not care what became of such beauty. Oh, he had told her so much—too much— and what could she do about it? Remembering Polli's long, plump, soft hands, she shuddered. Her brain whirled and her heart fought fear while nine dollars' worth of the world's finest food was set before her and taken away, and it might just as well have been sowbelly and cowpeas.

What a blessing was home! She sat long evenings trying to think out many things, trying to plan her wagon route, figuring, figuring, and thinking, thinking. She cherished the sense of serenity; the ticking of the clock, Hancy sleeping in her little bed, Selah finishing the dishes, or perhaps gone to her own shack but leaving her presence in that blessed sense of loving care which gleamed in starched curtains, glistened in dark green floors, and shone in the crystal cleanness of the lamp chimneys. Sometimes she could forget the worries and bask in the feel of home. Home, she realized, meant more than ever before, meant something rooted, something flowering, something reliable. She would knock out that wall and add two rooms and a bath and someday she would enlarge Selah's little house and put in a bath, just for the pleasure of seeing Selah's eyes when she beheld it. Yes, sometimes she just basked in the sense of home, but mostly she felt an undercurrent which endangered it. Most of the time underneath all else she did and said, a tiny stream of consciousness stirred like an ever-present thing which prodded her to find the strength to do the things she must do. So she planned her wagon route, persuaded Bije Peck, Tim's eldest, to start out as a traveling merchant.

Sometimes in the evenings she sat quiet and alone in the soft yellow lamplight, in the midst of a swarm of whispers, no one of them clear and outspoken, but buzzing—buzzing. Night after night she tried to single them out, to understand what her heart and her spirit were trying to say to her mind. And through these times Hank's word "nictitate" haunted her, an opaque presence, an unexplainable dark nebula. And through it all, like a thousand-volt wire, live and burning with its power, ran the longing for Hank. Sometimes in that soft yellow lamplight she crumpled the papers which were covered with figures on the cost and profit in ging-hams and calicoes, linseed oil, and rouge; crumpled them in fingers tense and nervous with the need for the feel of Hank. Sometimes so great was her longing, so hot that wire, that she slammed out the door and ran across meadows and atop the knoll, or ventured toward the bayou where fierce night creatures of the woods might prowl. Sometimes she took her need to the great live-oak tree and sobbed her longing against its strength. These were the times when Flamingo and Sylvia Hylen floated before her and she singed her heart on that burning wire, and pulling back from it, found herself in the shadow of that haunting dark nebula. Sometimes the nebula was only a shadow and sometimes it was a misty composite of Hank's hazed-over eyes as he said, "Then I'm a-nictitatin'," of Polli's soft, soft hands; of the scathing, curdled stare in the gooseberry eyes of Robert Castleberry; of the dream in Swith's face, the flailing 'gator pole; of the big Flower hurrying to the parched Jenny.

After these sessions with herself the little iron monitor told her anew that she did not want to live on money that came from drawing a third eyelid at will, from the power of men like Polli who controlled bootleggers and whores, and, through these activities, the "gentlemen" of place and power who bought these wares. She could not live on that kind of money, nor would she have Hancy do so. But, cried her common sense, this means separation from Hank! No! cried all her intuitive knowledge. And she knew that this "no" came not only from her own desire for Hank, but from the true love, the greater love. She knew that Hank needed her; knew that she must try to keep within herself the high mountain, the still, still glade. With this thought came despair. How could she keep herself as she was? Would she lose those qualities in the fight for her own strength, so that she fail no one, not Hancy, not anyone? In not failing Hancy or herself or others, was she failing Hank? Had she failed him in the past and not known it?

And what does one do when one fails? She pondered it over and over. If I have already failed, what can I do? And only after weeks of pondering did one clear whisper come singly out from the buzzing swarm—"I have to rise again and start again from where I seem to fail." It was a clear whisper straight from her spirit to her mind. And her heart took courage and she looked at Selah's garden to see if it would sustain them, and she bargained with Picayune Potter to build her two rooms, knowing well that she need not wait to ask Jules for permission. She went to Delamore and learned about septic tanks and cesspools. She thumbed her mail-order catalogues and counted over the money on hand and waited anxiously for Bije Peck's return from the first wagon trip so that she might judge the profit after he received his percentage. She chose the cheapest enamel bathtub in the catalogue, but not the cheapest toilet. She could not have piped running water, so perhaps that toilet would sit there, unused for a long time. But even if the water had to be carried, she would have a tub that would drain out and she could again know the luxury of an all-over bath.

Often as she planned the new rooms and drew diagrams, and talked with Selah, she wished Jules would come home. He must be very busy with his light and power company to stay away from the plantation all through the summer months. When she drew her final plans, she carefully made them to meet Jules's suggestion that there be a patio.

She had an idea Hank would think all this foolish. He was so much nearer to his palace, all marble and shining, that this share-crop house would seem more temporary than ever. But she was fortifying her soul with a home, and every woman fiber of her approved it. She just did not have a third eyelid. She, Verity, was simply a wingless mate.

Throughout these days Selah watched over her with a look in her eye which reminded Verity of her own mother. The same concern was there. Concern for her proper growth, it seemed. And though Selah could not have put it in words, Verity knew Selah sensed her hunt for a spiritual stance. And she was grateful, for this loving quality in Selah gave Verity much strength. By the end of the summer they had chickens and a few hogs. Selah took their cane to Jules's grinder and vats and made their syrup. Tape butchered for them and under Selah's guidance Verity helped smoke and corn their own pork.

As voting time drew near, the folk of the Bend came oftener. Hope came alive in their eyes as they talked, and with their talking the tiny confidence which Verity had built dwindled. She looked at the new rooms. They were just pine walled and smelling fresh and woodsy. They were really ugly little square rooms, completely dependent on color for their small share of beauty. She looked at the gardens, the full shelves of canned goods, the pork, the dried corn, the dried beans, the cowpeas. She saw that it was all so little and realized she had done it because it was the only thing she knew to do. But with Hank's coming drawing nearer it dwindled to insignificance. Hank would soon be home again!

Each day now she dressed with great care. Each day, often several times a day, Hancy was dressed and washed, her dark curls carefully combed and placed, "in case your daddy comes today!" If it was Selah talking, "yo' pappy, he lak ter come dis day!"

Throughout the early fall months when rain fell heavily or even just lightly, she thought of Hank, his fear of rain on election day. When election day was within a week's time, her first act each morning was to hurry outdoors, look off toward Tim's shop, and read the weather signs as Tim had taught her. If the smoke from Tim's forge was climbing high in feathery double O's to the sky, and the birds, too, were high, ignoring the shelter of trees, then it would be fair and dry all that day and night. But if, in the early morning, the birds flew low, or cheeped from the trees instead of spiraling to greet the sun, and the smoke flattened out, then it would rain. No matter how bright the sun shone at the moment, it would rain before the next morning.

This morning, the day before election, she stood in her little yard, in her warm yellow robe, breathing the sweet frost-flavored air, shading her eyes to see the smoke. There it was, looping its way joyfully heavenward, and birds, mere specks, seemed literally able to peck the face of the sun. "He'll be elected," she said aloud. "He'll be elected." And she turned and looked again at her little home and her little efforts, trying to realize all that smoke and birds forecast. "He'll be elected," she repeated, feeling dumbfounded by the news. Leaning upon her gate, she looked off over the meadows toward the knoll. The night dew, whitened to rime, silvered the grasses and stubble, and the warming sun graciously set the world with diamonds for a few lovely minutes before redressing it in daytime brown and green. She seemed to see the little boy Hank, running across the fields while the little things of the earth scurried before him and pleasured him; as he ran swinging his arms for blood warmth in the chill of the early mornings while the "rime was still on the grass"; running for warmth as he troubled his baby brain about his mother being some strange captive. She looked back at the high-sailing smoke. "And tomorrow," she told herself in great awe, "tomorrow he'll be elected!"

13

By now everyone knows that Hank Martin sometimes wore an iron vest, but few know of the first time he wore it.

The need for an iron vest rose that very first election. Yes, it was election eve and the huge campaign tent stood on the meadow in front of Hank's little share-crop house. A great party for the followers of his home parish was in progress when terror was struck to the hearts of all, for news came that nine men were out to kill Hank. They were the Davols from Delamore, and Marcus Davol had been a partner of Robert Castleberry's in the Delamore cotton gin. . . .

HANK came in the late afternoon. Verity and Selah heard wagon wheels crunching the hard rutted roads. It could only be Hank's outfit, for there were mingled with the tromping of many hoofs the sounds of brave singing.

Flying to the mirror, Verity patted her hair, powdered her flushed face, grabbed a shawl for her shoulders, and ran outside. All four of the wagons came down the road and all voices were raised in one of Hank's favorite "fightin' hymns," and over all she could distinguish, as always, Hank's voice so powerful and tuneful.

"Children a' Zion, awake from thy sadness;
Awake, for yore foes shall oppress you no more—"

She felt herself stirring within, coming sharply to life, coming keen with the pure joy of being, feeling in herself a brilliance and at the same time a power to observe, as if she saw and heard as well as felt with greater awareness when Hank was near.

"Bright o'er thy hills dawns the day star a' gladness;
Arise, for the night a' yore sorrow is o'er!"

It was like a personal message to her. Her hungry heart opened to the words, "the night of your sorrow is o'er." "Oh, let it be so," she asked of her God silently, "let it be so. All these months here alone. Such a long, long night!" She clung to the gatepost while the thousand-volt wire came singingly alive, reminding her . . . reminding her . . .

Hank's uplifted arm saluted her, and handing the reins of the first team to Flower who rode beside him, he leaped from the wagon and came running ahead of the horses. Stopping outside the gate, he looked down at her with all the anticipation with which one sees the spread of Thanksgiving. Almost as if unable to believe the fact of sight, he put one finger to her cheek in his characteristic way, marveling, reverent, and passionate.

"Hank—" she breathed softly.

"Lord save us!" His whisper was low, just a passionate throb.

"We'come ter y', Mistuh Hank," called Selah from the little porch. "Y'all bin a powe'ful time gone."

Pulling his eyes from Verity's, he came into the yard, looked at Selah, and grinned broadly.

"Selah, even you are a plumb joy t' a man as is honin' for home." He was full of the joy of return. "Yes, sir!" He nodded his head in emphatic admiration as Selah's broad face beamed. "Even you are a sight for home-hungry eyes, y' great big black skinful a' sin!"

"Go 'long, Mistuh Hank," laughed Selah; "I is a deaconess uv de church."

"Well, it don't seem t' do you no harm," said Hank, teasingly. "You don't yet look too godly for t' comfort man."

Selah's full-gathered skirts did a little jig of pure pleasure as her big stomach moved to her laughter.

"Doggone," she giggled, "you gone so long, Mistuh Hank, I neah 'bout forget whut sugary deelight you dishes."

"Doggone," he mimicked, "I been gone so long I near 'bout forgot what a close second you run me in the dishin' a' such. Where's my girl-child?"

"She sleepin'," Selah replied. "Usn starch dat chile up fresh ever' hour for de pas' ten days an' now you kotch her rumpledy."

"Well, iffen she's sleepin'," said Hank to Verity, "let's you 'n me go out t' the folks 'n tell 'em where t' set up the tent. I reckon there'll be some fandango tonight."

"Law!" cried Selah, "looky yonder, Miz Verity! Mistuh Hank shu' 'nuff home! De whole place done turn inter a hullabaloo! An' looky dere, Miz Verity—dere dat li'l ol' Mistuh Swith jes' a-standin' wif his gun, an' dere t'ree mo' men, all sizes, jes' a-standin' wif guns! Ever'body workin' 'cept dem. Ain' dey gwine do nothin'?"

"They're my bodyguard," said Hank.

"Bodygua'd?" Selah puzzled over this one, then asked in wonder, "Law, Mistuh Hank, you hones' t'ink yo' body worth dat much gua'din'?"

Up and back went Hank's head in delighted laughter. "You're dang tootin', since I'm the one as lives in it."

Selah nodded. "Reckon so," she said, seeming a bit doubtful. Then, becoming her practical self, "Say, is I gwine hafter feed all dem folkses?"

"Nope," Hank replied. "We got a cook. Great big fine darky feller. Make four a' that there skinny Tape."

Selah's great eyes rolled naughtily. "Um-m-umph!" She gave the wordless exclamation all the meaning her race can give and with a capering whirl went into the house.

It was wonderful to feel gay and lighthearted. Everything in Verity bubbled in excitement. She looked over the activities, saw the familiar faces of the campaign tour.

"Jenny stop in the village to see her boys?" she asked.

"Yeah. With Sophy. They'll all be comin' along come nightfall. Folks comin' a long way can stay the night in the tent. I aim to have some dancin' in the tent tonight."

"That'll be fun."

Into his face came the intent, desiring look. "For others, mebbe. But me, I'd like t' be inside four walls—just you 'n me, man 'n wife, agin."

His words, reminding of their parting, brought the little iron monitor alive for a fleeting moment, but she pushed it back into darkness and gave herself to the sweetness of Hank's nearness.

"I've missed you so—" she murmured.

"Yeah," he whispered, "sometime you 'n me is goin' t' make up for a lotta lost time. Right now, I gotta work with the men 'n you gotta greet yore friends fitten 'n proper." Laughing, he tucked her arm under his. "Cut a caper with the Commissioner a' Public Works 'n Highways?" he asked, laughing.

"You bet I will—Commissioner." She was almost solemn-sounding, but not because she was solemn. It was because so much gratitude for this fun was in her heart that her mind was filled with the wonderment of it.

"One-two, prance to the right," Hank chanted. "Three-four, prance to the left—"

The last of her cares took flight for a time. Oh, it was wonderful to be young again with Hank! Wonderful to be gay again with Hank! She lifted her face and smiled up at him, marveling at his ability to play after such intensity of work. As they went gaily to his three-four prance to the left, she noted on all the faces the flush of excitement, the slightly haggard look of weariness. But no weariness showed on Hank even though he had worked harder, longer hours than any other. She smiled up at him, trying to thank him for having the energy and the understanding of a need for play.

As she greeted each man, she felt again the glow that was Hank. These men reflected him as tinsel takes the sun. They loved him. Aside from the gain they hoped for themselves, they loved him.

After her greetings, he said to the crew, "You-all gotta forgive me for desertin' of y' tonight t' supper. I wanta be a-eatin' alone with just my wife 'n young'un."

"Shore y' do, Hank," and "A-course y' do, Hank," they replied.

Walking back to the house, Hank said as he looked over the place, "'Pears like you made a heap a' changes here. Hogs 'n all. 'N the house plumb doubled in size. Why'd you do this, Verity? Don't y' think I'll be elected?"

"Oh, I know you'll be elected. You always said you would be if it didn't rain; and it's going to be dry."

"Well, now, I know right well y' ain't done all this 'cause y' knowed it would be dry. Couldn't you be tellin' me how come?"

"Oh, I guess after being in a tent for a few months I wanted to feel I had a permanent home," she evaded. "I'd like to keep this place always."

"This li'l ol' no-'count share-crop house! You're a-funnin' me!"

She shook her head. Her face clouded.

"It ain't Jules? It ain't that dang Jules?" he pleaded low and earnest. "Tell me honest true. Don't be foolin' me."

"Oh, Hank," she replied softly, almost indulgently, "you know it isn't. Jules hasn't even been home all summer."

"Was sure it wasn't," he said, puzzled. He stopped in the path and looked at the little house critically. "Didn't you know we're like to move after I take over the office a' commissioner?"

"Even if we do I still want this place. I—I want it. It's home to me. I—I need to feel it's here to come back to." She could not bring herself to go into all the reasons, all the doubts, but stout stubbornness was in her voice.

He looked at her sharply, searchingly. "Come back to a—" he murmured. "I just don't get it. God'lmighty, we're on our way t' palaces! Still, there was a queen in one a' them hist'ry books as couldn't stand palaces all the time, neither. She hadda have a playhouse. But near as I could figger she didn't play in that there house alone. 'N I'm damned iffen I can think that a' you."

She simply stood and let him search her face, beginning to steel herself to fight for this if it came to an issue. But she hoped it wouldn't. Hank's first day home and she had to get all involved in principles again.

"It ain't that you misdoubt I'm a-goin' t' make a heap a' dollars, is it?"

"You told me to do something I wanted to do—and I have." But even as she spoke, she thought she was weak to evade. "I have also sent out your wagon with Bije Peck driving."

"The hell you say!" Then thinking this over, he said, "Dang iffen that ain't plumb smart. Hank Martin shouldn't oughta never get too uppity t' peddle, mebbe. Leastways not yet. That's mebbe smart a' you, Sweetface! 'N keepin' the li'l ol' country farm is too, come t' think on it. Hell, ain't I allus readin' 'bout presidents 'n such a-goin' back t' the old farm place for restin'!" Putting an arm about her waist, he squeezed her enthusiastically, relieved at having solved this poser. "Lord God'lmighty allus give me His best," he praised fervently, and went happily on to the house.

Hancy stood near the stove in a fresh little dress of pink-and-white gingham, contentedly chewing a fried hog rind. Her dark curls were freshly brushed and her little face was flushed with the stove's heat. She raised her dark eyes and looked at Hank unconcernedly. He stopped and stared admiringly.

"Ain't she a lovely! Come here, Hancy, 'n gimme a kiss."

The child took the rind from her mouth. "No!" she said decisively.

"She don't know me!" cried Hank. "Me, her own paw!"

"Lawd uv mercy, Mistuh Hank, whut you 'spects uv a baby jes' 'bout t'ree year old!" Selah defended. "Such a foolishness. Looky heah, Hancy honey, dat's yo' pappy."

"It's your daddy, darling," coaxed Verity.

But Hancy remained unimpressed.

Dropping on his knees before her, Hank looked at her with the air of one pleading for recognition from his favorite goddess. He brought a harmonica from his pocket and held it up.

"Lookit, Hancy," he coaxed, "ain't that a pretty, though?"

Her eyes fixed on its shining tin sides. Putting the harmonica to his lips Hank ran all its notes up and down. Hancy's eyes widened with wonder and longing.

"More!" Hancy commanded.

Again he ran the little instrument across his mouth. With a sudden change of mood, so like Hank, the child broke into wild, glorious laughter, ripply and shrill. Immensely pleased, Hank held the thing out to her.

"You can have it—iffen y' give me a kiss for it."

The baby laughter dwindled and stopped. Her little hands went behind her and she stood in a pose typical of Hank when defied; head forward, chin jutted, she glared at him.

Disconcerted, Hank exclaimed, "What the hell!" Then, "Don't you like it?"

"Yeah," replied Hancy firmly.

He puzzled over this, then asked gently, "Don't you like me—Hank, yore paw?"

He looked like a pleading giant before a Lilliputian, Verity thought, wanting to put an end to this and make the child kiss him, though she knew it would probably only make matters worse.

"Don't you like me?" he asked again softly.

Hancy stared at him. "Yes," she said very low.

"Well, what's the matter then?" Hank asked.

Some of Hancy's belligerence left her. She twisted her toes, flipped her dress hem this way and that but continued to glare.

"Hancy want it free," she blurted, and, turning abruptly, ran outdoors.

Hank stared after her, then rose from his knees. In his face was the look of one who has had a revelation.

"Iffen that ain't wonderful!" he marveled softly.

Selah was chuckling, but he paid no attention to that; he just looked at Verity and in his whole bearing was some quality which made her feel more joined to him, more united with him, than at any other time. It was a fleeting feeling but its flash was sweet.

"Wonderful?" she asked.

"Yeah," he said, "yeah. The young'un is like to seein' a little a' myself a-standin' there. She's like me, ain't she?"

Verity laughed. "She's exactly like you."

"No. She ain't. You plumb birthed my young'un with a somethin' extry special as is just how I'd like a girl-child t' be. She ain't a-givin' for no shiny piece a' tin even withen the music throwed in. Like you, she is that-a-way. 'N I plumb gotta admire it even whilst it maddens me." He grinned sheepishly. "'N her a wee mite of a baby! Purely seems like the Maker's last whisper to her afore she come t' us was, 'Love yoreself big; hold yore-self high; 'cause iffen y' do, ain't ary man can lay you low.' "

Striding to her, he grasped her shoulders firmly. "She's like to her maw," he said very low. "Somethin' in her stands strong 'n ungivin'. Yeah, you birthed me a young'un as is somethin' special. Like Maw birthed me with somethin' special she prayed into me as was different from the rest a' her litter." He hawked a choke out of his throat. He searched her face anxiously. "There's times you mind me a' Maw—when there's a pullin' 'n a reachin' in you. You feelin' held captive by somethin'?"

The pity of it. Why did that something in her stand ungiving, though not always strong? Why could she not go wholly with this man who had enough tenderness to sense this in her? There was strength in his very tenderness, passion in whitened lines from nostrils to mouth, desire in the heat of his hands.

"I'm held captive by love," she whispered.

"Someday," he threatened huskily, "I'm purely gonna capture all a' you. Every bit a' you. So's nothin' pulls 'n reaches away from me. I purely am, iffen it's the last thing ever I do. By God'lmighty, it's a somethin' I gotta have like bein' governor. It purely is. It makes a fierceness in me." The intent of union was in every line of him.

She became aware of the fact that they had not been alone a few minutes ago. But Selah had tactfully, quietly vanished. Now her voice was heard on the porch with the unnecessary loudness of warning as she talked with Hancy. Verity pulled away from Hank just as Selah pushed open the door and entered with the child.

"Suppah ready," she said. "An' dem folkses down by de tent dey askin' fo' you, Mistuh Hank. Um-umph! Look lak dis gwine be a big night. Um-umph!"

Hank grinned at Verity and winked teasingly. "Iffen we didn't have no stommick nor no brain to be allus havin' to be fed, what a time a feller could have in this world."

Giggling at this, Selah said, "I is partial ter my stommick, an' so is you."

"I'm plumb partial t' everything I got," laughed Hank. He took the harmonica from his pocket and proffered it to Hancy. "Here, my little special, it's yores—for free!"

The child did not move, did not go to him for the gift. She stood, her little hand out and open, waiting, as she gave him the solemn going over of babyhood. Going to Hancy, Hank bowed before her with great flourish and laid the instrument in her hand.

"And t' think," said Hank largely, "that there's likely a boy somewheres in this here world as is gonna draw her. Ain't he gonna have a wonderful time!" he gloated. Then, realizing what he'd said, he howled with outrage. "Roarin' thunderbolts! Think a' that, Verity! Us raising a girl-child for to pleasure some unknown sonuvabitch!"

While they ate, their attention was constantly drawn by the sounds of wheels and hoofs, to mule-drawn wagons, or cane carts with children peering between the slats of the upflaring sides. Some family groups came on foot. Often the mamma and papa were barefoot, their shoes hung by laces around their necks, their children herded before them, a baby in mother's arms, a toddler in father's, the older children carrying boxes of food and bundles of blankets.

Verity sat at her table staring out the window. She couldn't eat; she was choked and hushed with the immensity of this. In Selah excitement and wonder grew until she couldn't stay away from door or window. She made her little sounds of amazement, "Tch-tch—Lawdy, Lawdy, Mistuh Hank, suh, you is a somepin'! Tch-tch—I declah you mus' be a somepin'! Yes, Lawd!"

Through all this Hank ate heartily. Looking out the window, then turning his attention back to Hancy, he made his comments; comments which were all mixed. "Lookit that—there's the Scanlons. Fourteen miles they've walked. 'N they ain't failed me—seventeen young'uns they got. 'N every one a' them is there. The oldest, he's voting age. That's three votes for me now 'n sixteen more votes for me some time in the future." Then looking at Hancy, "God'lmighty, ain't she a lovely, though! I've seen more young-'uns 'n probably any other feller in this state—'n I ain't never seen one sweet as her. Well, well, lookit there, Verity, there's the Ribidoux'. A-drivin' there, see? Old Hilbert's got hisself another mule! Bet he's a-feelin' plumb rich." Hank chuckled. "I bet it's purely a sight t' see the swamplanders a-goin' t' the polls in their pirogues. Wisht I could be every place in the whole state," he said wistfully.

Verity looked at him—Hank Martin, her husband. She looked out the window again, noted that his followers eyed the house with curiosity, wandered to the barn and peered inside, leaned against the fence and looked at the garden, the hog and chicken pens. But with a natural courtesy they did not bother Hank now; they waited for him to come to them. She had seen people pour into the campaign grounds, but this was the test—tomorrow they would vote. They would go in a great stream like a pilgrimage to the polls and, using Hank's instructions about the Grandpappy Law, would recite the name of a forebear and cast their vote for Hank. The evening sky was gently purpling its reds and golds, and against it the tent was blackly blocked, a huge and awkward pyramid of a captive people.

Only the main tent of Hank's outfit had been set up, the platform as always at one end, but along one side of it, by Hank's directions, Cookie's stoves and ovens had been lined up. On the tent benches arranged around the walls, mothers sat persuading their little ones to sleep. Men stood in groups talking of crops and of tomorrow, and joking with each other as to who was his voting father or grandfather. The Cajun folk clung together asking anxiously, "Your *grandpère* who has made the vote, his name you know, yes?" The old folks clustered around the heat of the coal-oil ovens, sitting on up-ended boxes and sipping of Cookie's *café au lait*, Selah and Tape helping, with Selah throwing arch glances at both men. The orchestra, consisting of three fiddles and a concertina, played from the platform, and the crowd danced on the ground. A slight dust rose from the stubbled earth, and, like so many earthy things, gave body to the light, shedding false haloes from the hanging, swaying lamps.

To enter this tent with Hank gave Verity a taste of being a queen. Mrs. Ribidoux was one of the first to greet them. She threw her fat arms around Verity, then around Hank, laughed with an immense pleasure.

"The good papa you give to me, what make the vote so long time gone, I know his name—is Jean Bourdette, yes." She winked with glee over this lovely deception, waved her hand at the crowd, and said, "Is *le grand fais-dodo*. Is finest ever I go to, you bet. Hilbert and me, we feel once more young."

"That's the stuff," said Hank heartily. "You're a long ways from bein' old, Miz Ribidoux. Dance whilst y' can. You Cajuns got a song as says it exactly right. You know, the one as says 'Soon m' daughter'll make me a grammaw 'n instead a' dancin' the gavotte I'll have t' be a-settin' just gossipin' 'bout the sins a' my youth.'"

"Is fine song, you bet," cried Mrs. Ribidoux, and rolling her eyes naughtily and swinging her thick hips, she sang:

> *"Bientôt arrivera que ma fille me fera grand'mère,*
> *Au lieu de danser la gavotte—"*

Mrs. Ribidoux waved to them gaily as Hank took Verity in his arms. They danced over the rough ground and the smell of clean earthy dust was in their nostrils, excitingly blended with fragrances of gumbo and coffee, with the odors of oilstoves and exercising bodies. Verity felt herself grow warm under Hank's clasp, felt beloved and giving.

"Lord save us," whispered Hank against her ear. "Lord save us! I gotta get busy with them there sample ballots I got in my pocket. Iffen I don't do it quick I'll be a-pickin' you up 'n runnin' for home. Some time, Sweet-face," and his voice was very low, "some time I'm gonna take a week off for t' do nothin' but the courtin' 'n lovin' a' you. . . . God'lmighty, I bet-ter get me some a' Cookie's coffee."

As Selah gave them coffee, she said, "I hafter be two womans, Mistuh Hank, fo' ter he'p wid de servin' 'n watch dat Miz Hancy. Dat chile wanter run in de crowd."

"Well, take her 'n find Swith. Tell him to follow her. 'N iffen she so much as stubs her toe I'll have his neck."

"Yes, suh, Mistuh Hank," grinned Selah and grabbed up Hancy.

Verity stood by the serving table and, as Hank moved away explaining the sample ballot, she heard those little muted whispers that, in a crowd, indicate the arrival of an important person. She turned and saw Jules coming toward her. The refracted, dust-diffused light seemed almost like veils through which he walked with sureness, finding no need to part them. She had seen this eager sureness in him before, had felt that any minute he would reach out and take his full share of life. She liked the immaculate look of him, the handsome, conservative tweed suit, the covert topcoat, the way his hair lay as he removed his soft felt hat, liked the studying con-cern in his eyes. She went toward him, hands extended.

"Jules," she said softly. "Jules."

"Verity, my dear." Crushing his hat under one arm, he took both her hands in his for a moment, then raised one to his lips.

"I wondered if you would come home to vote for Hank."

He smiled crookedly. "Well, that is the reason I gave myself for coming. 'Jules, old boy,' I told myself sternly, 'you must go home and vote for Hank.' " He laughed a little. "But I know now that he would never have missed my vote." He looked around appreciatively. "Looks like a Cajun *fais-dodo.*"

"That's what Mrs. Ribidoux called it," said Verity. "What does it mean exactly?"

"It means go to sleep." At her astonished look he said, "The go-to-sleep part applies to the children. With children asleep parents can be people again until dawn." He shrugged in a truly French manner. "Since I have been mingling more with the people, I realize what a remarkable folk we are."

She studied him. "You speak as if you thought of yourself as one of them, Jules."

"Yes," he said. "Since I have been working with them I find I am deeply concerned with their welfare—with the welfare of this state." His eyes looked into hers with a soft intentness.

"Tell me all you've been doing. I want to hear everything."

"And I want to tell you—because, you see, I stopped at your gate and admired all you have been doing."

"You didn't mind my building onto the house?"

"Mind! It gave me heart. It made me think that Cypress Bend meant something permanent to you."

She looked away from him, feeling again the agonies of the past months.

"You have not been happy this past year." It was said simply yet with concern.

"Oh, yes—yes, I have, Jules," she said quickly. "It's—it's—well," she tried to laugh lightly, "Hank's on his way to palaces, all marble and shining, he says. And I—I guess I just have to have something my size to cling to. I—" she hesitated and then added, "I'm just not a big person, I guess."

"You are a great person, Verity." His tone dropped a note lower. "Once upon a time," he began, smiling, "there was a beautiful little cow who took her duties most seriously, so seriously that in time of famine she exhausted herself trying to supply all the people of the valley with nourishment, and as a reward she was turned into a beautiful goddess with just the hint of two lovely golden horns upon her forehead—lovely little horns to mark her past services, and, of course, to warn all adversaries."

She had seen Hank coming toward them, knew that he stood just back of Jules, listening to the last phrases, saw him make an effort to be jovial and welcoming. He slapped Jules on the back.

"Tellin' them dang parables a' yores agin, Jules?" As the men shook hands, Hank said, "I plumb despise them parables."

"Why, Hank," laughed Jules, "after that splendid one about the seventh angel clothed in a cloud!"

Hank looked a trifle uneasy, then, with great affability, said, "Leastways, you come home t' vote for me."

Jules looked over the crowd. "My vote will neither make nor break you. That's evident. Tell me, Hank, are all these people actually voting tomorrow? How have you overcome the property and literacy law?"

Hank chuckled. "That there law has plumb turned into my Grandpappy Law. Now lookit, Jules, here's what I done—"

Verity saw amazement in Jules's face as Hank talked with a childlike self-delight. When Hank finished, Jules asked, "And if the vote of your people is challenged?"

"Then I'm a-goin' into court 'n fight. I'll make the whole country read about me on the front page, 'cause I'll fight to prove that such a law ain't got no right in the statutes of a democracy, 'specially when there ain't never been a chancet for these here folks t' get a edgucation."

Jules was silent for a moment; then, "Probably the vote will not be challenged. With this sort of thing going on all over the state . . ." he shrugged, "it has the proportions of a rip tide. It can sweep over the land and wash it clean, or," he hesitated and looked directly at Hank, "or it can prove to be democracy's Frankenstein monster. Do these people know how to use the privilege of the vote?"

"God'lmighty, Jules, you make me steam nigh t' the splittin' a' my seams!" Hank roared. "They're a-goin' t' vote same way the upper crust votes—the way somebody tells 'em to vote. But this time the somebody as tells 'em is me!" He pounded his chest and glared.

"The things you have promised these people would benefit the entire state. So far, so good, it seems. We need good roads and better schools." Then, in the friendliest of voices, Jules shot his arrow. "Our old friend Saber Milady may be up here tomorrow. He tells me he has persuaded his editor to let him get the up-country story, as he calls it. Milady says there is no point in his staying to cover the events in Crescent City, since he knows exactly what can be expected from Guy Polli." Hank's head jerked back ever so slightly; he started to speak, but Jules went on, "Remarkable man, Milady. I have met him several times lately with a most gorgeous young person. Well, I must speak to old friends whom I see here—"

Verity watched him moving through the crowd, stopping here and there to speak to someone of the Bend. Hank put a hand on Verity's arm.

Musingly, Hank said, "I don't know why I put up withen Jules. He scalds me like to a mustard plaster. He plumb raises my phlegm. Mustard plaster is right, I guess—I keep feelin' I gotta use him sometimes. But I can't right squarely catch that Jules's mind." He sighed. "Well, I gotta get goin'."

But he did not move away. He stood fingering the sample ballot and she knew he was concerned with the fact that Saber had somehow learned of the tie-up with Polli.

She turned to Hank but he was standing as if entranced. Following the line of his gaze, she saw Hancy quite near, wandering through the crowd with Swith following. The countryfolk stopped her often, querying, "Ain't that Hank's young'un?" "Shore," Swith would reply. "Shore his spit 'n image, ain't she?" Or they addressed Hancy, "Ain't Hank yore paw?" "Ain't Hank yore pappy?" Or, "You're Hancy, ain't y'? Ain't Hank yore daddy?" After Swith answered for her several times, she learned that Hank was all these things, was hers, and was very important indeed. She made her way to the platform and beat her feet to the music, put her harmonica to her lips, and helped the musicians get bigger volume if not better time and tune. Being Hank's young'un proved delightful, and Verity conceded, as she watched, that it was cute and sweet. She was enjoying some coffee as Hank talked to a group, painstakingly explaining the sample ballot.

Hearing a harmonica blasting with complete disregard for tune, Hank looked up. Then slowly he went forward.

The tune was ended. Hancy jumped up and down and screamed at the players, "More!" But Swith said, "Here comes Hank." So the musicians waited. Turning, Hancy saw Hank just as he reached the platform. He stood looking at Hancy. So different, thought Verity, from the last time I saw him looking up at a girl on that platform. There was something in his attitude that clutched the heart. Hancy beamed, and still feeling the time and tempo of the music, chanted in her shrill, carrying baby voice, "He's my paw, he's my pappy, he's my daddy, he's my Hank!" and threw herself at him. He grabbed at her frantically to save her from falling, and held her tightly. "She's a somethin' precious," his attitude said plainer than shouted words. Hancy continued her chant while she hugged her father, her little face glowing with the same intense delight which Hank could show.

By now the people had come to a hushed silence, the sort of sacred silence which can come over a crowd when the last veil is drawn and the innermost throb of a heart is shown and found sweet.

With his back to the audience for once, Hank stood, just enfolding his child while she, with her arms around his neck, her head tight against his face, faced the audience, saying over and over her little chant, "He's my paw, he's my pappy, he's my daddy, he's my Hank!"

It was Picayune Potter's piping voice that broke the spell. Catching Hancy's rhythm and words he shouted out, "He's my Hank!" and set the crowd on fire. "He's my Hank! He's my Hank!" they chanted.

Turning, Hank seemed to find it difficult to come out of his mood, seemed almost embarrassed. To Verity this was amazing—Hank, embarrassed at being caught showing an emotion!

Putting Hancy down, Hank jumped to the platform and motioning for silence began going through the letters of his name as he had done twice every day for months.

"I'm yore Hank all right, but you gotta learn yore alphabet. You gotta be rememberin' this here is a off year in politics, since it ain't a year for electin' a president nor a governor. But two years from now is a year for electin' the governor. I gotta run then or wait six years, 'n you know I ain't never been one as can do a heap a' waitin'! You-all gotta get so's I can tell you the names of fellers I want elected to the house a' representatives. Can't no man, not even Hank Martin, pass laws withouten some fellers as will say, 'Yes, Hank, b'God'lmighty, I'll vote it liken you want.' 'N you fellers, iffen y' want all the things I'm promisin' t' get for y', have gotta leastways learn your alphabet.

"Right now all you gotta know is Hank Martin—now remember, the first letter H is built like to a gate, two poles a-standin' straight up 'n a crossbar between. I'm a-openin' a gate a' riches t' you! A is like to a church steeple, two lines a-slantin' together makin' a peak t' the sky withen a crossbar halfway, leavin' long, hangin' eaves for the birds t' nest in."

As he talked on the spelling of his name, he took huge cards with big, heavy letters on them, then set them up one by one until his name was spelled.

"Law," murmured Selah, "I cu'd learn ter read iffen Mistuh Hank learnt me."

All over the state, Verity realized, eyes that had never focused on a printed page could now recognize an N " 'cause the crossbar slants liken the supports of a rail fence 'twixt posts."

Hank was now picturing his last name. "This R is like to a woman 'bout t' give with child. You know how they allus rear back makin' 'em look flattish in back with them two rich bulges to the front. 'N this here T is like the cross as Jesus was—"

He stopped. A group of frantic, panicky men were shoving and pushing through the crowd. With them were Flower and Jep and Vince, who had left off their guarding outdoors to come in with these men.

Craning, Verity saw it was young Bije Peck and three of Hank's key men from Delamore. Bije's face was white with fear, as were the faces of the other men. Sophy, Tim, and Verity began pushing through the crowd to get to Hank and Bije. But before the men reached the platform, Bije shouted out.

"Hank! Hank!" he called, "Hank—they're gonna kill y'—the Davols—they're gonna kill y'!"

Hank dropped the big letter cards, his face whitened, his lips thinned, his eyes became mere slits.

"What the hell you sayin'?" he blustered. "Who's gonna kill me?"

"The Davols," said a Delamore man. "The Davol girl's kin. There's nine a' her men kin," he declared.

"The Davols!" exclaimed Hank, bewilderment in his voice. "The Davol girl's kin? Well, who the hell are the Davols? 'N what's a Davol girl t' me?"

At the words "Davol girl" Verity had felt throttled with agony, but now some triumphant knowledge soared in her—"He actually doesn't know her," it sang.

Flower went to the platform edge, beckoning Hank to lean down so he could whisper. She couldn't see Hank's face as Flower talked, but she felt Jenny's small, friendly hand on her arm.

Hank suddenly stood up. He jumped up and down in rage, flailed his arms.

"Tell it t' everybody!" He yelled his command at Flower. "It's a goddam lie! 'N I ain't a-feared t' let everybody hear it!"

But Flower stood red-faced and tongue-tied.

"All right—I'll tell you all!" Hank shouted. " 'N as the Lord is my judge —I'm a-tellin' you for a fact—I don't even recall this girl they're a-talkin' 'bout. Janie Davol, they say her name is, 'n she's dead. Abortin', they say. Her men kin is out t' kill me—layin' for me at the polls, they say—tomorrow mornin'."

Everything in Verity was sagging to nothingness—the 'gator pole of Lula May's words was beating her down—down—

Hank stopped talking for a second. He looked at the men from Delamore, studying, and then shouted, "Davol! Ain't Marcus Davol the feller as owns a interest in Castleberry's Delamore gin?"

"Why, sure," said one of the men from Delamore. "Sure. He's the girl's uncle. 'N he owns a fifth interest."

"God'lmighty!" howled Hank, "God'lmighty! I didn't never dream there was men low enough t' do the likes a' that! Is this here girl dead—actual dead?"

"Dead 'n buried!" said the man.

" 'N they lay the blame on me!" Hank beat his chest. "Me! That never even knowed she lived!"

Hank's words had the blessed effect of stopping the 'gator pole, as Spurge's bullet once had. They gave her a steel-stayed corset for her love and her pride. She felt it pulling her straight and upright as Hank laced it tighter and tighter with his words.

Like Hank, she could not imagine men being low enough to make up such a story on which to hang revenge. Gasping with anger, she walked in a proud fury toward Hank. Seeing her coming, he stopped his denunciations, his words petering off as he searched Verity's face. The crowd took on a new and curious edge as they waited for Hank's wife. Verity extended her hands to Hank in a gesture meaning "you and me, darling—you and me—" He jumped from the platform to meet her faith, took her hand, and held it in fierce possession.

Strong in her steel-stayed pride and love, she wanted desperately to give him greater strength, and she said, "Don't you worry. We'll find a way to stop those men. I know we will. Why—just knowing you're right makes me feel all safe—sort of ironclad and upheld."

"Sort of ironclad 'n upheld," he repeated. "Yeah, that's how a feller should oughta feel times like t' this." Then suddenly into his face came that pouncing look. "Ironclad," he murmured. "Ironclad!"

He dropped her hand and stepped past her to Tim.

"Tim! You hear that? Ironclad, she says, Tim! That's what I gotta be! Ironclad!"

Tim stared, uncomprehending, but Sophy's face lighted. "Ironclad!" said Sophy in awe. "Paw, you could do it!"

"Sure y' could, Tim!" said Hank, low and urgent. As Tim still stared at him, Hank almost shook the big man. "Ironclad, Tim, she says. 'N you could do it—y' could clad me in iron. A iron vest, sorta. Immune I'd feel then! Ironclad 'n upheld, by God'lmighty.''

Understanding at last, Tim clasped Hank in his arms a second, then turning, he placed his hands upon Verity's shoulders and with all the unction of blessing he said, "You're purely his buckler 'n his shield."

"Ironclad," murmured Hank. "Ironclad in the law, too. That's what I gotta be. Protected agin a actual bullet 'n protected agin bein' put in jail like t' pore Harry 'n gettin' kilt there." Lifting his head, he bellowed out, "Where's Jules? Where's Jules Bolduc? Fetch me Jules!"

From the back of the tent came Jules's answering voice. He came to them swiftly, his eyes on Verity.

"Jules," said Hank, "Jules, old friend, I gotta depend on you to go t' Delamore 'n see that the sheriff makes me 'n all my men deputies. I ain't goin' t' risk the law 'n jail 'n be like to pore Harry. Them blue-bloods like t' kill when a feller's back a' bars 'n defenseless."

"I'll get the sheriff and arrest the Davols for threatened murder," said Jules.

"Arrest them! God'lmighty! Don't you do no such a thing!" said Hank fiercely. "Arrest 'em! Put 'em in jail a spell 'n then turn 'em loose so they can be a-layin' for me anywheres, any time! Why, god-damit! Iffen they're a-comin' t' kill me, let 'em come. Me 'n my men'll mow them Davols down. Just don't you dare put 'em in jail where they'll be all safe. You just cover me 'n my men by makin' us deputies. Just you fix us up withen immunity from the law. Immunity—that's all I want. You fix up a somethin' that gives us immunity—somethin' ironclad 'n upheld!"

Jules stood stunned. Verity cried out a stricken "No!" but Hank did not hear her. He jumped to the platform.

"Lissen, friends—hark to me careful now! You men from Delamore, here's yore job—you get a-goin', 'n you find a way t' get the news to them Davols that Hank Martin aims to be the first man to cast a vote in the mornin'. Make it clear 'n plain. Then we can have the shootin' over 'n the rest a' you will be safe, 'n can come to the polls 'n vote withouten no fear." A great hum of Ohs and Ahs and many protestations rose from the crowd, but Hank waved them to silence. "Now, you-all mind what I'm a-tellin' you. I aim t' walk outta Squeeze-nickel's store t' meet them Davols just as soon as the votin' place is open. 'N the votin' place is acrost from Squeeze-nickel's store, almost. Now you as live near, go home. 'N you as come a long way will bed down in the tent just liken you 'spected t' do. 'N don't none of you, 'cept them I choose, come nigh to the polls tillst the shootin's over."

He squared his shoulders, turned, and passed through the crowd, the proud, sure prophet of a people who had not felt they were captives until Hank pressed it in on their minds.

"All he wants is immunity!" said Jules. He turned a stricken face to

Verity and in her flamed a need to defend the qualities that make a woman love a man, and a need to speak the truth and to fight him in order to make him more nearly what he should be.

"What has been growing in Hank? With all his ability!" Jules spoke with a great, almost cosmic sadness. "What has been growing in him that I have not surely sensed until now? What?"

"A third eyelid." The bitterness in her tore the words from her against her will. "He calls it nictitating." Tears rolled down her cheeks. "Save him, Jules. Save him from killing. Arrest those Davols."

Jules's hands grasped her shoulders, and he was the intent, idealistic soldier he might have been when he lifted his bayoneted gun in salute to France.

"Did you say nictitating?—Answer me, Verity."

But he did not wait for an answer. He turned and ran from the tent.

Jenny came up with many questions but Verity couldn't hear her, couldn't answer, because she didn't know anything. She just didn't know anything—she couldn't make anything come clear to her. She turned and walked stumblingly out and home, a numb and empty thing, and she threw herself in her unwordable grief upon the bed.

Hours later she stole from the house. She knew men were posted far down the road and were fanning out through the fields, guarding the tent and this little share-crop house. The air was sharp from chill and damp and the dew lay thick on the gatepost. The huge tent stood black and solid against the sky's starred blueness, the chimney of Tim's shop shot up thick burning sparks which spiraled high toward the cloudless heavens, and plain and ringing over the chorus of small insects came the clang of Tim's anvil as he beat into shape the iron vest for Hank.

She fell on her knees among the broad, strong elephant-ears and clung to the pear vine which grew over her fence, and while big leaves drained their dew over her back and thighs, and the vine baptized her anew with each shuddering sob, she called to her God, her words rocketing skyward on her despair.

"Oh, God, it's that blindness—it's that blindness—oh, God, forgive me, but I'd rather see him killed than killing—and I couldn't live without him—" Through wrenching sobs, she added, "Oh, God, make him see— don't let him kill for power—for power—"

Black, hopeless despair came on her. But Hank's men were not the only ones on guard, for Selah came and put her strong arms around Verity protectingly.

"Dere, dere, honey-chile," crooned Selah, "dere, dere." Rocking back and forth in the misery sway of her people, Selah held her and whispered, "You feels low, I know. An' I knows why. Mistuh Hank he ain't no diffrunt fum lotsa men. He love evabody w'en dey is persons, but in flocks

258

aey jes' blackbirds." She smoothed back Verity's hair. "Us culla'd folks, we knows how dat is. White man usn serves can love us 'cause usn is persons, but in flocks, usn jes' blackbirds."

And through Verity's mind ran Hank's words as he spoke them the day after their marriage, "Lookit 'em, Verity, ain't airy one got the gumption of a nutted cockerel—but in herds they got a use t' a man like to me— sometimes I feel myself full t' runnin' over withen love for the dumb sons- abitches—" She shuddered and cried out, "Oh, no—oh, no—!" And Selah held her tight and swayed and swayed, syncopated with the ring of Tim's hammer on red-hot iron, while the insects buzzed and the forge belched redly at the sky.

14

A dozen stories could be written about just one day in Hank Martin's life, for on that first election day there were terror and valiance and devotion, all set in a scene that staggered the imagination. For out from the hinterlands came Hank's followers . . . men and women to cast a vote in spite of the fact that most could not read nor write. Some walked barefoot through the night to get to the polls. They crossed alligator swamps; hyacinth-choked lagoons; they came out of the trackless wastes of the pine hills.

All over the state election officers were stunned and stupefied by the horde, each reciting the name of his father or grandfather, while Hank's watchers stood by to. . . .

WITH the first break of light in the east, Verity was again in her yard as she had been yesterday morning. Once again the coldest hours before dawn had transformed the dew to silver, and the tent, so black last night, was now held to the ground by ropes of rainbow hues. The quiet of yesterday morn was gone. Though the world itself was still and windless, there were the bustle and tenseness of many nearby people, the small movements and swishes of tethered animals. And like sounds of peace and plenty rolling mellowly over the knoll from Jules's place, came the lowing of a cow, the barking of hounds. In no time at all the polls would be open. Had Jules and the sheriff arrested the Davols? Would he send word? "Oh, God," she called silently out of the pressure of her heart, "Oh, God—" but she could go no further. The aching tortures of the night were on her. And always, throughout all these hours there was the dreadful pressure of feeling she had missed an important part in the whole picture. Why should Hank be threatened?

Several men emerged from the tent. Talking mutedly, they went stolidly to tend their mules. Mamma Ribidoux, shushing the chatter of her flock, herded them to the trough where they lined up and splashed their faces while she pumped vigorously. The men led the animals to water, and the stretches between tent and barn and outhouse became alive with people. They saw Verity but they did not speak, only questioned with their eyes—"Have you heard?"—"Have you heard anything?" She seemed to feel thousands of eyes bearing down on her, begging for release from this strain. The children were not completely hushed. Their chatter mingled with the snorts and whinnies of horses and mules, with the deep bass grunts of Verity's hogs, the cackles and crowings of chickens, and over all, through the frosty air, came the redolence of Cookie's coffee, of corn pone and grits. But only the smaller children were called by these fragrances. The older ones and the adults stood on the rainbowed meadow looking off toward the Bend, where their Hank was, stood praying for the man whom only yesterday she had visioned as a little fellow running while the rime was on the grass. Through her mind flashed many of the homely beauties as he had expressed them—a thrush all soft 'n brown on a red haw bush; a mocker a-fillin' the dark withen his song— "Oh, God —oh, God—" and this time her crying heart pushed the words out in sound. He must not die and never see the world's loveliness again. So many people couldn't see it at all—it's a pore heart that don't never find nothin' for t' be rejoicin' over—oh, he could always do that!

She became suddenly aware that the sun had come over the world in all its full, round glory, had dimmed its heralds of color, and the polls— the polls would be opened any minute. Right now Hank might be staring out of Squeeze-nickel's window, might be peering over the rack of overalls and skimpy calico dresses, waiting to step out as soon as the election officers unlocked the forlorn little building which was to serve the voters. She had to get to Hank—no word from Jules—if Jules failed—

With desperate passion she flung wide the gate and ran and ran and ran, only half hearing the calls of the men and women, only half hearing the feet of those who followed.

She made the last turn in the road just as Hank stepped out of the store, flanked by his bodyguard, looking warily up and down the street. She knew that Hank wore the iron vest, for he walked stiffly and had a strange stuffed look. From a distance she heard the roar of a motor and at the far end of the little town she saw a gray car. Jules. Jules! . . . It was then she saw the Davols. Nine well-dressed men came from back of the election office, revolvers in hand. In a flash she saw that they were not yet in the line of Hank's vision and with all her might she ran faster. The Davols would have to shoot from the narrow areaway between the election building and the harness shop, and to that narrow opening she ran and stopped, facing the nine strange, intent men. She came upon them with startling suddenness, the last thing in the world they expected to see, and she prayed, "Oh, hurry, Jules—"

"God'lmighty!" Hank roared. "God'lmighty—no shootin' for God's sake—no shootin'." And forgetting all caution he ran as fast as he could in his cumbersome iron. She felt the touch of his hand and with it sagged, all strength gone. His arm braced her while he glared at his enemy. His men came and guns pointed at guns around the bodies of Hank and Verity. One of the Davol men stood out before the others, and this man and Hank locked stares.

"You are under arrest." It was Jules's voice.

She felt the slight jerk of Hank's arm, but he did not move or shift his stare. The lead Davol man tore his eyes from Hank and looked at Jules.

"Who is under arrest, Jules?" he asked.

"Why, you are, Marcus," said Jules smoothly. "And very fortunate you are. But for Mrs. Martin you would, I assure you, now be dead. I was just a trifle slow, it seems." Jules shrugged. "I have with me the sheriff and his men. I suggest we go across the street to the store and talk this over."

As they moved out into the street the sheriff took the revolvers from the Davol men and herded them into Squeeze-nickel's. Hank motioned the excited crowd back.

"God'lmighty, Sweetface, ain't you got no sense? None a-tall? You coulda been kilt."

She nestled a bit closer, loving the feel of his arm about her waist, loving the knowledge that he was well and whole.

"So could you," she said softly.

"No." His voice was low but apprehensive. "Likely them dressed-up highfalutin' Davols couldn't hit a bull's ass withen a fly swatter. Here I am in a iron vest, b'God'lmighty, 'n nary bullet a-shootin'. It's humiliatin'. It purely shames me. 'N here you've fixed it good—you 'n Jules—so's there's gonna be nine men as hates my guts runnin' loose in this here state t' snipe at me any time, anyplace. God'lmighty, 'n it could all 'a been finished up. I aimed t' learn this here state right now that not nobody's stopping Hank Martin. I aimed t' show Castleberry I got a charmed life. He framed this, 'n don't you never forget it." He squared his shoulders and walked determinedly and awkwardly into the store. She followed.

Inside the door, Hank stopped and looked over the crowd. There were the nine Davols standing before the scarred and pitted counter. Sheriff Mulland from Delamore stood in front of them, obviously hating to point a revolver at a Davol. Swith, Flower, Jep, and Vince stood by, their firearms ready. Jules lounged against a case of hard and stale-looking candies, and back by the paint counter stood Jenny, Sophy, and Tim. Jenny came instantly to Verity's side. Hank just stood, stiff and awkward in the vest. Marcus Davol and Hank Martin measured each other. Verity felt herself held in a tense moment.

Marcus Davol was a long, broad, sandy-haired man. In fact, Verity thought, everything about him was sandy. His suit was a sand-and-brown tweed, his shirt, of no definite color, had a glistening, smart casualness of cut as well as shade, a putty or sand-colored handkerchief with monogram in brown perked from his breast pocket. His hat was a correct and stiffly blocked brown felt and his tie a blend of browns with just a scratch of blue showing in the weave—as his eyes were just slits of blue. But he was no more drab than is a long stretch of sandy beach.

Hank sighed. "Men," he said, "I would shore as hell 'druther 'a kilt y'."

Marcus Davol's narrow, piercing eyes looked long at Hank and then turned on Verity. "My apologies, Mrs. Martin. I hope my kinsmen and I may serve you as well in the future as you have served us today."

A shiver ran through Verity.

"Now, sir," said Davol to Hank, "this matter is not for gentlemen to discuss before crowds. Would you trust me enough to step outside—just you and I? I'm unarmed."

"Why not?" asked Hank largely. Plainly he felt himself once more on sure ground. Verity knew Hank was judging this man and wondering at his value. "I'm not armed but I'm sure armored." He laughed and struck his iron vest a resounding thump. The tenseness of the group was instantly broken. People shifted positions and were more comfortable in mind as well as body. Only Jules remained exactly as before, the quizzical expression neither more nor less.

"Hm—" said Marcus Davol thoughtfully, "armor, bodyguard, Jules Bolduc, and the law. . . . Hm—thorough. You have been underestimated, Mr. Martin."

"You been lied to, Mr. Davol," said Hank.

"Of that I was convinced the instant your wife dammed up the passageway like a brave little thumb in a dike," said Marcus Davol. He walked to the window. "Amazing," he said, admiration in his tone. "Amazing. I would never have believed it possible." He gestured toward the door. "Before you, I presume?"

"Shore," said Hank, laughing. "I still aim t' play safe, iffen it's possible."

Verity watched them through the window, bewildered and groping. And again the name "Janie Davol" whirled in her brain and then, like a magic lantern, her mind slid everything in place and showed her a plump brown-haired girl standing beside Sylvia Hylen in the tent at Delamore; her mind heard the silken voice exclaiming, "Why, Janie Davol—" She felt all hollow and cheated. Hank not recall that name until just now —with his memory! Impossible! She had to get out of here. She looked wildly about and started for the back door. Her eyes were caught by Jules's eyes. In them was a realization of her need for escape. He walked to the back of the little store and opened the door. She hurried out, Jenny following, and like an automaton she walked around the back way to Tim's shop. She hadn't the strength now to go home. In the warming sun on the bench in front of the shop she sat, staring off toward home. Jenny walked in front of her, back and forth, and finally stood before Verity, feet spread, fingers interlaced.

"Lookit, Verity—lookit—you gotta git some iron in yore guts. You jus' gotta! 'N a-course it was that Sylvia Hylen as showed the Black Skimmer how t' rile them men t' killin' Hank." She pressed her hands together so tight and hard they looked like thin strips of gristle. "When this thing happened t' Janie Davol that Sylvia must 'a just seen how t' turn things round 'n say Janie Davol used t' take her along t' see Hank."

"Don't!" said Verity. "I can't stand any more. I can't stand any more."

"You ain't got it so bad!" Jenny was pleading and anguished. "Gawd! You got it soft 'n beautiful in a kinda way. Any woman should oughta know it's better t' have a whole man part a' the time than a pulin' critter alla the time. Bah!" She spat out her disgust. "Ain't nothin' so cankerin' as a pulin' man-critter that a woman has alla the time gotta prop up t' make him think he's man-size, whilst he ain't nothin' but a overgrowed young'un as won't wean." She drew a long breath and plunged ahead. "You're a somethin' special t' Hank. Full-growed, real man he is. 'N you're actual the only woman he's got a real need for, seems 's though. I tell y', Verity, you got it soft 'n beautiful in a kinda way. You just gotta git some iron in yore guts."

Jenny sank onto the bench beside Verity. "'Sides," she said, "you knowed 'bout Sylvia Hylen long time ago." Jenny drew a long, shuddering sigh. "Flower, he swears Hank didn't never lay her. Flower says, 'Hell, Hank was in a plumb dangerous spot whether he does or don't, seein' she's kin t' the Skimmer 'n a-stalkin' him.' More 'n more I lean t' Flower's notion. But me—" She took Verity's hand and said with simple sincerity, "I was worse'n her, it sometimes seems 's though—'n you was wonderful. You washed me clean. It's a somethin' y' seem t' be good at." She said it so softly and then added, "You jus' gotta do it fer Hank—y' jus' gotta do fer alla us."

Deeply touched, Verity couldn't speak. She squeezed Jenny's hand and the two sat in silence. Somehow what happened between Sylvia Hylen and Hank was not the point. She wished she could talk about it to Jenny but she was too weary. Still her mind pursued the point, trying to find it with exactness. It seemed to be the terrifying quality in Hank that enabled him to turn everything to his benefit and yet—and yet—she thought it all seemed connected with that willful blindness. He would have let nine men die—maybe more, secure in his own immunity.

"Well," said Jenny, "let's usn go vote. Jus' think a' it, Verity—folks votin' like's if they can spell 'n got money."

The small village was made into a sight she would never have deemed possible. Even though she had seen Hank's followers many times, she could never have envisioned this. The very atmosphere was charged with crosscurrents: solemnity, as seen in the solemn-faced people waiting in line to vote; a picnic joy in the yelling, playing children, and in the excited adults coming out of the polling place, having successfully named a forebear and marked a ballot. Hank's instructors stood the legal distance from the polls, showing each and every voter exactly where to put his mark on the ballot, while their assistants barked like side-show ticket sellers. "Everybody come up here and get your sample ballot—Step right here—see how it's done—don't risk votin' for the wrong feller—Hank Martin for Commissioner—right here, get your sample ballot. . . ." And as always, there was given the definite sense of menace by the armed guards standing near the instructors to see that they told it right.

Through the window of the little building she could see the dazed faces of the election workers, two men who had expected to lounge easily through the day. They were strangers to her and she asked Jenny if she knew them.

"No," said Jenny, "not t' say howdy to. They're planters from north a' the Bend. Highfalutin'. Not, though, like Mr. Bolduc is highfalutin', 'cause he's really high. But they got money. Not heaps, but a-plenty."

The upper middle classes, thought Verity, the ones Hank didn't quite know how to handle. Hank was standing in front of Squeeze-nickel's and with him were Jules, all the Davol tribe, the sheriff and his men. Hank talked earnestly to Marcus Davol, whose narrow, piercing eyes were studying the scene with the air of an analyst charting an all-telling graph.

"When I was working Delamore for Hank," said Jenny, "I used t' hear 'bout them Davols. They're uppity folks. They're blue-bloods, I hear tell. They ain't rich, though."

"Marcus Davol is planning on being rich soon, or I'm not learning as fast as I think I am," said Verity bitterly.

She went toward them.

"There y' are," cried Hank, "I was just a-wonderin' should I oughta start worryin' 'bout y'. But Jules, he said you was with Jenny." He drew her to him and said, "This here Marcus Davol is a most remarkable feller. Him 'n me is goin' t' be friends. Ain't that amazin'! Iffen anybody had tolt me that a few hours ago, I woulda had 'em put in a strait jacket. 'N speakin' a' strait jackets, by God'lmighty, I'm in one now. Come into the store with me, Verity, 'n help me outen this thing."

Everyone laughed easily except Jules, who stood engrossed in the scene.

In the dim cavern of the store Hank peeled his coat and asked Verity to stand on a chair so she could lift the crude vest over his head. It was a strange-looking thing made of strips of iron which had originally been intended for wagon rims. It hung in two sections from heavy leather straps, held to the metal by rivets such as are used in a horse's harness.

As she lifted the weighty, awkward thing, she wanted to cry, to give way to hysterics; she understood suddenly how people could break and shatter and let fear of future anguish drive them into a beaten withdrawal from life. And in one second a revealing vision blazed forth like a facula and she saw all Hank's followers, the captives of the world, as he called them, as descendants of some forebear who had fled from anguish. She was not going to be that kind of ancestor. If anguish was her portion, so be it, but she would not quit. She called on all the puissant stamina of her mother to help her, and she threw the crude armor to the floor.

"Iron—iron," she said low and fierce, "iron monitor in my brain and iron in my guts—to match you in a vest of immunity!"

Hank jumped at her words and the clanging of the vest. He stared up at her, a strange excitement, almost an exalted ruthlessness showing in face and attitude. He came up on his toes, thinned his abdomen, expanded his chest, beat upon it with his fists, lifted his head, and gave out a joyous howl, reboant with the sounds of conquest. She had seen him do this before, and as always, it reminded her of something—but now she again remembered words overheard in Delamore.

"She was right," said Verity harshly. "Sylvia Hylen was right when she called you a big untamed lion."

"Yeah. The big lion—that's me, 'cause I'm sure as hell king a' this jungle!" He beat his chest again and laughed. " 'N, by God'lmighty, this here whole state'll know it come nightfall. Hank Martin, the Big Lion, starts ruling this here jungle right now!" He caught her up in his arms and held her close, rubbed his face in the curve of her neck, and growled gently. "I'm a big lion, all right. By God'lmighty, I feel like t' one today." Nibbling her ear he whispered, "But you're of a size t' stalk me, Sweetface. You purely are. Nearest I ever felt I come t' dyin' was when I seen you a-standin' there, arms outspread, a-facin' down nine guns for t' keep me from bein' kilt."

She struggled in his arms and turning her face so she could look directly into his eyes she said, "Hank, I didn't do it only to keep you from being killed—but to keep you from killing. It's that blindness—"

"Aw, mudlarks," said Hank huskily, "aw, mudlarks! A lion's mate don't never run t' save the prey." He grinned teasingly. " 'N iffen y' think y' did, then I'm nictitatin' t' that there mental angle right now."

A fury went through her. She jerked from his arms and, standing before him, slapped him deliberately.

He howled with a pleasured excitement. "Y' dang little pepper pod. You're a-ripenin' t' red-hotness." Grabbing her by the shoulders he held her firmly. The pride of vision came on him and as if showing her the loftiest, profoundest destiny which man could attain, he said, "Lookit, Sweetface, you don't like killin'. Well, hell, I don't like it neither. 'N the day is come when mebbe I can do without it. It's this-a-way—remember way before even we was married? D' y' recall I tolt y' peddlin' 'd mean everythin' t' me 'cause I'd know just how much them dam swamp angels 'd have t' have give t' 'em afore they'd gimme their vote? Well, I'm a-catchin' onto other folks now, too. Once I'm in power, the fight'll be over. There won't be no killin'. 'Cause, by God'lmighty, I'll know how to wangle laws so's there won't be no ifs 'n ands." He grinned widely and the softness of cunning was in his voice as he added, "There's more ways t' climb a pinnacle than by powder 'n shot. Already I know how t' control every cannery on the waterways, 'cause they're highways, by God'lmighty. Why, Sweetface, I'm a-goin' t' carry you up such high pinnacles as to make you plumb dizzy. Yes, sir, plumb dizzy!"

"I don't think I want to go up those pinnacles, Hank."

"Aw, mudlarks," said Hank. "God'lmighty, here you save a most valu-able man for me this mornin' 'n now you say such a thing. Why, d'you know what I'm thinkin'? I'm thinkin' that there Marcus Davol is the exact right feller for t' be a sort a' buffer. You know, the feller as knows all the Who's Who in the state, the feller as can see all comers first 'n tell me what is their weakness 'n what is their bank account, 'n what is their wants, 'n what is their followin'."

She turned from him and walked heavily toward the door. Hank, still in high humor, followed. He stood on the steps of the little store, gloating over the scene, and in the joy of conquering he thumped his chest, grinned with delight, and declared loudly, "Who but me could 'a made a thing like this t' happen! I'm the Big Lion! I purely am."

Jules turned sharply. "Big Lion?" he asked. "Did you call yourself the Big Lion?"

"Yeah." Hank laughed. "Me, the describin'est man in the state, 'n yet Verity, she calls my name."

A wave of sick heat burned Verity. In Jules's eyes she saw understand-ing of far more than Hank had told in those two words.

"Say, Marcus," said Hank, "I been a-wantin' t' ask you what you know 'bout Varick Kirkendall. Now, I allus thought mebbe he might make me a good lieutenant governor when I run next election. You got the low-down on that feller?"

"Well—" Marcus's voice lowered to secrecy, and as they talked Verity realized that each man was scenting fruitful winnings.

Jules came to her. "I have always maintained," he said, "that love meant taking the responsibility of the greater, the higher action. But un-til this morning I had seen it only in war, motivated by love of right and love of country."

Her head flew back, startled by the impact of this thought—love of right and love of country. She stared at the crowd in the village, and while the barker bawled, "Step this way—get your sample ballot! See just where to mark a cross for Hank Martin! Don't risk a mistake. Get your sample ballot—" she looked into the past. She saw now that Hank had, just as he'd said in the store, told her plainly how his mind worked; had told her time and time again. There in the schoolhouse, and on their wedding day, "Allus remember you can kiss their ass today 'cause you're a-plannin' t' kick it tomorra"; in his use of Jules's satire; in the canny, computing look that crept through his prayerful attitude after his first speech in Tim's shop when he learned how to trade a mite of hope for a dollar a year. She felt that in the beginning he had wanted to help people, maybe truly help them; but even then his eye was on the power and the pinnacle.

She realized that she had fought back at this in-creeping knowledge, doing her best as a girl in love to see him as she wished to see him, to hear what she hoped to hear. She saw that all his followers were like her in some degree. Marcus Davol interrupted her revery to say good-by, to thank her for being a thumb in a dike. She shook hands and tried to smile.

As Hank and Marcus clasped hands, Hank said, "Now, Marc, you get busy with Varick Kirkendall 'n repeat good 'n accurate my words."

"He's in a very tight spot, Commissioner," replied Marcus. "He may feel he wants more than words."

Hank slapped him jovially on the back. "Hell, Marc, iffen you're a-goin' t' partner up withen me, you gotta learn fast that a politician is a mite like t' a god." He laughed and added, "You know, liken it says in Genesis—In the beginnin' was the word."

Marcus laughed in the quiet, almost soundless way he had until Jules wiped the laugh away by asking, "And in the end was the flood?"

Hank whirled on Jules. "The trick is t' be the feller withen the ark."

"Exactly," said Jules, smoothly. "Are you building one?"

"God'lmighty, Jules," roared Hank, "you're fast becomin' like t' alum 'n bile! Who, but me, could 'a—"

But Jenny stepped up, pulled Hank's sleeve, and said plaintively, "Gawd, Hank, let's usn vote. Years we been workin' just t' make our cross."

15

Hank took pride in never wasting time on nonessentials such as becoming the perfect grammarian. He said simply people understood him and they did indeed. He became known far and wide as the most describing man in the state—which is what his friends had always said of him. Indeed, with his voice and his expression they might well have understood him in any language.

The opposition party headed by Governor Rordan, the then incumbent, tightened and worked hard to keep in power, but Hank gave a demonstration of his farsighted planning when the gubernatorial election rolled around. The opposition prayed for rain—and planned. He always said he knew how to lick the rain. Within a few days after he was elected commissioner. . . .

HANK sat in the corner of the big black limousine, seething over the nerve of Guy Polli sending this car for them. Verity half lay against the other corner, her eyes on the necks of the three men in the front seat; the thin, sleek, high-shaven neck of Polli's man, Willie, whom she had met before; the rough, red neck and cauliflower ear of Flower; and the thick bull neck of Vince. She would have preferred to have Swith with them, but Swith had been white with exhaustion.

They had been home only long enough to eat and rest a few minutes when this car had drawn up at the gate and Flower had come in with the message that Guy Polli hoped Mr. and Mrs. Martin would come to his country place just five miles out of the capital. Knowing that Hank had arranged to have a car come from Delamore to take him to the party committee's headquarters later in the evening to watch the returns roll in, Polli had suggested that Hank come over earlier and talk over their bargain. Hank was furious. "A deal is one thing," he had said, "but the nerve a' that feller thinkin' I got a wife as is the kind t' hobnob withen the likes a' him!" But after some thought he had decided he had better not slight Polli just now and so they would go. Polli, Hank explained, was a feller most sensitive to slights.

Ordinarily, to get to the capital from the Bend was quite a journey. One went by wagon to Delamore, then by train to Loder City, where a change must be made before continuing on. And so it came to Verity as a great surprise that the trip could be made by car, even over these rough roads, in less than three hours.

Each little village or settlement through which they passed cheered Hank considerably, for the places were still filled with the strange voters and, as Willie drove slowly through, the voices of the barkers could be heard, the men with guns were in evidence, and the watchers with the names of voters prior to 1867 could often be seen. In some places astonished, well-dressed townsfolk stood in groups talking excitedly or staring in bewilderment.

"Looks like we done a swell job, don't it, boss?" Flower would call.

"Shore does," Hank would answer. "Shore does."

He was still angry when they turned into a long private, well-graveled driveway lined with magnificent oaks. The noble trees met overhead and half a mile from the gate at the end of this drive there gleamed the white pillars of one of the old mansions of the South. Acres of well-groomed park spread out on both sides of the drive.

"I'm damned," said Hank under his breath as he looked around. "Well, I'm damned. Hey, Willie," he called, "this where Polli's got that there acres-wide, mile-high birdcage a' hisn?"

"This is the joint," answered Willie.

"I allus supposed he stayed near Crescent City."

"Nope," said Willie. "Polli likes to forget them sordid things. And when he forgets, he forgets. Nothin' my boss can't forget when he sets his mind to it."

They crossed the wide gallery and in answer to Willie's knock, the door was opened by a huge Negro. He was well trained. He did the right things, but in his attitude was disdain for these white folk. He ushered them through great, spacious, and once-gracious rooms, now desecrated, for they lacked the simplicity of elegance and glared with cost.

"Mr. Polli, he out back," said the Negro, "hit 'bout feedin' time fo' de birds."

They went through the house and out through French windows onto a fine lawn. About fifty feet from the house a wire fence rose higher than the treetops. It was vine-covered, but the door of woven wire on a frame of iron pipe was bare and through this Verity caught glimpses of color while the Negro twirled the gate knob first this way then that, as if opening a safe. At last he flung wide the wire door and as they stepped inside, the beauty within this enclosure came on them with all the force of a blow. Verity gasped. With all Saber had told her, she was not prepared for this. Hank stopped, drew in his breath in a long, slow amazement. "Lord save us," he said softly. Vince and Flower stared with eyes that seemed to believe nothing of what they saw. A huge L-shaped summer house sprawled handsomely off to the left, and from this Guy Polli called.

"So glad you got here." He bowed slightly. "I had you brought out here because it's almost feeding time."

"God'lmighty," said Hank, "don't even talk t' me, Polli; just lemme set 'n look a spell."

Polli, immensely pleased, beamed and said, "Yes, it affects some people that way." He waved at fine lounging chairs of bamboo and reed handsomely pillowed in bright blocked linen. The floor was tiled in blues and yellows, and fan doors of glass which could be drawn against rain and dew stood wide and glittering in the sunset gold. One whole wall was a fireplace in which great logs now burned, warming the chill fall air.

"Mix some drinks, Willie," said Polli.

"Don't never drink," said Hank firmly. "Just lemme look, like I said."

A large lagoon lay placid and sparkling, a great blue jewel reflecting the day's fine colors, its far side carpeted with lilies and hyacinths. Back of this, like loyal but crude sentinels, stood the rank, rough kex so common to the swamps. Fine late-flowering shrubs mixed with the mean Spanish daggers grew at its edges, and a dead, moss-draped cypress had been left—a thrilling touch of artistic reality in the midst of so much cultivation. Birds indigenous to this country stood at the edges or flew about. The air was full of the sounds of them and off in the far parts of this park Verity could catch glimpses of moving color among the majestic oaks and the glistening magnolias.

Flamingos whirled and ducks zoomed and pelicans made their raucous sounds, blending voices with great bright birds she could not name.

"What's that thing?" asked Hank.

He pointed at a wide, down-swooping trough which came through the fence at the right and seemed to empty into a huge barrel. They were scarcely discernible with their green paint against the foliage.

"That trough comes from my fish hatchery," said Polli with pride. "I have to have fish for the birds. When the keeper stands on the platform by the barrel, he can pull the sluice gate on the fence and the little fish come down. Thousands of them every day for my birds."

Verity turned and looked at Polli. He sat forward in his chair, excited anticipation in every line of him.

"This end of the aviary is only for the big birds." He rubbed his long, plump, soft hands. "I'll take you back and show you the others after feeding time. My keeper has them trained to eat at sundown. I can't bear to get up early in the mornings."

"Well," said Hank, "ain't y' got no 'gators?"

Polli smiled. "Nothing vicious here, Hank."

"Ain't this place a somethin', though!" said Hank. "What the hell makes feedin' time so wonderful?"

"You wait and see." Polli beamed and rubbed and rubbed his hands. "Those gorgeous things fight and scream and dive to get their food. To beat another bird to a fish. You wait and see." He looked at his watch. "Keeper should be here any minute."

The gate clicked. "There," said Polli and then added, "Oh, it's you."

A voice, a most melodious voice, a voice that could be only the Little Flamingo's, answered, "I'm not too late, am I?"

"No, just in time," said Polli.

A chill ran through Verity. She pulled her coat around her, rose, and went nearer the fire. She could now see Flamingo, and to her great relief saw that Saber was with her. At the moment she gave that no thought except for being glad to see him. Hank jumped and ran to Sunny Lou.

"What the hell you doin' here?" he cried.

"Oh, I come here often," said Flamingo. "I adore this place. Guy lets me feed the birds. I'm so glad to see you, Hank. Saber and I have been all over the state, seems as though. We've just come from your house. Saber came on here because he knew he'd catch you tonight at the headquarters in Sherman."

Hank glared at Saber. "How'r'y', Saber?" He turned and glared at Polli. But the gate clicked again and the keeper, in white ducks as pressed and sterile as a surgeon's, stepped in and walked down the path on the right of the lagoon to the trough and the barrel.

"Wait a minute," commanded Polli, "the young lady wants to feed them."

Flamingo ran to the summer house; stopped short when she saw Verity.

"Oh, hello," she said.

"Hello," said Verity flatly. But as the girl flung off her coat, she felt the beauty of her. She was not dimmed in this place of color; in fact, she seemed to draw from it as if gifted by some strange magnetism which pulled the very virility and color from the earth and all its living things. Flamingo turned, dismissing Verity, and came abruptly face to face with Hank, almost colliding. Both stood still. The feel, each of the other, was on them. Every atom of Flamingo reached out toward Hank as tangibly as forks of lightning, and seeing, Verity realized the girl invited the senses as surely as does the glow of a deep-red rose.

Saber stepped in front of Verity, blocking out the sight of these two.

"Come, sit over here with me," he said, "it's been a long time since we've had a chat."

But she moved to watch the girl, who turned slowly from Hank and then ran fleetly down the path to the fish barrel. She wore a full-skirted dress of soft turquoise jersey, and Verity thought bitterly she had chosen almost the only color this place did not grow. Her magnificent hair flowed to her shoulders and as she stood beside the barrel she threw her head back and her arms out in a gesture of wild delight. Then she made strange, piercing, calling sounds, pulled the lever of the sluice gate, took a big net, dipped it into the barrel, and tossed hundreds of small silver-bellied fish in the air. From a distance came the shrieks and caws, and as if by magic the air filled with whirling, screaming, diving color.

Polli rubbed his hands, almost danced with excitement, and his strong white teeth gleamed in his smile. Hank stood staring a minute while from the very roots of him a fermentation of pleasure seemed rising, and he ran to Flamingo shouting, "Lemme do it! I'm the feller as is throwing bait these days. I'm the feller! Lemme do it!" He grabbed the net and tossed the little fish into the air and the world became a cyclone of color that dipped and swirled and fought and screamed. Some bled and some fell. And the face of the blue lagoon was completely hidden by voracious beauty.

Verity clutched the chair back and turned her face away.

"Nothing vicious here!" said Saber. "Oh, no, nothing vicious here!" Then seeing Verity he said, "That's how it affects me. I'll get you a drink."

"Just get me out of here, Saber. Just get me out of this place."

He took her arm and hurried her to the gate. But the gate would not give. He fumbled and swore and finally managed the safety bolt which the keeper must have turned. Just as she went through the gate she saw Flower. The big fellow stood with back to lagoon and birds, fists clenched.

The Negro threw open a French door for them. "Cain't heah dem birds so plain heah," he said.

"Thanks, Hugo," said Saber. "Could you rustle us some good strong tea?"

"Yas, suh, right away, suh."

Saber sat down at the grand piano. "Sit there." He indicated a chair with a jerk of his head. "Where I can see you."

He strummed idly and she felt the kindness in his action for it helped shut out the screams of the birds. She sipped the tea and Saber played. Not well, just played.

"You've heard Jules play, of course?" he asked.

She shook her head.

"He plays excellently. . . . Now there is a man." Saber stopped strumming. "He's doing most constructive things, Verity. We've grown to know each other quite well down in the city. Jules believes that the whole country shows indications of a great depression. Says the cities are overcapitalized and overindustrialized. Declares there's a frightening adverse balance of trade between agriculture and industry and that it must be offset, since this is a machine age, by finding new uses for agriculture's produce and by electricity which will make possible country industries. Make sense to you?"

"I don't know," she said wearily. "I'm too tired to know anything."

"Poor kid." He swung his legs over the piano bench and picked up his teacup. "How are you going to like being the wife of a public officer?"

"I wish to God it had rained and rained and rained!" she said huskily, and her face burned with the speaking of this truth.

He sat still a long minute, then slapped his knees in anger and impatience. "Verity, I know it's not cricket for you and me to be discussing your husband—by man-and-wife rules—but some loyalties come before even that loyalty—" He hesitated, hating to speak these words, but he took a deep breath and went on. "This morning you put yourself in front of nine men and nine guns instead of putting yourself in front of Hank. How significant is that action, Verity? Maybe it was a deep mother, or protective, instinct—to—well, to talk in clichés—keep blood off Hank's hands."

Confusion was swallowing her and she lowered her head. But Saber rose and, standing before her, gently tipped up her head and said, "I have a terrible feeling that we have seen only the beginnings—what Jules once called the hidden consecutives. As I look back, I think all the indications were there—to one who could read the score. What I'm trying to say is that I am your friend. Yours, I mean. But I am going to have to fight Hank. I feel it coming on."

She knew what he said and she knew what he meant but she couldn't digest it just yet. Saber sat down again on the bench and hitched it nearer her.

"Jules helped Hank a lot. I helped him a little. Why did we do it? Verity, I've thought about it all day. He has such great ability, such great power to stir." He struck her chair arm with a clenched fist. "Dammit, Verity, Hank has a positive genius for giving one answer in words and another in action! He stirs the emotions so! Why, when he quotes the Bible in that rich voice of his, he absolutely makes people feel that here, at least, is the one man in the world who loves people with a Godlike greatness."

Saber rose and paced back and forth. "I spoke of that to Jules and Jules said a most revealing thing." He stopped for emphasis. "Jules said Hank's religion is not religion but an appetitive expression."

She looked at Saber in bewilderment.

"You don't understand, do you?" he asked almost gently.

"No," she murmured, "no."

"Neither did I." He laughed with a self-deriding bitterness. "Took me all day to figure that one out. Hank hungers for religion. It's a part of his psychological picture of himself. But, as he once told me, preaching pays off in picayunes. And so—it's the appetizer before the worldly meal, and the digestive aid afterward."

Her head went back as from a knockout blow and a daze and numbness came on her such as fighters sometimes know while yet they go through the motions.

"Forgive me, Verity. Please forgive me," pleaded Saber. "Perhaps I shouldn't have said that. But good heavens! Someone must prepare you against hurt."

No more hurts, her heart pleaded—no more—no more; and she sat like a frozen dummy staring at the deep, thick pile of the rug.

"I'm so sorry, Verity." Saber kicked a carved chair leg. "Stupid fool that I am! I don't want you hurt, so I inflict a helluva wound!"

He took her hand and held it a moment in comradeship and understanding, then slid into a chair and smoked cigarette after cigarette and looked at his watch again and again, finally murmuring something about phoning his editor, he left the room.

Returning after some minutes, he said, "Well, Governor Rordan is preparing to contest this election." She made no answer. "Do you hear me, Verity?" he asked.

She simply nodded. Saber crossed the room to a huge ornate cabinet, twirled dials, and soon the room was filled with soft music. It was the first time she had ever heard or seen a radio and yet, so deep was she in dumb misery, she didn't feel the wonder of the instrument.

But when Polli and Hank and Flamingo came in she had the feeling that all the color and wildness of the birds were again thrust upon her and her nerves instinctively braced and tightened against this foin.

"When I come here t'day I was a-feelin' the need for hibernatin' a spell, 'n now here I am, all perked 'n refreshed," Hank said. "You should oughta stayed, Verity. You never did see such birds. From all over the world he's got 'em. Shore makes a feller hone t' see 'em in the places as is their natural homes."

"Oh, pshaw," Flamingo's remarkable voice rolled softly through the rooms, "I wouldn't go out of the Magnolia State to see nothin'."

"Flamingo," said Hank, "yore voice is like to small thunder all fringed with cymbals 'n bells."

Verity's heart clutched and everyone was too still. Hank cleared his throat and, sensing the feel of error, pushed on expansively. "Well, now, it purely is," he asserted. "It purely is."

An intense fervency glowed in Flamingo and leaped plainly forth as she smiled at Hank.

"I just talked to my editor," said Saber, "and he tells me Governor Rordan is preparing to contest the election. Court, I mean. Not a recount."

Hank whirled and shook his fist heavenward. "Let him do it! By God-'lmighty, them folks got a right t' vote!"

"Just thought I'd tell you." Saber grinned. "Give you something to worry about. Come on, Sunny Lou, I have to go."

"Oh, don't go," said Polli. "I've ordered dinner for all of us."

"Not for me," Saber replied. "And not for Sunny Lou. When I bring a girl she leaves with me. She's due back at her school tomorrow. See you at headquarters tonight, Hank."

"Now, you know," Polli reminded Saber, "everything you see or hear here is off the record!"

"But I knew about your deal with Hank before I saw him here. Remember? That was just adding the old two and two," said Saber.

"You can't prove it," said Hank.

Saber shrugged. "I can always allege it," he laughed. He took Flamingo's arm and pulled her out of the room while she set her feet against going and laughed, "I don't want to—I don't want to!"

As the door closed after them, Hank drew a long, whistling breath. "Polli, I dunno as I like her bein' here. Her paw's one a' my best friends. Iffen she comes t' harm from you—"

"Now, now," Polli's voice was as soft as his hands, "she's very beautiful. Like one of my birds. You saw that, long ago."

"I'm a-warnin' y', Polli."

"Now, now, don't be hasty, Hank. She comes only to feed the birds. And she can take care of herself, that one."

Hank grinned. "Reckon so. Well, let's get down to business. You heard what Saber said. I ain't goin' t' have that vote brought into court iffen I can help it. But iffen it has gotta be, why, I wanta be sure a' the judge. How many judges you done business with already, huh? You must 'a had t' find out which judges could be made t' hear the sound a' silver."

Suddenly uneasy, Polli turned to Verity and bowed slightly. "May I have Hugo bring you some dinner on the tea cart while your husband and I have a talk as well as dinner elsewhere?"

"Why, shore," said Hank. "That'll work out fine." He looked at her, really looked at her for the first time since morning when she lifted the iron vest. "Roarin' thunderbolts, Verity, what ails y'? Y' look as if y' been consortin' with ghosts. You ain't sick?"

"No—no, just tired," she said harshly. "I'm all right."

"You plumb shore?"

She nodded.

"Well, I reckon y' are, at that. Feller don't get the pleasure a' strainin' through a election day but oncet every few years. Better'n Christmas, by God'lmighty." He turned and left the room with Polli, his words trailing back to her: "That's a thing I purely gotta do when I'm governor, is control the courts. Iffen somethin' should get into court, y' gotta have some judges as will interpret the law yore way. Now withen the list you get—"

She held firmly to the chair arms and bit her lip, and told herself over and over—"Iron in your guts—get some iron in your guts—"

They were in Sherman several weeks in a fine suite in the best hotel. The sitting room was always full of men and smoke, and bellhops seemed forever bringing sets of glasses and ice and soda and ginger ale to serve the good whisky which Polli sent in cases. But Polli never came. Both he and Hank knew their alliance must not now be known as a proved fact.

Hank made the front pages of the newspapers almost beyond his hopes. To Hank his sunbonneted women and his barefoot men of the swamps and the hills had long been an accepted fact, perhaps the best known fact in his life, but to the editors and to the opposition party, and even to his own committeemen, they were a miracle. That any man had ever trod those swamps and hills long enough and hard enough to make these reticent, clannish backwoods folk his friends—that any man could find the mortar that would make them stick together and fight for and worship him—was a thing almost past understanding.

Papers sent reporters out to find some of these voters in their homes. The *Evening News* of Sherman ran columns on how they intended to choose several voters' names just at random throughout the state, send reporters to find these voters in their homes, and in this way determine in some degree whether Governor Rordan was right in contesting this vote which Commissioner-elect Martin had brought out. And when the paper listed the names chosen, Hank howled with glee.

"By God'lmighty," he roared to Verity one night as he paced through the two rooms of their suite, "that there paper couldn't 'a done me a better turn. Lookit there, Verity, one a' the names they picked is Elly Lanson. Old Elly allus said he guessed his real name was Ellsworth, but he ain't never been called nothin' but Elly. You ever heard the name Ellsworth Naughton Lanson?"

"No." She shook her head.

"Elly's paw," Hank grinned, "was a soldier in the War Between the States. A officer, b' God. 'N Elly's paw fought the carpetbaggers brave and fine after the war. Him 'n his family was so persecuted that, after he was shot through the shoulder, 'n his wife nigh 'bout took by looters when them looters burned the Lanson house in Crescent City, that Lanson took his family into the swamps, and with him he took twenty-two other families who either hadda flee or leastways felt they did."

Verity's heart went out to these people. These were the things that swung one around to Hank's outlook, these were the things he was going to right. And these were the things that revived hope for the good, for the fine, for the best.

"These here folks went in rowboats 'n fair shot their way through the 'gators, which was as a nothin' compared t' them drunk 'n crazed carpetbaggers, both white 'n black. All a 'gator could do t' a man's wife 'n daughter was kill 'em. But Lanson died afore his house on stilts got proper finished." Hank looked at Verity with eyes that saw again the Lanson shack, and he went on softly, "There's books lined up agin old Elly's wall that ain't been opened for fifty years. Life got so hard didn't nobody have time for readin' 'n book learnin'. Old Elly's a-goin' to stand straight 'n proud 'n look at that there reporter. 'N I know just 'bout exactly what old Elly'll say." His voice dropped to a sweet softness and he swiped at his eyes. "Old Elly'll likely say, 'Hank come t' us fair leapin' from tussock t' hummock. Bold 'n fine, he come t' us. His heart allus callable by ourn, 'n ourn'll ever be callable by his. 'N our answer won't never be in carnal love. Nor withholdin'. We won't never offer Hank the pindlin' bit, but allus the great fardel.' "

Tears rolled down Verity's cheeks.

"Old Elly tolt me just that 'bout myself oncet." He walked to the window and looked out on the little capital city of his state. " 'Not the pindlin' bit, but allus the great fardel.' " Then turning, he came to her, lifted her in his arms and laid her on the bed. "That's what you allus done—you didn't never give no pindlin' bit a' love; it was allus the great fardel. Why, Sweetface," he murmured, his face against her neck, "you even done better'n that. Yes, sir, you plumb added unto. You added the high hill 'n the still, still glade."

He wiped the tears from her cheeks and asked, "What for you crying? Don't never salten yore eyes for what's done 'n over. I ain't a-leapin' from tussock t' hummock no more. I'm 'bout t' make the pinnacle."

"But the scheming, the using of people to get up that pinnacle—it's terrible."

"God'lmighty," he exploded, "you goin' into that agin? D'you think I didn't use people 'n scheme t' get past 'gators from tussock t' hummock! You just be my wife. I'll carry y' up the pinnacle. I'll do the climbin'. I've tolt you afore there's some things that has just gotta be." Looking down into her eyes, his nostrils pulled downward, his lids half closed, his hands slipped under her and pulled her body against his own. " 'N this is one a' them." He kissed her and whispered, "That's kissin' afore lovin'—'member? Yes, sir, this is one a' them things that has just gotta be."

The papers became a source of never-ending interest and bewilderment to her. Some carried editorials championing Hank's remarkable ability and declared that actually the old voting law had, as he said, been intended to outlaw the Negro vote which was then larger than the white vote, but, the editorials always added, regardless of all else, regardless of past wrongs, a voter should be able to read and write, no matter who his father and grandfather were. Hank laughed at the editorials, saying, "Who the hell reads them editorials anyhow? Only a few folks as wanta talk learned t' their neighbors. The place t' get somethin' across to the mob a' plain readin' folks is in the news columns."

Verity's picture was also in the papers as snapped beside Hank at the headquarters election night. Those pictures of her annoyed Hank. He couldn't see why she had to look so peaked and so full of misery, but added that leastways she looked like a lady.

But the pictures which bothered Verity most were the ones of the party committeemen. To Verity they showed the strangest assortment of faces that a group of men could show to the world and yet have a sameness, for in each she saw a sleekness, an overlayer of joviality, and as she stared at the picture, the highlight in every eye became a dollar sign.

Throughout the days in Sherman she felt like a prisoner on a different planet. She had felt strange during the first days when campaigning with Hank, but there the tone and fiber of Hank had been those which she knew and to which she was accustomed. But here he seemed changed in hue; here he was always sitting before maps pointing out where this shrimp or oyster cannery was. During these days she developed a morbid penchant for knowing all. Instead of going to the movies or on an orgy of spending, as Hank urged her to do, she sat in the bedroom sewing on little dresses for Hancy and listening to the talk from the sitting room, coming only a little muffled through the thin door. Sometimes Hank took her in to meet the men and his pride in her shone clear and fine; and sometimes as he talked, she felt a great pride in him and a rising hope—and at such times she found herself listening to him and leaning toward the idea that Hank was right. And then she would fall to the depths again as the maps came out and chairs scraped nearer to the table and whisky glasses clinked in toasts to the Commissioner, and to the sunny days that were now not far off, since in only a few months Hank would take office. Then, reminding them that time was a-wastin', Hank would trace the road maps, point out the territories each man present was to look after in the matter of finding in each little town a keyman who would have some vote pull, to whom should be given the easy job of scraping the dirt road once a week—in dry weather only, of course. There was nothing like putting people on the pay roll, to make them and all onlookers jump on the band wagon and vote right from then on. The fellow who scraped a ten-mile stretch once a week in dry weather would get a tidy sum each month, whether it was wet or dry, and it would take but a few hours. Just manna from heaven. To the objection that the state didn't have that much equipment because now folks took turns doing a little road work instead of paying all their taxes in cash, Hank bellowed, "Don't y' think I know that! Why, I'll just take away all the money allotted t' Mayor Appleby's Crescent City, 'n allot it to the villages, since I can only control a part a' that city anyways. 'N, hell, don't y' think I know exactly how much there is for road upkeep? Iffen I can't get more from the state, we'll pay it outen our own pockets." Men protested at this but Hank bawled them to silence. "God-'lmighty, ain't you willin' t' part with a half a' the money you'll be gettin' for nothin' from the canneries in order t' get in power where the pickin's are hundredfold?"

Each day while at Sherman, Verity felt as if her inner self was growing colder and colder, and yet she punished herself with more of this knowledge as if doing penance. She heard it all, but she couldn't make it seem real, couldn't actually visualize Hank carrying out these plans. When she thought back on the heartbreaking labor he'd put in to achieve this, she couldn't believe it was what he wanted. Election day was only just past and yet every plan laid was pointed toward the next election day.

Election day—election day—those words became the most onerous words in the English language to Verity. Rain was the one thing Hank feared most—if it should rain at election time—if it should rain. He paced the floor long into the nights, hunting the solution in case it rained a few years hence, come the gubernatorial. And then one night he laughed and laughed in the way she had come to recognize as triumph.

"Beats all, Verity," he laughed, "how simple everythin' is. 'N how really the answer t' everythin' lays either in nature or in a man's past. Here I been a-workin', 'n a-worryin' 'bout rain, 'n then I think about my tents 'n all the folks as stayed overnight just a few nights ago. 'N there it is."

"There what is?"

"The answer. Iffen the voters can't come thru' the rain, I'll house 'em—for as long as I hafta just so's they're at the polls, rain or no rain. 'N will I keep this one quiet t' surprise the country! Oh, glory and throne chairs, won't them dang papers have a somethin' for to make news out of then!"

"How can you house people all over the state?" she cried. "At every poll?"

"Easiest thing y' can imagine," he grinned. "There's all them hundreds 'n hundreds a' tents the state militia uses only durin' summer encampment. I can sure find a way t' wangle them, iffen I gotta swipe 'em for a spell. 'N there's all the highway trucks for t' haul 'em. God'lmighty! It pure beats all how everythin' works out t' help me, iffen I just think 'n work long enough. Lord God Almighty allus gives me His best." He pranced about exultantly. " 'N then there's my organization money as has rolled in dollar b' dollar—'n then I can allus force the feller as owes his state job t' me t' pay into a sorta welfare vacation fund. 'N election time is when my members will be a-takin' of vacations. They'll shore like that. They don't get vacations."

She stared at Hank. "You mean you'd make a man pay you for the job you get him?"

"Shore," said Hank. "Only," he grinned, "you call the kickback names like 'welfare fund.' "

"Don't start that sort of thing! Hank, I beg you not to start doing that sort of thing. Rulers who have done that have just kept creating more and more jobs, taking more and more back to themselves." She felt she was pleading as she had never pleaded before. "That's the sort of thing that made once-great countries fall. Countries like Rome—finally people lived by fear and favor, and men held office by homage and tribute. Sometimes I think that's the most vicious thing I ever read in history."

"God'lmighty, what's vicious 'bout that! Iffen it does what I'm after—'n that's keep me in office—I can do great things."

Sadness filled her. "You know better!" she cried. "You know better. You're being blind again! You're nictitating!"

"All right, so I'm nictitating!" He sighed. "God'lmighty, I been a-wantin' for the two of us t' get outen this hotel at the same time afore you went home, so's I could show y' the Capitol 'n the Governor's Mansion. You ain't scarce been out a' doors sincet election. The Capitol building is a hideous old thing but the Governor's Mansion is a lovely. But I'm thinkin' you better pack 'n go home." He put his hands on her shoulders and shook her gently. "I just plain can't see what's the matter with you times like t' these. I've tolt y' 'n tolt y' there is some things as has gotta be. Mebbe," his voice softened, "it's just that a Venus girl shouldn't oughta go into battle. 'N that 'minds me—you keep away from that dang Jules. Him 'n his damn fables!"

He swooped her up in his arms a minute and holding her close said, "Afore God, Verity, you make a man's gorge t' rise. You purely do. Here I work night 'n day tillst I ain't scarce ever had time to love y' brimful 'n splendid, liken I—"

The telephone rang. "Roarin' thunderbolts," he howled and put her down. "The committee's downstairs," he said as he hung up the receiver. "They'll be right up. Allus there's somethin'."

He paced the floor, getting himself into his hail-fellow mood, and when a knock came he threw open the door with great joviality. But the committeemen were uneasy. They made their greetings and went into hemming and hedging.

"Well, what is it?" demanded Hank. "A blinded halfwit could be a-seein' there's somethin' on yore minds."

As if strings pulled them, all heads turned toward Mr. Angleman, who shifted unhappily and adjusted his very proper dark suit and licked his set, almost prim lips.

"Well, my dear fellow," he began, "it's—ah, well—it's your English."

"My English, huh?" Hank asked cautiously. "Ain't you allus understood me, even when I wasn't showin' y' where 'n how t' make money? 'R haven't you ever come near me, 'cept for that fine 'n noble purpose?"

The question of Hank's English had crossed Verity's mind many times when first she knew him and she had thought that with his reading and studying it would be just another thing he would conquer. But the matter slipped her mind. To her Hank's speech had become Hank and she loved it.

"The rest of us are not in accord with this, Commissioner," one man declared. "We have all tried to tell Angleman so."

"Well, yes, it was my idea that we speak of it," said Angleman. "It is not too bad, perhaps, in a road commissioner—but in a governor—ah—well, how is one really to command respect—"

"Command respect, huh? Now you lookit here, Angleman—just answer me this—which a' us, 'twixt you 'n me, is commandin' the most respect? Ain't I the one as you been a-takin' orders from? Ain't I the one as is fattenin' yore pocket?"

"Well, now—no offense, Commissioner." Mr. Angleman was placating and nervous. "No offense. I—I mean it for the good of the party."

"Good a' the party! Hogwash! D'y' honest think a feller smart 's me ain't give some thought as 't whether I should oughta speak what you're a-callin' 'good English'? Well, lemme tell you somethin'—I come a' the people a' the hills, 'n I live 'mongst the people a' the swamps, 'n all this state knows it. Would I be like t' you 'n yore 'good English'? Why, hell, you fool, such a act would be like t' a mockin'bird discardin' his vocal box in favor a' takin' on that of a sparrow! Like t' a scarlet tanager a-pluckin' his feathers in order to don them of a wren!" He drew himself up and said scornfully, "Far 'n wide I'm knowed as the most describin' man in the whole state—'n would I change t' be like t' you?" Contempt curled his lips. "Who is it can speak from a platform 'n plumb drown a thousand folks in fervor? Is it me—'r is it you? The day'll come, 'n soon, when I'll be a-drownin' hundreds a' thousands over the radio. Would I cease t' be me, so's t' be as you? You—who plumb prove by every 'good English' word you let drool forth that you ain't a nothin' but a pusillanimous pewit withen a pisiform brain, 'n capable only a' pis-antin' around!"

The committeemen sat paralyzed. Quietly, Verity shut the bedroom door and went to the window. She laughed in spite of her low spirits. The faces of those men! The harried amazement—and the dollar sign fading right out of Mr. Angleman's eye! He knew he had probably seen his last Martin-made dollar. She looked out on the placid little capital city of the Magnolia State, sighed heavily, and turning from the window, pulled a suitcase out of the closet and began packing for home. Oh, Hank had considered his speech all right! Yes, he had indeed. In the beginning was the word.

16

*Yes, Hank Martin was elected governor by the shrewdest bit of
foresight and planning against rain—his old enemy, rain. Yes,
Hank Martin always knew how to bring the mountain to Mo-
hammed.*

*As governor he seemed to sweep all before him with his passion
and his purpose. Many a passionate fight was fought on the
floor of the state senate and in the assembly, for Hank had
bitter enemies as well as stanch friends. But in the end Hank
always got his bills passed just as he wanted them.*

*From the very beginning Hank became famous for his disre-
gard for party lines. If a member of the opposition had ideas on
finance or roads, or on almost any subject, that man was put on
a committee to offer advice to the lawmakers of the state, and
Hank always said, "The state comes before the party."* . . .

VERITY'S life through the next years seemed lived on two levels: the top
level of activity, and an underplay of sad speculation, like background
music which sometimes swelled into great discordant rolls of fear, or into
powerful, magnificent yearnings of passion; sometimes into a cacophony
of jealousy, and sometimes thinned to a tremolo of self-misgivings.
Through it all she went her daily rounds of home and friendliness, and
through four hours daily of reading and study. Her studies were a strange
mixture. Each day she read Saber's column; thought on what he said. But
whatever he wrote of Hank and Hank's activities she clipped and filed
away. She went through three newspapers daily, clipped news and comment on Hank, and news and comments on conditions in the state gen-
erally. Why she did this was not clear to her except that she must learn all
she could. After the papers she turned to books on economics and
sociological progress. She did not at first understand any of it but with
dogged determination she emulated Hank's persistence in his study of law.
Her newspapers began to carry considerable news about Italy, and

sometimes a picture of Italy's worshiped leader. As she studied his strutty bull-like posture, his jutted chin, his menacing fists, his bemedaled chest, a wandering sadness invaded her, wafting itself around through the maze of her being as if hunting the emotion in which to root long enough to show clearly its flower and its fruit.

Every few months she heard the reverberations of Hank's activities in the Bend. The man to whom Marcus Davol gave the road-scraping job was one of the election officers. His name was Seymour and it was known that he had always been a registered member of the opposition party. Hank's old friends saw the wisdom and bigness of this—didn't it show that Hank put some things above party lines? Now Seymour would bring in other members. And wasn't Hank doing the best he could the cheapest way until he got good cement roads like he promised?—for after all Seymour owned wagons and horses to do the work. So once a week in dry weather Seymour's eldest son drove a wagon over ten miles of road, dragging a dust-raising log, like a whiffle tree on the wrong end of the rig. And too, the humble folk were well paid by the unworded, but clearly recognized fact, as shown by Seymour's pleasant greetings, that Seymour owed this windfall to them, to their chosen leader. The more people Hank snared from the opposition, the quicker he could really get everybody to that lovely place where the riches were to be divided. But one day while Verity was in the store, Squeeze-nickel said, "I was jus' a-sayin' t' Tim 'Don't it beat all! Here's Seymour, as don't need the cash, but Hank ha gotta give the job t' a rich feller afore he can fetch us all t' the point a gittin' riches divided.' Don't it, Verity? But, ain't no doubt though, Hank knows what he's a-doin'."

Sometimes her love rose and soared, iridescent and beautiful, but then she would read a bit of history, a comment, that would plunge her into thought.

The story in the papers about old Elly Lanson was a masterly piece. To the city dweller the story read like an adventure tale out of another age and old Elly said almost the exact words Hank had quoted. There were other stories of folk not so picturesque, folk ground down to lives having only one privilege more than a work mule has—that of breeding their own kind—in the reporter's opinion an ability the world could do without.

Reporters came to the Bend, took pictures of Verity and Hancy and of Selah, of their tidy white-gleaming house, the well-tended garden, the thriving patches of cotton and cane; also, of course, of the horse and cart. The fat, pink cardboard baby, now a little faded, still looked scared at the sight of its booteed foot. This cart, so well known through the back country, caught the imagination of the village and city folk. There was no doubt about it—Hank was now news.

Governor Rordan went ahead with his intention to contest the election and when Hank heard this he howled with glee; declared he'd show

Rordan whether that vote was authentic, whether those people had a right to vote. Rordan could spend his life in court proving the ancestry of thousands of folks if he wanted to! But time went on—and somehow the courts always found some small troublesome technicality. One postponement followed another. Verity, reading her newspapers, knew the case would probably never come up unless Hank felt it to be to his advantage after he was in the governor's chair.

Then came Hank's big fight with Governor Rordan over control of the waterways. Waterways were highways. A law of the state decreed that they were. "But this state has plumb been cursed with governors as has ignored the law 'n just plain took things in their own hands," Hank was quoted as saying. "Some governors can't keep in office withouten overplayin' the old game a' patronage. Rordan has separated the waterways from the roadways, 'n give the control a' waterways as a appointive job! 'N, by God'lmighty, I aim t' wrest it away from a feller as gets the job by appointment 'n personal pull, 'n put it back under the control of a feller as the people has elected! . . . 'N, yes, I mean me! All over this state people has showed they put their trust in me! By God'lmighty, I plumb got a mandate from the people!"

The law was the law and the waterways became a part of Hank's responsibilities. Then, Hank pointed out that actually every fish and shrimp and oyster taken out of waters within fifteen miles of the shore line belonged to the state because of that law which defined waterways as highways, and another law which defined highways as state-owned and state-controlled property. Therefore, all commercial fishing boats must account for their take. This, Hank pointed out, was only good sense. When he was governor he would, in the interests of conservation, get a law passed that would put this control of the fish catch under the jurisdiction of the conservation department. But until then he would care for it himself as the law decreed.

Everywhere there were echoes of the people's amazement that they could ever have elected a man like Rordan to be their governor. Why, Rordan was just what Hank Martin said he was—a pompous old mossback, a dumb fellow who didn't know what laws were on the books of the state, heavy in the belly and heavy in the head. Governor Rordan wanted to keep the state in the horse-and-buggy era.

Verity wondered about Governor Rordan and what kind of a record he had actually made in the governorship. She sent for old papers and to her amazement found that Governor Rordan had several times proposed bills to appropriate more money for schools and had been gnawing away at the problem of roads. But Governor Rordan had felt that the building of roads must be a slow process in the Magnolia State, since it was an agricultural state and as such was feeling the pinch of readjustment; for though the Kaiser and the Huns were handsomely licked in the war, world markets for cotton were not what they once had been. Verity felt like Diogenes, the cynic, and it gave her a lift to find that she could put her lamp up to Governor Rordan's face and find more than a trace of honesty. She had begun to feel that there was no such creature as an honest governor, or statesman, or politician.

The opposition tightened its belt and worked and prayed for rain, and Hank worked and cared not a damn whether it rained or not. That Varick Kirkendall would be Hank's running mate came as the greatest of surprises to the public. The name of Kirkendall was linked with the glories of the state. Marcus Davol's name began to appear in print. It too made a flurry. At campaign meetings in the cities Marcus was often the first speaker, introducing Kirkendall next and Hank last. "Kirk," as Hank called him, was a tall, lean, impressive-looking man, with thin graying hair, much older than Hank. His wide blue eyes looked out of the news pictures with an air of being unhappily startled out of sleep. But his gray-haired wife had the austere, set-mouthed look of an ambitious and hard-driving woman.

Jules's company, the Southern Light and Power, brought electricity to the Bend, and Hank bought a radio. The night on which Hank was to make his first radio speech, Verity's house was jammed with his friends. For two days Selah baked for this event and the little house was like a nosegay with its new electric lamps softly shaded and its fragrances of spices and cake. Jenny, the first to arrive, looked about appreciatively.

"That there Governor's Mansion you're a-goin' into can't be a heap prettier'n this."

"No," said Verity, "perhaps not as pretty to me. And by the way, you may live in the Governor's Mansion, too."

"Me!" gasped Jenny. "Aw, you're a-funnin'!"

"Why, no, I'm not. Hank has to have his guards. What better than that you and Flower live there? A lot will depend, I suppose, on how the house is laid out and how much room there is. But I'd like to have you near, Jenny."

"Gawd!" said Jenny softly. "Gawd—t' think you'd ever be a-sayin' such t' me! Me, that don't b'long in no governor's house! I ain't no lady like you."

"You and Selah are my only friends." The deep sadness welled in Verity as she spoke. "I'll be very lonely."

"No, you won't, Verity. All them hoity-toity folks'll be a-kowtowin'."

"Exactly," said Verity. "Kowtowin'."

The folk of the Bend marveled at the music and words coming from the big gleaming radio. They turned the dials, exclaiming at the wonder of hearing Hank in a few minutes talking into the air—over a station into which their very own dollars had been put. Verity thought of Swith coming through the misty morning, harnessed to his wheelbarrow. She could imagine the little fellow as he looked tonight at the radio station with Hank, his face lustrous with the sheen of dreams and miracles.

The hands of the clock drew near the hour of seven. Verity set the dials for the best reception and sat where she could watch the faces of her guests. Selah sat back of the stove, trying to keep Hancy quiet.

As the announcer made the little introductory speech there were Ohs and Ahs, and when Hank's voice came forth, vibrant and rich with music, the thousand-volt wire flamed so whitely hot within Verity that she rose and went back beside Selah, and Hancy cried out, "That's my Hank! Mamma, where's my Hank?"

"Sh!" said Selah softly. "Yo' pappy, he talkin' t'rough de box. Sh, now."

And from the radio came, "This here's yore friend Hank Martin. Hank Martin. Everybody hear that name? I'm yore friend Hank Martin. Right now I'm commissioner of public works 'n highways 'n I'm a-runnin' for governor.

"Now, I ain't a-goin' t' say nothin' a' no importance for three minutes, mebbe five, so all a' you as has telephones run to 'em quick. Ring up yore friends 'n tell 'em Hank Martin is on the air, 'n tell 'em the station.

"Now while you're a-doin' that I'm just a-goin' t' tell you some a' the wonders a' this here Magnolia State. Beauteous it is in its richness. Why, here in this state we got only about one-seventh a' the land under cultivation. 'N yet ours is a agricultural country. But even on just that there one-seventh we're a-growin' crops as total nigh 'bout two hunderd million dollars . . ."

As Hank went on telling of the wonders of richness, Verity knew that in spite of inviting people to tear their attention from the radio long enough to do some telephoning, he was working up to the high pitch of pointing out that with these hundreds of millions in this state, "mebbe you, like me, didn't have enough t' eat when you was a young'un. Mebbe you, like me, look around y', 'n are a-seein' of great riches. 'N mebbe you, like me, are a-thinkin' them riches should oughta be divided so yore young'uns'll have the chancet you didn't never have—well, I'm yore friend! I'm the feller as comes a' the plain people. I can see that not merely has the pore a' the hills 'n the swamps never had the right chancet —but you fellers in the towns 'n the cities ain't had it neither! Should you oughta be workin' for some rich 'n mighty feller a-lettin' him take a profit off a' the salt a' yore tears!

"Are y' just gonna set still, come election day? Or worse, are y' gonna go t' the polls 'n cast a vote for the feller as is now governor—that poor dumb feller as don't know the laws he's supposed t' be administerin'? The opposition smears my name 'n calls me a grafter 'cause I done took the job a' lookin' after the waterways. They say I bullied 'n threatened them rich purse-proud owners a' canneries— Well, roarin' thunderbolts! I did! Yes, sir, I purely did! Not no man—no, nor not no army a' rich capitalists are a-goin' t' scare Hank Martin into lettin' the natural sources a' food in this here state be used up faster 'n a fish can fertilize a egg!

"The governors a' the past should oughta put a stop t' that long ago!— 'N Rordan, he should oughta done somethin'! But, no! He ain't done nothin'! Not nothin'!

"But I'm a prophesier—yes, I am, friends. I'm like t' Joseph—him that got sold by his brothers into slavery. But whilst he was a prisoner in a strange land the king had a troublesome dream, 'n Joseph was brought t' interpret it. So Joseph saw that a famine would come on the land after seven years of fatness . . ." Here Hank's voice went into thickest sarcasm. ". . . the fattest of all would be the capitalists then, just like now, I got no doubt . . . but Joseph, he wanted t' save the people. He sold the king on the idea a' storin' surplus grains 'n food agin them lean years. 'N so Joseph, he was the first feller t' look toward the future 'n conserve the resources.

"Now, liken I said, Rordan he smears me, 'n he vilifies me. But I got confidence in the people!—I got confidence that through the people's vote I can one day say, liken Joseph said t' his brothers—them same brothers as sold him into slavery. . . . They come t' Joseph t' beg for grain. They didn't know the great man was their brother when they come. 'N when they recognized him they fell back in fear. But Joseph, he says, 'Ye meant evil against me; but God meant it unto me for good.' "

Hank's pause here was the pause of the finished orator. The little house pulsed with the magnificent roll of his tones, as an organ leaves its throb in a church. Then, in a beautiful, sweet glissando from great volume to the melodious theme of his hymn, Hank went on.

"Yes, friends, I got confidence. Confidence that after the election I can say t' them as vilify me, 'Ye meant evil against me; but God meant unto me for good.' But God is a mite handicapped, friends, unless'n them a' you as can hear will hear my plea. Go then to the polls 'n vote for yore friend Hank Martin. Remember now, yore friend Hank Martin, for governor. 'N bless y'—everyone."

A prayerful, thrilling enchantment was in the room until Hancy exclaimed, "That's my Hank!"

"Lawdy, Lawdy," breathed Selah fervently, "dat man a somepin'. Iffen I cud vote, reckon he git my mark on dat papuh. Um-ummm!"

"That's our Hank, all right," said Tim. Sophy was trying not to cry and Tim patted her knee consolingly. "Don't mind a-bawlin', Maw," he said gently. "Lotsa us is a-snivelin' more'n a mite. 'N t' think," he looked over the group, "t' think usn here is the first members Hank had. 'N Swith, a-course. 'N t' think he made his first real campaign speech in my shop."

"I bet that'll fetch them city fellers over t' Hank," Squeeze-nickel nodded emphatically. "That there speech was purely a sockdolager. That's what I tolt that young offshoot as comes t' sell me some canned foods fer n' shelves. Here he's a-askin' six cents more fer a can a' oysters 'n he usen to be a-askin'. So I says why's that? 'N he says I oughta know since the feller as causes it lives right here." Squeeze-nickel wrenched his thin torso into a strange backward S, doubled his fists, and shadow-boxed a bit. "I says, 'Iffen you're a-layerin' muck over the name a' Hank Martin, Squirt, you-all gotta fight me.' "

"That was a-tellin' him!" said Whale Cruze. "What'd the pulin' offshoot do then?"

"Aw, he says, take 'em 'r leave 'em." Squeeze-nickel deflated to normal size and posture. "I tuk a couple jus' in case Mr. Bolduc wants 'em." He sighed, "Them oysters was allus a treat t' me 'n Maw fer extry special. But I reckon now we can't have 'em no more."

"What the heck," exclaimed Picayune. "Usn done withouten more'n oysters. Iffen it's right fer Hank 'n the country, what the heck."

A few weeks before election time two huge trucks stopped before Verity's gate. When she answered the knock on her door three burly workmen greeted her courteously. On the sleeves of their khaki work coats were appliqués of white magnolia and the words "Public Works and Highways."

"Miz Martin?"

"Yes."

"The Commissioner told us t' stop by here 'n pick up some tents he says is stored in the barn. Can we go right out there 'n find them without botherin' you?"

"Didn't Mr. Martin get the militia tents?" asked Verity.

They grinned. "Oh, sure he did. You know 'bout that then?"

"Yes," she replied. "Well, you'll find the tents in the barn just as Mr. Martin said."

"O.K. Thank you, ma'am."

They turned, but as they reached the road the voice of one came clearly back. "Christ's sake, who'd think the boss would have a high-grade icicle for a wife!"

"She's kinda beautiful, though."

"So what? So's statues. Here we was all expectin' t' see a yummy little mamma, all sweet 'n hot. You coulda blowed me down with a—"

Verity stepped back in the house and closed the door. An icicle, she thought bitterly. Yet she knew she was constantly feeling more aloof, more removed. It bothered her too—this strange feeling of heaviness within her, this sense of needing to hunt and hunt all the time for the real things in life.

Jules helped a lot when he came on election evening as she and Selah listened to the returns. It had rained for three days and the opposition gloated while at the same time warned the public not to take anything for granted. But, oh, the pleasure the rain gave Hank's enemies! The rain, the blessed rain would keep the immense country vote at home, hemmed in by the deep old blackjack. And Hank had made a speech in which he nicely covered his use of the militia tents. "I requisitioned additional equipment for t' work the roads. 'N I was refused. Here we got a state militia in this state as has all kinds a' tools 'n other equipment. But, no— Rordan refuses t' let my workmen use them tools. No, by Christmas, they tolt me I hadda wait tillst I was give more a' the taxpayers' money for t' buy stuff just for the highway department. Just double the expense on the taxpayers! But I'm tellin' y' plain, friends, that I plumb raised a ruckus as made that pulin' li'l ol' Capitol buildin' shake t' its foundations. 'N that was all right, too, 'cause one a' the things I'm gonna do is build a Capitol buildin' this here state can be proud of. Yes, sir, when I'm governor this state's a-startin' clean 'n shinin'.

"Well, like I was sayin', I did finally get that there equipment from the militia, so's I could put the roads in shape best I can for folks t' travel over come election time. Why, you'd think from the way Rordan acted that he didn't expect a single feller as traveled over them roads t' cast a vote for him! Well, I don't expect many of 'em will—but I aim t' play fair."

Governor Rordan was going to be a most surprised man, thought Verity, when he found that tools were spades, but that "other equipment" was tents—tents which had lain in some friend's shed or yard, and which were put up only when the weather signs read rain within twenty-four hours.

She knew Hank's friends would be reading the weather signs every day for weeks before election. And when rings round the moon, or birds cheeping from shelter while smoke flattened out thin and vaporous forecast rain, she knew that all over the state swampers and hillbillies left their homes with an almost animal instinct, like lemmings pouring out of their holes on a certain hour of a certain day intent on marching to their death.

Verity had not gone to the polls. She had done her household duties and now sat knitting a coat for Hancy when Jules came. At the sound of his stamping feet on the porch Selah threw wide the door.

"Law, Mistuh Jules! Hit Mistuh Jules!"

Verity ran to the door. "Jules," she cried, "oh, it's been so long since we've seen you!"

Removing his dripping hat he took her hand and kissed it lightly.

"Come in, Jules. Come in."

He looked down at his boots. "I took the liberty of putting my horse in your barn. I gathered all that mud just from the barn to your door."

"Don' y'all min' de mud, Mistuh Jules," said Selah heartily. "Ain' nary person I druther scrub after. Um-umm! You is a treat, Mistuh Jules. Miz Verity 'n me livin' year in an' year out, seem lak, in dis nothin'-but-woman's house! Um-umm! Usn lak dem nuns. 'Ceptin' dey leastways does it uv dere own free will—so folks says."

Jules laughed, laughed his free and merry laugh. Verity stood very still trying to feel the old gaiety bubbling within her. But she was only reaching toward it. The spontaneity was not there. Selah took Jules's dripping coat and he stood before the glowing stove, looking about with the air of one seeing again a place he longed to see. He reached out to the shaded light, turned the switch off and on, and smiled.

"I like seeing electricity in this house, Verity. And I like your flowered shades. Just right in this room. Is Hancy sleeping?"

"Yes, and I wish she weren't. I'd like you to see her."

"Yas, suh, Mistuh Jules, usn shu' got us a fine chile. Dat chile a lovely. Usn proud uv her. You mind dat mouf organ Mistuh Hank fotch her las' ee-lection? Well, dat chile shu' blow an' puff fine tunes now."

"Real melodies?" asked Jules.

"Yas, suh. She gwine be good. Tape 'n me, we nigh 'bout th'ow down our hoes in de ga'den fo' ter do a mite uv struttin' w'en Miss Hancy a-breathin' music."

"I would really like to see that," said Jules softly, adding, "You look robust, Selah, and it seems Hancy is fine. But—" He turned to Verity, studying her. "Actually, I suppose you look well. Your cheeks are rosy and the glow of the country is on you, but—"

"But not in me," said Verity. "Fix some coffee and cake, Selah."

"Yas'm. I shu' do dat. How you want yo' coffee, Mistuh Jules? You want whut Miz Verity call Pennsylvania coffee wif cream, 'r does y'all want it French lak dat Cookie uv Mistuh Hank's make?"

"I prefer *café au lait* if it is all the same to you."

"Yas, suh. Say, Mistuh Jules, whut dat mean—dat 'oh lay' after coffee, huh?"

Jules laughed heartily and again the sound was so pleasant to Verity's ear that she just stood still.

"It refers to nothing more than the hot milk." His smile was wide and happy.

"Shu' 'nuff? Tch-tch—"

Verity and Jules sat before the radio with their coffee and cake. She tried to get some music but the programs were constantly interrupted to give the election returns. Hank was not carrying Crescent City, though the foreign quarter had done well by him. He was running a little behind in Sherman, the capital. Loder City gave him almost no votes at all. Yet the village and country votes were carrying him on a good margin right into the Governor's Mansion. Verity turned the switch and they sat in silence, just the two of them, for Selah had gone to her cabin.

"The next time I call on you I will have to go to the Executive Mansion," said Jules. "How does it feel to you, Verity? Soon you will be the first lady of the Magnolia State!"

"It's funny, Jules, but it doesn't feel at all. Nothing seems real to me any more. From the beginning Hank said he was going to be governor and I his first lady." She sighed. "But something in me just— Oh, Jules, I just can't make anything come real any more." It was a cry for help.

He leaned forward and took her hand in his. "I understand that feeling," he said. "I was just a spectator of life when first we met. Remember? Well, my dear, I had been to war." After a moment's silence he went on, "A man cannot see brave men fighting for an ideal—see his comrades die —without shock. He cannot rise on wings to carry death to men, though they be enemies, without the ever-constant prayer that he be right. And right or not, a kind of soul shock comes after war to a whole people, to a whole nation. Something inside one waits for the stone to be rolled away; waits hungrily for that higher and finer life for which he fought. And then—" He stopped short.

"Go on," she said. "Go on, Jules. I have to know what you were going to say."

"No," he said gently, "you don't have to know that just now. But whenever Armistice Day rolls around—I again grow bitter. Armistice Day, indeed! Just after the war I was so bitter I felt that by the very word 'armistice' the leaders of the countries were prophets or fools. After all, armistice is defined as meaning a brief suspension of hostilities by agreement. . . ."

After a long silence he said, "All this, my dear, because you said nothing comes real to you. Something will suddenly come real to you—something will suddenly become worth while." Here he laughed with a little of the old bitterness. "Above all things, do not lapse into cynicism, as I did, and write a satire."

She said nothing. She wanted to tell him that Hank would have found an idea on which to carry people whether he had written a satire or not, but she couldn't bring herself to say it.

"I am anxious to hear the returns on the election of representatives," said Jules. "Do you think the people will give him the representatives of his choice?— Do you think they will vote Hank's ticket straight?"

"I don't know," she said dully. "He has certainly worked hard at it. And he has a way of working hard enough to make the angel bless him."

Jules laughed. "Well, I must brave the mud and get home. All the returns will not be in until morning."

As he left, he said earnestly, "I hope to see you often at the Capitol."

"Do. Please do, Jules."

"I shall try. Good night, my dear."

She watched him plow through the mud and rain and wished she'd had the courage to talk more openly about Hank. She wanted to, she wanted to know just what Jules thought, but she could not ask.

Hank's good fortune held. The voters did well by him in the matter of representatives. Hank had not even come home to vote but had exercised the right of the absentee ballot, telling all listeners that, after all, he was still commissioner and as such would stick to his job. Verity had laughed when she heard this, for he had spent months campaigning. The use of the militia tents caused a mild furor, but the majority of people grinned and said Hank Martin certainly tickled their funny bone.

So Verity did not see Hank until she and Selah and Hancy arrived at the railroad station in Sherman. Hank greeted her jubilantly, and the news hawks gathered round, the cameramen flashed their bulbs, and the movie newsmen ground their cranks. To the great delight of their story sense, Hancy hugged her father with a wild and possessive joy and cried, "You're my Hank! Aren't you? Selah and Tim and Sophy says you're everybody's Hank. But you're my Hank, ain't you?"

Hank held the child and beamed with a pride that was truly lovely. Hancy, in her soft pink broadcloth and Hank in his handsomely cut blue suit with a too-bright purple stripe, lavender silk shirt and purple tie, made a real picture. Verity beside them served only to point up their color, their vitality, for she stood modestly garbed in the coat Hank had brought her years ago, her face still and remote.

They rode in an open car from the station to the hotel where they would stay until the inauguration. Selah sat up front beside the colored chauffeur; Hank, Verity, and Hancy in the back. And standing on the running boards were Swith on one side and Jep on the other. Vince and Flower rode in an open car ahead, one eyeing the crowd on the left, one eyeing the crowd on the right of the street. Hancy jumped up and down on the seat and screamed her delight; Hank howled an answer to all who cheered or called; Selah clung to the side of the car and squirmed in a fearsome delight; and Verity sat still, her eyes fastened on Swith's profile. The little man beamed with the glow of saintly satisfaction as he viewed this concrete evidence of the coming salvation. Verity's heart ached for Swith and all the simple, loving folk whose faith lay in the young Hank, the Hank whose heart was callable by theirs.

Inauguration Day startled the capital city and indeed the whole state as they had not been startled since the Civil War. Hank's horde poured in by wagon and mule cart, and a veritable army of pirogues came out of the swamps and lagoons, followed small tributaries, and converged into the great river. They poured into Sherman as if by planned siege.

Even Hank was surprised, for some of his sturdy followers had come almost two hundred miles by the devious water routes.

He came bursting into the hotel suite where Verity and Selah were packing the last of their new clothes and personal belongings into new alligator bags which were to be sent to the Governor's Mansion.

"Put on that there new suit you're a-wearin' t' the ceremonies, quick," he howled. "Selah, put some fine pink thing on Hancy. God'lmighty, I want you should see my people on the river. Some is a-comin' down easy on the current, 'n some is struggling hard agin it—but they're all a-comin' t' me." Tears welled in his eyes. "God'lmighty," he said softly, "it's purely wonderful t' be me 'n have folks love y' so."

Hastily Verity put on one of the new suits Hank had bought her. Softest of larkspur blue it was, and yet it had an overtone of gray. She wore a hat of matching straw, crowned with yellow flowers and enhanced by a blue veil. Hank's love of color and beauty was a never-ending wonder to Verity.

In Hank's car with sirens screaming and Sherman police on motorcycles clearing the way, they tore through Sherman traffic to the levee. Excitedly Hank helped Verity and Hancy up the levee's slick, grassy sides. On reaching the top, Verity gasped at the sight. As far as the eye could see pirogues by the hundreds and hundreds came on the breast of the river upstream and downstream.

Hank had not forgotten to call his new publicity man, one mouse-colored, sharp-eyed Bob Walker, and soon Walker came up the levee with reporters and cameramen, for this was news—colorful news, news that could tug the heartstrings of a nation.

Running up and down the levee in his magnificently tailored pale gray suit with the gaudy green stripe and the shirt of too bright a blue for good taste in men's wear, with Hancy jumping and screaming at his side, Hank bellowed at his friends.

"Hey, there, Les Pecot—lookit! It's me, Hank!—Georgie Croom—Hey! God'lmighty! You shore do me proud!—Lookit that! Verity—lookit! That there is old Theo Dauzart! Him 'n his woman has come two hundred miles iffen they come a inch! Through the god-damdest fiercest 'n most beautiful country ever the eye a' man could behold! More beautiful it is than Polli's birdcage. Damn if it ain't." He swiped at his eyes. "Full t' runnin' over withen love for the sonsabitches, I am."

He ran wildly among his friends, Hancy clinging desperately to his hand, and repeating the names of these people after her father.

The swampers—or, as the city people called them, the batture dwellers—lifted their pirogues out of water and hauled them up the levee. The sun was creeping toward midheaven and the stream of pirogues was thinning when Verity saw Spurge and Lula May. They came with many from their settlement, following Spurge's lead here as they did at home. It came to Verity's mind that as a people the swampers were superior to the average cropper, stronger, more vital. Perhaps because they lived by their own laws and none other; perhaps because their selected leader must be able to live according to the laws which he set for his community. As she looked at Spurge, she was again impressed with the grace and magnificence of him. And Lula May in her stiffly starched full-gathered dress of green percale, with her gay flowered shawl and her flared sunbonnet, glossy and bright with starch, was a figure of dignity and pride. Fit parents, thought Verity, for a beauty like Flamingo.

Verity pulled on Hank's sleeve. "Hank," she said, "here come Spurge and Lula May."

Into Hank's face came a slight unease. "Hell," he said softly.

She was surprised. "Why, I thought you and Spurge were devoted to each other."

"Oh, shore, shore we are," said Hank. "Ain't no man in this world I got more respect for. But God'lmighty, the sun gets high. Time we got back t' the hotel and took off for the park. Oh, well—" He ran down to the river's edge and yelled, "Hey, Spurge—hey, Spurge! You're nigh 'bout late! I ain't got time t' wait t' greet y' proper."

"You go 'long, then, Hank," Spurge called back. "It'll take a spell t' wedge in 'mongst all them pirogues. Usn'll see y' later."

Verity waved, and Spurge, standing in the little boat, bowed graciously without causing the pirogue to roll an inch.

Hurrying back up the levee, Hank took Verity's arm and Hancy's hand, helped them into their car, and with guards and policemen they screamed their way back to the hotel.

The inaugural ceremonies took place in the park at high noon. Verity sat upon the platform just to the right of the microphones, between the grimly pleasant Mrs. Kirkendall and the excited, squirming Hancy.

When the national anthem was to be sung, Hank grabbed Hancy and held her up to the microphones. Clearly through the loud-speakers the delighted crowd heard their new governor say, "Sing for yore Hank, Sugar. 'N beller it out good 'n strong." Hank sang, too, and the voices of father and child blended with vital clarity through the loud-speakers over and above the voices of the crowd.

> "Oh, say, does that star-spangled banner yet wave
> O'er the land of the free . . ."

A prayer rose in Verity's heart. Now surely—oh, surely, the fine and wonderful things would begin. For Hank was "in" and the schemes could now be forgotten and the true work begun. Oh, it will be so, she told herself, as Hank, his voice rolling out gloriously solemn and rich, took the oath of office: "I pledge allegiance to the Flag, to the Constitution of the United States; and I do further pledge to faithfully serve this great and sovereign State . . ."

The mansion sparkled with light and fine orchestral music, and the great wide lawns were gay with colored lights and the music of fiddles and concertina. Hank's famous tent, its sides up-rolled, stood on the wide treeless sweep of green on the east side of the mansion, and Cookie stood in spotless cap and coat cooking at his oilstoves. The countryfolk danced, but this time on a specially built floor. They began their dancing long before the hour of the formal reception and Hank had danced with them to the delight of the photographers and the newsmen.

While Hank celebrated with old friends through the sunset and twilight hours, Verity sat before the huge vanity mirror having her nails lacquered and her hair done by two young women whom Hank had hired and instructed.

"Now lookit," he had said to them, "don't put nothin' flamin' on her fingers. Just a glossy pink. See? And now, lookit—lookit the way she carries her head. Straight up from her backbone 'n proud. Her head ain't stuck out afore rolls a' fat like t' some old work mule who has wore a heavy yoke. By God'lmighty," Hank beamed, "she carries a head as a crown could stick onto. She's the first lady a' the Magnolia State. 'N I allow she's the only one ever to look like a first lady should oughta." He shook a playfully menacing fist in the faces of the delighted and amazed operators. " 'N mind you don't turn her out withen them Annie-'n-Lizzie hussified frizzes, or I'll have yore life." He gnashed his teeth and grinned at them. "I'm the Big Lion, remember. 'N iffen she ain't a queen when I come back up them stairs, I'll eat y' for breakfast." He winked and gave his head the sidewise twist and opened the door to the hall, but before closing it completely he stuck his head back in and growled.

Verity laughed. Hank could shed hard work and tenseness when a job was done and get down to the business of having joy. Why, she had been stuck in the country waiting—waiting—filled with apprehensions, thinking herself into her grave. Maybe this was the beginning of feeling alive again.

The two beauty operators looked at Verity with a new interest. Plainly they wouldn't mind being Hank's breakfast at all.

"What I'd give to have my husband think of me like that!" one sighed. "He's wonderful, Mrs. Martin."

"Yes," she said gently, "yes, he is." And, oh, he is very wonderful, she told herself. Being with him all the time here would surely make her feel happy and alive again. Her thoughts jumped to Jenny out in the cottage which had been the home of the head gardener. Hank had made the gardener move in favor of Flower and Jenny, and Verity knew that a beauty operator was now giving Jenny a going-over too. She laughed as she thought back on the way Hank had had salesmen and saleswomen pouring into the hotel bringing gowns and dresses and coats to try on her and Jenny. Little Jenny-wren should have a whole new wardrobe, too, by God'lmighty; nothing too good for Harry's widow and Flower's wife.

Hank chose their daytime dresses and suits with little trouble, but the stores had nothing to his taste in evening gowns. Finally Hank roared, "What the hell's the matter withen you dressmakers? Can't y' see Mrs.

Higgins is like to a thrush? But only not quite. She should oughta be dressed in somethin' that's soft 'n in shades a' tans, 'n with some surprise scarlet t' it. 'N my wife—can't y' see she is a changing person?—Sometimes like to a larkspur 'n sometimes like to a stormy sea. But mostly like t' the sun that'll come up sure 'n glowin' every mornin'. A gentled-down gold or a white as is almost blue or almost pink. Somethin' fitten for a lady."

A vision came into the eyes of the nervous little man who was the state's most famous designer.

"I see what you mean," he exclaimed. "Yes, I see. Why, Governor, you would have been a great designer."

"Hell," said Hank, "iffen you fellers'd tromp the woods 'n look good 'n long at the colors nature blends for her critters, it'd be purely a blessin' t' man. Roarin' thunderbolts! A man's eyes grows hungry in the city. Women is the only flowers a' the city. 'N be damn iffen they ain't all stove up withen high heels, swaybacks, 'n grass bellies. All swaddled in drabness, a-lookin' soured enough t' be on the hunt for their own coffins."

As the little man grabbed up his boxes and scurried out in a dither of nerves, Hank grinned.

"Well," he said, "iffen that don't fetch somethin' fitten, reckon you girls're gonna stand in that there reception line in yore skins. Look better that-a-way, too. Dang if it wouldn't."

Verity looked at the dress spread out over the satin counterpane of the bed. It was a white that had in its texture the blush of pink, and fine gold stitchings emphasized its lines like hints of a coming sun. Tender love and excitement gathered in her. She had been too long away from Hank. Here in this gracious house surely—oh, surely—that fine sense of wholeness and reality would come to her again.

To Verity this bedroom was a miracle of bigness and beauty. Its thick ivory rug and its crisscross curtains, its flowered chairs and glowing furniture spoke to her of many fine ladies who had been privileged to live here. She heard the door of the adjoining bedroom slam and a minute later the water running in the bath, and then Hank's voice raised in glad and boisterous song.

"Oh, there's pork on the table 'n grits in the pan,
'N the pone's oozin' grease through the crust . . ."

The operators stopped a second, enchanted by hearing their new governor singing such a strange song, and Verity's whole being stretched forth its hand trying to catch the happiness she'd had when the floors were newly green and the pone oozed grease through the crust.

A knock came on her door and Selah entered.

"I ain' got ter knock on only shut an' upstairs doors—" She stopped and stared at Verity, her eyes popping. "Lawd—Lawd—Miz Verity, I declah—I do declah— You de purtiest t'ing in dis worl'—I knows you is!"

Selah cocked her head this way and that and eyed Verity with beaming pleasure. "Um-ummm! Yo' hair dat-a-way! High t' de top an' low t' de back—um-ummm! Plumb puts dem church-winder halos ter shame. Umummm, it do!"

"I'm ready for my dress now," said Verity, smiling.

Selah lifted it from the bed and slipped it over her. The operators adjusted a strand above her ear and Selah fastened her up. Verity turned to the mirror. "'Someday, Sweetface, you'll have silks 'n satins 'n velvets. Things fitten for a lady,'" she murmured, her eyes misting.

"Dere, dere," said Selah, "y'all gwine ruinate dat paint dey got on yo' face."

She blinked and smiled.

"Mistuh Hank, he got dat uppity Jackson a-helpin' him inter tails— yas'm, dat whut Jackson say. Whut usn comin' ter, I wants ter know, w'en Mistuh Hank he need dat kinda help?"

The girls giggled.

"Go 'long wid yer, now," Selah commanded them. "Pick up dat litter uv boxes an' paints an' go 'long."

When they had reluctantly gone, Selah said, "Miz Verity, I has got ter askes you. Dat uppity Jackson—he say he de 'major-domo.'" Selah carefully pronounced the syllables exactly. "Yas'm, dat whut he say. He de 'major-domo.' He say dat mean he de boss heah."

Verity was amused. Selah had no intention of getting into the Governor's Mansion only to be bossed by a colored man. Verity considered Jackson a real blessing, for he had served in this house since he was a young man, and now old Jackson was major-domo and had been for almost twenty years. Jackson knew how state dinners were served; Jackson was informed on how to seat visiting celebrities according to precedence and rank. She knew she was very dependent on this old colored man and had much to learn from him. But she couldn't have Selah hurt or feeling her place less secure. Why, she couldn't get along without Selah.

"He is major-domo." She put an arm around Selah's shoulders. "That is, he runs the house. But you—you're Hancy's and my major-domo. You run me and Hancy just as you always have. Let Jackson have all the work of this great big house, and the worry with the cooks and the maids. You're my major-domo just as you've always been."

Selah nodded and smiled. "I tell him dat fust time I cotch him in de hall 'r de kitchen. I is major-domo uv people, not uv no great big ol' house. Um-ummm, I bet dat fotch him down a peg. Miz Verity, has you seen de kitchen? Law, Law, dat kitchen a somepin'! Yas'm, I shu' glad I ain't got ter cook dere. Law, hit mos' as big as our whole house in de Bend."

The door to the adjoining room flew open and Hank posed in the doorway. He stood, chest puffed, howling, "Lookit me! Me, in monkey tails! Iffen this here shirt didn't have a high shine on it, afore God I wouldn't wear it."

"Oh, Hank," said Verity, "you're handsome!"

"Ain't I, though! Best lookin' penguin ever caged." He looked at Verity and came slowly toward her, circling her, wonder growing in his eyes. "Lord save us," he murmured. "Lord save us." He touched her cheek gently. "Purely a thing for a man t' fall down 'n worship. You purely are."

He bowed before her and his shirt front popped up and open and he howled with a pleasant fury. "Jackson! Jackson! Come here, y' stiff-backed soul a' correctness, 'n flatten the bulge on me. Roarin' thunder-bolts, I ain't no nursin' mother!"

Jackson came hurrying in from the other room, dazed by this new governor. Hank opened his waistcoat and Jackson worked over studs and shirt. As Jackson finished, Verity said, "We are depending on you, Jackson, to see that everything goes well. We come from a small and simple farm. All this is new to us."

Jackson bowed and smiled. "Yes, madam," he said.

" 'N don't call her 'madam,' " said Hank. "It don't scarce sound decent outside Cajun country. Call her Miz Verity, iffen you feel friendly—leastways Miz Martin."

"Yes, sir, Mistuh Governor." Jackson bowed and left.

Verity noted that it was only on certain words that Jackson lapsed into the broad dialect such as Selah spoke. Jackson, she decided, was quite a person.

"Well, let's go down," said Hank. "Jackson tolt me there's a few folks there. We're gonna stand in a line 'n greet folks, seems 's though."

"I go wake Miz Hancy 'n fotch her down. How long you gwine let her stay a-lookin'?" Selah asked.

"Oh, just a little while," replied Verity.

"Let her stay as long 's her legs'll hold her up," said Hank. "Ain't every day a young'un's father gets made governor."

"Yas, suh, Mistuh Hank," said Selah. "Law, you shu' is a fine pair. You shu' is!"

"Coming, my lady?" Hank asked and extended his hand.

She put her hand in his and together they went down the broad curved stair to face a new future.

She had been standing in the receiving line between Hank and Lieutenant Governor Kirkendall, becoming wearied and a little upset by seeing in the eyes of all guests as they arrived the look of startled surprise when they met and spoke with the Governor's wife. At first it had been fun. But now it was becoming so repetitive as to be insulting. What kind of a wife had they expected Hank to have? She wished Jules would come.

Jules had nicely avoided being invited to stand with them to receive by sending Hank a note immediately after election day, saying business would keep him in Crescent City on Inaugural Day, but he would make every effort to drop in at the ball. Saber had come early and was now standing at the far end of the room talking with other newsmen and Hank's new publicity manager, Bob Walker.

When Jules came earlier than she had hoped, Verity's spirits picked up.

"Jules," said Hank, "I shore am glad t' be a-seein' y'. I broke all them precedents 'bout folks not puttin' nobody but 'ristocrats in this house."

"Indeed you did not," said Jules, taking Verity's hand. "I bow to one." He kissed Verity's hand. "Magnolia Mansion is very proud of you, I'm sure."

"Is this house called that?" Verity asked.

"The name has not been used much lately, but in my father's and grandfather's day it was always called Magnolia Mansion."

"Now, say," said Hank, "that's a nice tidbit for my publicity man t' remind them news fellers about."

Jules smiled. "The eye is on business, as usual, isn't it, Hank?"

"Well, you're dang tootin'." Hank grinned.

Jules smiled at Verity and moved on. "How are you, Kirk? This is a pleasant occasion for you, isn't it? Good evening, Mrs. Kirkendall . . ."

Verity thought on the strange conglomeration of people in this line. Marcus Davol, the state committeemen and their wives—and Mr. Angleman not among them—old Judge Esterbrook from Delamore, several very haughty men and women who were kin to the Kirkendalls—and Jenny.

Verity had been most interested in the state senators and in the members of the House of Representatives. She was studying their faces, wondering if she could pick out the ones whom Hank called his rubber stamps, when a stir in the room caused her to look toward the door. Flamingo stood there, looking over the crowd with the air of seeing an enchanted land.

She wore, Verity knew, a dress Hank had bought. No one else, she thought, would have found so right a gown. It was a pale, lustrous green, not snug, yet every glorious bit of her was displayed, and it hung from a strange yoke of topaz jewels. It set off the startling, the elemental, and yet the natural Flamingo. It gave her the effect of a wild swamp hibiscus coming gloriously up from a sun-drenched sea.

Verity caught her breath as did most of the guests.

"Flamingo!" said Hank, and taking her hand, drew her near him. He lowered his voice. "What the hell you—" He stopped, realizing that his lack of welcome did not sound right. "What the hell you so late for?" he asked and added, "Here's Flamingo, Verity."

Verity and Flamingo eyed each other and shook hands while Verity murmured the names of Sunny Lou and the Lieutenant Governor.

Kirkendall looked as if surely she was a vision, and Verity had to repeat her name three times before he could let go of her hand and present her to his wife. Mrs. Kirkendall blinked unbelievingly before her grim face became grimmer, and her hand took a hold on her husband's arm as if about to hustle him off to shelter. Marcus Davol came alive, every little fine grain of him taking on sparkle. Saber came hastily toward Flamingo, and Bob Walker pursed his lips and wondered about the wisdom of pictures, while the cameramen present were already flaring bulbs and snapping lenses open and shut.

"God'lmighty," said Hank, "ain't we passed folks around like as if they was peace pipes long enough? Let's break this thing up. God-'lmighty!" He stepped out of line.

The orchestra broke into the grand march, and sighing, Hank took Verity's hand and led off. Mentally Verity thanked old Jackson for telling them what would be expected of them. She had thought Hank would strut a bit at this point, but he did not. She saw Saber with Flamingo; Jules bowed gallantly before little Hancy and took her as his partner. All Hank's attention was turned toward the windows, his anxiety plainly showing.

"What's the matter with you?" Verity whispered.

"Spurge is out t' the tent," he said. "Supposin' he takes a notion t' look into the windows 'n sees his young'un surrounded by them oglin' jackanapes. Spurge, he's like to think it ain't fitten—him out yonder 'n his young'un here unbeknownst t' him. Well, hell," he sighed, "I reckon I'll have t' bring 'em together. 'Druther take a lickin'. Hell, they ain't seen nor heard tell a' their young'un sincet Spurge took her down river withen her hair shoe-blacked."

"Why, Hank," Verity exclaimed, "you mean you've never told them about sending Flamingo to beauty school?"

"I ain't seen Spurge since that," said Hank.

"You have so," said Verity. "You planned to go near Spurge's after I left at Mundro."

"Oh, yeah," said Hank vaguely. "Well, hell, I was plannin' for t' surprise 'em one day."

"This seems to be the surprise," said Verity with sarcasm. "What is so troublesome about this meeting, anyway?"

"Well, you know Spurge. He's a judge in a way. By God'lmighty, we ain't got none 'round here like t' him, don't seem 's though."

The instant the orchestra abandoned the march for waltz time, Hank took Verity into his arms and danced over to Saber and Flamingo.

"Flamingo," he said, "I gotta talk with you."

"Sure," said Flamingo, "after the dance."

"Now," said Hank. "God'lmighty, yore paw's out yonder 'n I don't want him sightin' you by surprise."

At the mention of her father Flamingo stopped and stared wide-eyed at Hank. Verity's mind went back to the swamp when it had been Spurge's whistle, not the 'gator, which had put fear in the girl. Now, she ran her hands uneasily over her thighs, seeming conscious of her clothes, and in her eyes came a blend of fear and love and longing.

"And Maw, too?" she asked softly.

"Yeah," said Hank. "Come on. I gotta talk t' you a minute." He turned away and Flamingo followed.

"Dance?" asked Saber.

"No," Verity replied, and Saber led her through the dancers to a settee against the wall.

Sensing drama, Saber leaned forward in his seat, watching Hank and Flamingo as intently as Verity was watching. What was the great trouble, Verity wondered, with Spurge being here? Surely Spurge would be glad to see his child well and prospering after so long a time. Lula May certainly would. But something troubled Hank deeply. Hank and Flamingo talked earnestly, and unwelcome surmisings bubbled in Verity. In spite of their unease over facing Spurge, an awareness, each of the other, leaped now and again like a flame escaping its banking of ashes. Verity saw between them the mystic looks which pass only between a mated man and woman, a sort of communion of possessiveness, when in spite of all other urgencies they hunger each for the other; and envy came desolately in Verity's breast.

Desperately she shifted her eyes and looked at Saber, but seeing in his face pity and understanding, she braced herself, murmured her excuses, rose, and walked toward Hank.

"I'm gonna fetch in Spurge 'n Lula May now," said Hank. "Verity, you take Flamingo into that there library back yonder across the hall. I'll fetch 'em to the side door. 'N you stay there too, Verity. I gotta have you there."

She wanted to cry out, to scream, but with head high she turned and led the way. In the library she closed the door and stood leaning against it for a moment. Flamingo, intent on her own thoughts, walked up and down the room. The philosophies of the ages stood bound in old leather on shelves from floor to ceiling, and Verity wished she could unerringly choose one that would help her now. But she crossed to the desk, sat down, and watched this girl.

There was nothing of the self-conscious, slinky siren in Flamingo. She was vital and natural. Her stride had an easy, springy grace. At other times Verity had seen the shine of delight in her, the same kind of young delight a puppy can show. Yes, Verity thought, Flamingo is a magnificent and natural young savage. She realized Flamingo's great appeal for Hank —this girl was the embodiment of the swamps and the earth, their beauty and their fierceness. She answered Hank's fundamental need for these things here in the city. She had a savage and straightforward way of taking what she wanted. But aside from all else, Verity felt she was bad for Hank —satisfying the elemental in him and at the same time promoting its growth.

Suddenly Flamingo whirled, facing Verity directly.

"You hate me, don't you?"

"Yes," said Verity coldly, and turned her head.

"But you didn't drop me off the cypress stump for the 'gator to get any more than you'll let me down now. And for the same reason—'cause you'll lose Hank complete if you do." Flamingo turned, dismissing Verity as of little consequence, and resumed her pacing until the door opened, then she whirled, but took not a step forward.

Lula May looked at Flamingo and gasped. Spurge stood erect, jaw set, staring at his daughter.

"Go on in. Go on," said Hank. "Lemme close this door."

Flamingo looked at her father. Her eyes misted. Lula May ran to Flamingo, threw her arms about her, crying, "My baby! My Sunny Lou! Oh, my pritty one—my pritty one!"

But even as Flamingo embraced her mother, her eyes pleaded with her father to forget her banishment and make her again one of his flock.

Love and yearning were in Spurge's face, but he stood still, getting complete control of himself.

"Stand away from her, Maw," he said sternly. "Lemme look at the girl."

Flamingo stood like a prisoner in the dock, her hands touching uneasily her beautiful dress.

"How come y' t' be in such fine raiment?" It was Spurge, the judge, demanding an answer.

"I bought that there dress for her," said Hank, adding easily, "bought it special for this here ball."

Lula May stood clasping her hands, her eyes pleading with Spurge to see their child's goodness.

"Where at you a-livin', Sunny Lou?" asked Spurge.

"Crescent City."

"Crescent City?" Spurge asked astounded. "Crescent City! That ain't no fitten place. Whole streets they got I hear tell, for nothin' but fornicatin'."

"Well, God'lmighty—" Hank began.

"Oh, Paw," cried Flamingo. "Oh, Paw, the city is just like the swamp. You know where the 'gators are and you don't need to go there—" She stopped, horror-stricken as Spurge's hand went up signaling her to silence.

"Yeah," he said with sternness and grief. "I 'member well a time when you did go t' the 'gators 'n not withen no honor nor bravery in yore heart."

In spite of herself, Verity felt a vague touch of sympathy for Sunny Lou.

So plainly did she want her father's love and approval. So plainly did she esteem and fear him as a great and just man.

"She had leastways bravery," said Hank.

"No." Spurge was firm and sure. "That kind a' bravery is the 'gator's own kind." He sighed heavily. "You was ever one as leaned t' the carnal, Sunny Lou."

"Now lookit, Spurge," said Hank earnestly, "lookit, the young'un loves y'. Purely loves y', she does. She's worked hard 'n she's goin' t' school. I been a-helpin' her. I woulda tolt y' iffen I'd seen y'. But I was campaignin'. She wrote t' me, 'n I put her in school. She's yore young'un, Spurge. She's got a education." He took a deep breath and plunged. "I aim t' give her a fine job here where I can look out for her."

Spurge looked long at Hank, then suddenly he put his hands on Hank's shoulders. "You was allus a bringer a' great gifts, Hank," he said.

"Oh, Paw!" cried Flamingo. She flew to Spurge's arms and kissed him ecstatically. "Oh, Paw!"

Lula May wept. Hank tried to get his handkerchief out of the pocket in the tail of his coat. "Helluva place for a man's handkerchief t' be put." He backed up to Verity. "God'lmighty, Sweetface, fish that thing out for me."

Verity could hardly move. She hated Flamingo, she told herself, but knew it was not wholly true. She was touched by the deep bond between Flamingo and Spurge and she thought, Flamingo is elemental, but sometimes the elemental qualities are the most unwavering.

"God'lmighty," said Hank, "let's usn all be gay 'n happy now."

"I ain't had no true happiness," sobbed Lula May, "tillst this minute. Not since she went down river. Neither's Spurge," she added, flashing a look that dared him to deny it.

"You're right, Maw," said Spurge gently. "You're shore right. But a feller can't just have happiness, Maw. A man has gotta live just 'n right, 'n deservin' of it. 'N it's happy I am this night—'n so's Sunny Lou."

"Paw, come out in the ballroom and dance with me," pleaded Sunny Lou.

"You want I should? Bad?" asked Spurge.

"Yes. Please," she begged.

He turned. Sunny Lou clung to his arm. Proudly she walked across the wide hall and into the great ballroom.

"A waltz?" called Hank.

She nodded. Hank hurried to the orchestra leader. The music stopped abruptly and then went into a soft waltz. Spurge, in his carefully creased fresh denim trousers, loose denim jacket, soft white shirt, wide gun belt with two revolvers in low-cut holsters, his magnificent daughter in his arms, made a sight Magnolia Mansion would never forget. Hank took Lula May out on the floor. Other dancers stopped and stared and wondered. Lula May in her full-skirted percale, her gaily flowered wool shawl about her shoulders, danced happily with the dress-suited Governor.

The two couples on the floor danced a back-country waltz. It was a regulation waltz step punctuated now and then with the couple holding hands while the lady retreated a dainty, coquettish three steps, then after two beats marking the man's hesitation to overcome his lady, he glided forward in one long step on the third beat, took his partner in his arms, and whirled her again into the dance.

Like marriage, thought Verity, a few steps back and the heart grows heavy and the mind probes, and then one is swooped up into the whirl again.

The guests were gone. Only Marcus Davol, Bob Walker, and three of Walker's assistants remained. Swith sat in a fine big chair running his finger tips luxuriously over its silk upholstery, his gun across his knees. Flower lounged on a wide davenport looking admiringly at Jenny, who sat stiff and upright, her dress spread just so. Verity wished they would all leave. She needed some time alone to think, and yet she wanted, in spite of Flamingo and all else, to go up those lovely stairs this first night arm in arm with Hank.

"Now here's the point, Walker," Hank was saying. "I asked y' t' stay so's we could get this here thing well in mind tonight so's you can start a-goin' come mornin'. You lissenin' t' me?" he asked the drooping Walker.

"Sure," said Walker, "get to the point, Governor. My flesh longs to spread out on the inner-springs."

"Hell," said Hank, "ain't nobody but me got no stayin' powers? Well, I want y' should hire extra offices in some business building—there ain't no room in that damned old Capitol building—'n set up one a' them clippin' bureaus. I want y' t' get every paper that's published in this here state. I want every line read. 'N every time a feller is mentioned in connection with politics, I want that article clipped. Them articles is then t' be sent to Marcus. Then him 'n me will decide how t' clip the wings a' that feller. 'N if the feller belongs t' the opposition—why, then we sure go t' work on him."

Walker sat up sharply at this. "What do you mean, Governor?"

Hank grinned. "Why, just this—" His voice dropped to the emphasis of secret schemes. "I don't aim t' give the opposition time t' grow nobody of a size t' even compete with Hank Martin. No, sir, by God'lmighty, iffen a man's able to make gophers lissen to him, we invite him down here." Hank waved a hand expansively. "Hank Martin is a feller as rises above party— see?" He winked at Walker and Marcus. "If this feller has ideas on finance, 'r on schools—why, then we put him on a state advisory committee on finance or on schools. Y' got me?"

Walker shook his head. "No." He was puzzled. "Afraid I haven't got you."

"Roarin' thunderbolts," cried Hank, "we put that feller on a committee 'n then we put on two men a' our own to vote him down. 'N in no time flat we have discredited this feller's idea. His home folks that would mebbe voted him t' be an assemblyman sees he ain't set the world on fire, 'n he's out. Don't you see that in four or eight years, come time for elections, the opposition just can't find no men of a size t' oppose me?"

"Well, I'm damned!" said Walker.

Marcus hit Hank on the back. "That's using your head, Hank!" he exclaimed, admiringly.

"Why, shore," Hank beamed, "the sheep's-clothin' tactics. You know— we put on sheep's clothin' 'n sidle up t' the lamb all sweet 'n full a' honey, tillst we get plumb cuddly, 'n then—" Hank made a magician's gesture of legerdemain, "'n then—bingo!—there ain't no lamb!"

Verity sat held by a nebulous terror, while Marcus laughed his almost silent laugh and Walker and his assistants stared at Hank.

"I'm damned," said Walker again, softly. "I'm damned. I've been a political publicity man all my life but this is the first time I've seen anyone smart enough to start right in impoverishing the opposition party of all human material."

"It certainly is subtle," said Marcus. "If it works it'll kill the robust two-party system."

"You're damn right," said Hank. "I aim t' show this state who is indispensable—I'm the Big Lion, 'n I'm a-runnin' this here jungle from now on."

Verity and Jenny stared into each other's eyes a second. Verity rose from her chair and went slowly up the great stair of Magnolia Mansion. She threw herself on the wide beautiful bed, and the mattress was soft, not made of crackly moss; and she wept bitterly. Hank came in, fresh and vigorous with anticipation.

"God'lmighty," said Hank, "what for you a-bawlin' on a night like this?"

"What for! What for!" she sobbed. "I'm bawling for a moss mattress and fresh green floors and for pone oozing grease from the crust."

Hank pulled her up from the bed and stared at her. "God'lmighty!" he cried, "what the hell you a-sayin'."

"I was a whole woman then," she cried. "I wasn't half swallowed up by a nictitating Lion and his sheep's-clothing tactics!" Her hands went to her breast. "I didn't have just a heaviness in me then."

A sadness came in him. He touched her cheek gently with one finger. "Sweetface," he said, shaking his head, "that Venus girl shouldn't oughta never go into battle."

Sighing heavily he took her into his arms. "Lookit, Verity, lissen t' me. In every man—'r leastways in every politician—there is four critters, seems 's though. Like it says in Revelations. The first beast is like t' a lion, and the second like to a calf, and the third has the face of a man, and the fourth is like to a flyin' eagle."

"The eagle would come last," she said bitterly, catching her breath in a sob.

"Shush, now—shush." He kissed her lips gently, then said, "What I want you should know is this—some things has just got t' be, seems 's though, iffen a man ain't t' stay a pulin' thing, not fitten for domination. But—'n here's the point—you got the power t' turn the face of the man toward you. Yeah, allus toward you the face of the man is turned. So shush now—shush."

But her life went on with that strange sense of disconnected coreless levels. She saw the first roads stretch over the country; saw the skeleton of the new Capitol building reach gauntly skyward; entertained the druggists and the mayors, the bankers and the storekeepers, who came to consider and accept Hank's invitation to serve on a committee, to give their counsel and advice for the good of the state.

Living now was just an outward thing. No longer were the currents of her life like spokes, well socketed in the hubs, or core, of being—the core which gives to life its import and its substance. The more she thought, and learned, the more she saw and heard—the more numb and still and heavy the core.

Desperately she clung to her determination not to withdraw from life; not to refuse to face its anguish, or pain, or action. But like a little caterpillar—like a true child of the moth—she spun a cocoon for the essential core of her. And like the caterpillar, she spun it with threads which were pulled from her head, every thought and every dim perception making another winding, encasing thread. It was an instinctive process born of the knowledge that the creature she now was, was a creature unable to live through the coming tomorrows; and, in Nature's own way, her inner being began its years of lying quiescent, encased—not sending out into the various spokes of her life that indefinable quality which makes for significant and meaningful living, not able to pull into itself the highest and best in joy. She was not quitting. She was not withdrawing. The self of her merely lay in its strange pupa stage, not exactly growing, but developing, developing, waiting for freeing—for that lovely, or perhaps terrifying moment, when the cocoon should be rent and some new thing be born.

17

By the middle of Hank's second term as governor the roads he had promised ran the length and breadth of the state, and then Hank promised himself that he would go on to Washington. . . .

THE MAGNIFICENT new Capitol building was being dedicated. Verity sat upon the platform and only half listened to the speeches. The platform was built at a right angle to the wide marble entrance steps, across which were stretched glistening satin ribbons of green and white, the colors of Magnolia State. The river could be plainly seen, and Verity noticed that it was still pushing at its levees, swollen with carrying to the sea the melting snows of northern states.

Saber sat at the press table. Before him, as before each reporter, was a pile of prepared releases which Bob Walker and his helpers had put out. She looked over the crowd, wishing Jules were there, but she could not see him. She had missed Jules and Saber. Her life had been dull indeed. She had long since ceased attending women's clubs, or any women's activities, feeling she was not truly welcome. The politeness of the ladies held a hint of fear, a currying of favor.

A few rows in front of the platform sat Flamingo, glowing and vital and proud, her lustrous face shaded by a wide-brimmed felt of cobalt white, exactly matching the trim on her blue suit. Hank had created a Department of Cosmetic Sanitation and had appointed Flamingo "Commissioner" of the new division, and Commissioner Sunny Lou McMenimee traveled all over the state examining beauty parlors and barbershops. No cosmetics, no creams, no equipment could be used without Flamingo's O.K. Verity knew that all the shops in the state paid off to Flamingo. Hank had once called her the smartest female in the country, and Verity had retorted that she'd had the best teacher in the school of graft, no doubt. And though Verity knew these things for a certainty, she often thought she must have been wrong in her feeling that Hank and Flamingo were lovers, for throughout these past six years since the first inaugural ball, no breath of scandal, no rumor linking them, had ever been whispered. And, Verity had asked herself time after time, how could two such outstanding people get together and no one know it? But always when she saw them in the same room, she felt the same way.

And too, there were Spurge and Lula May—they came to Sherman twice each year now with their settlement's catch. They had a key to the two modest rooms which Flamingo occupied in a most respectable and high-grade rooming house. After Spurge sold his catch to the trader, they walked to their daughter's place and spent one night. Usually they returned to their swamp the next day.

Two pretty girls dressed in colorful cotton hoop skirts walked up the marble steps of the Capitol and cut the ribbons. The huge bronze doors of the building opened magically, and a horde of Hank's state employees marched up the steps and disappeared within while the band played the state song:

> "From our hills and from our swamplands,
> From our rivers, from our fields,
> We take our blessings—richer far
> Than other lands will yield. . . ."

The crowd broke into applause. The Capitol was now open to the sight-seeing taxpayers. People crowded into the building, and Verity, wishing to avoid the handshakings, the cameras, and all the talk of Hank's yes men, slipped from the platform and joined the crowd. It always gave her a childish delight to lose her bodyguard. Wishing to avoid the crowd around the elevators, she started up the stairs. The building rose twenty-six stories, but the governor's offices were only one flight up, just above the assembly chambers.

When she was halfway up the flight, she heard someone behind and thinking it was her guard went on until Jules's familiar voice called, "Verity—"

She turned. He was running lightly up the steps two at a time. Six years had fined him to greyhound leanness. She thought, as always, how extraordinarily splendid a person he was. She had seen him but rarely through the years.

"Verity, my dear," said Jules, and kissed her finger tips as he always had.

"Jules—Jules—oh, I'm so glad to see you!"

"Going to look at the Big Lion's den?" he asked.

"Yes," she said. Then, "I've missed you, Jules. You and Saber. My, how I've missed you!"

They were on the second floor now. At the end of the hall to the right were huge double doors to the governor's suite. Jules stopped and turned Verity about, facing him. He looked at her searchingly.

"Verity—Verity, my dear, I have missed you, too. And so has Saber. Saber and I came up from Crescent City together today—over one of the finest roads in the country." He hesitated a second. "You've changed, Verity," he said softly. "I watched you all afternoon. You sat there so still —so terribly still. You looked like a lost Madonna. Get away from all this for a while," he urged. "Go to the Bend and stay for months and months."

"I can't," she said. "I don't know why I can't, but I just can't. I feel like a guardian—only I don't know of what. Silly, isn't it?" She made a futile little gesture.

"No," he said. "Nothing you do is silly."

A door just behind Verity flew open and Flamingo flashed out into the hall. At sight of Verity and Jules she flushed slightly.

"Oh—oh, hello," she said.

"Is that your office?" asked Verity.

"No. Oh, no. The Department of Cosmetic Sanitation," she grinned impishly, "is on the floor above. This is just a little storeroom for supplies." Then, as if chiding Verity, she flung wide the door to display the shelves of stationery and big jars of paste and bottles of ink. She shut the door, put a key in the lock, and turned it. "How have you been, Mr. Bolduc? Long time no see."

As Jules spoke courteously to Flamingo, Verity's face burned. She had thought Hank had put Flamingo's office right next to his own—and she had shown she thought so.

As Flamingo flitted up the stairs, Jules said, "Saber tells me she is growing rich."

"Yes, indeed." She was very bitter.

"Ah—where's Hancy?" asked Jules.

"She just happens to be convalescing from a cold," Verity replied. "I wouldn't let her come out for this affair. To tell the truth I was glad she couldn't come. Too much of this sort of thing is bad for a child."

"Um . . ." murmured Jules.

He opened the door to Hank's outer office. The fine room was loaded with flowers, and the young man who was one of Hank's secretaries ushered them into Hank's private office. This room was also crowded with great floral pieces, but in the midst of all this profuse splendor Verity's eyes fastened immediately on a beautifully fashioned flamingo of blown glass which stood with long neck stretched gracefully upward and holding a single red rose in its beak. She walked to the desk and looked at it.

"My goodness," said the secretary, "isn't that lovely! I didn't see that when I was in here before. I must have been blind. It's prettier than all the rose-and-gardenia horseshoes in this room."

"Yes, yes, it is," said Verity. As usual, she tried to speak casually of Sunny Lou. "Miss McMenimee brought it, no doubt. It's her symbol, you know."

"No, I don't think so," said the secretary. "I haven't seen her."

Verity shrugged the matter aside. A flamingo from the Flamingo, it was, and Verity knew it.

The secretary left. Jules and Verity looked around. The room was definitely magnificent; a huge rich Oriental rug upon the floor, high, wide windows fitted with Venetian blinds and set off by rich drapes of lustrous, muted satin in stripes of Burgundy and an off shade of blue. There were fine paintings, deep divans and easy chairs, Hank's immense mahogany desk, and his cushioned desk chair. One side wall was lined with lawbooks and the other with cupboards for the filing and storing of the governor's papers. A door opened into a small hallway off which were a complete and elegant bath and big cedar-lined closet. Jules laughed at the sight of the closet.

"The architects must really have thought Hank a lion of size if he needs that for his overcoat."

"Hank works so late sometimes," said Verity. "One of the things he insisted on was a bath and closet so he could change and rest a bit if he chose." She laughed a little. "But cedar lined! Isn't that typical of government, though! There isn't a cedar-lined closet in Magnolia Mansion—but the moths shall be kept out of the governor's overcoats!"

"Not getting a little cynical, Verity?"

"More than a little, Jules," she laughed, "but I have not yet written a satire."

The office door slammed.

"Verity!" Hank called. "Where the hell are you?"

"Right here," called Jules. "We're hunting a moth in this closet of yours."

Hank bounced into the little hallway. "Well, get outa my closet."

"I know now where to store the blankets during the summers," said Verity.

"Oh—oh, yeah," said Hank. "Ain't this place a piperoo! How'r'y', Jules? Ain't seen y' in a helluva spell. Was plumb surprised when I seen you going up the steps after my wife. Her bodyguard wasn't behind her, but old Jules was. I says t' myself, says I, 'Hank, y' shore have had a time keepin' a bodyguard for yore wife that she can't lose. By God'lmighty, you should oughta hire Jules for that job! He'd be there, you bet!' That's what I says t' myself."

"How right you are," said Jules gallantly. "I would even fall in line with your policy, Hank, and pay you a kickback of munificent size."

Vexation flickered in Hank's eyes as Verity laughed, but almost instantly he was again genial.

"Same old Jules," he said. "Funnin' aside, you been plumb avoidin' us, Jules. How come you to be at the ceremonies today?"

"I want to talk with you about the financial condition of the state. I feel

I have to make one last effort to make you see—" Hank flopped into his desk chair, his eyes on the glass flamingo. Jules leaned over the desk and went on. "Hank, do you realize that you have put so many people on the state pay roll as to be fantastic? Do you realize that the producers of actual goods, such as cotton and cane and lumber, are fewer in number than the people now occupying nonproducing jobs?—Do you realize that such an unbalance means that a smaller and smaller portion of the consumer's dollar buys actual goods and that a larger and larger percentage of the consumer's dollar goes to the spread which must cover the cost of keeping the nonproducers?" Jules stopped significantly for a second—"Such as the people on the state pay roll."

Hank leaned back in his new swivel chair and listened closely to Jules. Verity realized that she could understand Jules. Her years of stubborn study had done something for her.

"Well, Jules," said Hank, "I don't reckon I do realize all that. But I'm shore willin' t' realize it, iffen you can make me see it clear 'n plain. There's a lot 'bout money I don't understand. Now," he said earnestly, "I only just set up a committee for t' study them very questions of how much of a dollar goes to the real producer, 'n how much just goes t' God-knows-where. 'N I'd be mighty proud, Jules, iffen you'd head that committee. Yes, sir, I'd be proud. 'N I'd know the state was gettin' the good a' the best brain in it." Hank leaned forward with all the air of earnest and sincere hope. "You take that committee over, Jules. Will y'?"

Verity held her breath a second. She opened her lips to speak, but Jules straightened, laughed, looked at Hank with the old sardonic grin.

" 'I give the answer Reynard gave,' " he quoted, " 'I cannot like, dread sir, your royal cave: because I see, by all the tracks about, full many a beast goes in, but none comes out.' "

Hank almost let chagrin show plainly on his face before he said, "What y' a-talkin' 'bout, Jules?"

"You understand me perfectly," said Jules. "I, too, am a describing man."

"Roarin' thunderbolts," howled Hank, "I offer y' a chancet t' serve yore state 'n you come back at me withen a carkin' rhyme!"

The door opened and Saber came in.

"How'r'y, Saber?" said Hank, and then almost yelled, "You're another one I'm purely gettin' fed up with!—But I'll get t' that. Here I offer this dang Jules a chancet t' serve his state 'n he talks t' me like as iffen I'm still a peddler. I'm Governor Hank Martin, the Big Lion, by God'lmighty! You're a-talkin' fancy about the size a' the state pay roll—why, lookit what I done!" He waved his hands toward the windows. "Roads we got, 'n schools, 'n all kinds a' things! I plumb carried the people a' this state on my back from the backwoods t' modern glories! Plumb carried 'em on my back! I purely did."

"Ah, yes," said Jules smoothly, "and 'they who ride lions can never dismount.'"

Hank leaned back in his chair and said with great satisfaction, "Yeah. That's it, exactly." He grinned at Jules. "You quotin' that—'r did you actual think that one up?" His voice was scathing.

"No," said Jules, pursing his lips, "it's an ancient proverb."

"Huh!" said Hank. "You at last brought forth one as has some meanin'. That's one the people a' this state is purely gonna remember. Yes, sir," Hank laughed and winked. "They can't never dismount."

Verity realized that Hank actually did not get the meaning of the saying. "Hank!" she cried.

Hank looked at her and then back at Jules. "Now don't be a-tellin' me," said Hank, "that I done took a inverted viewpoint agin."

"You have indeed, Hank," said Jules, almost sadly.

"Well, thank God," said Saber fervently, "in this country we can dismount at the polls." Hank laughed. Saber took a newspaper from his pocket, unfolded it, and laid it on the desk before Hank. "Heard the latest news, Hank?" he asked.

"Nope," said Hank affably. "Too busy today with the dedication to give a tinker's hoot in high hell what the rest a' the world was a-doin'."

It was a morning paper and the two columns on the right were devoted to a story of the preparations for the dedication of the new Capitol building; the center of the page carried a picture of the resplendent structure with an insert picture of Hank.

Hank looked up from the paper well pleased. "Fine stuff," he said, "nothin' t' what the evenin' papers'll have, though."

"Great God!" exclaimed Saber. "Read the last column on the right! The citizens of the Saarland today climbed on the back of a Lion. And if he doesn't take them for an unforgettable ride, I miss my guess." Saber's voice rang with bitter vehemence. He flipped the paper over to the picture page. "Look at those people greeting their hero!"

"Well, God'lmighty," said Hank, "what the hell you so hot over? Them folks went over t' Germany by plebiscite. Why ain't that all right?" he asked, grinning.

"It would be quite all right," said Jules, "if it were an honest vote. But—" he pointed at a paragraph in the story, "reliable journalists point out that for years now German men and their families have been pouring into the Saarland, becoming residents—voting residents—outnumbering the old inhabitants almost two to one."

Verity caught her breath. "The old sheep's-clothing tactics," she murmured.

Hank whirled in his new swivel chair and thundered at her. "You keep outa this," he howled. "'N I mean it! God'lmighty, you're my wife!"

She turned her back on all of them and looked out the window, trying to keep her poise and temper. An ominous stillness was in the office following Hank's roar at Verity, and then Jules spoke.

"A whole nation suffers soul shock from war, and while they are dazed and longing to find that better and finer life for which they fought, men like you—men expert in catching the pulse of the people—sense their hopes and deliberately misguide them."

Verity turned to watch Jules. He stood before Hank's desk, intense and pleading, as once she had seen him in the Delamore court. In Hank's face the furies gathered, but this was Jules Bolduc speaking, and plainly Hank was trying to restrain himself. Hank's clenched fists, his whitening face showed his struggle and his anger.

"Another war brews in Europe," Jules went on. "If after the next war we again mistake the false for the true—" he lifted his shoulders in a gesture of hopelessness, "then it will take centuries for the slow evolution of culture to overcome the damage of these years. The next war will be a terrible war of the air. Men will carry death on wings to whole cities—"

"God'lmighty!" roared Hank, jumping to his feet and shaking his fist at Jules. "God'lmighty, Jules, you talk like as if everything terrible is t' be laid t' me. God-dammit, there's allus been wars 'n there allus will be. Just every so often, just by instinct, seems as though, men come outa their holes like t' ants 'n start a-fightin'. Yeah," he said slowly, "like t' ants. 'N iffen hereafter they want t' be plumb like t' 'em, why, I reckon the males'll just fly tillst they die, 'n the females'll have t' break off their wings at the thorax and be worker ants the rest a' their lives. Hell," said Hank, almost pleased with himself again, "can I help it iffen human critters follow their instincts?"

"Yes," said Jules firmly, "you can help some. The chief job of all so-called leaders is to promote reason. But they grow drunk on power. You had the gift, Hank." Jules's voice was heavy with sad regret. "As I once heard you say—this is the generation in which much could have been done."

He walked over to Verity and, bowing almost formally, he said, "I make no apologies for speaking in your presence. I meant you to know my stand if I had to come to Magnolia Mansion to state it." He turned to leave.

"Jules—" Verity said, and took a step toward him, holding out her hand.

He turned and took her hand and lifted it to his lips.

"Thank you, Verity—thank you."

"God'lmighty," said Hank hoarsely, "what is this anyhow?"

"It is my declaration of war," said Jules. Turning to Saber he said, "Please feel free to publish whatever I have said here; preferably in the form of an appeal to the Magnolia State to dismount from the Lion at the next election."

He opened the door to the outer office but Hank sprang like the lion he called himself and slammed it shut.

"Saber," Hank hissed, "iffen you publish what's been said here, by God-'lmighty, I'll run you outen this state!"

The shining quality in Saber gleamed forth, and in his jaunty, mocking way, he bowed and swept his hat low as though it were the plumed hat of a knight of old.

"I am but a humble recorder of truth, sire," he said. He opened the door, and as Jules walked into the outer office, Saber spoke softly, " 'Care not, while we hear a trumpet in the distance pealing news of better, and Hope, a poising eagle, burns above the unrisen tomorrow.' "

He sauntered out after Jules and closed the door silently behind him.

An odd excitement held Verity. It was a vividness of the mind; something almost illuminating. She stood still, trying to catch that which she could almost perceive.

Hank kicked out his right foot viciously. "I'll plumb kick their asses up t' their shoulder blades iffen I gotta," he muttered. " 'A trumpet in the distance'—hell, I'm the feller as blows a trumpet folks can hear. Clear 'n loud, by God'lmighty! Nothin' distant 'n uncertain 'bout the trumpet I blow 'n I sure call 'em t' battle!"

"But only the people should blow the trumpet in America. Only the people," said Verity softly.

Hank turned to her. "God'lmighty, Verity, you a-gettin' jaw teeth like t' knives, too?" he asked almost tragically. He spread out his arms in his platform gesture of humble appeal and his voice was heavy with sadness. "You allus been a somethin' special t' me. Time was when my love for you had a fine 'n churchy feel. 'N now, here a' late, it's all shot through withen alum 'n bile. Afore God, Verity, you changed somethin' terrible. There used t' be a high mountain, 'n a still, still glade in you."

"Oh, Hank," she cried, "who leveled them out to a long barren stretch?"

He walked to his desk and sat down. Automatically, unthinkingly perhaps, he reached out and, taking the rose from the glass flamingo, he said, "Not me. It shore wasn't me."

The buzzer sounded. Hank flipped up the key. "Yeah?"

"There's a group of our citizens here. They've been looking over our new building. They've asked if the governor's suite is open to inspection. Is it, Governor?" The secretary sounded doubtful.

Instantly Hank was the cordial politician. "Why, a-course it is!" he exclaimed. "Whole buildin' is open for the taxpayers t' look at. Hell, ain't it their buildin'? Show them folks in."

He flipped the key off, sighed, rose from his chair. "Didn't never expect anybody'd go this far in their dang sight-seein'," he said. "Hell, they was invited t' go up t' the tower 'n see the view a' the city from there. Be dang iffen I don't sometimes think I got a-holt a' some a' that honey as is bitter in the belly."

He opened the door and stood waiting to greet his voters. "Welcome," he called out genially. "Now this is shore right nice a' you-all. You're a-takin' the kind a' interest as folks should oughta take." Then his face clouded, for the last ones to enter were Guy Polli and his man, Willie. Hank shook hands with all the callers, asked their names, introduced Verity, and told the ladies to help themselves to some of the flowers.

Polli shook hands with Verity and smiled widely. As the last of the sightseers straggled out again, Polli said, "Fine building you got here, Hank."

"Yeah," said Hank glumly.

"Now, Hank," said Polli, "let's you and me talk over the situation about me being put on your ticket next year for mayor of Crescent City."

"You lookit here, Polli," said Hank, "you well know I can't be a-doin' that. The mayor is elected every two years. God'lmighty, Polli, you should oughta know that's the way things is. You gotta wait for a off year. That's only three 'n a half years t' wait. Roarin' thunderbolts, you're a-pullin' in yore take regular. Only today Jules Bolduc, he—" Then remembering Verity, Hank said, "You should oughta go home, Verity. Hancy's home alone alla this time."

"Please don't leave on my account," said Polli. He rubbed his long, soft hands together. "You sat in on our first deal, why not on what may be our last?"

"Now lookit," said Hank tensely, "you gotta be reasonable. Since prohibition got repealed you fellers are gettin' t' be plumb troublesome. Wha'd'y' expect, anyhow!"

"One tires of being slighted socially," said Polli. "I wish to forget bootlegging. Yes, I wish to forget." He walked to the window and looked out at the river. "Ah," he said with what seemed to Verity an odd significance, "the river is still turbulent, but in a few weeks Flamingo's strange parents will come down it, no doubt."

A wary unease was on Hank's face as he glanced toward Verity. "Nothin' strange 'bout Flamingo's folks," he said.

Polli turned to Verity. "You have not been out to see my birds in years, Mrs. Martin."

A creepy discomfort came over Verity. "I go out so seldom," she replied. "I must go home. Good afternoon, Mr. Polli."

Polli had picked up the glass flamingo and stood holding it to the light admiringly. He bowed. "Good afternoon, Mrs. Martin."

She looked at Hank, but Hank's attention was all on Polli. She opened the door and went out; walked down the hall past the rooms full of clerks and typists and secretaries. In the outer office her bodyguard jumped to his feet and followed her out into the main hallway. She was deeply vexed and troubled. Polli, she knew, had some hold on Hank which was stronger than any knowledge of deals in graft and judges, and she felt it was something in connection with Flamingo. "The river is still turbulent," he had said—the river is still turbulent. . . .

Jules's announcement caused a stir. The opposition party took up the words, "They who ride lions can never dismount," until they became the slogan of their campaign. Hank seemed driven by a fury into harder and harder work. He bought time on a nation-wide hookup, saying to Verity one day as he stood at the window of their bedroom, admiring the tower of the Capitol, "Lookit there, Sweetface—lookit there—ain't that purely a thing a' beauty, though! There it is, Sweetface, the pinnacle I been a-climbin' to, all marble 'n shinin'!" But after a moment, he added, "But now I look on it, I see it ain't big enough nor high enough for t' satisfy Hank Martin." He beat his chest. "No, sir, Verity, I see now I gotta climb to that round glitterin' dome in Washington. I purely have." He kicked out his right foot angrily. " 'N now," he said, "I gotta have troubles withen that damn Polli. Here I gotta sponsor that gangster for mayor a' Crescent City. As if things ain't bad enough withen that dang Saber a-writin' 'n a-writin' agin me. Not to mention that Jules! By God'lmighty, I plumb rue the day I brought him outen his sleepwalkin' t' do pore Harry's trial. I purely do."

"Why do you sponsor Polli?" asked Verity. "Is it something to do with Flamingo?"

"Why, a-course it ain't," Hank bellowed.

"You're lying, Hank," said Verity calmly.

"Now, you lookit here—don't you tell me I'm a-lyin'. Use yore good sense." His voice dropped to normal. "Polli's got hunderds a' gangsters 'n off-shade fellers tied up withen him. I gotta play ball, that's all." He added, "Aw, hell, I can get away withen Polli, I reckon. God knows he ain't much worse'n Appleby, 'n folks are tired a' Appleby. Thousands 'n thousands a' folks ain't gonna wanta vote for Polli, but we can shore as hell make 'em wanta vote agin Appleby. Folks is sick a' bein' run by big business—men like t' the Black Skimmer."

"All big-business men are not like Castleberry," said Verity. "And anyway, why should you hate Castleberry? It's the occasional Black Skimmer, it seems to me, who furnishes the springboard for a Lion's first leap."

He threw his head up and back and howled with laughter. "Sweetface," he said, "you're a-gettin' sharper'n a horned toad." He flipped his blue-bordered handkerchief from his breast pocket and wiped the tears of laughter from his cheeks. He grinned widely, swooped her up in his arms, cakewalked to a chair, and sat down, perching Verity on his knee so he could look into her face. "I'm a-goin' t' tell y' a secret," he said with a mock playfulness such as he might have employed with Hancy. "The truth is that deep down inside me I was allus filled withen gratitude t' Castleberry. But I didn't never 'spect nobody t' catch on! Why, roarin' thunderbolts, what'd folks like Abe Lincoln 'n me do iffen it wasn't for the greed a' the Black Skimmers! Hell, we wouldn't scarce have no chancet t' greatness a-tall!"

He chuckled softly, his eyelids drooped half-closed, his nostrils pulled downward, and he took a long, deep, savoring breath, ran a finger up the line of her cheekbone to her ear lobe, and pinched it gently. He pulled her head down on his shoulder and nuzzled her hair.

"Lord save us," he whispered. "Lord save us, but it pleasures me t' bite unexpected into pepper! For years now, seems though, I ain't found yore flavor." He rose with her in his arms and carried her to the bed. "Lord save us, Sweetface, I'm purely a-goin' t'—"

A knock came on the door and Selah called, "Mistuh Hank, suh—"

"Get away from that door, y' black skinful a' sin," howled Hank.

"But, lawsy, Mistuh Hank—Mistuh Flowah, he say scare you outta heah. He say y'all gwine haf ter drive too fast ter git t' Crescent City on time now."

"Roarin' thunderbolts!" Hank kicked the bed. "Roarin' thunderbolts! My first national hookup 'n me a-goin' t'— Aw, mudlarks, I gotta get a-goin'. At a time like t' this I gotta walk outta here 'n make millions a' slothful sonsabitches think I purely love 'em." He leaned over Verity and touched her cheek gently. "You stay here 'n wait for me—a-glowin'." He sighed, and hurried from the room.

Verity lay on the bed. Tears gathered and flowed across her temples and into her hair. She wept with the desolation of all women when first they realize their most poignant loss—the loss of the glory and grandeur of ardor.

Throughout the following year Hank spent much time in Crescent City trying to prepare the city to accept Guy Polli. The papers fought him bitterly, Saber more sharply than any other. But nothing annoyed Hank so much as the organization of women which Sylvia Hylen started against him.

Sylvia made her first appeal before the Crescent City Women's Civic Club. In it she asked for donations to print pamphlets. "Empty your purses and take off your jewels—put them in my hat—a fund to fight Hank Martin! Don't be afraid he will persecute your husband and run him out of business as he has many others, because we are not going to tell the names of donators. The newsmen here are not going to get pictures of your faces. If you hold your hats over your faces, ladies, how can Hank Martin find out who you are?" And the pictures of ladies with one hand dropping jewels in Sylvia Hylen's hat, while the other hand held their own hats over their faces, sent Hank into a rage. Verity realized that the guiding hand behind this move was that of Robert Castleberry.

The opposition party scrabbled around frantically to find a man who stood a chance of being elected, but Hank had absorbed the opposition's men into fat state jobs, or had put them on committees and discredited them. Several times the name of Jules Bolduc came up. Jules stated that he had no wish to hold any office, but he added that he would accept the nomination if it seemed he must. Promptly Hank gave out a statement to the effect that if he must lose the next election, he would rather lose it to Jules than to anyone else, since he owed much to Jules Bolduc. Hank cunningly pointed out, in statements to the press, in speeches, and in pamphlets by the hundreds of thousands, that it was Jules who had guided him in his study of the law; it was Jules who hád taken up the fight of the Harry Disbro case; Jules who had taken that means to expose the dishonesty of Robert J. Castleberry, the "Black Skimmer." Hank chuckled over this. He knew it would scare the opposition, and it did. "Caught old Jules withen my sheep's-clothing tactics after all!" he chortled. " 'I do not like, dread sir, yore royal cave,' " he mimicked. "By God'lmighty, iffen they'd decided t' run him, I'd 'a had a job on my hands. I purely would! But the opposition's committee is as dumb as my own. I knowed I could count on a committee's dumbness."

Hank raved and roared at the press; declared that the press abused the right of free speech; no one had the right to call the slandering of his administration free speech—no speech should be as free as that! He bought his own printing plant and flooded the state with his own newspapers, using the highway department to distribute them. State bureaus, factories, stores, were given these papers free, and across the top of each a screamer read: "The people of this state should thank God for Hank Martin."

The confusion of the people was complete when the opposition finally chose Warren Poussom, a grand old man, a former senator, now sixty-nine years old, to head their party.

Hank howled with glee over their choice. "God'lmighty!" Hank roared to his audiences, "they tell us he's honest; they tell us he's good. I'll go them one better! I'll tell them he's not even tempted—he's too dang old! Why, the pore dodderin' old feller, he's been a-playin' possum every time death comes his way, 'n death passes by thinkin' he's already fotched him!"

It was the following fall, election was drawing near, and Hank was worried and distraught. The Polli-for-Mayor business was harder to lick than he'd expected.

Whenever Verity went out, even if only downtown for lunch or to do some shopping, she felt the strange confusion of the people as they looked at her. She hated to leave the grounds of Magnolia Mansion and spent most of her time in the library. This afternoon she sat there as was her habit. It was past time for Hancy to come home from school, and Verity sat listening for the car, for Jep, who was Hancy's guard, to open the side door and say, "Home again, all safe, ain't we, Hancy?" Almost always Hancy replied, "Sure, what the heck you expectin' all the time?"

Verity had begun to dislike this bit of dialogue, for unease stirred within her constantly and the words took on an apprehensive significance. She looked at the clock.

Selah came into the library. "I declah, Miz Verity," she said, "hit a somepin' w'en a chile cain't be a few minutes late withouten a body got ter stew is somebody shootin' at her 'r not, lak Mistuh Hank seem all time 'spectin'. Jackson, he a-peekin' out de front winders, an' de cook, she a-peekin' th'u de pantry winder onter de driveway." Selah made a face of disgust and despair. "Law, Miz Verity," she said earnestly, "I jes' does long sometimes fo' de Bend, where de house is cramped an' de mind is free. Um-uummmph! dis am powe'ful wearin' on a body. Um-uummmph!"

Clenching her fists, Verity walked through the wide rooms to the front. "Do you see the car, Jackson?" she asked.

"No, ma'am, Miz Verity," said Jackson. His big, liquid black eyes looked at Verity with kindness and concern. "Shan't I call the school for you?"

"Yes, yes, please."

But just then the car came through the gate and Jackson called, "They're here, Miz Verity, they've come."

"Now don't look too anxious," Verity warned Selah and Jackson. "I don't want Hancy to feel this fear."

"Yas'm, das right," said Selah.

Verity stood still, calming herself. Selah picked up a small statue and dusted it on her apron. The side door flew open and Hancy came in screaming.

"The next time I'm fightin', Jep, you lay off—you hear?"

The child was battered and bruised, her once-pretty blue dress torn from one shoulder and the skirt half torn from the waistband. Her thirteen-year-old sweetness was not now sweet, but a dynamo of thwarted fury.

"Darling!" cried Verity, running to her.

"Honey-chile!" cried Selah, "whut low-life blackbird done dis ter my baby!"

Jep removed his cap and mopped his face.

"They was arguin' when they come outa the school," said Jep. "'N a great big lunk, leastways fourteen, swung at her and she lit into him. Nearly had him licked when four other boys jumped on her. I had a damn good notion t' shoot every one a' them. But I think mebbe I better not. So I hauled 'em offen her 'n threatened 'em good 'n hearty."

"You mind your own business," yelled Hancy. "I'm gonna beat them up good. Maybe kill 'em," she sobbed.

"Hancy—Hancy—" Verity put her arms around the child, her heart crying out for help. "Tell me about it, darling. Tell Mamma. Come, sweetheart, tell Mamma and Selah."

"That big old Tommy Penrow—he said my father was nothin' but a traitor! He said my Hank's a Big Lion all right and that half the people of the state are gettin' ready to bag him!" She threw herself in her mother's arms and sobbed hysterically. "I'll kill that Tommy Penrow— I'll kill him!—I'll kill him!"

Jenny came running in. "The chauffeur told me Hancy's hurt." Her words preceded her into the room. Jenny and Verity and Selah looked at each other. A terrible sense of being trapped closed in on Verity. Hancy's love for her father was a beautiful thing, a thing necessary to the child. Verity felt if that love was shattered, if Hancy was disillusioned, that something essential to her would be forever lost—that Hancy might never get over it.

It was Jenny who came to the rescue. "Afore Gawd, Hancy," said Jenny, "you're plumb old enough t' know that a man can't be great with- outen he's got a heap a' enemies. Like 's not, there's a heap a' folks 's do talk that-a-way 'bout yore paw. Why, pshaw, Hancy, you gotta git some iron in yore guts. Why, yore paw's been knowin' that—since most time when you was borned. 'N it ain't got him down."

"Jenny's right, darling," said Verity, giving Jenny a glance of grati- tude. And then in a flash Verity realized that Hank must never know of this, for Hank would set about systematically persecuting the fathers of these boys, feeling that certainly they had heard that talk in their homes.

She looked at Jackson and Jep and Selah and said distinctly, "Now, Hancy, your father mustn't know about this. It would hurt him to think you heard anyone speak that way. And also," she added shrewdly, "it would hurt your father to see that you are so upset. He wants you brave and big and able to face life as it really is. Your Hank knows the risks he takes, and he knows the risks he asks you and all of us to take. And we must take them because we love him."

"Das right, honey," said Selah. "Jackson, you run git Miss Hancy some raw beefsteak fo' her eyes an' den—"

"Then you pack, and tomorrow we'll go to the Bend," said Verity. "Only this morning I promised your father we'd go home and look after the farm for a while."

Selah beamed. "Das right, honey. Dis mo'nin' yo' pappy say ter yo' mammy, 'Ain' long now till ee-lection time, an' you an' Hancy an' Selah go ter de Bend an' make it fine fo' pitchurs in de newspapuhs—so's folks'll see Hank Martin's got a farm lak all presidents!' Ain' he say dat, Miz Verity? Um-ummph! Dis very mo'nin'."

You lovely liar, thought Verity, and said, "Yes, he did."

Hancy stilled her sobs somewhat. "Everybody in the Bend loves my Hank," she said. "Gee," she asked wistfully through her tear-filled, swollen and blackening eyes, "could I maybe ride horseback over the meadows without a man with a gun in back of me?"

"Yes, darling," Verity answered softly. "And your riding is not exactly expert. You've always wanted to be a good horsewoman and we'll ask Jules's groom to teach you. Maybe I'll ride with you. I'd like to learn to ride, too."

"Oh, gee, Mamma, will you really? I never have any friends," she said, and with the admission the sobs broke forth again convulsively. "The kids make fun of me. I never could play hide-'n-seek, even. When I'd hide that old Jep just went nuts. Just imagine how I felt, Mamma, playing hide-'n-seek and getting hunted by Jep! Of course I'm too old to play those silly games now, but I'm too old to be tagged all the time, too. Gee whiz! I didn't even get invited to the school party. What boy wants to take a girl, and a man with a gun, too?"

"Law," cried Selah, "ain't dat de truf!"

"Humph!" said Jenny. "I bet I know two boys'd be glad t' take y', gun 'r no gun. You ain't seen Pete 'n Perk fer most four years, have y', Hancy?"

"Nope," said Hancy.

"My, but they're shore handsome. Ain't they, Verity?"

"They certainly are," said Verity.

"I'm a-takin' them boys outa their fine school, 'n a-goin' t' the Bend fer a spell," said Jenny. "You reckon I can find a house there, Verity?"

Verity looked into the eyes of her friend. "We'll find a house for you, if we have to build one," she said.

"But they're over sixteen," said Hancy. "Gee, they wouldn't look at me."

"I'd shore hate t' depend on it," said Jenny. "You're a somethin' when you're all prinked up, 'n not fiesty."

"Gee!" said Hancy wistfully. "It'd be wonderful t' have some friends. And sixteen years old!" She looked belligerently through her swollen eyes at old Jackson. "Well, Jiminy kraut, Jackson, get me some beefsteak for this mug of mine!"

The cloud of commiseration lifted from Jackson's face. "Yes, ma'am, Miz Hancy," he beamed. "Beefsteak comin' right up."

Hancy ran for the stairs, Selah following. "I can put beefsteak on my own face," said Hancy. "I don't have to have you following me all the time, either."

"You ain' gwine go uppity on me," said Selah, "even iffen you is fixin' t' snaffle sixteen-year-olds. I bosses yo' mamma an' I bosses you. I'se de major-domo. An' don' you dish me no fancy back talk!"

As they disappeared up the stairs, Verity said, "She's been bitterly lonely. Poor little thing. This is no way for a child to live. Oh, Jenny, how can I thank you! Do you think Pete and Perk will . . ."

"Shore," said Jenny. "Them boys 'n all the young 'uns at the Bend'll help make Hancy feel liken a young'un should oughta feel. Kinda free, you know."

"Yes," said Verity. "Yes."

Jenny had gone to her own cottage and Verity was in her bedroom looking over her clothes, deciding just what to take to the Bend for this vacation, when she heard the knocker resounding through the house with a fierce and unceasing urgency. She stepped into the upper hall, heard Jackson's voice, and recognized Lula May's as she said, "Miz Martin— I jes' gotta see Miz Martin!"

Verity ran down the stairs. Lula May stood just inside the door, leaning on the jamb, panting as from great exertion and great fear, her face white, and yet in it was the look of strong acceptance of whatever must come.

"Lula May," cried Verity, "what's the matter?"

But Lula May looked hard at Jackson until he turned and left them. She looked up the stairs.

"Where's yore young'un? I don't want she should hear."

Into Verity came the certain knowledge that the matter was Hank and Flamingo. She gathered her forces as Lula May had done and took on the saving stoicism which she had learned through the years. She led Lula May into the small reception room.

"Quick," commanded Verity. "What is it?"

"It's Hank 'n my pritty one," said Lula May with piteous bravery. "Spurge, he's gone t' a big birdcage with a feller named Willie. Spurge is like t' kill Hank. Mebbe even—" Her voice broke. She braced herself and went on, ". . . mebbe Sunny Lou. Usn don't hold with fornicatin'—'n nine years this Willie says they been meetin' there." Lula May clenched her shawl and moaned. "That Willie, he met us at the levee. A big birdcage, that Willie said. A birdcage—a birdcage, he said. Oh, how can that be?"

A queer fatalistic acceptance mingled with Verity's fear. She felt she should have known it all the time. It was a natural setting for Hank and Flamingo. She turned from Lula May, rang frantically for Jackson, and called, "The car! The car! Quick!" She opened the hall closet and grabbed a coat.

Lula May stared at Verity, put her hands on Verity's shoulders and shook her. "You knowed this!" she hissed. She pushed Verity from her and wiped her hands across her dress as if she had befouled them.

"No!" said Verity, a fierceness rising in her. "But I know the place!"

She took Lula May by the wrist and went outside. The car came around the drive and Verity's bodyguard came running across the lawn. Verity pulled Lula May into the car, commanded the driver to go, to go fast, and to blow the siren.

Verity leaned forward, directing the driver, and through the screaming siren she heard the sad soliloquy of Lula May: "Oh, my pritty one—my Sunny Lou. Allus she loved him. Iffen you hadn't 'a come she would 'a wed up withen him in a year 'r two. Oh, my pritty one. 'N that Flower feller, a-settin' outside a birdcage a-waitin' for 'em. A birdcage, he said! A birdcage—oh—"

As they neared Polli's place, Verity ordered the driver to turn off the siren and creep as silently as possible up the driveway. She saw, parked before Polli's front door, Hank's car and Flamingo's green roadster. The lovely grounds were serene and deeply shadowed by the setting sun and the windows of the fine old house were goldened. As the car stopped at Verity's direction, she flung open the door and ran around the house to the back, Lula May following.

Flower stood outside the heavy wire-and-iron gate, big and helpless, not knowing where his duty lay. At the sound of Verity's running feet he turned, and his face burned with misery and shame.

"Is Spurge in there with them?" Verity whispered urgently.

Flower nodded. "Polli, too."

"Where's Willie?"

"He just opened the gate for McMenimee 'n then went back into the house," Flower whispered. "Gawd, Verity, Gawd! What'll I do?" He shook his fists in maddened futility. "Goddam, I hate this place!"

Lula May reached the gate. She flattened her face against the heavy wire and called, "Paw! Paw! You there? Spurge!"

Verity called, "Hank!"

"Sunny Lou," came Spurge's sad, stern voice, "it's yore maw 'n Hank's wife. Reckon they got a right t' be here. Go you, Sunny Lou, 'n open the gate."

"Spurge!" cried Hank. "God'lmighty, are you a-goin' t' take the word a' this scruff? You're too just a man for t' condemn withouten a hearin'!"

"He saw you both come here." It was Polli's smooth voice. "Seeing is believing."

Then Flamingo appeared on the other side of the gate. For one fleeting instant Verity and Flamingo stared at each other, through the wire. Flamingo's face was white and her eyes blazed commandingly at Verity as she whispered, "Don't you let me down! You hear?" She turned then and called, "I can't fetch this lock around. Polli, come here and open this gate."

No answer came from Polli, but Spurge said, "Go open yore gate, man."

Just as Polli came into Verity's sight, Flamingo turned the lock. She grabbed Polli's wrist, hissing, "Paw's like t' kill us all. Come on, run! Let him kill Hank—we gotta run for it!"

Sick terror came into Polli's face. Flamingo ran, helping the lagging Polli to fleetness.

"Wait, Paw! Wait!" screamed Flamingo.

Lula May ran through the gate. Straight to Spurge she ran. She stood in front of her husband and put her hands on the handles of his revolvers. Lula May was giving her child a chance.

Verity moved slowly into the aviary, clinging to the wire, for the terror of the 'gator and the swamp were on her. Flamingo had another outlander at her mercy. Verity knew Flamingo meant to save Hank from Spurge—but watching the girl running with Polli she grew sick with horror—what could she possibly do to the man? What? What? There were no 'gators here—no 'gators here—the words flailed at Verity like the 'gator pole itself—nothing vicious here—no 'gators here . . .

Straight to the chute and the barrel Flamingo ran with Polli, then stopped short. Polli slipped on the wet planks of the platform on which the fish barrel stood. Flamingo turned on him, and with one lunge pushed him off the platform into the blue lagoon. Almost in the same movement she pulled the sluice gate, made her loud, piercing calls to the birds, drowning the screams of Polli. Thousands of silver-bellied fish flooded down the chute and into the barrel. Flamingo dipped the long-handled net into the barrel and threw net after net of shining fish straight at the white face of Polli—the wet face that shone almost as whitely as the bellies of fish. From everywhere came the great brilliant birds, gorgeous and terrible, like a plague from out the skies. The world was filled with the beating of wings and the rending, screeching screams of the fighting birds as they dived at shining things. Polli screamed and beat the lagoon with his arms as the 'gator beat the swamp, but the fish rained on him and his screams were lost in the screeching of fighting birds—birds and more birds until they blanketed the lagoon—swirling, diving, sharp-beaked, sharp-taloned. Verity remembered Polli, dancing, excited, rubbing his soft hands, pleasured by voracious beauty.

After an interminable time, Flamingo ceased throwing the fish. The screams of the birds lessened, many flew away satisfied, and some bled and some fell, but there was no sign of Polli on the face of the blue lagoon.

Everyone seemed rooted, unable to move, save Flamingo. She turned and with head high and proud she came down the path with stately stride, so like her father's. Directly to her father she went and stood before him, once more a prisoner waiting for sentence.

"Polli's the man that took your daughter," lied Flamingo. "Polli, he wanted Hank killed and disgraced. You would've killed the wrong man, Paw."

Hank stood, a ghost of himself, only his eyes burningly alive. Spurge stared at his child, covered his face with his hands for a second, and stared again. Verity leaned weakly against the vine-covered fence, and the tears streamed down her cheeks as Lula May, with no sign of weakness, lifted her hands from her husband's guns and went to stand beside her daughter.

"She's our own young'un, Spurge," she said stanchly. "I birthed her 'n you sired her. Iffen she's wrong, it can't be that there's no fault t' lay t' us."

"Say no more, Maw," commanded Spurge sternly. "The will t' right, 'r t' wrong, lays in the girl herself, it does. Sunny Lou, how come you t' tell me Polli's the man? There wasn't the look t' him of a man you'd take t' yoreself."

"I hated him, Paw," cried Flamingo. "I hated him! He threatened t' kill me, Paw."

"How long has such been a-goin' on?" demanded Spurge.

Flamingo hesitated only a second and then said, "Almost a year, Paw."

"A year!" Spurge was aghast. "A year you lent yoreself t' such in this here place 'n ain't kilt him tillst this day!"

"God'lmighty, Spurge," Hank gasped. "In a city, you—"

"Silence, Hank! You was ever one t' be too forgivin' of her. 'N now I think on it, how come you t' let this go on?"

"He never knew it, Paw. He never knew it till now," Flamingo declared. "Oh, Paw," she pleaded, "I know I'm wrong. I know I'm terrible wrong!" She looked at Hank and then at Verity, and added shrewdly, "But, Paw, it was only when I saw Verity through the gate that I thought how t' kill him. It brought back the 'gator, and the ways of swamps and lagoons, Paw."

"Mebbe so," said Spurge, "mebbe so."

"Sentence me, Paw," said Flamingo softly, "only don't banish me from you. I'll need you so bad, now, Paw."

"God'lmighty, Spurge," said Hank urgently, "let's get outa here afore we gotta kill a dozen more!"

But Spurge was not impressed. He put his hands on his revolvers. "Sunny Lou," he said sternly, "you purely forgot how t' kill varmints timely 'n clean, seems 's though. One year you let a varmint poison you with carnal shame. Leastways three years it'll take t' wash y' clean, I reckon." He squared his shoulders and pronounced sentence. "You'll go home withen yore maw 'n me; you'll be a-huntin' every day withen yore brothers 'n me; a-wearin' yore strength agin the 'gators, 'n a-learnin' t' strike quick at the viper."

Such vast relief and gratitude shone in Flamingo's face that Verity's heart was wrung as it had never been before.

"Oh, Paw," said Flamingo softly. "Oh, thank you, Paw."

Lula May swiped at her tears and smiled at her husband. She linked her arm through her daughter's. "Usn can go home now, Paw?" she asked.

"Yeah," said Spurge, turning to Hank. "I didn't know a viper soon enough myself, seems as though. I should oughta knowed that was a lie. I'm humbled with shame for puttin' guilt on y', Hank. I should oughta knowed better. You're my firmest friend."

"Yeah," said Hank, "yeah—" He looked at Flamingo and the tears ran unashamedly down his cheeks.

The girl stood dry-eyed, proud and at peace. The last of the sun's rays made a brilliant corona of her hair and laid the purples and golds of majesty upon her blue dress. Her eyes flashed Hank one last message of love.

"You always done only good to me, Hank," she said softly. "And now I've done good to you. Polli'll never threaten you again. Now you won't have any trouble with election."

Hank could not speak. His hands went out in a simple gesture of acceptance of her gift. Spurge offered his hand to Hank. Automatically Hank clasped it.

Spurge then bowed to Verity. "I'm a-humblin' myself for yore forgiveness, ma'am." He spoke to his womenfolks. "Come," he said, and turned toward the gate.

Hank put out his hand to Lula May, but Lula May crossed her arms over her bosom, running her hands under her shawl. Her mouth hardened, her eyes looked accusingly into Hank's. She bowed ever so slightly, turned with Flamingo, and Spurge's womenfolks followed him out of the aviary.

Hank jammed his hand into his pocket. "Now everybody walk outa here like as if nothin' went on but a reg'lar bird feedin'," he warned. He took a deep breath, struggled for the curing effect of pulled-in guts pushing on a chest full of air. Then he looked at Verity. "Breathe deep," he said, " 'n hang onto yoreself tillst we get home."

But Verity knew she did not need his warning. She had not lived almost sixteen years with Hank Martin without learning many things. Also she had iron in her guts, and she now knew she had. She pulled herself to her full height and followed the McMenimees across Polli's lawn. In that walk from aviary to car, an assurance came to Verity. She knew she no longer had to fight to make herself endure the anguish; she could now do better than that. She was strong. She was strong enough to blunt the sharp edge of anguish against the rock of reason and understanding.

Hank put the McMenimees in his car. "Take 'em wherever they tell y'," Hank said to the driver.

The car moved away and Flamingo did not look back.

Hearing the motor, Willie came out the front door, amazement plain upon his face.

"Hi'y', Willie," said Hank.

"Where's Polli?" asked Willie.

"Out yonder withen his birds," said Hank and got into the car. Flower, in the front seat, sat tensely forward, and the driver, knowing nothing of the happenings, started the car unhurriedly and went slowly over the driveway and out the gate.

Verity sat well over in one corner of the seat, her eyes on Hank. As they turned onto the main highway, and the siren began its screaming in preparation for the swift, mad driving, the color came back into Hank's face. He sat back in his seat, put his elbow on the armrest, and covered his eyes. Looking at him Verity realized she had no blame in her for Flamingo. The girl's love for Hank was an integral part of her.

Hank sighed. He turned to Verity, a haunted look in his face.

"The scent a' Eve's apple plumb keeps a man a slave—with his honin' 'n his reachin' for it," he said simply. "She loved me whole 'n of a piece. She saved my life at the hands of her paw, but I see clear 'n plain it's mebbe gonna take all the money I got to pay off Polli's gang. I ain't got a minute t' lose. I gotta get Polli's records of our deals iffen it's the last thing I do." He waited for Verity to speak, but as she said nothing he added, "My life ain't worth a spent nickel tillst I clean that gang up. I don't mind 'bout the money; there's more where that come from. But it's the old iron vest for me."

Again he waited for her to speak, but she was marveling that even now his thoughts were on immunity, immunity for himself.

"Well, Verity?" he said almost testily, wanting to have this matter over and done with.

"Well, Hank," she said.

"What the hell you mean 'well, Hank'—that ain't all you got t' say? Jealous women ain't never wordless."

"But I am only sorrowful," said Verity firmly. "I see that everyone pays too high a price for loving you. I, your wife, have paid too much; Flamingo, your mate, has paid too much; Hancy, your child, has paid too much."

"Hancy! Wha'd'y' mean by that! I done everythin' for my young'un. She's mine. 'N I love her past everythin', I sometimes think."

"Yes," said Verity. "That love stays pure. But she's paid with her freedom—just like every citizen in the state, it seems to me. She has no freedom—but she doesn't quite realize it is your fault."

He looked at her as at a stranger. "There was allus somethin' unknown in you—a somethin' ungivin'," he muttered and turned to the window.

Still conscious of the strange, almost stirring strength within her, Verity sat quiet and upright in the car. Jackson must have been on the alert for them, for he swung wide the door of Magnolia Mansion before the car came to a full stop. Hank sprang out and into the house. Verity stepped out of the car. Flower stood still a second as if getting his bearings again, gave Verity one glance of sick misery, and turning, went swiftly off to Jenny.

Hank was at the telephone.

"Now lissen careful, Marcus," Hank was saying. "The chief a' police'll play ball—god-dammit, he knows who butters his bread. Pick only the policemen we can be sure of. Get the proper papers made out. Go into Polli's house 'n take the records." He lowered his voice somewhat. "They're in the attic behind a false partition on the north side a' the house. . . . Yeah, the attic— Get goin', now. I'll get out there whilst you're still there, so's t' check on them records— Or mebbe join up withen y' at the police station. Get a warrant t' hold Willie on suspicion a' murder tillst I get to him. You understand? Yeah . . . yeah . . . yeah . . . that's exactly right."

He hung up the receiver, saw both Verity and Jackson waiting. He glared at Jackson and howled, "When I'm talkin' on the phone, get the hell out!"

"I been trying to tell y'all, suh," said Jackson, "that Lieutenant Governor Kirkendall is waitin'. In the library, suh." He turned and went to the back of the house.

From the big living room came the voice of Kirkendall.

"No, I'm here. I heard you come in, and—"

" 'N so you come a-snoopin'. Well, I've had all I'm of a mind t' stand today. I gotta get a-goin'. Go on away 'n leave me be."

"That is what I want to do for all the rest of my life," said Kirkendall. "I came here to tell you, Hank Martin, that I'm not running for office again on your ticket! I'm resigning."

"Resigning!" Hank's lips curled with disgust. "You ain't upsettin' my plans 'n makin' no stir now! 'N I'm a-tellin' you so flat 'n short. The people are used t' you, 'n they don't expect nothin' from y'. I ain't a-wastin' time a-huntin' somebody else t' sell t' the voters."

"To sell out the voters, you mean," yelled Kirkendall.

No longer was there in Kirkendall the look of the sleeper.

"That'll be all from you!" roared Hank. "Why, you pulin' pip-squeak! Who are you t' talk! Everybody comin' at me, Hank Martin, a-sayin' I ain't fitten, 'n I ain't honest! I also ain't had no trouble a-findin' plenty a' dishonest fellers t' go along with me. You stir up so much as a riffle, Kirkendall, 'n, by God'lmighty, I'll expose you. I'll show just how much it took t' buy you—I'll show just how much—"

But Kirkendall stood so silent that Hank stopped. Then Kirkendall spoke with a lofty remoteness.

"All that you can do," he said. "I do not care. I took your money. But it was my own self and my own soul I was selling— But now you persecute man after man who opposes you. There is no sense of peace or security. It fills the air. Men cannot make decisions. You manage, by throttling business, to keep so many dependent on the state that fear rides our citizens—fear that their children will starve if they have not Hank Martin to lean on. I hate the sight of you!" Lieutenant Governor Kirkendall stood erect. "And I hate the heart in me that let me help betray a proud state into your hands."

"You'll stay on that ticket, 'n you'll play ball," Hank hissed, "iffen I gotta put you under lock 'n key tillst election is over. You think well on yore moves, Kirkendall. You got a proud wife 'n four young'uns t' think on. 'N, yeah," said Hank, slowly, pointedly, "yeah, 'n well you know that in my records 'n in my own personal files I got the proof that'll send that oldest boy a' yoren t' prison for years on end."

"He was framed!" screamed Kirkendall. "You did that to my son just to make me sign a—"

"Shut up!" yelled Hank.

"I'd kill you to get those records!" Kirkendall shook with rage. "I'd kill you to get them—and so would some others. Marcus Davol would kill you to get them—and then he'd have the control. I tell you, Hank Martin—"

"You ain't tellin' me nothin'!" Hank howled. "After election you can resign 'n be damned t' you. Tillst then, remember my special records—'n you'll do my way."

Kirkendall turned and went out of the room, a broken man. Verity watched him walk heavily through the hall and out the front door, aware that within herself, where once had been an inert heaviness, there was now a violent rending. Her very being seemed rending apart. She saw that she had, for ten years, nursed a sick and ailing man, and, unbelieving and ever hopeful, had watched him turned by the black magic of power and more power into the Big Lion.

She felt a wild and flying fury, an almost supernal strength. She turned on Hank, crying, "You—you, and men like you all over the world have pillaged this generation! You've pillaged our faith and struck at our freedom. By giving one answer in words and another in action, you've made yourself into an all-powerful executive—a Big Lion! And when a country has a Big Lion—the people lose all! All they have of freedom! You've pillaged this generation—and perhaps you've done the same for generations to come . . ."

"Stop! Stop!" Hank cried out. "You're my wife—you're my wife!"

"Maybe generations to come," she blazed at him. "You once said politicians have four faces! And one of the faces you named was that of a calf. Well, I've read lots of ancient history in these recent years. You meant the golden calf, or the Moloch, no doubt! The calf with the arms that reach out for a living sacrifice of the young to be placed within them! The face of the Lion I know well, the face of the calf I have glimpsed—" She caught her breath on a sob. ". . . The face of the man I have loved—but I've never seen the face of the eagle—no, not once!"

"A'right!" Hank bellowed in a blind fury. "Let's say you seen the face a' the eagle, too. The eagle's a nictitating bird! You're allus a-hollerin' about me a-nic—"

She pulled herself out of tears and in a cold, hard voice she half whispered, "Don't you dare stand there and tell me our national symbol is a nictitating bird! Don't dare say a thing like that. Our eagle is kin to the phoenix; our eagle will take new life from its ashes every time!

"Law by law you grind out a sickness on this state. You and your nictitating!" She threw the words from her with disguest. Hank's eyes took on an unbelieving, stunned glare. "You could have been great. Yes, truly great—almost as great as Lincoln, perhaps. You could have been, Hank." Sobs caught her again.

"Verity—God'lmighty—you're my wife!" cried Hank.

"No," she said, "I am not. I refuse to be the Big Lion's wife. I married a man whose heart was callable by mine. I married a man whose only records were on the cost of pins and calicoes and peppermint candy for knobby-kneed children." Sobs choked her. "I married a man who—"

"The records!" cried Hank. "God'lmighty, Verity, I got no time for this now. I gotta get a-goin'." He stood a second pulling air into his lungs, thinning his abdomen, then ran from the room.

They drove to the Bend in a gentle rain. Soft and fine and straight it fell on the cane fields and the cotton stubble; on the timberlands and the wide, lush meadows which were not yet brown. An exhilarated look of wonder shone on Hancy's face as she settled happily between Jenny and Verity and said, "Gee, Mamma, not a man with a gun among us!"

Hank had been gone all night, and though Verity delayed leaving until late in the afternoon, he had not returned. She called his office and left a message saying she was leaving for the Bend and toward late afternoon his secretary called back to tell her that Governor Martin had phoned in, and on being given Verity's message he had said to tell her he was all right and to go on. But Verity had left a note for Hank. She had written: "We are going to the Bend where Hancy will live as a child should—with a little freedom for play and friendships. I shall be there if the man I married has need of me. Verity."

The feeling of sure strength was still in Verity, though all the strength seemed to be walls around a well of sadness. She had done all she could where Hank was concerned—all she knew how to do. It was Hancy's turn now. She thought on the words, "strength of one's convictions," and she concluded that a conviction must be more than a thought. It seemed to her that a conviction was a conviction only to the exact degree that one acted upon it. She was doing what she must do. It was a great pity, she thought, that there were not more men in the world like Spurge. It seemed to her that the only positively good thing in the world was the will to follow one's inner sense of moral duty regardless of profit or loss or happiness or censure.

That night Hancy said, as she sat on the edge of the bed, "It's such a funny, boxy little room, Mom. I'm sitting here laughing at it, but it laughs right back at me. Can you hear it laugh, Mom? This whole house laughs, seems as though."

"You is tellin' de Lawd's truf," said Selah fervently. "Dis whole house laffs. But w'en usn git dat bathroom piped, 'n we ain' got ter skip ter de privy, dis house gwine be plumb disgustified. 'Cause you know whut, Miz Hancy?"

"What?" asked Hancy, grinning.

"Dis am de kind uv house as ain' never 'spected ter see de day w'en folks do such t'ings inside it."

Hancy rolled on the bed with laughter. "Selah, you black skinful of sin!" She said it so like her father that Verity felt the tears burning. She kissed the laughing youngster and left the room.

Selah came out after tucking Hancy in bed. "Law, ain' de ways uv de Lawd wonderful!" she exclaimed softly. "Dat chile got all de good an' de beautiful dat's in Mistuh Hank an' a lotta whut's in you, Miz Verity. Usn rich wid goodness in dat chile. Um-uummph!"

Jenny, who was sitting beside the stove, looked up at Verity and smiled. "Do we plan t' stay here in the Bend, Verity? Just kinda settle here agin? Flower, he says he's a-comin' soon as Hank'll leave him off. Do we just kinda plan to send the young'uns t' school in Delamore on that new school bus?"

"Yes," said Verity. She noticed that Selah went to the door several times and turned back to some unnecessary job at the stove or table. "Is something wrong, Selah?"

"Aw, I reckon not," said Selah. "Hit jes' I so used ter gua'ds, hit don't scarce seem safe ter leave y'all heah."

"That's just habit, Selah. I know how you feel, though. It seems really strange, doesn't it? Go on, now, you're tired."

"I ain' tired," Selah denied, "but I fixin' ter git up wid de sun. An' iffen dat string bean, Tape, ain' kep' up dis place lak he been tolt, you gwine heah a long lean man doin' heap uv hollerin' come mawnin'."

With one last, anxious look, she opened the door and went off to her own little house, and Jenny and Verity sat together in friendly, wordless silence, a silence possible only between women when there is kinship of spirit.

Next morning Verity was up to watch the first sky golds in the east. She stood at her gate hugging to her heart the sense of home. This was her land. The country looked green and new after the rain and the lights of the coming sun spangled the wetness. The sounds of the earth's fullness came sweetly to her—the cackling of chickens, the lowing of the cow, the distant bark of Jules's hounds—all dear and familiar sounds. The birds spiraled high and there was the fragrance of the blue, sweet smoke from wood in Selah's stove. Currents of air, fresh off the bayou, fanned her face; thin little currents as if from small wings fluttering. Verity felt as if the world were new with an innocent sweetness fresh from a creating hand. Everything was as it used to be except the splendid cement road, a glistening gray satin ribbon in the wetness and the light. She pushed open her gate, crossed to the road, and stood looking up and down the stretch of smoothness. She loved this road. It belonged here. It was a vital part of the dreams and visions she and Hank had known in the little white share-crop house. She stooped and ran her fingers over the cold, hard surface of the cement and smiled tenderly as she thought of the young husband who had walked nineteen miles in the sucking, clinging black-jack to come home strong, and not weary, and hold his child up to the Lord, saying, " 'N don't stint on the strength, Lord." Yes, she loved this road.

Jenny's boys were handsome big blond fellows, and Hancy bloomed un-der their companionship. Jules did not come home, but he talked over the telephone with Moses regularly, and Jules's groom came to Verity's gate each week-end morning with horses for the youngsters to ride. Often Verity also rode. They enjoyed their lessons in horsemanship, and through the weeks a healing began in Verity. She began to feel a realness in life again, to know the bubbling of joy, could again laugh with her child.

Each morning the youngsters took the school bus. To see the big yellow vehicle coming down Hank's road with a load of country children always gave Verity a thrill.

Verity found she had accumulated almost three thousand "honest" dol-lars from her interest in the peddling. Three thousand dollars in eight years and, of course, the wagon's present stock. She talked matters over with Selah. Selah declared it was riches. The farm would keep them and the "cash money" would buy all other needs. Verity kept the car in which they came from the capital. The chauffeur had stayed a week to teach her to drive. Driving over the countryside gave her a great sense of freedom. Like Hancy, the feel of having no man with a gun trailing her was deli-cious beyond words.

The campaign for reelection was in its last days. Hank made good cam-paign material out of the roundup of the Polli gang. He said Polli had almost fooled him into thinking he was the right man to be mayor of Crescent City, but that was when he, Hank Martin, discovered certain facts about Polli and had threatened to expose him. Polli's body had been found in his own lagoon and some of Polli's gang were now in jail, and though he had not been able to prove that Willie Rizani had murdered Polli, at least the state was rid of him.

The tents of the state militia were again distributed and kept in readi-ness to house the countryfolk, but election day came fair and bright and that night Verity and Jenny, the youngsters, and Selah pulled cane-syrup taffy and listened to the returns. By midnight it was evident that Hank was in. It was not a landslide, by any means, however. His margin was narrowed.

"They can't lick my Hank!" said Hancy triumphantly, through a mouthful of taffy. "They sure can't lick my Hank!"

"Well, now we know," said Verity, "you kids get to bed in a hurry. That school bus will come around awfully soon."

"Aw, heck, do we have to go to school tomorrow?" asked Pete.

"Lissen t' that, will y', Verity?" cried Jenny. "Usn work our guts out for t' get schools, 'n that's what they holler at us!" She grabbed up Pete's coat and threw it to him. "You get in them coats so's usn can trek for home. You ain't a-missin' ary day a' school unless'n you're busted out with a fever rash as is bigger'n dollars."

It was midafternoon the following day. Verity and Selah were in the smokehouse with Tape, preparing hams and bacon for smoking, when they heard both the voices of Moses and Jules's groom calling urgently.

"Miz Verity! Miz Verity!"

"Selah! Miz Verity!"

"It's Moses!" cried Verity. "Something's wrong!"

They ran out of the smokehouse.

"Oh, Miz Verity," wailed Moses, "y'all ain' bin lissenin' ter de radio—I sees dat! Oh, Miz Verity—Mistuh Hank, he been shot!"

Verity stopped as if she too had been shot. The terrible, unbelievable pain of those words froze her. Selah's arms went around Verity.

"Shush yo' mouf, man," cried Selah, "whut you a-sayin'?"

"I is tellin' de Lawd's gospel," said Moses sadly. "He shot, but he ain't daid. He mebbe dyin', t'ough." Moses went on while Verity stared at him, trying to understand all this meant. Hank dying! It had come! In a way she had felt for years that it might come like this. And yet—and yet— Hank dying! It was impossible! "Hit de truf! De Lawd's truf, Miz Verity. Mistuh Hank, he step out his own autymobile, he do. He got all his gua'ds 'round him. Dere's a shot. Folkses sees a man whut's blond, seem lak, in black overcoat an' dem black glasses a-runnin' inter de Capitol an' up de windin' stairs. Big crowd dere is, all sudden lak. An' de big doah, hit git swung to. Some uv Mistuh Hank's gua'ds' bullets done hit de do', dey say."

Verity stood, seeing it in her mind's eye as Moses talked; the way the marble stair wound round back of the elevators would get a man out of bullet range from the rotunda in just a second. She could see the huge bronze inner doors, the magnificent doors with their bas-relief magnolias.

The groom spoke up. "I is come ter drive y'all, Miz Verity," he said. "Y'all ain't gwine be fitten fer ter drive."

"Yes, yes," Verity murmured. "Come, Selah, quick. Help me dress."

Selah dressed her in a suit which Hank liked, a dark green with red-fox fur, and with tears rolling down her black cheeks she said over and over, "Mistuh Hank, he lak you purty."

"Listen carefully, now, Selah," commanded Verity as she stepped into the car. "Get Jenny. Moses, you please phone to Delamore and arrange to hire a car. Get the children from school, Selah, and you and Jenny and the children come to Magnolia Mansion. Hancy'll need the twins."

"Yas'm, Miz Verity," said Selah. "Usn be dere."

The car moved, and into Verity came that feel of being transported into the past—that feel which a sameness of season combined with the same degree of sunlight, the same crispness and scents in the air can produce. It was election time as it had been on that day when she and Hank rode in another big black car behind another driver. She seemed again to be riding behind Willie, Polli's man. The scenes of election day were clear. The air was charged with crosscurrents. She saw again Hank's instructors at the polls, heard them barking like side-show ticket sellers: "Everybody come up here and get your sample ballot—step right up here —see how it's done—don't risk votin' for the wrong feller—vote for Hank Martin—step right up here, get your sample ballot." And over all was the feel of menace; she could see again the armed guards, could see, rather than hear, the almost soundless laugh of Marcus Davol.

She shuddered. Why was that day so clear to her now? she wondered. Ah, yes, perhaps if she had not left Magnolia Mansion she could have stood between Hank and death this time, too, as she had on the day the barkers cried, "Right this way—see how it's done—" Could she—if she hadn't come to the Bend? Hank dying! How could she endure the loneliness of knowing he was nowhere in this world! Hank dying! Hank never coming home again! She remembered her terrible need for Hank when she lost her little son and the tears streamed down her face; and she remembered her resolve never to fail others because of her need for Hank. Never to fail others because of her need for Hank! What an immense resolve!

She walked through the cold marble halls of the hospital leaning on a young doctor's arm. When at last they stopped before the door of Hank's room, she took a deep breath, pulled in her abdomen, conscious of Hank's training on preparing to deal with fear. The doctor held open the door. Several physicians and nurses clustered around the bed, but at the sound of the opening door they turned, and she could see Hank. He lay—almost sat—propped by pillows, his face white, his dark hair catching blue lights even in this dimmed room. His eyes had a luminous clearness. Verity stood just inside the door, held spellbound by the look of Hank—for here, once more, was the man she loved. The doctors and nurses filed past her and closed the door soundlessly.

Into Hank's pale face came that look of marveling, of reverence.

"'And to the woman were given two wings of a great eagle,'" he whispered huskily, "'that she might fly to the wilderness, where she is nourished for a time from the face of—'" he hesitated, then went on, "from the face of the Lion."

"Oh, Hank," she sobbed. "Oh, Hank!" She ran to his bed and fell on her knees beside him, and between them bloomed again the sweetness of shared love and parenthood.

He touched her cheek with one finger. "Shush, now, Sweetface, shush." There was still the feel of vibrancy in his muted voice, still the push of life. "Don't never salten yore eyes for what's done 'n over. Shush, now—it's a pore heart that don't find somethin' t' be rejoicin' over. 'N d'y' know what, Sweetface? I got a somethin' t' be rejoicin' for."

She put her lips to his and kissed him gently, fervently.

"Yeah, rejoicin' for, Sweetface—" He stopped and breathed heavily and with effort. "I must 'a clean forgot t' admonish the Lord t' lead me not into temptation. But the Lord God Almighty allus gives me His best. Yeah," he gasped, "yeah, folks got a way a' rememberin' men as get kilt whilst in office. That's a somethin'. . . ." His breathing was becoming very labored.

"Don't talk, darling—don't talk. Save your strength to get well," she pleaded. "Oh, Hank—my Hank!"

"Gotta talk, Verity." He grinned a weak but valiant grin. "Words— you know. But these here words is honest words. Folks blame me 'n men like me—'n we got a lot t' answer for, mebbe. But the people, Verity—the people—they're so dang slothful. Liken it says—'The slothful man turneth on his bed as a door on its hinges'— Yeah. I been a-thinkin' a lot sincet you went away. 'N so a lion comes, a-trumpetin' loud 'n in no way uncertain . . ." His voice almost died out. He struggled to keep consciousness. "There's a bleedin' in my guts. I feel the fast hot stream a' it. . . . My Hancy—she'll love me allus, won't she?"

Verity couldn't speak, but she nodded and kissed him again on the cheek.

"My young'un, 'n my wife—God!" he moaned. "I'm a-leavin' you plumb penniless. God! Cleaned I am withen the pay-off t' that bastard Polli's gang. Scarce more'n enough t' pay for the coffin I'm needin'." Then he stared at her wildly a second. "God'lmighty!" He cried it out with the virility of fear and horror. "God'lmighty! Them records! My records 'n all a' Polli's!" He hoisted himself with a mighty effort and clenched at his bandaged breast and stomach; the tearing pain was in his face.

"Hank!" she cried. "Don't move—Hank!"

"Get 'em, Verity! Them records. God'lmighty, don't let Marcus—not nobody get 'em—" Death wrenched him back on the pillows in a last agony. "They're behind the ce—" He fell back, unable to speak. He fought for breath, struggling for a few minutes more.

"Where, Hank, where?" she pleaded.

He struggled pitifully with his agony, his eyes glazed with pain. At last he smiled. The look of the young Hank came on him. He smiled, and from the edge of death he murmured, "I plumb gotta find some stillness in me—I ain't heard aught but the caterwaulin' for years, seems as though. Purely gulled I been, Sweetface—Sweetface—" He sighed, a struggling, gurgling sigh, "purely gulled—" His eyes rolled upward and Hank Martin, the Big Lion, was dead.

She knelt beside him a long time, her hand on his marbling cheek. A bitterness almost beyond bearing filled her, for she knew he had hastened his death by minutes, perhaps hours, when he pulled himself up in fear to tell of the records. The records—those terrible documents which could guide another lion into power! That a man would so live that, after being shot, he should have to rob himself of his last minutes, his last hours!

Then to her came the realization that he had given her a last job to do for him and also, she thought bitterly, for the state. If those records fell into the ruthless hands of Marcus Davol—or one of Polli's men, or any of a number of Hank's associates, there would be no end to the tyranny. What had he meant by the "sea"—"behind the sea"—or would the word be spelt "s-e-e"? Oh, what had he meant?

At last she rose. Gently she covered his face with the sheet, rang the buzzer, and went to the door. A doctor entered. She passed him by wordlessly and went out into the hall. The hall was filled with hushed and waiting people, among them Jules. Seeing Verity he came quickly to her and took her arm.

"Hank is dead," she said hollowly. "Dead." The thought came to her that almost exactly ten years ago she had said she'd rather see him killed than killing and the memory of those words smote her and weighed her down. But she had a job to do, and she pushed all other thoughts away. Erect and strong she walked out of the hospital beside Jules.

The Capitol building had been closed since Hank's death. After the shooting all employees were searched and made to leave. No one had been allowed in the building since, except on special business, and then only under constant police guard. How Hank's assassin had ever got out of the Capitol building could not be explained, but the police had searched the building several times. Jules, at Verity's request, had questioned Hank's bodyguards and his secretaries on the whereabouts of Hank's records, but had learned nothing of any help.

Jules reported that Saber declared many men stayed on the Capitol grounds and on the Capitol steps, "men who have not the look of natural mourners for Hank." Saber felt the assassin must still be in the Capitol, that these men must know who the killer was and that he had never come out of the building. Hank's receptionist gave the only possible clue. He said,

"When I heard all the commotion, I ran out into the hall. I bumped into a man who seemed to have come up the stairs. I think he wore a black coat. But I couldn't be certain. Where he went I don't know. And I never saw him before."

It was very late the night of Hank's death when the committeemen came to call on Verity to get her O.K. on their plans for the funeral. Hank's body was to lie in state in the Capitol rotunda. . . . Verity looked at the circle of men and agreed to this. Hank would want it so. She brought up only one objection.

"But the Capitol building is still closed, isn't it? No one has been allowed inside—isn't that right? Not even well-known employees?"

"No one has been allowed in without police guard," replied one of the men, and added, "Ridiculous! How could the assassin still be in the building! It's been searched and searched. No one is even allowed to go to his own desk without a guard."

A cold fury gathered in Verity. The records, she thought. The records. These men wanted the records, too. She looked at their faces and wondered if one was the assassin.

"Is that all?" she asked coldly.

"No, no, it isn't." The committeeman cleared his throat and put on his professional beam. "We have made arrangements for a national hookup over the radio. The whole world is interested in Hank Martin and wants to hear more about him. Now, Marcus Davol is a good speaker . . ."

"Marcus Davol!" she cried. "Never!"

The committeemen looked at each other.

"But Marcus was a close associate and a good friend," said the chairman.

"No!" she said.

"Well," the chairman temporized, "there's Judge Drury."

"One of the bought-and-owned judges, no doubt," she spoke flatly.

A look of amazement and confusion spread over their faces and she thought, oh, yes, an obituary which shall be splendid propaganda for the organization—well, I won't have it—I won't.

"The man at the microphone," she said firmly, "shall be Saber Milady."

"Saber Milady!" It was a unanimous gasp.

"But, Mrs. Martin," protested the chairman, "that's impossible! Milady is one of Hank's bitterest enemies!"

"Not exactly." She was prepared to fight. "Saber Milady could tell the drama of Hank Martin, the man—could tell as much as the public is ever told—and he would tell it without making it a build-up for another Big Lion. And after all," she hesitated before she gave them the next blow, "you're a little handicapped both in your efforts to build another lion and in your efforts to protect your standing and reputations until—and unless you find the records. Am I not right?"

The chairman jumped to his feet and standing before Verity, demanded fiercely, "Have you got the records? Have you?"

"No," she replied wearily.

They did not quite believe her. Fear was in every face and Verity looked on them with contempt.

"It is agreed that Mr. Milady shall be at the microphone?" she asked.

After a moment the chairman perked up a bit. "It's not such a bad notion, at that," he declared. "Somewhat like Hank's methods. He'd know how to capitalize on that. Hank'd know how to make it look as if that damned Saber Milady had climbed over into our pasture."

She sighed. But she could do no more. In one thing, at least, she was triumphant. Saber would tell the drama of Hank, the man. He didn't know it all—not by any means. He knew little of the hidden consecutives, and that was well. But Saber would not load the obituary with machine politics. Without another word she rose and left the room.

From then on she stayed in her bedroom, waiting on herself to bring forth some hidden, inner knowledge. She knew that Magnolia Mansion was full and running over with vultures—waiting, watching, hoping to learn something from her moves which would tell the all-important thing as to where the private records of Hank Martin were. Judges stood in groups, each eyeing the other with suspicion, anxiety plain on every face. Marcus Davol had his kinsmen posted at the two entrances of the Capitol, and he himself stayed, in the name of sympathy, at Magnolia Mansion.

Knowing all this, Verity felt if she knew who the killer was, she might know all. She felt she had to know who killed Hank. It wouldn't be Spurge. Spurge would have walked straight up to Hank and shot him. One of Polli's gang? A hireling of Castleberry? Castleberry himself had been in Loder City that day. That had been ascertained. She had to find that man. She had to know. Was it Marcus Davol? Was it Lieutenant Governor Kirkendall?

18

Yes, Hank Martin was a man of action. When he said he was going to do something, he did it. There were people in this state who declared that if Hank Martin said he was going to move the river, it would not occur to them to doubt it: they would not ask why, nor how, nor when. They would only ask, "Where do you suppose Hank will put the river?"

During Hank's administration more laws were passed than in all four preceding administrations. The records show laws. . . .

THE RECORDS! the records—where would he put them? "Behind a false partition in the attic," Hank had said when designating the hiding place of Polli's records; and on his deathbed he had said, "Behind the . . ." She knew! She knew where the records were! And then came a terrifying, an astounding thought. . . . She caught her breath at the immensity of it. She began to tremble, and clenching her fists, she took a deep breath— iron in your guts, Verity—iron in your guts—she told herself. She began to feel again that calm, cold strength which she had known before. She switched off the radio and hurried to the door, opened it a crack, and whispered urgently, "Selah, get Jules and Jenny and Flower and bring them to me. Quick!"

She donned the new black coat, put on the small mourning hat with the veil which fell softly in the back, making her face startling in its white, repressed calmness.

Selah came in. "I sent fo' 'em," she said. "Whar you gwine? Huh? Whar you gwine?"

"To the Capitol," said Verity.

"Uum-uummph! Den you shu' needs dis." She took a small white packet from her dress pocket. "Dis ol' Granny's chawm. Ain' never fail usn yet. I gets dis chawm w'en I has de mournin' miseries—an' now you gets it, honey." She kissed the packet of hummingbird's wing and goofer dust, kissed it soundly. "Do yo' stuff, chawm!" she incanted. "Do yo' stuff!" She pinned it inside Verity's black dress. "New life whut usn need now—yes, Lawd, it is." Tears spilled down Selah's cheeks, but she shook her head emphatically at Verity. "Mistuh Hank, he give dat chawm ter me an' he say, 'Now, raise up, woman, an' claim dat new life!' . . . He say dat, an' now, Miz Verity, honey, he a-sayin' hit agin, like's not."

But Verity scarcely heard. Her whole thought was on making herself strong and equal to whatever lay just ahead. She had a job to do for Hank.

A few minutes later she went down, with Jules on one side and Jenny on the other. The callers in the great rooms stared and the cameras clicked; the public would want to see how the Lion's wife looked when she decided to go to the Capitol, in order to see the last great tribute which the people paid to her famous husband.

Jackson opened the door and they stepped into the waiting car. Flower had called for motorcycle police to get them through the crowds; so police rode ahead, and police rode alongside of them, and police rode in back of them. Swith and Vince and Jep in one car; Flower, a chauffeur, Jules, Jenny, and Verity in the other.

"What makes you so sure we're gonna find the killer?" asked Jenny.

"Hush!" said Jules.

No one must know what they thought. No one must know except Jules and Jenny and Flower—and, yes, Saber. Verity felt they would need Saber to protect them from other news hawks.

As they neared the Capitol, the motorcycle police shot ahead and cleared the way. The cars stopped. Hank's bodyguards jumped out and with the aid of the police cleared a broad path through the crowd. From the loud-speakers came Saber's voice:

"Yes, yes, it is Mrs. Martin! She is coming up the steps of the Capitol . . ."

Verity saw him turn and speak to a colleague and then come hurriedly toward them. In an instant another voice spoke to the crowd:

"It is natural that Mrs. Martin should want to see Hank in the midst of—"

"Come with us, Saber," said Jules.

The policemen went ahead clearing the way. There, in the magnificent rotunda in the silver casket, lay Hank. Verity stopped a second. My Hank, she thought, my Hank. I loved you so terribly, Hank, she said to him silently. The great crowds stood quiet and awed. Verity turned and went into the elevator. The police had gone ahead and now stood by respectfully in the upper hall, one holding open the door to Hank's office. Flower ordered Swith and Jep and Vince to stay in the hall with the police.

When inside the reception office, Jules whispered to Saber, "Verity thinks Hank was trying to tell her about a false partition in the closet off his private office. She thinks that's where his records are—and if the killer did not get out of the Capitol—"

"Good God!" exclaimed Saber.

They hurried into Hank's private office. The fine new door swung silently on its hinges, and the handsome Oriental rug stilled their footsteps. Jenny stood, her fingers intertwined and clutched to a bloodless whiteness. Verity crossed the room to Hank's chair and clung desperately to it. The little glass flamingo stood in the exact center of the desk, its long, graceful neck upstretched, its beak flowerless.

The men hurried into the small hallway and into the cedar-lined closet. Verity waited, caught in a dread intentness.

"She's right!" It was Saber's voice.

There was a faint grating sound of an opening panel. Then came Flower's fierce command, "Put up yore hands 'r I'll shoot!"

Verity heard the next words—Jules's words—as once before she had heard Jules's voice; as if the words came from a long way off, as if they were heard by a kite mind, as if they traveled to her by slow motion down a long kite string. Jules spoke only three words but they meant so much. They meant that the unknown blond, black-coated, dark-bespectacled man was actually unknown! Jules's three words were a question: "Your name, sir?" Yes, those three words had great meaning; Jules's addition of the word "sir" meant that in the unknown man was some quality which commanded respect.

"Gawd!" cried Jenny, and running to the hall door she slammed it shut, put her back against it, and spread her arms out as if to bar new pain and new knowledge from her friend.

Verity needed help. Hank—Hank—where are you, Hank? And Hank gave her help. From out of the walls, from the drapes, from the thick rich rug, from desk—yes, even from the glass flamingo, came Hank's voice, vibrant and echoy and urgent: "Breathe deep, Sweetface. Don't never let nothin' upset you. Ain't nothin' so curin' as pulled-in guts a-shovin' up on a chest full a' air. Sends somethin' t' the brain that's right confidence-givin'." She breathed deep. Through the closed windows came the rumble of words from the loud-speakers, and through the horizontal slats of the Venetian blinds she saw the vast crowd on the Capitol grounds. She lifted her hands from the back of Hank's chair, took another deep breath, and then sat in the chair. The little secret room nagged at one edge of her consciousness. Hank had just had it walled off—probably by country friends to whom it meant nothing more than a pleasure to do a secret job for Hank. Surely the records were also in that room. Clarity and strength came to her again. Stonily quiet she waited—waited.

Jenny stepped away from the door and waited—waited.

At last the door opened. Saber and Jules came in. Verity sat slightly forward in Hank's chair and studied them. Their faces wore the look of men who have seen a vision; of men who have found the spirit at the end of a long arid journey following the star. After their eyes collided with Verity's, some hopelessness and bafflement crept into their faces.

Slowly Saber walked across the room and laid a paper on the desk before Verity, but she kept her eyes on Jules and Saber, trying to understand, to analyze that uplift which first they wore as they entered.

"Who is he?" she demanded, her voice hard and cold.

The look of beholding a vision came again to Saber's face. "He's all the men of the Boston Tea Party; he's the men at Valley Forge"—Saber's voice was soft and vibrant—"he's all the liberty-loving men who live by Patrick Henry's words."

"He killed Hank!" Verity cried out bitterly. But even as she spoke the little iron monitor came alive and fought back, saying: No! The Lion sidled up to Hank full of power and honey, and then—bingo!—there wasn't any Hank!

She dropped her eyes and looked at the paper which Saber had laid on the desk. It was a crudely drawn lion lying prostrate with many little people dismounting from the lion's back. She stared at the picture while the full meaning of it tied in with Saber's words. Jenny came and looked at the paper and gasped a muffled "Gawd!"

"Yes," said Jules, "he simply drew it. Pulled it out of a hat."

"Verity—remember?" Saber was pleading. "Remember I said there were lots of men around this building who did not seem to be natural mourners for Hank? Well, I was right. They were waiting to help this—this unknown man." He sighed. "There are thousands and thousands like him—men who do not hold with killing. But when a ruler, be he governor or king, has spread an organization like a choking octopus—when the courts are corrupted and there is no justice, when he has blackmailed and bribed the judges—when his organization is so great and corrupt that a people cannot get rid of him at the polls—how else do a people dismount such a lion?"

She sat stone-still. Like a judge she looked with her coat of mourning black falling loosely from her erect shoulders, and her face so stern, so bleakly austere.

Saber turned away. Jules spoke softly: "Who shall be tried here when a man lies already dead?" Jules's voice, low and echoy, ushered the past into the room. "The qualities which made the man have been poured into the world. Justice must weigh the validity of honor, of intent, of spirit, and of thought! Was this man valid? Did he pour into the world that which is honorable and that which is good?— These are the questions."

There was a mighty stillness. Verity thought: Why, there's no caterwauling, no caterwauling at all; there was only the high mountain from which one caught the far vision: and Verity saw that Hank had been tried for years—tried by more than twelve good men and true—tried by the people and found guilty.

"Justice," she said firmly, "is the same today as it was in our yesterdays."

"Thank God!" breathed Saber, "at last I've met truth."

Tears came to Jules's eyes and his hand trembled as he took his kerchief from his pocket. Jenny sobbed softly.

"But—the records?" asked Verity in a low, steady voice. "The records?"

"I'll guarantee you the records with my life," cried Saber. "They're in there—big locked files all bolted to the floor."

"But how'll the feller get out?" sobbed Jenny.

Jules cleared his throat. "The—ah—the records will be taken out to-night through the supply closet which opens into the main hallway. Saber and I—we'll manage everything. The records will be in Cypress Bend tomorrow morning."

Verity rose. "Call Flower," she said. "We will leave now."

"Gawd!" said Jenny softly. "Gawd!"

Verity stood waiting, her eyes on the little glass flamingo. When Flower came, she turned from the desk and walked ahead of the others out of Hank's private office through the reception office and on. Out in the hall Hank's bodyguard and the policemen fell automatically into the business of protecting. Verity walked straight and strong, but as they passed through the rotunda where Hank lay, she hesitated. She loved him —she loved him; but justice was justice. She breathed deep and walked on.

A great choir was assembling on the Capitol entrance steps to sing for the nation, at the close of Hank's story, some of Hank's favorite hymns. The low sun fell richly on the vast crowd and on the scarlet vestments of the choir. The policemen spoke the magic words, and Verity and her party walked through a parted and stilled red sea down the wide marble steps. Jules handed Jenny and Verity into the car, then stepped back beside Saber. The red sea of choir flowed together again and in a magnificent blend of voices they sang:

> "Take time to be holy,
> Speak oft with the Lord . . ."

The motorcycles spit and popped; the cars started almost soundlessly. Slowly the Governor's widow and her party moved up the broad, paved, tree-lined street, and the singing came clearly over the loud-speakers for more than a block:

> "Oh, clean is your heart then,
> And sweet is each day . . ."

For Verity, the choir needed Hank's jubilant and boisterous voice on the last lines of the verse.

> "Take time to be holy,
> Take time, then, to pray."

They turned the corner, picked up speed, and went swiftly to Magnolia Mansion. Jackson opened the front door and stood, respectfully waiting while Verity and Jenny stepped from the car, crossed the gallery, and entered.

Verity ascended the wide, lovely stair, not blinking at the flash of cameras, not looking toward the crowded living rooms. At her bedroom door she hesitated and looked into Jenny's eyes. The two friends communed silently for a minute. Then Jenny found words.

"You're kin t' the people, seems 's though," she said. She put her thin hand in Verity's. "Hank didn't never go for no pulin' critter." Then she turned and walked slowly down the hall to the children.

As in a trance Verity went into her room, crossed to a window, and looked out at Hank's pinnacle "all marble 'n shinin'." The glow of the western sky pinked the leaves of oak and magnolia, and in the distance was the sheen of the silvered river. A great love of this country swelled and pushed within her. Spreading her arms toward the world she pleaded silently, Don't—oh, don't turn on your bed as a door on its hinges. You're my kinsmen—you're the people! Only the people can blow the trumpet— the incorruptible trumpet of faith and justice, of equality and truth. And blow certain, she pleaded. Oh, trumpet, blow certain!